THE
LOST
COLONY

THE
LOST
COLONY

A.G. RIDDLE

An Ad Astra Book

First published in the UK in 2020 by Head of Zeus Ltd
An Ad Astra book

9 7 5 3 1 2 4 6 8

A catalogue record for this book is available from
the British Library.

ISBN (HB): 9781800241510
ISBN (XTPB): 9781800241527

Typeset by Divaddict Publishing Solutions Ltd

Floor plans redrawn by Jeff Edwards

Printed and bound in Great Britain by
CPI Group (UK) Ltd, Croydon CR0 4YY

MIX
Paper from
responsible sources
FSC   FSC® C020471
www.fsc.org

Head of Zeus Ltd
First Floor East
5–8 Hardwick Street
London EC1R 4RG

WWW.HEADOFZEUS.COM

To time and its magical healing properties.

Emma

The rolling thunder wakes me.

I lie in the bottom bunk, listening in the darkness. The narrow mattress is just big enough for James and me, but he's gone. He has been for most of the last six months.

"Mom," Allie whispers from the lower bunk on the opposite wall.

"It's okay, sweetie. It's just a storm."

The thumping in the distance grows louder. The walls vibrate. I'm sure of it then: this isn't a storm. They've returned.

I push up and pull on my suit. It's made from a specialized material that blocks the heat from my body. We used the 3D printers to create the suits, and they've saved dozens of lives in the last few months.

Sam climbs down from the top bunk as Allie swings her feet over the side.

"Where are you going?" Sam asks.

"To work."

"Mom—" Allie starts.

"Stay quiet, you'll wake your brother."

It's too late. In the bassinet, Carson rolls back and forth, breaking free from the tight swaddle wrapped around his tiny body. He yawns, and a yell follows. That noise could be deadly. For all of us.

I grab Sam's shoulders. "Get a bottle from the canteen. Give it to Carson and keep him quiet."

He shakes his head. "I'm coming with you."

"Do as I say, Sam."

"Where's Dad?" Allie whines.

"Be quiet—both of you. Now go, Sam. Hurry."

He scowls as he marches out the door. Allie looks up, lip quivering.

I lift Carson out of the bassinet and hand him to her. "I'll be back soon."

Across the hall a door opens, and my sister, Madison, sticks her head out. "Everything okay?"

The pounding beyond the barracks is growing louder by the second.

"Sure," I lie. "Just try to keep quiet."

Sam is racing back down the corridor, bottle in hand. I pause just long enough to hug him and whisper, "Thank you."

Outside the barracks, I march toward the command post. Overhead, a canopy made of parachute material blocks out the sun, making it feel like night. During our first few months on Eos, the lack of night here in the valley disrupted our circadian rhythms, so we built the canopy to simulate the setting sun and darkness.

There are fourteen long barracks buildings under the domed canopy, and people are pouring out of each one, mostly army troops in green fatigues. A few wear the insulated suits like mine, but we only have twenty, all fitted specifically to the owner's body. If we had more of the necessary raw material inputs for the 3D printers, we could make more, and in moments like this, when I wish we had more, I think maybe what James is doing is truly important enough to risk his life for. He's spent countless hours away from Jericho City, scouring the dark side of Eos for material we can use in the 3D printers.

Inside the small habitat that serves as the command post, Colonel Brightwell is issuing orders rapid-fire, her voice low, the British-accented words snapping out like suppressed gunfire.

"Launch both surveillance drones."

At the long table in the middle of the room, Corporal Aguilar types quickly at his terminal, then looks up. "Drone launch confirmed. Initiating startup."

"How long until we have line of sight with Carthage?"

"Another hour," the young man responds.

"Launch the relay balloons."

"All of them, ma'am?"

"All of them, Corporal. We need eyes in the sky, and Dr. Matthews may want to issue orders to the ship before it reaches line of sight."

Brightwell pauses, seeming to consider her options. "Activate Alpha Tac Team. I want them in the jungle ASAP—in that group's vector. Orders are to take up defensive positions and await further instructions. No active measures until authorized."

Another technician relays the order over the radio.

Brightwell turns and realizes I'm here. She nods slightly and eyes the troops following me.

"Major," she calls to a man behind me. "Lockdown protocol."

"Yes, ma'am!" His loud, crisp voice makes me wince.

The command post is a one-room habitat that's only about five hundred square feet. Every inch of it falls silent.

Brightwell sighs. "Quietly. All of you."

The troops turn and creep away, leaving only the pounding in the distance, like a great battle at sea drifting closer to us.

"Drone telemetry incoming," Aguilar says.

The wall screens switch from the perimeter cameras to video feeds from the drones flying above the city. The domed canopy is a giant white circle in the vast blue-green plain. It ripples from the vibrating ground, reminding me of a pebble skipping across a pond. A cluster of white comm panels lies nearby. Those panels are our only link to the colony ship orbiting above.

The grassy field around our city is bordered on the south by a wide blue river with white-capped waves. The stream has surged since the storms began. But the water isn't our greatest concern. To the north, east, and west, the grass ends in jungle, a thriving ecosystem that reminds me of the rainforests of Earth.

Yet for all its similarities to Earth, Eos still feels foreign to me. The sun it orbits is dim and orange-red, a red dwarf that burns less than a tenth as bright as the sun we left behind. The temperature is about the same as the temperature on Earth since this planet orbits closer to its star, but I may never get used to the alien quality of the sunlight.

Eos, like Earth's moon, is tidally locked—one side always faces the sun. The sun never sets on that side. It's boiling there, a vast desert. The dark side is the opposite—an expanse of ice and mountains that reminds me of my last glimpses of Earth, an ice ball devoid of life. It's only here, in the dividing line between the desert and the ice, that Eos provides a habitable zone, a band where conditions are just right for human life. This Goldilocks valley runs all the way around the planet. It's beautiful. A paradise. Or so we thought.

We made one miscalculation. There's a dwarf planet in this star system with a highly irregular orbit. The scans we performed when we arrived didn't detect the planet—it was too far outside the system at the time. But that planet is now moving closer to Eos. It won't collide, and it won't drastically change our orbit, but its gravitational pull has caused Eos to turn slightly, just enough to shift the Goldilocks valley, causing a minor ecosystem disruption. An event that may well be our undoing.

On the screen, the drones fly toward the western jungle. The canopy over Jericho City passes out of sight, leaving only the thick expanse of trees. The first time I entered one of those jungles I was shocked by how dark and cold it was. The leaves and branches overhead are so thick it almost feels like night.

"Switch to IR," Brightwell whispers.

The colors on the screen change to blue and black—and red. The red dots are life signs, and they cover the screen from edge to edge.

"Zoom out," Brightwell says slowly.

The image widens, but it's still covered in red dots.

"Again."

Finally, the entire group of red heat signatures is revealed. The dots form a diamond, and they're moving quickly through the jungle, directly for this city.

2

James

On the icy plain, Arthur stares at me with exasperation.

"Go home, James."

Ignoring him, I glance down at the tablet, confirming the location. It's here. Right under my feet.

At the ATV, I pull a shovel from my pack. A cold wind kicks up, blowing snow like tumbleweeds through a ghost town. To the west, snow covers the towering mountains that separate the dark side of Eos from the habitable valley. The valley we call home, a valley that I fear is in danger from an enemy unseen and unknown. But the answers are out here. I can feel it.

"What do you tell them?" Arthur asks.

"About what?"

"About why you're out here."

"What does it matter?" I mumble as I walk back to the location on the map and begin shoveling snow.

"My guess?" Arthur says, pretending to contemplate. "My guess is that you tell them you're searching for material for the 3D printers. You bring back just enough matter to assuage their suspicions."

"Your deductive powers are breathtaking. It's almost like you're a machine capable of running infinite calculations of the possibilities."

Arthur smiles. "Touché. But I'm much more than that. And I'm telling you that you should go home, James." He stares at me, serious now. "Listen to me."

"I'd already be at home if you'd help me."

"I just did."

The shovel breaks through at that moment, catching air below the snow that covers the entrance to the tunnel. I dig faster, uncovering the mouth of the passage. It's dark, a jagged corridor carved into the ice at a descending angle, just big enough for me to walk in if I stoop a bit.

In the distance, beyond the mountains, I hear a faint rumbling. Probably another storm coming in from the desert.

"Go home," Arthur says. "I told you the storms of Eos are dangerous."

"I'm not worried about the storms."

"You should be."

I trudge down the tunnel, my headlamp lighting the way. "Come on," I call back to him.

After a moment, I hear his heavy footsteps crunching in the ice.

At the end of the tunnel lies a black metal sphere, slightly larger than a basketball. It's the third one I've found. I take a measurement and confirm that it's larger than the other two. But only slightly.

A symbol is carved into the ice on the wall beside it.

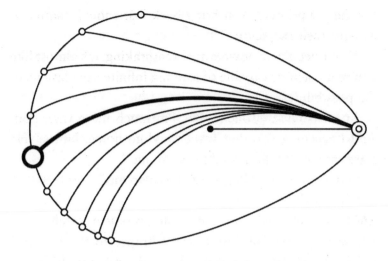

Harry made this mark. Was it a message to me? Or simply a marker for him and his team?

He's dug around the device on all sides, allowing me to examine it. Like the other spheres, this one has no markings, only a single door that lies open. The hollow sphere is empty inside. The other two were as well.

The first time I saw the symbol—the Eye of the Grid, Arthur calls it—I thought it was a map. I still do. My working theory is that these spheres are points on the map—specifically, the closed circles on the top arc. Before, with only two points, I had no way to verify my supposition. The Eye has no scale, no points of reference. The two locations could have been any of the two points or none of them.

But having three points changes that.

On my tablet, I plot the points on a map of Eos, then overlay the symbol.

They match.

Using this, I can find every one of the spheres—if that's what's out there. Things will go faster now. I don't need the rovers combing the tundra looking for metal readings.

I turn the tablet to Arthur. "It is a map. What will I find at the other locations? More of the same?"

He rolls his eyes. "I imagine you'll find that you're wasting your time."

"That's cute." I study the map a second longer, considering which point to search next.

"There's only one line that terminates on this map. Is it the start? Or the end?"

"Who says it can't be both?"

"That's not an answer."

"It's the only one you're going to get."

I exhale. I'm tired and cold and sick of being in the dark—figuratively and literally thanks to the permanent winter on this side of the planet.

"We're going to the point in the middle. It's different, isn't it?"

Arthur shakes his head, disgusted.

"Why do you call it the Eye?"

He stands there, looking uninterested.

"I think I know why. Because the eyes see everything."

I pause, but Arthur doesn't respond.

"No. It's more than that. The eyes see something very special: the beginning and the end. Is that your little secret?"

His gaze snaps back to me, but he remains silent.

I press my point. "What it sees in the beginning, it doesn't understand. We don't remember the first thing we see, when we're born. We can't recall or understand what we see for years. But we see the end with our eyes wide open, like the arcs in the Eye."

Arthur's face freezes. His eyes go glassy. I know this expression. He has paused all bodily control functions. Every bit of his processing power is focused on some calculation. I've only seen this a few times. He's reassessing. Something I said has rattled him.

Suddenly he reanimates, as if waking up. "Interesting."

"What is?"

"You, James."

"You didn't think I would figure it out."

"The probability was so small as to be indistinguishable from zero." He shakes his head. "It doesn't matter. Don't go to that point or any other."

"Why?" I step closer to him. "There's only one reason you wouldn't want that: because it might harm the grid."

"That may be, but consider this: What if that's not the only reason? What if it could harm you?"

"You don't care about us. You've said so. You only care about the conservation of energy. The grid's great work, whatever that is."

"People change."

"You're not a person."

"Not by your definition, but it doesn't mean the grid can't change."

"So the grid cares about us now?"

"Is that so hard to believe?"

"Very."

Arthur stares at me. "You've changed, James. In prison, when this all started, you were unafraid, even in the face of a riot that could have killed you." He pauses. "Maybe you would have even welcomed it. You had nothing to lose then. Your family hated you. The world didn't understand how valuable you were. They rejected you, locked you away. But now, you have it all: your brother's love, a wife, three children, a band of people who celebrate you and trust you. You have it all, and you're terrified you're going to lose it again. That's why you're out here—your own fear, this sense of doom you've invented in your head. You've been fighting the Long Winter so long you don't understand that it's over now."

"It's not over. Now start walking."

Arthur doesn't move.

I draw the energy weapon from my pocket and let it hang at my side. Grigory made the device. One shot will completely disable Arthur.

"You can walk or I can strap you to the back of the ATV. I don't care which."

He turns and marches out of the cave.

The wind has picked up and snow is falling. It feels like a storm front is forming, moving toward the mountains and the valley beyond.

Arthur lifts his chin to gaze at the sky.

"You don't want to get caught in this storm, James."

"Then we better hurry."

He jogs beside the ATV on the plain and walks when we enter the mountains. The origin point on the map—our destination—lies in the mountains at the edge of the dark side. If a sphere touched down here, it might have been crushed by the rocks and scattered as it fell. Wreckage might be hard to find.

As we travel deeper into the mountains, shafts of dim light break over the peaks in the distance. The barren, frozen ground slowly gives way to life—shrubs at first, then giant trees that reach into the sky, trying to catch the meager scraps of sunlight. The branches have no leaves, only a blue-green spongy substance that hangs like ripped-up curtains. They remind me of the Spanish moss on the trees in the South where I grew up.

The ground is black as soot, damp and soft. In the distance, I hear rattling and animal calls, but the only life visible to me is the tiny insects that crawl across the trees, making the bark seem as though it's shifting back and forth.

The tablet beeps, and I check the map. The location is a hundred feet away. I stop the ATV and dismount, hiking the rest of the way, Arthur plodding along in front of me. Up ahead, I spot the mouth of a cave. It's wide, tall, and dark, an opening that goes right into the side of a mountain, near its base. The destination is somewhere inside.

Arthur stops and opens his mouth, but I draw the weapon and motion him forward.

"Keep moving."

He shrugs. "I thought maybe you'd want to go in first."

"I don't. It might be dangerous."

"Finally, he's right about something."

A gust sways the trees, sending pieces of the moss-like substance drifting down like confetti in a ticker-tape parade.

"The storm's coming," Arthur says as the moss collects in his hair.

I wave the weapon again, and he continues into the cave.

Within a few feet, the darkness is complete. I turn on my headlamp and study the walls. They're rock, black and damp like the forest floor. After another wave of the gun, Arthur marches forward. The cave turns, and when I round the corner, the headlamp rakes over piles of bones.

I grip the gun tighter as my heart thunders in my chest. Slowly, Arthur turns to me, his face half in shadow.

I step back until I feel the cold of the cave wall on my back. I glance left, then right, searching for any predators that might live down here. But I don't see any. The cave is dead silent.

I move my light to the bones once more. The piles stretch out so far I can't see the end. Only then do I realize they're human.

"Who are they?" I whisper.

Arthur's voice is loud, echoing off the rock walls like a megaphone. "You know who they are."

"What is this?"

"*This* is the end of the road you're traveling, James."

3

Emma

For a long moment, the command post is silent. All eyes study the drone video feed on the screen. A sea of red heat signatures is moving through the jungle, heading directly for Jericho City.

We'll never survive contact with this many E. rex.

Even before we came down to the planet, we knew that the Eos rex was the most dangerous predator on this world. We call them E. rex because they resemble the T. rex from Earth's past. Both are lizard-like, with thick, scaly skin. The E. rex also runs on two muscular hind legs. But whereas the T. rex had two small arms on its torso, the E. rex has four: two longer arms and two shorter. It also has a long tail with a sharp spike at the end. We've seen it spear its prey with that spike, then use the arms to rip it apart.

To date, the E. rex have killed seven of our people—five soldiers and two adults who were hunting in the western jungle. We've killed twice as many of the E. rex, though it wasn't easy. Their skin is tough, and the bone in their skulls is tougher. It takes two or three shots to pierce the brain. A shot through the eyes, nose, or mouth will do as well, but as fast as they move, that's a tall order.

Their vision is principally infrared, which, along with a heightened sense of smell, is how they locate their prey. Once we figured that out, we created the suits like the one I'm wearing. That enabled us to move unseen and to defend ourselves. Against a few E. rex, a team of cloaked humans stands a chance. Not against what's coming for us now. The herd of E. rex moving toward Jericho City must number in the thousands.

Brightwell breaks the silence.

"How long before the leading edge reaches us?"

Corporal Aguilar chews his lip as he studies his terminal. "Thirty minutes, give or take."

Troops are continuing to arrive at the command post, men and women apparently not needed for the lockdown protocol—and not subject to it. The crowded one-room building is overflowing out into the street, people shuffling and elbowing as they try to catch a glimpse of the screens.

Brightwell turns to a tall captain standing just inside the doorway. Her name is Rachel Harris, and she's third in the chain of command for Jericho City's armed forces.

"Captain, execute Omega Protocol. Form up on the herd's vector and shoot anything that breaches the tree line."

Omega Protocol mobilizes our entire army and arrays them at the city's perimeter for its defense.

As the captain departs, Brightwell nods to me and cuts through the crowd to join me in a nook at the back of the room. She keeps her eyes on the screens and her voice low.

"We don't have the firepower to stop a herd this large."

"Can we evacuate?" I ask.

"Not everyone. And those who do get out might be overrun."

Brightwell's piercing eyes betray no emotion. It's as if she's just recounted today's lunch menu. We can't fight and we can't run. What does that leave? One thing is certain: it's my decision to make.

It's been six months since we completed the buildings of Jericho City and began settling our families here. Four months ago, we held elections. To my shock and horror, I was elected mayor. I don't know exactly why. James thinks it was my experience on the ISS and, in his words, my leadership during the Long Winter, when we were trapped in the Citadel and in those difficult months before we left. I think he was glad I was elected—it's given me less time to wonder about what he's doing.

We've had our share of challenges here on Eos, but I never imagined we would face a conflict like this.

In our last year on Earth, we endured similar crises— but we fought them as a team. Fowler, Harry, Charlotte, and Earls were all at the table, giving their opinions and sharpening our plans. They're all gone now, as are the rest of the colonists from the *Carthage*.

Vanished.

Their settlement, almost a mirror image of ours, lies deserted, the buildings crumbling and caved in by tree limbs. Is what's happening here the same thing that happened to them?

We searched the Carthage settlement several times for clues about what happened to them. We found several data drives, but they were all damaged beyond repair. Our best guess is that they decided to leave for some reason and never returned. Time and weather have demolished many of the buildings.

We made the conscious decision not to build our settlement next to those ruins. There were the practical considerations: that there might still be a pathogen buried somewhere in Carthage City and that crumbling buildings are a bad place for kids to play. I think there were also psychological considerations. Eos is a new start for all of us. Building our city in the shadow of Carthage City would have reminded us every day of the friends we lost—and that Eos harbors dangers even the best of us couldn't survive. Maybe we should have heeded the warning of our lost colony more, but after what happened on Earth, we were all anxious to start over, to get back to a normal life—and a future for our kids.

At this moment, that future might be slipping away.

Keeping my voice low, I ask, "What are our options, Colonel?"

"Our best chance is to divert the herd. But we also need to know why they're stampeding. It might be a predator, but my guess is they're running from a storm. Either way, anything that's bad enough to send the E. rex running could be a bigger threat to us than the stampede itself. I suggest we use the video feeds from the drones and the telemetry from the *Carthage* to survey the area. And if it is a storm, we'll need Dr. Morgan to predict its course asap."

"If that herd does go through the city, what are our chances of survival?"

"Impossible to say, ma'am."

"Best guess?"

"Low."

I chew my lip, contemplating this impossible decision.

"Start making preparations in case we need to evacuate the city. And let's figure out why that herd is stampeding—and where they might be going."

"Yes, ma'am."

With that, Brightwell turns and begins issuing orders. A few minutes later, Aguilar calls out, "Ma'am, the relay balloons have reached altitude. We have active comms with the *Carthage*."

"Retrieve aerial imagery," Brightwell says.

Izumi, Min, and Grigory arrive at the command post in time to see the first image from Carthage, which shows Eos's dark side from orbit. Ice covers everything but the mountain peaks that border the valley and the wide rivers that stretch across its expanse. But that's not what's drawn everyone's attention. There's a massive storm on the dark side. It looks like a hurricane, with a wide eye and spiral arms lashing out. It hovers at the intersection of two major rivers.

My first thought is of James. My fear gets the best of me. In my mind's eye, I see the storm rolling him across the tundra like a rag doll, smashing him into a tree or tossing him into the mountains. There's nowhere to hide out there.

I grab a radio from the table and speak quickly. "James, this is Jericho CP, do you copy?"

I wait, but there's no response.

"James, do you read?"

Still no response. Was he close by when the storm formed? Is he still out there? If so, he's in danger.

I turn to Brightwell. "We need IR from the *Carthage*."

She nods, and Aguilar types quickly at his terminal. "IR overlay requested." He pauses. "Delta image caps downloading."

A second later, the image on the screen updates, showing the storm's arms churning counterclockwise. It's moving upriver, toward the mountains and the valley. I don't see any human life signs. Did James already flee the storm? Or has it already hit him?

Things are even worse for us. The E. rex are coming at us from the western jungle and this deadly storm is approaching from our east. It doesn't make sense: why are the E. rex charging *toward* the storm? They must be running from something else. Another storm to the west?

At that moment, Dr. Morgan enters the command post. "You called—"

He stops in mid-sentence, his eyes wide as he stares at the screen.

Charles Morgan was one of the top climatologists in the United States before the Long Winter. His team at the National Oceanic and Atmospheric Agency, or NOAA, modeled the Long Winter and made some of the most precise predictions. I'm hoping he can do the same for us now.

"Doctor?" Brightwell asks, snapping him out of his trance.

"Is this all you have?" he whispers.

Aguilar hits a few keys, and the delta image caps join to make a choppy video that shows the massive storm moving along the river toward the mountains that border our valley.

Morgan leans forward, adjusting his thick glasses. "This is... unexpected."

"Will it impact us?"

"Definitely."

"How?"

"How fast is the storm moving? And what's the top wind speed?"

Aguilar answers a few seconds later. "It's moving at ten klicks an hour. Max wind speed is one hundred kph."

Morgan shakes his head. "This is bad."

Brightwell exhales impatiently. "Can you be more specific, Doctor?"

"Not really. Not with this much data." He throws his hands up. "We lived on Earth for millions of years—studied its climate for thousands of years. We've been here a year. We still have no idea what Eos is capable of. We don't even know—"

My voice calm, I lock eyes with Morgan. "Doctor. Tell us what you do know. Please do it quickly."

He takes a deep breath. "Eos is turning slightly because of that rogue planet passing by. Its gravity is exerting a pull on us." He cocks his head. "The *effect* is that our valley is being turned toward the star—just slightly, but enough to cause some major issues. Namely, it's making the valley hotter and more humid. Warm air from the desert is spilling into the jungles. The worst is what's happening to the rivers. This valley serves as a natural filter between the warm and cool sides of the planet. Warm water flows from the desert into the valley, where it cools before it reaches the dark side. With this change, the water reaching the dark side is now warmer."

Morgan points at the screen. "That storm is going to travel up that river, feeding on the warm water like a power source. If it reaches the mountains, the storm surge will send water back into the valley, and the storm could possibly shear the icecaps from the ridges, allowing even more warm air out of the valley and onto the dark side. It's a spiraling process until that planet passes."

"What does that mean for us—here?" I ask.

"I'm guessing the city will see a lot of rain. Snow will fall in the eastern jungle. The rivers will surge. The valley might even flood. That's probably why this area is grassland—and why I told you we should have studied the planet for longer before we settled here—"

"That's enough, Dr. Morgan. We've been over this. We didn't have enough rations on the *Jericho* for a prolonged study—"

"We could have settled in the mountains."

"This is not the time, Dr. Morgan."

This discussion has reared its head more and more since the storms began. When we arrived at Eos, we briefly considered settling in the foothills or even the mountains, but it would have been harder to farm there. That's likely the same reason the *Carthage* colonists settled nearby. We never imagined the climate would change so drastically, so quickly.

"The storm is a problem, but it's not the reason we called you," Brightwell says to Morgan. "As I'm sure you're aware, that sound in the distance is an E. rex stampede." She motions to Aguilar, who brings up the drone footage that begins with the canopy over Jericho City and continues on into the western jungle, displaying the sea of red heat signatures. "Given the E. rex are moving *toward* the storm on the dark side, I assume it's not what's causing the stampede."

Morgan seems stunned. Finally, he says, "Doubtful. Show me telemetry from the desert."

"It's seven hours old," Brightwell says. "That's when *Jericho* last flew over. Those two drones will reach the desert in..." She eyes Aguilar, who says, "Less than a minute."

"Show us real-time imagery from the drones."

On the screen, the drone footage shows the canopy of the western jungle, which is decimated. Massive trees have been thrown to the ground, shattered and strewn about like toothpicks. Many E. rex also lie on the ground. Some were crushed by the falling trees, but others are seemingly unharmed. Their heat signatures glow on the screen. They're alive. So why aren't they getting up? Fear?

Again, I wonder: What are they running from? What has forced this many to flee, more than we've ever seen before? And why have so many fallen?

On the screen, the western mountain range looms at the edge of the jungle. Beyond the mountains lies the vast desert that stretches across the light side of Eos. Above the ridge line, a wall of sand and wind spreads out.

"A sandstorm," Brightwell says quietly. "Is that what the herd is running from?"

"Maybe," Morgan whispers. "At least one of the sandstorms breached the mountains and flattened some of the jungle." He steps closer to the screen and points. "There, look. Focus on that downed E. rex."

The image zooms in on the fallen beast. It's not moving. Deep cuts run all over its body, as if a razor blade sliced into it a thousand times.

"I'm guessing this is why they're running," Morgan says. "It's not the sandstorm—it's a predator that is following

the storm and the warm air from the desert into the jungle."
Still pointing at the image of the dead E. rex, he turns to
Brightwell and me. "If this predator can do that to the E.
rex, we don't stand a chance."

James

A whistling sound screams from the mouth of the cave, reaching down into the darkness like a ghost calling for me.

Arthur turns slightly toward the sound. "The storm has begun, James. Leave now."

"There's something down here you don't want me to find."

"Or maybe I just don't want you to get yourself killed."

I push off from the wall and step toward the bones, my headlamp illuminating them. It's the saddest, most grotesque thing I've ever seen: the remains of people lying in piles, the skeletons of children hugging the adults.

I recognize the clothes. These are AU uniforms. The fatigues have been dyed green, just like ours back at Jericho City.

The wind grows louder by the second. If there is a storm out there, it is indeed picking up.

I skirt the edge of the bones, careful not to disturb them, and cast my light deeper into the cave. The bodies there are better preserved. The skin is gray, the hair and nails brittle.

They look almost like corpses in a morgue. Indeed, the cave provides an almost ideal place to preserve them—it's dark and cold. The moisture, however, isn't ideal.

I squat beside the first bodies, the skeletons, to inspect them closer. Tiny insects are crawling over the bones. That's what took away the flesh. No doubt bacteria did their share of the work too. Moisture enables the bugs and the bacteria to survive down here.

As I stand, my headlamp passes over a pair of blue coveralls similar to the ones I wore in the warehouse in Camp Nine. The face above is gray and sunken, but I recognize my old friend lying among the dead.

"Harry," I whisper as I move to his body. Fowler is beside him, and Charlotte is a few feet away, hugging two smaller bodies.

These are the *Carthage* colonists. Our lost colony has been found. But why here? At the origin—or termination—of the Eye of the Grid?

My light glints off something in Harry's hand. I reach down and gently move his stiff fingers, wincing as I touch his cold, dead skin.

It's a small data drive.

I stare at it a long moment. For some reason, I instinctively sense that it's a message he's left for me, here where he knew I would find it, deep in this cave that is safe from the storms and predators and whatever else lies in wait for us on Eos. But I dread what it will tell me. And I can't possibly ignore it.

I plug the drive into the tablet. It brings up a list of hundreds of files. Documents. Charts. Logs from medical devices and test results. At the top of the file listing is a video named _Hello-World. I open it.

Harry's face fills the screen. He's sitting in a cave—this cave, by the looks of it. A dim light shines on his face from below. His voice is soft, as if he doesn't want the people nearby to hear him.

"Welcome to this week's episode of *Tales from the Crypt*." He raises his eyebrows theatrically, then settles into a somber smile. "That's probably not as funny as I think it is, but hey, how many times does a joke like that present itself? Actually, that show was probably before your time anyway."

He stares directly into the camera. "I'm leaving this for you, James, because I figure you'll be the one who finds this place. I hope learning what happened to us will help you. It'll become obvious soon why we didn't go back to the camp. Why we came here."

He swallows, as if gathering his thoughts.

"It all started with the storms."

5

Emma

I feel all eyes in the command post staring at me, waiting for my orders. I want to pick up the radio and call to James again, but my first duty is to this colony.

I've been here once before, in a similar situation, where seconds were the difference between life and death, when the people I was responsible for were under attack. That day was my last aboard the International Space Station. I watched my entire crew die in the blink of an eye. I've replayed those seconds a million times in my mind. I know I will do the same with these seconds.

Brightwell drifts closer to me, turning her back to the eyes on us, her voice low.

"Given the predator that's driving the E. rex, and the storm behind them, I don't think we can divert the herd. Not all of them. And the storm on the dark side might just drive them right back to the city again. One way or the other, odds are we'll be overrun."

"You said before that we can't evacuate everyone before the herd arrives. That means we can evacuate *some*, correct?"

She nods. "Maybe half, possibly more. We'd need to hurry."

"Proceed, Colonel. Evacuate as many as you can and make preparations for those who will have to stay."

Brightwell barks orders at the soldiers around the room, no longer trying to be quiet. We're not hiding anymore. Leaving will be noisy.

When the stampedes began, we created an evacuation plan. A scouting team identified a cave at the base of the eastern mountain range that we believe will serve as a viable shelter. The team hasn't had time to return to the cave and do a thorough survey—or even explore far beyond the entrance. I pressed them to at least venture farther and map the passages and chambers, but the expedition leader insisted that they would only find "more cave" and that even if the cave isn't big enough for our population, there are a dozen more close by that could be used for the overflow. The evacuation prep team has instead focused their efforts on clearing a path to the cave—their reasoning being that if we don't have a way to get to the cave, it doesn't matter how large it is. I suppose they were right. I just hope the cave will hold us.

Most of the colonists will walk—or run—to the cave. We'll use the ATVs to transport those who can't make it on foot. The plan is to station troops in the woods to guard against E. rex and other predators attacking the convoy. I fear those troops may be nothing more than sacrifices left along our path to slow our enemy.

James knows the location of the cave. When he sees what's happening, hopefully he'll meet us there.

"How far out is the herd now?" I ask.

Aguilar responds. "About twenty-five minutes, ma'am."

"What are our options for slowing them down?" I ask Brightwell.

"I've got a tactical team in the jungle along their vector. The alphas will be at the head of the pack. We take them down and hope that the herd disperses or changes course. We'll also fire along the northern flank of the formation, trying to force them south. As you know, the evac cave lies to the northeast."

"Do it."

Brightwell gives the order as I stare at the blue dot on the map, the cave that is our best hope of survival.

"Other options?" I ask.

Brightwell shakes her head. "I don't see any. We don't have any heavy artillery."

"We do have something that will burn though."

Brightwell cocks her head, confused.

"The field. Burn it."

Brightwell's eyes go wide with surprise. She quickly brings her reaction under control as I lay out my plan.

"Use the grass hooks to cut a perimeter around the city, then light it up. If we're right about the E. rex's visual ability, they'll see a wall of red and smell the smoke long before they reach the city."

"That might keep them away," Brightwell says cautiously. "But the fire won't stop at the tree line. The jungle could burn too. And the wind could carry the flames back into the city. The canopy is fire-retardant, but it will provide limited protection."

"Let's worry about getting out first. If we live, *then* we'll worry about where we're going to live."

"Yes, ma'am."

Brightwell issues the orders and turns back to me. "Your vehicle will be ready—"

"I'm staying."

She takes a deep breath. I know what's coming next.

"I'm staying," I repeat. "'Til the very last person is out of this city. So let's focus. What's next?"

Over the command post speakers, a man's voice whispers, "CP, Team Alpha. We're in position. Awaiting fire authorization."

Brightwell clicks the microphone at her station. "Team Alpha, CP. Fire at will."

On the screen, I watch the red dots of the herd, the diamond formation moving through the jungle. Ahead of it are five green dots—our people, hopefully safe in the trees above the stampede.

From the drone's non-infrared images, I see trees tumbling as the herd moves. The canopy above us ripples. The ground shakes.

My mind drifts to Sam, Allie, and Carson. I hope Madison or Abby is taking care of them. They're probably scared to death. I'm scared to death.

Aguilar's voice breaks the silence. "Ma'am, one E. rex confirmed kill. Herd is shifting."

The diamond formation breaks. Several of the E. rex at the head of the herd slow, but those behind keep pace. They transform into an upside-down triangle that slowly breaks in two.

Brightwell grabs the microphone on her desk. "Alpha Team, move north and engage the herd splitting off. Drive them south—at all costs."

When the response comes, I hear what sounds like someone moving down a zip line. "Alpha Team, Alpha One. Dismount and move north. On me. No time for elevated cover. Fire from the ground and keep moving. Use the trunks for cover."

The E. rex will overrun them, even if they hide behind the trees.

Brightwell turns and finds a captain in the group.

"Amelio, get Bravo Team into the jungle. Same orders, drive them south. At all costs, Captain."

With a nod, the man vanishes into the darkness. Behind him, ATVs are being loaded, kids are crying, and adults are yelling. Beyond the canopy, the thunder of the stampede grows louder.

I pick up a handheld radio and activate it. "James, do you copy? Please respond."

I wait, then try again. "James, a herd is moving toward the city. We're evacuating to the cave. Please respond."

As I listen for a response, I realize Grigory and Min are standing next to me, staring.

"What?"

"We want to alter the ship's orbit," Min says.

"Why?"

"We can't establish a geosynchronous orbit because the Hill sphere—"

"I know. What sort of orbit are we talking about?" I ask.

"Around the terminator," Min replies. "It will give us visual on the rest of the valley around the planet. We might find a better place to go."

"It's not perfect solution," Grigory says. "The ship will have to veer out of orbit to grab sunlight for solar cells."

"Do it. And disassemble four of the comm panels and protect them. The herd might destroy the field."

"Of course," Min says. "And we have another idea."

I nod to him, and he continues. "The canopy. We can detach it and bring it to the ground. Use it as a shield."

"That's brilliant. Get to it."

Outside the command post, automatic gunfire erupts.

6

James

In the video, Harry says, "I think I should probably start at the beginning, with the spheres. I think somehow they're connected to the storms, but I'm still not sure."

He holds up his tablet. The image is one I've come to know very well in the last nine months: the Eye of the Grid.

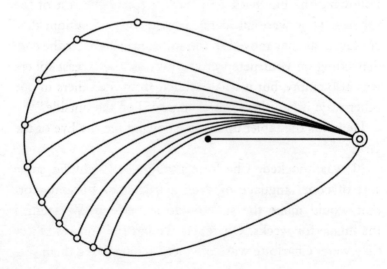

"I'm assuming you found the symbol I left at Carthage City. Or maybe you found the symbol without seeing my message. Let me tell you how I found it. Shortly after we arrived on Eos, I built a rover and started searching the dark side of the planet for rare metals. We were trying to manufacture incendiary rounds to kill or divert those giant dinosaur-like predators. We call them Eos rex—or E. rex for short. They weren't a problem at first, but the herds kept moving closer to the city. When the rover located the first sphere, I thought it was the core of a meteor. Imagine my surprise when I dug down and saw it—a smooth, hollow, obsidian sphere. There was no question it was alien in origin. It was empty, and there were no clues about who made it or why. I thought there might be other spheres out here, so I built two more rovers. I even tried to get the drones in on the search. I found a second sphere, then a third. By then, the pattern was clear. They were arranged in an arcing line, and the spacing of the spheres followed a formula. Following the line back and forth, I found the rest of the spheres. They were all identical, with one exception: they got larger as they moved to the start of the line. Or the end, depending on your perspective. Anyway, the largest sphere was also empty, but it was different from the others in one other way: it had this symbol engraved on the outside."

He holds the tablet up again, showing me the Eye of the Grid.

"I was shocked. Charlotte thought it might be some sort of code language or even a frequency of some sort that would make the spheres do something. We studied the image for weeks. Obviously we left the spheres where they were. Charlotte was convinced that moving them was

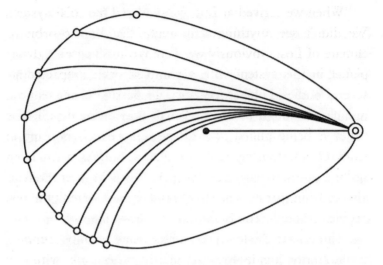

a bad idea—that they might need the cold weather or that displacing them could set in motion some security measure or other dangerous event."

Harry lets the tablet fall back to his lap. "But we got nowhere—with either the spheres or the symbol. The only thing the symbol gave us was two points we didn't have on the arcing line. At one location, the one on the outside, we found nothing. And at the location in the center of the symbol, where the line starts, we found this cave. I was excited then. I was sure it was the key to unlocking the mystery of the spheres."

He shakes his head. "I searched it from top to bottom, for weeks, but there's nothing here. It's empty. Maybe whatever was here has already been taken—a geocached treasure found long ago. Or maybe it's some sick joke the grid is playing on us. I never got to find out, because we soon had other problems."

Harry takes a deep breath, steeling himself.

"When we arrived at Eos, we surveyed the solar system. We didn't see anything that might disrupt the orbit or climate of Eos. Obviously we were wrong. There's a dwarf planet in this system with a complex orbit, impacted by several bodies. Long story short, it's passing near Eos now, just close enough to exert a small gravitational pull. The valley is being pulled toward the star. Heat is pouring in from the desert, bringing storms with it. And the warm front spilling onto the dark side, along with the warmer rivers, is also causing storms. The storms themselves weren't the real problem though. The E. rex stampedes were.

"They started slowly at first, small groups running through the jungle for the plains, coinciding with the storms. We thought they would pass. But then a massive storm swept out in the desert. It sent a massive herd of E. rex fleeing the jungle. It had to be thousands. We just ran. We put everything down and evacuated. Earls ordered his troops into the jungle, every last one of them. Hundreds of men and women. The plan was for them to shell the herds and divert them. The sounds over the radio..."

For the first time, I hear someone else on the video, coughing in the distance. Harry stares beyond the tablet and calls out, "Lawrence? You okay?"

He jumps up, taps the tablet, and the screen goes blank, but only for a second. It resumes with Harry again sitting in the floor of the cave. He looks different now. Empty. Beaten. His voice is a whisper, emotionless.

"The last thing I did when I left the city was put the symbol on the comm panels. In the event we didn't return, I hoped you would see it and figure it out. As I said, I think it's connected to what happens on Eos somehow. The orbit of the planets, the ecosystem disruption. Maybe it's a warning."

He pauses. "We never heard from our troops again. They must have been overrun. We didn't go looking—we knew what we would find. The predators in those jungles don't let carrion lie long. We retreated to a cave in the eastern jungle, at the base of the mountains. It was the logical place to wait out the herds and the storms. The complex was vast, and Earls liked it because it had only one entrance, making it easy to defend from anything out there. What we didn't know was what was waiting for us *inside* that cave. It changed everything."

Emma

It's absolute chaos in the command post. Brightwell is shouting orders. Grigory dashes through the exit, off to bring down the canopy. Min is typing furiously at the comm terminal, issuing new orders to the *Carthage*. Izumi is gone, probably prepping the sick in the infirmary for transport.

The ground vibrates.

The gunfire is unrelenting.

From the long table, Aguilar turns to Brightwell. "Five E. rex running ahead of the herd have reached us. They've slowed in the field." He pauses, listening to his headset. "One down, the other four are wounded. They're breaking off."

The gunfire will no doubt draw the herd's attention, but what choice do we have?

"Alpha Team, respond," Brightwell calls over the radio.

On the screen, the troops' green markers aren't moving. The drones can locate the transponders in the suits, but they can't tell us if the people inside are still alive.

Brightwell shakes her head. "Bravo Team, respond."

There's no answer. Both teams are down. Or they're surrounded and can't make a sound. I hope for the latter.

Outside, the gunfire ceases. In its wake, I hear other sounds: the roar of the herd in the jungle, voices yelling here in the city, vehicles speeding away. Through the command post doorway, I see ATV tracks kicking up dirt as they drive across the city's hard-packed streets. The evacuation has started.

We have a little over five thousand people in Jericho City. We would need a hundred buses to evacuate them. And we don't have any buses. What we have are ATVs with tracks pulling trailers. We typically use the trailers to carry material and food back to the city. Now those trailers are loaded with people—those who can't make the hike, mostly the young and the old. They're packed in tight, holding each other.

Brightwell was right: we'll never get everyone out in time. Waking up five thousand people and getting them out of the city in twenty-five minutes just isn't possible.

"Ten minutes," Aguilar calls out.

Outside, I hear Madison calling my name. I dash out of the command post, into the open. People are everywhere, thousands of them. The convoy leaving the city already reaches to the eastern jungle, the lead ATV out of sight. Troops are spaced out along the western side of the convoy, ready to engage any E. rex that come their way.

I snake through the crowd, following her voice. The heat is suffocating. Finally, I break through and find Madison holding Carson. Allie and Sam are beside her. Her own children, Owen and Adeline, are squeezed in behind her, holding hands, forming a protective barrier of sorts.

Madison's husband, David, is beyond the crowd, loading people onto trailers hooked to the ATVs. James's brother, Alex, and his wife, Abby, are also helping to load people. Their two children, Jack and Sarah, stand close to Madison, faces serious, hands held out to keep the crowd from pressing into her.

"There's room on our trailer," Madison says, holding Carson out to me. "I can get your things from your flat—"

I gently press Carson back into her arms. "I'm right behind you."

"What?"

"I have to help with things here."

Madison glances in the direction of the thundering herd then back at me, silently making her point.

"Mom!" Allie cries, reaching for me. I squat and pull her into a tight hug, then put my arm around Sam. They're puffy-eyed, still half asleep, both scared. Sam is putting on a brave face as usual. I kiss Allie on the forehead. Sam wiggles as I plant a kiss on him too.

"Listen to your aunt. I'll be along soon, and she'll tell me if you act up." I stare at them, my expression stern. They're used to seeing that. Right now, I'm hoping that warning them about getting in trouble for disobeying will subtly put them at ease, assuring them that my discipline is the only danger they face.

"The E. rex—" Sam begins.

"Will pass soon," I finish. "Now get going."

When they turn to join their cousins, I hug Madison and Carson in her arms. "Thank you," I whisper.

Alex walks toward us, squinting as he moves through the crowd. "Where's James?"

"On his way. He'll join us soon."

I leave it at that—and hope I'm right.

Overhead, the canopy groans, the sound of steel bending, the massive cover sliding sideways on its rails. I glance up and see Grigory at the top of one of the giant piers. Two of his technicians are atop other piers. At night, the canopy is positioned toward the desert, but now we need it to move slightly toward the western jungle—and to come down all the way to the ground. The steel groans again and the canopy shudders.

Just beyond the canopy, a small group of soldiers with grass hooks are felling the tall blue-green grass in broad strokes, making a sort of fire break that we hope will keep the blaze from the city. Another group of soldiers collects the fallen grass into stacks away from the city. Still more soldiers, holding rifles at the ready, creep forward as the grass falls, ready to fire on any E. rex emerging from the forest.

I hear the pitter-patter of rain falling on the canopy. The blue-green sea of grass sways in the wind. Suddenly, the blades begin to glisten as rain falls in sheets. Not great timing for our whole burn-the-field plan.

Rushing back to the command post, I hear Dr. Morgan's voice before I reach the threshold. "I have no idea. Without aerial footage, it's impossible to predict."

When I'm inside, Brightwell locks eyes with me. "It's raining."

"I know. Light the field up now."

Brightwell gives the order. On the screen, the herds are almost out of the jungle. They've slowed some. One group will miss us by a wide margin. The other is still heading for us, on a vector slightly north. They'll pass the city and overrun the convoy. It's a worst-case scenario.

"How long is the trip to the cave?" I ask.

Aguilar shrugs. "About fifteen minutes. The first vehicles should arrive in five minutes or so."

There's a crash outside the door.

"Canopy is in place," Aguilar says.

A minute later, the smell of smoke drifts into the command post, putrid and thick.

Brightwell steps close to me, speaking quietly. "We have to stop the evac. The people who've already departed might make it to the cave. And those leaving on vehicles now. But anyone leaving after might get caught out on the plain when the herd gets here."

I nod. She's right. Anyone out there between the city and the eastern jungle will be a sitting duck.

"What do we do with the people still here?"

"It's your call, ma'am."

I nod. "Get them back into the barracks. Crowd everyone into the flats away from the direction the herd is traveling. Have them crouch against the walls. I want guard teams at every entrance."

As Brightwell gives the order, I step out of the command post just in time to see the ATV pulling a trailer with Madison on it, Carson in her arms, Allie and Sam beside her. They're getting out. They'll reach the cave.

8

James

Arthur steps closer to me. "Stop the video now, James."

I draw the energy weapon and train it on him. "Back up."

He holds up his hands. "That's no way to treat someone trying to help you."

"This video is what you were afraid I would find down here, isn't it? Or something like it."

He glances away as if bored.

"How does me seeing this harm the grid?"

"Maybe it harms you, James."

"We'll see about that."

Still holding the energy weapon, I press play, and Harry continues his story.

"We evacuated nearly four thousand residents to the cave. About two hundred feet in, we noticed a spongy substance on the cave walls and floor. It was black, almost indistinguishable from the rock it grew on. Whenever someone approached a sponge, it would release a fine powdery substance, almost like pollen, but gray." He smiles ruefully. "Fowler and I called them regolith sponges. The color and fine powder reminded us of moon dust. We figured it was harmless."

Harry falls silent. His eyes fill with tears.

"The kids were the first to get sick. Coughing. Fever. By the time we figured out what was happening, everyone was sick. We had brought some medicine with us. We tried everything—antibiotics, antivirals, anti-inflammatories. We were even testing antidepressants and insulin by the end. Nothing had any effect."

He holds up a data drive—the same one plugged into my tablet. "All of our data is on here." He sets the drive down and looks into the camera again. "The first deaths occurred eight hours after we entered the cave. We fell like dominos after that. It was like a bomb went off. Our first instinct was to take everyone back to Carthage City and put them in stasis. But the herds had destroyed most of the buildings, and none of the troops were responding. Even if we found the stasis equipment intact, it would have taken days, maybe weeks to get everyone into stasis. And the E. rex were still everywhere. Going back would have been certain death. And worse, if you found some of our infected corpses, whatever this is would spread to you."

Harry takes a deep breath and glances away from the camera. "I thought about trying to get back to Carthage City just to leave a message for you—to warn you about the caves and the sponges. But I would have never gotten past the E. rex. I'm not even sure I would have made it anyway. At the rate we're dying, we've determined that we don't have much time left. Certainly not enough to find a cure."

He brings a hand up, covering his mouth as he coughs. "Our only hope was to get away from the regolith sponges and hope the disease went away. We covered the mouth of the cave with rocks to prevent anyone else from finding it, and we left. We couldn't go west, so we went east. To this cave. I knew it didn't have the regolith sponges. I hoped that maybe, just being away from the sponges might cure us. So much for that idea."

He shrugs, a sad smile on his lips. "James, you've got to stay out of the caves at the base of the eastern mountains. And the regolith sponges are probably in other caves, too. I think maybe it's too cold for them here in this cave. Or maybe there's a predator that feeds on them here. If someone from Jericho gets infected by the sponges, I hope the data we collected helps you find a cure. I don't know if you can contract the disease from our corpses, but the best advice I can give you, James, is to quarantine yourself until you're sure you haven't been infected. And whatever you do, don't go in those caves."

Emma

The sound of the herd blots out everything else. In the command post, Brightwell's mouth is moving, but it's like I'm watching a movie that's been muted. She's talking to the technicians, but all I hear is the herd barreling toward us.

Finally, she steps back and draws a hand across her neck in a kill motion. The technicians in the domed building scramble to turn off every machine, then race for the barracks. They don't have suits to hide their body heat from the E. rex. But I do. So does Brightwell.

To me, she holds up three fingers on one hand and makes an 'O' with the other.

Thirty seconds.

Thirty seconds until the herd reaches us.

Brightwell pulls on a face mask that covers her entire face except for the two pieces of plastic where the eyes are. From the outside, the eyes look black, but you can see perfectly from the inside.

As Brightwell puts her gloves on, I don my own face mask and gloves and accept the automatic rifle she hands me. Without a word, we march quickly out of the command post. Two other suited army soldiers fall in behind us. We proceed directly to the barracks on the edge of the city— farthest away from the herd.

Min and Grigory arrive there just as we do.

Min recognizes me only by the name tag on my suit. "They're coming—"

"We know," I say. "Get inside."

"Have you seen Izumi?" he asks quickly.

"No. She's probably in the infirmary."

He turns in that direction, but I catch his arm. "There's no time, Min. Get inside. We'll look for her after."

As they dash into the building, I glance up at the ripples in the canopy. At that moment, a screech calls out in the din, a wild, unnatural call like nothing I've ever heard. It makes my skin crawl, like hearing nails on a chalkboard.

The E. rex have seen the wall of fire.

Are they diverting? I hope so. It might be our only chance.

Brightwell motions for the two suited soldiers to take up positions at opposite ends of the barracks. She turns to me and points toward the door to a nearby flat.

I shake my head and hold up my rifle, then nod at the entrance where she's taken up position. I can't see her face, but I know she doesn't like it one bit. She simply points to the floor behind her and grips her rifle.

I squat and listen, trying to make out the herd's movements. The E. rex calls are closer now, louder. The thunder of the stampede shakes the barracks floor, bouncing tiny bits of dirt and rock near the baseboards.

Time seems to slow. My heart pounds in my chest. I feel my breath pushing against the mask. My palms feel sweaty and clammy, the gun suddenly like a lead weight in my grip. But I cling tight, watching the empty streets, the shaking canopy above, and the black smoke drifting beneath and into the city.

A strong gust of wind rushes past, carrying the smoke away and pulling at the canopy. Has the sandstorm reached us?

Then a boom explodes through the city—the sound of the canopy fabric breaking as the first E. rex hit it. Metal groans like a wounded animal as some of the beasts miss the openings in the canopy and strike the frame.

More waves of thick black smoke roll through the city. The smell of burning grass is overpowered by a new odor: burning flesh. The E. rex didn't make it through the field of fire unscathed.

The next boom erupts from somewhere much closer. The first E. rex has hit one of the barracks. More crashes follow, buildings crumbling as the massive animals plow into them.

I wonder then if the E. rex are still on fire. If they are, it could spread to the barracks. Our citizens hiding there would be forced to either put out the fire or flee. They would be out in the open either way. Vulnerable.

That's my last thought before Brightwell spins and points at the flat behind me, motioning for me to go.

When I shake my head, she sets her rifle down, grasps me by the shoulders, and spins me toward the doorway, pushing me, covering me with her body.

I realize what she's doing a split second before the flat across the hall explodes.

The debris slams into Brightwell's back, propelling her into me. I hit the floor hard, my hands barely breaking my fall. I expect Brightwell to roll off of me, but she lies there, limp.

Gently, I push up on an elbow, and she rolls onto the floor, face up.

Through the gloves, I can't feel her pulse.

I'm reaching out to her chest to try to feel for a heartbeat, when I see the E. rex across the hall, lying in the flat. It seems to be unconscious. Or dead.

Its thick, scaly skin is black from the fire that burned it. Around the hole it made in the barracks, a few small flames still crackle. But they're going out as the wind picks up.

Without warning, its eyes snap open and it springs to life, arms clawing for anything to help it stand, head thrashing back and forth like a battering ram against the walls. The entire building shakes.

I freeze, my hand hovering above Brightwell's chest. She still hasn't moved.

The E. rex freezes too—and slowly its head swings toward me, eyes raking over my body, until it's staring directly at me. Directly into my eyes.

Its nostrils flare as it exhales, and the warm air rushes over me.

James

On the tablet, Harry smiles. The lines on his face are deeper than I've ever seen them, his skin ashy.

"Good luck, James. You'll come through it, if anyone can."

He reaches down, taps his tablet, and the video fades to black.

I wait, expecting Arthur to react—to attack me or to try to destroy the tablet or make a snide remark. At this moment, I think I would shoot him if he did.

But he doesn't move. In the icy cave, he simply stares at the piles of bodies that stretch into the darkness.

There was something in this cave he didn't want me to find. Was it the video? Or something else?

Quickly, I scan the other files on the drive. There are no other videos, only medical files. I can read the charts and lab results, but I'll need Izumi in order to really do anything with it. I have to get back to Jericho City.

"Let's go."

Arthur turns to me. "Where?"

"Home. Just like you suggested."

"Might be too late for that."

"What do you mean?"

Arthur doesn't respond.

The moment drags on.

Wind howls through the cave opening. The cold air blows through me like a wind tunnel in a freezer. I stow the tablet and pull on my gloves.

"What do you mean, 'It might be too late'?" I ask again.

"The storms of Eos have returned, James. You should have left when I told you."

"Well, we're leaving now."

I motion toward the entrance with the energy weapon, and Arthur begins marching. The beam from my headlamp guides our way, and I can't help but rake it over the walls, looking for the regolith sponges. As Harry said, there are none here.

At the mouth of the cave, the cold is even worse. It seeps through my facemask, parka, and gloves right down into my flesh and bones.

The scene outside is beautiful. The wind carries snowflakes through the air like dandelion seeds floating by. The Spanish moss-like plants hanging from the tree limbs are coated with snow. I feel as though I've been shrunk and placed in a snow globe. Eos has never felt more alien than it does now.

A stiff gust knocks sheets of snow off the trees and sends flakes flurrying. For a moment, all I see is white.

I hear Arthur moving, footsteps going away from me. I raise the energy weapon.

"Freeze."

I can't see him, but his crunching footfalls cease.

If he's going to make a move on me, now would be the time.

His disembodied voice is calm. "If we don't move, we'll both freeze, James."

The wind dies down, and when I can see Arthur again, I realize he is halfway to the ATV.

Usually when I return to Jericho City from the dark side, I put Arthur back into the landing capsule and arm the explosives. It's an insulated prison cell, and it has been effective at containing him. Now, however, I feel that I might need his help. Emma, Allie, Sam, and Carson could be in danger at this very moment.

"You're coming with me."

He raises his eyebrows. "Not back into the cage?"

"Not this time."

I mount the ATV and motion for him to walk ahead of me. He trudges through the forest far more slowly than he's capable of.

"Get a move on," I call out.

He says nothing, but increases his speed slightly.

I draw the radio from my backpack. "Jericho, this is James, do you copy?"

The forest is silent except for the sound of the ATV tracks crunching in the snow, Arthur's footfalls, and the wind barreling through the massive trees. The gusts are gaining strength. Pieces of the moss-like substance fall around us.

"Jericho, do you copy?"

I'm within range. Why aren't they responding?

I push the ATV closer to its top speed and shout to Arthur. "Move it!"

The dense forest changes to snow-covered shrubs as we climb into the shadow of the mountain peaks. It's darkest here, but soon we'll crest the ridge and see into the valley.

When we're high enough to clear the tree canopy, I feel a strong wind at my back. I turn and get my first glimpse of a storm raging on the dark side. It's like nothing I've ever seen. It's a wall of snow, churning and spinning. A white hurricane on land. That's the first thought I have. A wide river lies beneath it, icy plains on each side. And it's coming this way. If it crosses the mountains into the valley, it'll be trouble for the city. If it catches me, I'll have to try to find a cave to hide in and ride it out.

I press Arthur harder after that. We bound through the rocky pass, finally arriving at a lake. It's the source of two rivers—one flowing into the valley, the other flowing into the dark side. The path around the lake is narrow and sparse. Today there's a thick film of fog hanging over the lake, as if it's a volcano about to erupt.

About halfway around the lake, I hear thunder in the distance. But this thunder doesn't stop. It drones on, growing louder.

On the other side of the lake, I peer down into the valley. The eastern jungle is still and quiet. But the canopy of the western jungle shakes. The leaves—green, blue, and purple—ripple like a body of water. What's happening?

What I see beyond the western jungle makes my mouth run dry: a wall of sand, churning and spinning. It shines brown, gold, and blood-red with the light from Eos's star. It's like a sand monster, burning through the jungle.

And behind me lies a storm of ice, also marching on the valley.

"What's happening?" I ask Arthur quietly.

"I told you."

"Tell me again."

"The storms of Eos have returned, James. You should have gone home."

11

Emma

Inside the barracks, it's dead quiet.

The E. rex stares at me through the open door of the flat. My hand hovers over Brightwell's chest. I'm terrified to move.

The flames on the beast's back are dying down, the wind extinguishing them. Still, the stench of burned flesh assaults my nostrils and turns my stomach. But I don't flinch. I don't dare make a move.

Outside, the stampede grows louder. The thunderous sound rumbles through my body.

The herd seems to bring the wind with it. The gusts turn to gale force, blowing through the city like a twister through a prairie town, tearing off loose pieces of the barracks and rolling debris through the streets.

My heart beats in my throat as I stare down the E. rex.

Through the din, a voice calls out. "Emma!"

It's Grigory, yelling from the flat two doors down.

The E. rex snaps its head toward the sound.

"Emma!" he calls again. "Are you all right?"

The E. rex raises its arms and claws at the interior walls, trying to free itself from the thick exterior wall it crashed through.

Quickly, I make my choice. I jerk my hand away from Brightwell. If she's dead, there's nothing I can do. If she's unconscious—and alive—I want her to stay that way.

I lean forward and crawl out of the flat.

"Emma!" Grigory calls out again.

Reaching out into the hallway, I grab my rifle and bring it to my shoulder. I train the sight on the E. rex's head and yell as loud as I can.

"Hey!"

As it spins toward me, I pull the trigger.

The gun kicks like a mule. My shoulder throbs as the rounds hit the E. rex. The beast cries out loudly enough to blow out my eardrums. With the noise of the herd and wind around me, I feel like I'm in the center of a hurricane.

Blood pours from gunshot wounds on the E. rex's neck and head, but the giant animal is still alive.

And mad.

It roars again, mouth open, and finally breaks free from the wall, its back legs propelling it toward me.

I pull the trigger again.

12

James

The blue-green field that stretches from Jericho City to the western jungle is covered with a thick cloud of black smoke. But as the clouds shift, I glimpse the charred expanse below.

They burned the field. A few small fires are still burning. Through gaps in the black cloud, I spot E. rex stampeding across the black soil, disappearing beneath the canopy of Jericho City, which now has a dozen large rips in it. The fabric ripples as E. rex crash into the frame.

Still holding the binoculars, I activate the radio.

"Jericho, this is James. *Do you copy?*"

No response.

A thought seizes me: What if the sound of the radio puts them in danger? If they're still in the city, they're hiding from the E. rex.

I pan around with the binoculars, looking for clues to what's happening. But the action in Jericho City is shrouded under the vast canopy and the cloud of smoke.

I scan the eastern jungle. At a break in the tree cover, I see an ATV pulling a trailer full of people—kids and elderly mostly. Adults with backpacks jog behind them. They're evacuating.

And they're heading toward the eastern mountains, to an emergency evacuation cave we identified weeks ago. It likely has the regolith sponges—beyond the entrance, beyond where the scout team ventured in during their brief survey.

I have to warn them, even if it risks giving away their position to the E. rex.

"Jericho, do you copy? Do not take refuge in the caves in the eastern mountains. I repeat—*do not* go to the caves in the eastern mountains!"

I wait, but there's no response.

For five minutes, I repeat the warning, watching as the E. rex herd dwindles and the smoke slowly clears from the field.

Standing at the edge of the cliff above the valley, Arthur turns to me. "You should have gone home when you could, James."

"What do you know about all this? Tell me."

"Nothing to tell, James."

"Is this what the Eye of the Grid sees?"

He smiles. "The Eye sees everything."

I'm sick of his cryptic answers and double talk. "Let's go."

"Home? It seems your neighbors are partying on your lawn again. Best to wait—"

"We're going to the cave."

He raises his eyebrows. "Cave?"

"The evac cave. It probably has the regolith sponges."

"Bad idea."

"We're going to make sure no one reaches it. Now go."

Reluctantly, he turns and begins down the mountain.

The sound of the herd grows louder as we descend. At the tree line at the base of the mountain, the sound fades significantly, as if the forest is an insulated sound booth.

In contrast to the sunlight at the lake, the forest feels dark and cold, almost like the far side of Eos. Creatures call and crawl around me, as if every single part of this jungle is alive. They all seem to be in motion, flowing by me, going south. Why?

This valley was here for billions of years before we arrived. It has its own rhythms, seasons, and supercycles. More than ever, I feel like a visitor here, a colonist in a foreign land, in over my head.

As we travel through the dense jungle path I cut months ago, I try the radio periodically. There's never a response.

Behind me, the wind picks up, a cool breeze that rustles the canopy and sends the animals scurrying faster. The faint rumbling of the herds grows, echoing through the forest. The E. rex are reaching deeper into the eastern jungle.

"We shouldn't be out here," Arthur says over the noise. "The storm has breached the mountains. It'll come fast now."

"Suggestions?"

"We need to take cover. The herd will be on us before the storm, but we can't survive either one."

"No. We don't stop until we reach the cave."

"James—"

"If those colonists are going there, they'll die. I'm not going to let that happen."

Arthur shakes his head, but he bounds forward, running now.

The wind howls at our backs. Icy rain pelts the forest canopy, then breaks through, falling like ice water blended and poured down on me. Leaves and twigs fall with it.

I push the ATV harder, standing as I ride, leaning forward. Arthur leads me, running flat-out with no further goading required.

The wind grows colder. The icy rain morphs into sleet and snow, and suddenly it's coming down in sheets.

The roar of the herd grows ever louder.

I glance down at the tablet. At my current speed, I'm thirty minutes from the cave. It'll be close.

A branch above me snaps in the wind and crashes to the ground behind me.

Through the din, I think I hear a voice calling my name. I glance around, but all I see is ice and jungle. The wind catches me, almost throwing me off the ATV, but I cling tight, grinding my teeth.

Just a little longer...

The voice comes again, faint, blotted out by the sleet and hail pelting everything around me.

I realize then where the sound is coming from: the radio. Emma's voice.

I'm pulling the radio from my pack when a gust catches me and throws me from the ATV into a thorny shrub at the base of a tree. Above me, limbs crack one after another, the sound like an automatic rifle firing in the snow-covered jungle. Through the white, I barely get a glimpse of the limbs before they bury me.

The world goes dark and the voice fades away with the herd and the wind.

Emma

The sound of the automatic rifle is deafening. It pounds my shoulder as it fires. Metal casings shower the ground, chiming like a slot machine paying out a jackpot.

The rounds dig into the E. rex's neck and mouth. Blood pours out as it screams. Then suddenly it collapses and falls silent. The gun clicks, and I release the trigger. I'm breathing so fast I might hyperventilate.

The only sounds now are the herd and the wind, both growing louder.

On my hands and knees, I crawl back to where Brightwell lies face-up on the floor of the flat.

She's breathing. It's shallow, but she's breathing.

"Tara," I whisper.

She doesn't move.

"Grigory," I call as quietly as I can.

"I'm here."

"Everyone okay?"

"Sort of," he says.

I don't like that response, but there isn't much I can do at this point.

"Stay where you are and stay covered."

I crawl back to the hall and grab both rifles. Glancing down the corridor, I see one of the other two soldiers peeking his head out of one of the flats. They took cover. Good.

Back in the flat, I take a magazine from Brightwell's pocket and reload the empty rifle, then cradle the other one, pointing it out the doorway, ready to fire.

Outside the barracks, the E. rex pound the streets of Jericho City.

Through the thunder of the stampede, I hear a man cry out. More voices join his—a woman; another man; then a chorus. A few seconds later, they all stop.

I swallow hard, heart beating fast. More than anything, I want to go out there. But I can't. I'd be trampled, and I might draw attention to the barracks.

The flat I'm in is a standard family unit with a queen bed on one wall and two bunk beds on the other. A table sits under the only window. Gently, I pull Brightwell toward the queen bed and slide her under it. Her head rolls toward me and she whispers, but I can't make out the words.

"Just rest," I tell her as I pull the mattress off one of the bunk beds and position it on the side of the bed, blocking any debris from hitting her.

Careful not to make any noise, I turn the table on its side and take up position behind it, rifle ready.

A second later, the barracks seems to explode. Two, maybe three E. rex collide into the building, screaming and clawing. I hear more shouts from another barracks.

I grip the rifle.

Two more crashes. They come faster then, E. rex colliding with the building and with the other beasts stuck in the side of the barracks. The thunder of the stampede is deafening. This is the main body of the herd.

To my left, I hear one of the animals break free, cross the hall, and begin destroying the flat next to mine, trying to escape the barracks. The bunk beds crumble, but the back wall holds as the beast bashes it with its head. It can't go forward, so it turns to its left, bashing into the wall that joins this flat. After a half dozen blows, the wall cracks, splits, and finally bursts open.

Two E. rex hands reach through the opening and begin clawing at the air.

I raise the rifle.

14

James

I wake to darkness and a cold I've never felt before, even at the depths of the Long Winter. The chill goes right down to my organs, seeming to freeze me from the inside.

I reach out, but my hand hits solid ice. The ache throughout my body is agonizing. It's as though I've been beaten nearly to death and left in a coffin of ice.

"Arthur!"

The word comes out scratchy and weak.

"Arthur!"

Stronger this time, but the sound simply bounces around in the dark like an echo chamber.

"Arth—"

A hand breaks through the ice, bringing light with it and a rush of cold air. The sporadic sound of E. rex feet beating on the jungle floor surrounds me.

The hand touches my chest and slides upward.

"Arthur, what—"

"Be quiet," he hisses.

I try to sit up, but the pain in my ribs overwhelms me just as Arthur's hand slams me back down. I grip his hand with one of mine, then throw a fist through the layer of ice, into the open.

Instantly Arthur moves his hand to my neck and squeezes. He is ten times stronger than me, but I fight him, squirming and pulling at his arm with both of my hands. His grip tightens.

I gasp, clawing at him, feet kicking, but he doesn't relent.

Darkness comes, slowly at first, then all at once, as if I've slipped off the edge, into a hole I'll never return from.

Emma

The short burst from my rifle rips through the E. rex's arms.

It instantly draws back from the crack in the wall, then surges forward, head first into the breach, widening it until I can see the animal's massive red eyes staring at me.

A bolt of fear surges through me as I pull the trigger again.

A crash explodes through the room—another E. rex trying to get through the barracks has blasted into the adjacent flat. Screeches and moans follow as the two beasts engage each other. The barracks shakes. The floor rumbles. The wall cracks and pieces crumble.

To my right, the mattress I put beside the queen bed falls to the floor. Brightwell crawls out, moving sluggishly at first, then pausing to listen. Through the crack in the wall, she sees the two E. rex fighting. She quickly motions for me to follow her out into the hall.

I hold my hands up, silently asking what she's thinking, but she ignores me, moving out, regaining some of her speed and dexterity.

In the hall, I get my first look at what's become of the barracks. Roughly half of the flats on the outer side lie open, their walls demolished from the animal impacts. The floor is covered in blood. E. rex lie dead in the doorways, trampled and cut up from the shards of the building.

Brightwell scampers to the utility closet in the middle of the barracks. Inside are a large water recycler and a rack for cleaning supplies and toiletries. She squats, grunting against the pain, and throws open a trap door.

"The crawlspace," I whisper.

"Only safe place," she replies, voice strained. "Go. I'll get the others."

Before I can protest, she's gone.

I drop the rifle into the dark pit, then quickly climb down the short ladder, only using a few rungs. The space is about four feet tall, with water pipes snaking to the shared bathrooms.

The floor above shakes as an E. rex bounds over the barracks. These are the stragglers, the ones trailing the main herd.

Another E. rex hits the building. This time the floor joists grind and buckle. Twenty feet away, an E. rex foot plunges through the floor and quickly jerks back above.

Staying low, I move to the back wall, farthest from the direction from which the herd is approaching. Why didn't I think of telling everyone to hide down here before—instead of in the flats? How many lives did that bad decision cost us?

I can't think that way. All I can do is make the best decisions I can in the moment and prepare myself to make better decisions in the future. Agonizing about them after the fact accomplishes nothing.

Another set of feet descend the ladder. Grigory. His face is bloody, but he gives me a tired smile. Min follows, then the rest of the command post team. They're battered, weary, and scared, but they're all alive.

We huddle at the rear foundation wall, watching the floor above. Suddenly the thunder of the herd starts up again and their feet pound the floor. It's a small group, not as large as the main herd, but sizeable nonetheless. The E. rex come in waves after that, more straggling groups of varying sizes.

The floors are soon warped. Debris spills down through the holes, pieces of the walls, bunks, and personal effects our friends and neighbors left behind.

As the herds dwindle, the wind picks up, whistling as it blows across the broken barracks and through the holes in the floor.

A loud pop makes me wince. It takes me a second to realize what it is: the canopy. The wind has snapped it off of its frame. Even the E. rex only made holes in it, near ground level. The wind is now strong enough to tear it away. It must be sixty miles per hour or more.

The whistle becomes a howl, bringing hard rain with it, pelting the crumbled barracks above us. Debris crashes into the building, an endless flow of collisions as the wind grinds away at what's left of Jericho City. The walls buckle and fall. Furniture slides across the floor, piling more and more on top of us.

The storm is destroying our home. I just hope we survive it. We can always rebuild.

16

James

I wake to a loud crack that I think is lightning.

It's dark and cold, but not as frigid as before.

My face is soaked, my body aches.

Another crack, followed by something crashing to the ground near me.

By degrees, my eyes adjust to the darkness. Ice still surrounds me. Dim light oozes from above. The tree branches encased in ice remind me of veins just under the skin.

I'm in a one-person igloo. It's trapping my body heat. It's probably the only reason I'm alive.

I realize now what happened. Arthur did this. When the tree limbs fell and knocked me unconscious, he packed ice around them, making this protective shell. It's a genius idea. It not only kept me warm out here, but the thick ice hid my body heat from the E. rex and kept me safe from falling debris.

Another limb crashes to the ground near me. I don't hear the wind anymore, but its damage continues to cascade through the jungle.

How long have I been out? It could have been hours, or even the entire night.

I realize now that Arthur actually saved me a second time, when I woke up earlier. He choked me to knock me out again. He was afraid my sound and body heat might draw the attention of the E. rex. He could have killed me, but he stopped cutting off my air when I lost consciousness.

I wonder why he saved me. And why he didn't want me to see Harry's video. For the life of me, I have no idea how to make any sense of his actions. After the cave, I was sure he was slowing me down, hoping I would get trapped out here in the storm and in the path of the herd. But when that happened, he came to my rescue.

Why?

He remains a complete enigma to me. I need to solve that puzzle. I sense that my survival—and the colony's survival—depends upon it. Even now, our fate is linked to the grid.

But at the moment, another danger is more threatening: the cave. I have to warn Emma about the sponges.

My backpack is gone. Arthur must have removed it when I was unconscious. I bet he turned the radio off to silence it. The heat from the tablet might also have drawn the herd.

I reach down and feel Harry's drive in my pocket. If someone has been infected with the regolith disease, the data on this drive may be our only chance of saving them.

"Arthur," I whisper into the darkness.

Outside the shelter, a gust rustles the fallen limbs and debris. Another cool drop of water falls to my face.

"Arthur," I call out a little louder.

Footsteps approach and his hand breaches the ice with a quick crunching sound. He stops short of touching me.

Then he draws his hand out and bends over, one eye peering down at me.

"The storm?" I ask.

"Passed. For now."

"The herd?"

"Also passed. There are stragglers though. And wounded animals lying about."

"We need to get out of here."

He nods and begins pulling the limbs and ice from the makeshift shelter, tossing them to the jungle floor in whooshes.

When he's finished, he offers a hand, and I wince in pain as he pulls me to my feet.

I'm awestruck at what I see.

A thick layer of fog fills the air, but the gaps reveal the storm's destruction. The jungle's canopy is completely broken. What had been a thick ceiling of limbs and leaves is now mostly open air. Around me, only the sturdiest trees are still standing—the rest, still massive, lie across the ground, half-buried in the snow. Around and beneath them, the bodies of E. rex litter the landscape, their glassy eyes staring into the fog that rolls over them. I count a dozen of the fallen beasts, killed by the stampede or the trees that fell upon them.

A falling branch draws my attention. I watch, but there's no further movement, just a wave in the cloud of fog.

The E. rex are the danger out here now. They can see just fine through this fog. They'll see me from far away. And hear me. I wish I had more than the energy weapon, but I didn't have reason to expect an E. rex encounter. They've never breached the eastern jungle before. A bear-like creature with three eyes is the apex predator here, and they only attack humans if their young are threatened.

I spot my backpack beneath a pile of limbs next to the now-deconstructed ice shelter. Its back is torn open. I reach in and feel the pieces of the radio. It's busted beyond what I can repair out here. So is the tablet. I extract a protein bar and wolf it down. I didn't realize how hungry I was until I saw it.

There's another crunch in the darkened forest, but I don't see any branches falling—or movement in the cloud of fog.

Arthur eyes it for a long moment before turning away, silently concluding that it's not a threat.

"The ATV?" I whisper.

"Crushed."

The fog overhead parts and a ray of sunshine lances down, briefly illuminating the space between Arthur and me. His face is half covered in dirt and scratches. His clothes are torn. What happened to him? He should have been able to shut his body down—to hide his heat signature from the E. rex. Did he take shelter? Or did he defend me?

"You saved me."

His gaze drifts over to me. "Don't ruin this lovely moment by getting sentimental, James."

"I'm not. I'm being logical. And logically, it doesn't make sense."

"It will."

"When?"

"Soon."

"I thought you just wanted to get off this planet, to get back to the grid."

"I do."

"Then why don't you?"

He takes the water bottle from the pack and pockets some protein bars. "We're wasting time. Let's go. Keep that gun ready—and hope it works on the E. rex."

He sets off into the fog, stepping carefully, trying to be quiet. I take the last bite of the protein bar, shove the wrapper in my pocket, and fall in behind him, still turning the mystery over in my head.

Arthur saved me.

Arthur wants to leave Eos.

Harry found something Arthur didn't want me to see.

How does it all connect?

Suddenly, Arthur freezes. He throws a hand up, urging me to stop. His hearing and sight are far better than mine. He's seen something.

I hear it then: a branch snapping, leaves rustling.

The clouds part, and an E. rex breaks into a full run, head forward, massive mouth open, teeth gleaming.

17

Emma

Shafts of sunlight pour through the holes in the floor above. It's cold and damp down here in the crawlspace. We're huddled against the foundation wall, crouched just above the pool of water left by the rain. The ground beneath us is sealed with a thick rubber sheet. There are drains spaced throughout, but I think they're clogged with debris from above. We considered making holes in the rubber sheet, but decided against it. Any sound might draw the E. rex.

Despite the shafts of light shining down, the water is frigid, like a swimming pool in a cellar.

The wind and rain have gone now. Occasionally a gust blows across the broken barracks above. For hours, we listened as the storm moved through the settlement and moved south, following the river. I wonder if it has dissipated now, or just moved on.

It's been impossible to sleep down here. First there was the noise of the stampede and the storm and the crashing debris, then the cold water pooling beneath us. This long night has been an exercise in endurance, squatting and leaning against the wall, waiting. I drifted off a few times, but snapped awake before I hit the water. We're all tired and agitated.

In the dim light, I had a chance to examine the wounds on Brightwell's back and remove the shards of debris. She's bruised and cut, but she'll be all right. The knot on her head is my biggest concern. I want Izumi to take a look soon. Assuming Izumi is alive. She was in the med center. I hope she thought of the crawlspace. I hope those in the other barracks did too.

"I think it's time to take a look," Brightwell whispers.

I nod, and we both don our masks and gloves. Brightwell's suit is torn, but I'm hoping it will provide enough cover against any E. rex that might be lurking out there. She wades through the water, still crouched. Pieces of plastic and wood float on the surface like the remains of a shipwreck at sea.

Grigory and Min make to follow us, but she waves them off. Only she and I and two of her soldiers have the infrared blocking suits. She signals for those two troops to follow us.

As I suspected, the trap door leading up into the utility closet is blocked, likely covered with wreckage. Brightwell moves to one of the wider holes in the floor and motions for the two suited soldiers to form steps with their hands. She and I balance in the makeshift stirrups and climb out, her first, then me. She grunts, which means she must be feeling immense pain.

Crouched on the floor of the barracks, I scan the city. What I see breaks my heart into a million pieces.

The barracks lie in crumbled heaps. The black solar cells from the roof mix with the white hard-plastic tiles and assorted debris from inside. It's as though I'm back at Camp Seven, staring at the aftermath of the asteroid strikes. Our city is ruined.

There's no question about what our first priority is. We have to find our people.

Between the piles of rubble that used to be our homes, fog covers the landscape, moving slowly to the east. Above, the metal spine of the canopy glimmers in the sunlight like the bones of this carcass of a city. Through a break in the fog, I spot the canopy material lying in the charred field, a torn and wadded-up white flag in the smoldering black expanse.

The city is silent except for the occasional sound of debris settling. The fog hides the jungle around us, but I hear no movement there either. It's like this whole valley is crouched—like Brightwell and me—waiting, hoping the worst is over.

In the quiet, she whispers a single word to me. "Orders?"

Before the storm, I made a mistake: my orders were too specific. I assumed hiding on the far side of the barracks was the safest place. The crawlspace would have been far better. I can't go back and change that decision, but I can improve with this decision. This time, I'm going to issue a general objective and ask Brightwell how it should get done.

"I want to secure the survivors and prepare for further storms and stampedes. When that's done, we need to make contact with the cave, then go there as soon as possible. Recommendations?"

"Recommend we drain the crawlspaces of the four most structurally sound barracks. We'll stock them and use them as fallback shelters."

I nod, and Brightwell leans over the hole in the crawlspace and whispers to the two troops below.

"Get the rest of the CP team out and begin search and rescue."

Walking quietly, we make our way to the remains of the command post. The domed building is a crumbled ruin. I'm once again reminded of the aftermath of Camp Seven as I begin digging through the rubble, trying as best I can to quietly set the shattered pieces aside. Around me, the command post staff begin scurrying between the barracks, calling out in low voices to survivors. Finally, I reach what I'm looking for: a radio that's intact.

I check the channel and switch it on.

"Evac team, Jericho, do you read?"

I wait, watching the search efforts. I'm relieved to see a soldier emerging from a hole in the floor of one of the other barracks. They thought of the crawlspace too.

"Evac, Jericho, do you copy?"

A fog cloud drifts by and I catch a glimpse of Min and Grigory searching the wreckage of the med habitat. It's larger than the command post, but just as battered. Min is calling out, his voice carrying. Grigory wraps his hands around Min's shoulders, urging him to lower his voice. Grigory has been there before. At Camp Seven, he and James searched the wreckage of the Olympus building only to find Lina dead. I bet this feels similar to him, except now he's watching his friend, Min, live the same nightmare.

"Evac, Jericho, do you read? Please respond."

More than anything, I want to hear my sister's voice, or Alex, or David, or Abby. I want to know that my children are okay, that my friends have lived. That the people I was charged with protecting made it. At least some of them.

Brightwell's troops are sorting the living and wounded from the dead. Which group will be larger?

"James, Jericho, do you copy?"

James doesn't respond either.

Standing in the foggy, ruined city, I wonder if I'll ever see him or my family again.

James

The E. rex extends its hands, reaching for me as it leans forward.

I stagger back, trying to draw the energy weapon from my pack. My hands feel like they're made of Jell-O.

My foot catches on a fallen limb and I topple backward, arms flailing. The thick parka helps to break my fall, but my head still slams into a fallen tree trunk.

The beast roars. I reach again for the energy weapon. But I'm too late. The beast is six feet from me, mouth open, close enough for me to see its back teeth.

In a flash, something collides with the E. rex, latching onto its neck and hanging tight.

It's Arthur. With one hand around the beast's neck, he raises his other hand, which holds a broken limb about two feet long. He plunges the spike into the animal's right eye with lightning speed and perfect accuracy.

The E. rex lets out a sickening howl and bucks like a rodeo bull trying to throw Arthur off. The android holds tight, removing the spike and plunging it into the other eye, bringing the E. rex to the ground. A gurgling sound emanates from its throat as it dies.

Arthur rolls off and crouches as E. rex calls erupt throughout the jungle. The entire forest seems to come alive, bushes rustling, fallen trees and limbs cracking, the remains of the canopy swaying as if the battle cries have set off a hundred unseen armies.

"Take cover," Arthur hisses to me.

He crouches, his head swiveling like a radar dish trying to pinpoint a sound. Suddenly, he snaps around to his right.

An E. rex lunges for him, clamps onto his right arm with its teeth, and tears it away.

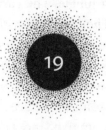

19

Emma

In the wreckage of Jericho City, the dead lay in piles.

The living are huddled together in groups of fifty, scarfing down the meager meals we salvaged from the wreckage of the mess hall. Our crops to the south near the river are ruined—burned and trampled.

Food will become an issue soon.

There's still been no word from James or those who evacuated to the cave. The evac team was told to turn their radios off during transit, for fear the noise might draw the E. rex, but I expected them to turn them back on in the cave. Yet still they aren't responding.

There's been some good news. Min and Grigory found Izumi and her patients in a barracks near the medical habitat.

Izumi has her hands full with the wounded. She's moving between the groups, taking stock and prioritizing care. I've also been moving around, trying to reassure people that we're doing the best we can. Many of the residents are separated from their families. All of them are tired, hungry, and scared.

Our biggest concern now is the herd doubling back, passing through Jericho City as they return to their natural habitat in the western jungle. The eastern jungle is cooler than they're used to. They won't stay there any longer than they must. As such, we're prepared to retreat back into the crawlspaces, which are slowly draining.

Brightwell has sent a team of her troops into the western jungle to look for the soldiers she sent there to try to divert the herds. Near the command post, she stands with her radio to her ear, the speaker at the lowest setting. I hear only phrases, but one catches my attention: "KIA."

Killed In Action.

As long as I've known her, Brightwell's face has always been a mask, rarely betraying emotion. But now the façade cracks for a moment as sadness overcomes her. A cloud passes through the ruined city, obscuring her. When it clears, the mask has returned.

I finish making my rounds in the current group of survivors, then return to Brightwell, who seems deep in thought.

"I'm sorry about your people."

She stares at the eastern jungle. "Thank you. How are the civilians?"

"Shaken up. Ready to get out of here."

"We need to send a team to the cave. Our first priority is recovering the vehicles so we can transport the remaining population and our food."

I raise my eyebrows. "You see us staying there for a while? Days or weeks?"

"I'd recommend we stay until this storm season passes, however long that takes." Brightwell motions to the city.

"We can't be out here in the open when those herds are on the move."

"I agree. But food will become an issue."

"True. But for now, evacuating is the bigger issue. I'm going to lead a team to the cave. Make sure the path is clear. I have three troops left here with suits. I'll take all of them with me. We've also found about half of the special ops team members I sent into the western jungle. We're going to bring their bodies back here and use their suits, assuming they fit other soldiers. Those troops will stay here to guard the civilians."

"I'm coming with you."

"Ma'am—"

"I have one of those suits. I killed an E. rex in the barracks last night. I'm not saying it was a SEAL-team-level takedown, but I managed. I'll follow your orders out there."

"I can't you put you in danger, ma'am."

"There's nothing more I can do here. I need to know that my family is okay. You know you can use an extra set of hands out there. And my suit doesn't fit any of your troops—I've been looking around. I'm going."

She nods, probably realizing that arguing will only waste more time.

At the remains of the armory building, Brightwell begins digging through the rubble until she reaches a metal locker. I help her move the rest of the debris covering it, allowing her to pry the door open. I wince at the sound of the metal groaning, and we both pause, eyes scanning around us for movement. Thankfully, the plain is silent and still.

Brightwell pulls a backpack from the locker. She unzips it and draws out a metal ball the size of a small apple.

"Do you know what this is?" she asks, extending the device to me.

"A grenade."

"We have three. I brought them against my orders."

"Good."

"Take one. Use it only if you have to."

"How do I know when that is?"

"If the time comes, you'll know it."

20

James

Lying on the damp ground, I watch in horror as the E. rex rips off Arthur's arm. The android's empty shoulder socket sparks. Wires hang free.

The E. rex chomps down on the severed limb, then pauses, seemingly confused by what it's bitten into.

That pause gives me the opening I need. Hands shaking, I draw the energy weapon and train it on the E. rex. I have one shot—and only one shot. If I miss, Arthur and I are both finished.

As the creature spits out the arm, I pull the trigger, sending a beam into the E. rex's chest. The beast squawks before going rigid and collapsing.

I have no idea how long it will be unconscious.

I don't intend to find out.

Arthur has the same thought. He bounds over to me, ignoring the mangled arm he lost. He leans toward the ground and whispers, "Get on my back."

I can't help but glance down at the energy weapon in my hand. Since I brought Arthur to the surface, I've always kept this loaded weapon with me in case he tried to attack me. It was my only countermeasure against him. Now it's gone. What's more—I'm not even sure I ever needed it. Arthur just saved my life. Again. Why?

"James, hurry. More are coming."

Reluctantly, still clutching the weapon, I climb onto his back. He dashes through the jungle, leaping over the massive fallen trees, ducking vines and branches, and adjusting course seemingly at random, parting the fog as he goes. He can see the E. rex moving through the dense forest. I can only hear the foliage rustling and branches snapping as they close on us.

Suddenly, Arthur changes course again, running faster now. The ground beneath him disappears as he leaps across a gully. Fallen trees lie across it like balance beams over a ravine. On the far bank, he slings me off his back and pushes me down into the wide ditch.

"Get down," he urges. "I'll hide you."

Near the bottom of the gully, a tree lies on its side, its roots in the air, leaving a massive hole. Arthur shoves me into the crevice and begins raking dirt and snow over me. He tears off a piece of his shirt and I close my eyes as he lays it over my face. The damp soil and ice fall upon me. I feel like a man being buried alive.

I don't dare open my eyes, but I hear Arthur dash away. In the distance, I hear him yell, "Who's afraid of the one-armed man?"

He's drawing the E. rex away. And the loss of his arm didn't take his sense of humor with it.

21

Emma

The path to the emergency cave is littered with fallen trees and branches. And beneath all that are the deep ruts the ATVs left during their frantic rush from Jericho City.

We've also found a collection of trinkets dropped along the way: a knit cap, a bag of food, a child's teddy bear. They're like bread crumbs leading the way. At the end of this trail, we'll find out whether our loved ones survived the trip.

In my mind, I keep picturing Sam, Allie, and Carson huddled together in the dark cave, wondering why I haven't arrived. That is, assuming they're still alive. With each step, I'm terrified that we'll start finding bodies.

Around me, Brightwell and her troops march carefully through the jungle, rifles at the ready. Every sound draws their attention. We stop and squat every few minutes, eyes trained on the disturbance. I always expect to see an E. rex, but we haven't encountered one yet. Perhaps they were all driven deeper into the eastern jungle. I hope so.

They won't cross the mountains to the dark side. At least, they never have. It's too cold there. The river to the south of us is too wide for them to cross—they can't swim. Which means they have to still be here, in this jungle, lurking. Or resting. Waiting to return to the far side of the western jungle, bordering the desert.

I expected Brightwell and her troops to clear the fallen trees on the path. The jungle is too dense for the ATVs to go around them. Instead, they merely step over them. It makes sense: she's going to gather more troops at the cave and return for the task. It's the right move. There's strength in numbers. For now, our sole priority is reaching the cave.

In the distance, I hear an E. rex roar. It bellows again, then suddenly stops. Another beast calls out—a different one, I think. There's a pop—not like a tree snapping, more like something metal breaking.

Brightwell stops in her tracks, turning toward the sound.

A bizarre hiss follows. The sound is faint. It's unnatural, more like a laser than an animal call. What could it be?

One of the soldiers takes a step toward the sound, but Brightwell catches his arm and shakes her head. For a long moment, the jungle is still and quiet, as if waiting to discover who or what is making the sound.

Suddenly, I hear movement all around us—from the north, south, east, and west. Massive animals, most likely E. rex, barreling through the forest, drawn by the sound like moths to a flame.

Quickly, Brightwell leads the team off the path and into a thick clump of fallen trees and brush. We crouch with our weapons ready, listening as the jungle thumps with the sound of E. rex feet beating the ground. The thinned-out canopy above shakes from the movements. E. rex roar every few seconds.

Amid the cacophony, I hear a voice yelling something, but the sound is too faint to make out. Is it James? I don't think so. One of the civilians or soldiers we evacuated? Or possibly someone who left the city when the herds came through? Doubtful—they would have been trampled by the stampede.

The voice calls out again, the tone almost taunting. It's familiar, but I can't place it. Whoever it is would have to be crazy to call out in this jungle filled with predators. Crazy, or desperate.

I lean forward and focus on Brightwell. We're both wearing our facemasks, which cover our eyes, so I can't see her expression and she can't see mine. But we know each other pretty well by now, and she interprets my unspoken question.

"We can't help them," she whispers. "There are too many E. rex." She pauses. "And I think whoever it is wants to draw them. I don't think they're in trouble."

For what feels like an eternity, we crouch in the thicket in the damp, cold jungle, listening as the last of the E. rex flock away from us. I feel like I'm back in that crawlspace waiting for the herd to pass.

Finally, Brightwell motions for us to return to the path, and we resume our march, now with more urgency, only some of the caution gone. She probably assumes the E. rex that hurried to the disturbance might come back. She's probably right.

At this point, we can't be more than five minutes from the cave. With every step, we get closer to finding out what happened to our loved ones.

I grip the rifle, scanning in every direction. My foot snaps a twig and the group stops, one of the soldiers peering back at me. I can't see his expression through the mask, but I'm sure he's scowling. I wonder if he'd make the same fuss if one of his fellow soldiers had made the racket. Brightwell motions for us to keep going, and we resume our procession through the jungle, stepping over more fallen limbs and trunks, brushing leaves out of our face.

Up ahead, the point soldier freezes and holds up a hand. Everyone crouches on the path, bringing their rifles to their shoulders, panning back and forth for targets.

Brightwell creeps forward, joining the point soldier, who's motioning to our left, toward a lump on the forest floor. As I watch, the lump rises, then falls. My mouth runs dry. It's a fallen E. rex, down but not dead. I scoot forward slightly, taking in more of the shape. It's young, maybe a third of the size of the adults. I have no idea how that translates into age. A deep gash runs from its back to its right leg. The wound is dry, the blood caked along the deep rut like a red canyon in the American west.

No one moves.

We're less than ten feet from the animal, practically right on top of it. Turning back to face us, Brightwell brings a finger to where her lips are behind the mask, urging us to keep quiet, then points forward. She takes a step, then another, slowly, careful not to make any noise. We follow suit, creeping like burglars in the night. I can barely take my eyes off the injured animal.

Behind it, a branch bends and pops as a massive E. rex head rises above the sleeping youth. This one is an adult. No question about it.

It isn't injured.

It peers directly at us. We freeze, no one moving a muscle.

Time stands still. The beast rises to its full height, towering over us. It leans forward, cocking its head as if puzzled by what it sees. Against my will, my breathing accelerates. My chest heaves. Beneath the infrared dampening suit, I break into a sweat.

The E. rex's nostrils flare. It pans left and right, scanning the group, and then raises its head to gaze past us, seeming to compare the two views.

It takes a step forward, leapfrogging the downed child—probably its offspring. To the soldiers' credit, no one flinches as the E. rex moves to within feet of us. It again scans back and forth. Finally, its gaze lands on the soldier closest to it. With its head, it moves forward and touches the rifle. It draws back, probably wincing from the cold steel.

It leans in again, mouth open, making for the man's head.

Suddenly, the soldier opens fire, emptying round after round into the E. rex. The beast roars and reels back, its left foot digging into the smaller E. rex. The other three soldiers begin firing as well. The creature flails and falls, screaming and thrashing in pain.

Brightwell's voice rises over the cries of the wounded E. rex: "Move!"

A strong hand grabs my arm and pulls me forward. We're running along the path now, ignoring the noise. Throughout the jungle, I hear movement. I'm blinded to it. All I see is the path forward, the soldier in front of me.

In a flash, that person is gone. A massive set of jaws clamp around the body and squeeze tight as the E. rex crosses the path in a full run.

The team turns and fires. Another beast roars to my right. Brightwell and the soldier next to her focus their shots on it. A bellow echoes behind me and I turn to see our last soldier open up with automatic gunfire, the rounds hitting the E. rex like a powerful wave, forcing it back but not felling it. The beast dives forward, coming down on the soldier, its head crushing him like a hammer, the man's rifle falling harmlessly to the ground.

I flick the safety off on my rifle and hold the trigger down, unloading rounds into the E. rex. But I'm too late. It's too close.

With its head, it sideswipes me, tossing my body like a rag doll. I land against a massive trunk, one of the few still standing.

My head swims.

Ache pulses through my body.

My gun is gone.

I hear the E. rex descending upon the fallen soldier. The man cries out, the sound agonizing.

I reach into my pocket and wrap my fingers around the cold, round object. I flick out the pin and toss it toward the beast.

22

James

Lying in the pit, I listen as Arthur leads the E. rex away. He calls to them, taunting, and they come running. There must be a hundred of them within earshot. Maybe more.

The dirt and ice cover me completely. The cloth over my face prevents the dirt from getting into my mouth or nostrils, which I'm thankful for because my breathing accelerates as the herd grows closer, my body responding involuntarily to my growing fear. Soon they're flowing around me, pounding the ground, and leaping the gully with a whooshing sound.

Against my will, I feel myself shivering—from cold, fear, or a combination of both. If one of those E. rex misses the mark and oversteps the bank, its massive claws will gouge right into me, gutting me.

Arthur's voice grows faint, drowned out by the herd rushing through the jungle. They're moving over me like a thunderstorm now, rumbling and rattling me as they pass.

Time stops. I lie there in darkness, the weight of the dirt upon me, the dampness of the ground below slowly seeping into me, as if this world has swallowed me and is slowly digesting my body.

After a few minutes—or what I think is a few minutes; it could be an hour for all I know—the flow of E. rex tapers off. And then there's silence again.

Out of nowhere, a paw presses down on the dirt above. It digs, shoveling the dirt off of me rapidly. For a second, I consider remaining still. But then I realize: whatever it is, it already knows I'm down here. I have to fight. My battered body won't be much use in that department, but if I'm going out, it will be swinging.

Lifting my arms, I rock from side to side as I rise from the dirt and ice. I grit my teeth against the pain and jerk the cloth from my face, ready to look the predator in the eye.

Arthur is squatting next to me, hand covered in dirt.

"You could have announced yourself," I hiss, rubbing the dirt from my neck and hair.

"I was scared you'd respond and call attention to us. Which you just did."

He holds his hand out. Is he offering to help me up?

The gun, he mouths silently.

"It's empty," I whisper. "It's a single shot."

"I know. Hand it over."

I can't see any harm in it, so I hand him the weapon. With his left hand—now his only hand—he deftly disassembles the device, using his knees to hold it.

What's he looking for?

He then grabs some of the wires dangling from his right shoulder, where his arm used to be attached. He pulls them out as far as he can, examines them for a moment, uses his teeth to strip them, and attaches them to the gun, near the battery compartment. Then he waits.

I finally realize what he's doing: charging the weapon.

"How'd you get away?" I whisper.

"I determined their visual range by changing course and seeing how they responded. When I was far enough away, I climbed a tree and waited for them to pass."

"With one arm?"

"And two legs. You made this body more capable than the Oscar unit."

"Oliver was a military prototype."

"Be glad. The extra strength probably saved your life."

He disconnects the gun from the wires, and to my surprise, he hands it to me. "We may need it," he says simply. "Can you walk?"

"I can try."

My body still aches from the tree limbs and brush that fell on me. And now I've been buried twice. That hasn't helped.

I stand on shaky legs, pain throbbing.

"I'll carry you," Arthur says.

"We're going to the evac cave," I insist quietly.

"The evac cave it is," he mutters, bending down.

Across the jungle, automatic gunfire erupts. More weapons join the fight, at least three or four people shooting at each other or an E. rex. An explosion overpowers the gunfire. It sounds like a bomb or a grenade.

It has to be someone from Jericho City. Possibly Emma. Or Alex.

"Let's go."

Arthur cocks his head. "Toward the gunfire? Bad idea—"

"I'm going. With or without you."

I slip the gun into my pocket and take a step up the bank, leaning forward, placing a hand on the ground to crawl up on all fours.

Arthur moves in front of me and stoops, offering his back. "Get on."

Up ahead the battle rages. Two more explosions flash in the distance, bright enough to shine through the thick trees. The canopy shakes from the blasts.

Arthur trudges along, me on his back, trying to stay quiet. I don't see the point—we're racing toward a battle.

"Faster," I whisper.

He complies, but I know he's still far from his top speed. He seems bent on keeping me out of the fight—on protecting me. Again, I can't see a reason why. That mystery is as thick as the fog surrounding us.

Soon I smell smoke and the odor of burning flesh. Arthur comes to a sudden halt, almost throwing me off. He squats, and I put my feet on the ground.

"They're fifty feet ahead," he whispers.

"How many?"

"Four dead E. rex."

"Humans?"

"Three."

"Dead?"

"Two. One dying."

That could be Emma.

I rise, but Arthur catches my arm. "There are three E. rex one hundred feet from us—twenty-five degrees from our current vector."

"Are they—"

"Devouring a dead E. rex. They'll be done soon."

"Then we better hurry."

I snake through the thick foliage, the damp, snow-covered leaves brushing against me. My feet sink into the mushy ground. Ahead, I catch sight of a body—mangled, unmoving. A deep pit spreads out beside it. Half an E. rex carcass lies nearby.

Holding the energy weapon in one hand, I make my way to the dead soldier, who's wearing an infrared cloaking suit. Emma has one too, as do Brightwell and some of her troops.

Gently, I pull back the facemask. It's a young man with a few days' stubble. He's a special forces soldier I've seen around, but I don't know his name.

I look around, taking stock. This is the path to the evac cave.

"Where's the live one?" I whisper to Arthur.

Crouching, he leads me down the path, past another dead E. rex.

Ahead, another suited figure lies against a tree trunk, unmoving.

23

Emma

The grenade lands on the far side of the E. rex. I expect it to go off instantly, but it doesn't. Time seems to stand still.

The beast roars and tears into the soldier.

Gunfire rakes over it.

The E. rex reels back, screaming, blood covering its teeth.

I try to push up, to crawl to my rifle lying on the ground, but the pain from my battered body keeps me pinned to the ground, wedged against the fallen tree.

Finally, my grenade explodes. The sound is deafening, then total silence.

The blast shreds the E. rex. Pieces of meat and blood spray across my body. Dirt falls like rain. The force presses my body into the fallen tree, crushing me for a split second. When it passes, I roll forward, face down. More dirt and debris land on my back.

A shrill ringing sounds in my ears, unceasing.

I feel sick, on the verge of vomiting.

I push up enough to turn my head toward the path.

Tracer fire lances out through the fog and smoke. Slowly, other sounds bleed through the ringing: gunfire and the cries of E. rex—shrieks of pain and anger. It sounds like a hundred of them are swarming us.

I try to stand, but the pain is so strong it's nauseating. Instead I crawl on my knees and elbows to my rifle. Cradling it, I roll onto my side, searching for a target. Three E. rex race across the path, making passes at the troops, who are firing mercilessly, then recede into the fog before attacking again.

I switch the gun to semi-automatic and train my sight on the closest E. rex, targeting its head. As I pull the trigger, another grenade goes off.

The blast rolls me like a barrel down a hill. My rifle flies out of my hand.

The ringing is louder now, all-consuming.

My heart races, my lungs gasp for air.

The incessant ringing and my ragged breaths are the only things I hear.

Another flash goes off, pushing a wave of force and heat into me. I stare straight ahead, unable to move.

Debris rains down.

I teeter on the edge of consciousness.

My head swims.

Vision blurs.

24

James

I take a step toward the fallen soldier, but Arthur waves me off. "Dead." He motions to a copse of trees off the path. "The live one's over here."

The forest is quiet now, but smoke still rises from the scorched ground like ghosts in a graveyard.

I creep carefully, mindful not to step on a branch.

Behind the bushes, another suited figure lies in the dirt, a man with a deep gash across his back. The mask is off, revealing short blond hair.

I squat down beside him and call out quietly, "Hey."

The man turns his head, looking up at me with bloodshot, weary eyes.

"I'm going to get you out of here."

Arthur grabs my arm and jerks me away. "James, they're coming."

I pull back from Arthur, breaking his grip.

To my right, I hear branches snapping. The E. rex are closing in.

"James," Arthur hisses. "We *have* to go—"

"I'm not leaving him." To the wounded soldier lying on the ground, I whisper, "Can you walk?"

"I don't know."

Arthur reaches into the pile of fallen limbs beside us, casting about noisily. I shoot him a glance, alarmed.

"They've seen you. They're coming anyway."

He rises up with a long, sharpened branch and hurls it through the jungle like a javelin. An E. rex cries out in the fog-filled forest, a scream of pain. Roars of anger follow—from other E. rex, I assume.

"Go," Arthur says, pointing to the south.

The cave is due east. "The cave—"

"Too far away."

Arthur grabs another limb from the pile of brush and throws it. This one must not have stuck—the screeching reply is far less anguished.

I grab the soldier's arm and pull him up, eliciting a strained grunt. The man's legs hang limp, unmoving. I wonder if the wound in his back severed his spine.

"Carry him, Arthur."

He flashes his eyes at me, but throws the man over his shoulder and begins pounding through the jungle. I follow behind.

The limbs and leaves scrape across me, slowing me down and soaking me with water and snow. I put my head down and keep charging. Just ahead, Arthur bounds deftly over the fallen trees and through the dense shrubs.

The beasts roar, and I chance a look back. There are two of them, towering E. rex, probably twenty feet tall. I stop, draw the energy weapon, and take a deep breath, aiming.

The shot hits the closest E. rex on the right side of its chest, spinning the animal to the ground. The other slows, turning to look back.

I don't wait. I turn and sprint, trying to catch up to Arthur.

For a moment, I think I've lost him. I don't hear his footsteps, or the sounds of him crashing through the brush. I hear only the wind. Except it's not the wind. As I burst through a thicket, I realize it's the river that bounds the eastern jungle to the south.

Arthur stands on the bank, the wounded soldier still draped over his shoulder. Ten feet below, the river is surging from the storm water. It's deep and wide here, and moving at twice its normal speed.

"Jump!" Arthur yells over the sound of the water.

"No way!"

Without a word, Arthur tosses the man into the stream.

Behind me, I hear a branch crack, then another. The E. rex are coming.

Without the use of his legs, I doubt that soldier will survive in the river.

And with no cloaking suit and no weapons, I probably can't survive here on land.

Staring at Arthur, shaking my head, I take three steps toward the river and jump.

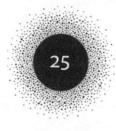

25

Emma

I just want to close my eyes and go to sleep. But I know if I do, I might never open them again, never see my children or my husband again.

I roll over and push up on my elbows, but I collapse quickly.

I'm too weak, too dizzy.

I crawl, elbows pulling me forward, feet pushing.

When I reach the path, the clouds and smoke in front of me clear. It's nothing but dead E. rex and soldiers strewn across the dirt road like rag dolls, unmoving.

I crawl, inches at a time.

Suddenly, I feel fingers wrap around my forearm and roll me over onto my back. The person lifts me and carries me through the fog, their legs weak, gait uneven. I can't see the face, but I know the voice.

"Stay quiet," Brightwell says as she staggers along the path.

I reach up and lock my hands behind her neck and pull, trying to take some weight off her arms.

After a minute, she stumbles and falls to the ground. I roll out of her grasp. The impact rocks my body, but the disorientation is the worst.

The fog is back.

Brightwell's voice is strained, a soft croak coming from somewhere inside the cloud. "Sorry."

I push up, ready to crawl back to her, to try to help her. At that moment, I realize I'm not alone. Three figures surround me, towering over me.

One bends down and lifts me up, carrying me with ease.

I recognize him—and the others. They're soldiers who were evacuated to the cave. The sound drew them.

"Wait," I whisper. "There's someone else. Over there. Save her."

As the soldier whisks me away, I hear Brightwell groan and see the other two helping her up.

Soon, the mouth of the cave looms ahead.

The temperature seems to drop ten degrees when we cross the threshold. ATVs and trailers loom thirty feet inside. Beyond them, the cave forks. The soldier carrying me switches on his headlamp, lighting our way.

I desperately want to put my feet down and walk. I don't want my children to see me this way. It will terrify them. Now, more than ever, they need to feel safe.

"Stop," I breathe out, voice scratchy.

He slows, but doesn't halt.

"Put me down. I need a second."

Finally, he comes to a halt and gently lowers me to the ground.

It takes a few seconds, but finally, I manage to stand.

Brightwell arrives at that moment, arm around a corporal who's helping her along, the third soldier bringing up the rear. Her mask is off, face bruised, steely resolve in her eyes.

"Thank you," I say to her.

"You're welcome." She turns to the man beside me. "Sergeant, there are three more in our party. Send a team to check for survivors." He nods and disappears deeper into the cave, probably to gather his team.

"James is still out there," I say to Brightwell.

She bunches her eyebrows, thinking. "We barely got here, Emma. If he's out there, he's probably hunkered down, waiting out the storm and herds."

I chew my lip, wishing there was something I could do.

Brightwell places a hand on my arm. "We'll look for him as soon as the herds leave the eastern jungle."

"That could take days. Or months. He's out there alone."

"If anyone can survive out there, he can."

"What about us? With the E. rex in the jungle, we can't get back to Jericho City—and the people there can't get here. We don't have enough food to stay in this cave for long."

She nods gravely. "We can only hope we have enough time to wait them out."

"Unless we can drive them away somehow." I think for a moment. "A fire maybe?"

Brightwell shakes her head. "A lot of trees are down— they're waterlogged from lying in the rain and snow-soaked dirt. A fire wouldn't burn far. It might even draw them."

We're trapped. But I'm not giving up. I can tell Brightwell isn't either. "Let's talk again after we've rested. There's got to be a way."

She nods. "Yes, ma'am."

I turn and head deeper into the cave. My gait is awkward, my legs still wobbly. One of the soldiers walks beside me, ready to catch me if I fall. With every step, I feel a little surer on my feet. Behind me, Brightwell is requesting a status update from one of her troops.

Her voice fades as the cave meanders and turns. The soldier's headlamp bores into the darkness, revealing the cavern in narrow swaths. The walls are gray and black, damp with condensation.

After a minute or so, I begin seeing a substance on the cave wall—a gray sponge I've never seen before. It looks almost like sea coral, but I figure it's a fungus of some sort. Or the Eos equivalent.

Up ahead, a side tunnel breaks off to the right. The soldier makes the turn and I'm relieved to see my fellow colonists lying on sleeping bags and sheets, gathered in groups of four and five. As we approach, they squint and turn away from the bright light.

A woman in the corner rises, an arm held up to block the headlamp. It's my sister, Madison. She snakes her way through the crowd and lunges when she reaches me, wrapping me in a tight hug.

I groan, and she instantly releases me. "You're hurt."

I pull her back into the hug, ignoring the pain. "I'll be fine. Where are the kids?"

"Over here."

Holding my hand, Madison leads me through the crowd to the corner, where Sam and Allie are lying next to each other, both asleep. My sister-in-law, Abby, is holding Carson, who's also asleep.

My heart bursts. Tears well in my eyes.

They're okay.

Across the way, a boy coughs, then an adult.

I lower myself to the floor of the cave. It's hard and cold and a little damp, but here on the floor of this cave is the only place I want to be right now.

I stretch out next to my children, and sleep instantly overtakes me.

26

James

I plunge into the water, sinking in over my head, the cold hitting me like an electric prod. For a moment I feel completely disoriented, as if I'm floating through the cold dark of space.

Finally, my body rises toward the surface. A current grips me, turning and flipping me. My head breaches the surface, and I gasp once before I'm plunged back underwater. Light and darkness flash in sequence as the river rolls me. I try to right myself, arms and legs spinning.

Arthur runs along the bank, eyes trained on me, his only arm clawing the branches and shrubs out of his path. His body is watertight and built to withstand punctures, but the massive hole where his right arm used to be makes all of that irrelevant. If he gets in the water, it'll flood right in. He has to stay on the bank.

He's not alone there. An E. rex emerges from the jungle where I jumped off, screaming as it stares down from the bank. The cold-blooded beast can't follow me in. For that reason, it was a good move by Arthur. Throwing the soldier

in was probably the only way to get me in the river—
and the river was probably my only hope of escaping the
E. rex.

Up ahead, the wounded soldier is floating face down in
the stream. I kick my feet and swim to him, the current
helping me along. My feet can't touch the ground. It's
awkward, but I manage to turn him over and get my left
arm around his torso.

His eyes open and he spits out water and coughs, the
sound barely audible over the rushing of the stream.

I paddle with one arm toward the bank, kicking my feet
furiously to keep us both above water, hoping to hit the
river floor.

Arthur points furiously downriver, urging me to stay in
the water. He's right. I need to get past the eastern jungle.
But my arms are giving out. My legs feel like lead in the
water already. I don't know if it's the extra weight of the
man I'm pulling, the water soaking into my clothes, or
the strength of the current, but I feel myself sinking, losing
the battle to stay above water. I have to get to the bank, if
only to rest.

Still jogging along the bank, Arthur points downriver
again.

I shake my head.

I can't do it.

I'm too weak.

I keep paddling toward the bank, making slow progress.

I wish my feet could reach the riverbed.

Arthur eyes me and disappears into the jungle.

My head goes under and I gulp frigid water, which seems
to freeze my chest from the inside. I fight with my free

arm, kick, and spit out as I break the surface. Water covers my eyes.

I flip onto my back, momentarily losing my grip on the soldier.

I turn and swim harder then, catching him and trying again unsuccessfully to float on my back with my arm around him. The current is whipping me around. I have to float. It's my only chance.

Emma

I wake to coughing all around me. The sound bounces off the cave walls, echoing without end. An LED lamp sits in the corner, casting faint light into the cavern where I lie, my family around me. Allie and Sam are sleeping. Madison sits with her legs crossed, staring, unblinking.

A gray haze hangs over the group of sleeping colonists. Is it a cloud of fog that has drifted deeper into the cave? It must be.

My arms are shaky as I push up.

"Hi," Madison whispers.

"Hi. Thanks for taking care of the kids."

"Sure. How is it out there?"

"Dangerous."

I barely have the strength for more words, and there really isn't much more to say. Between the E. rex and the storms outside the cave, it's quite simply dangerous out there.

"How long have I been out?" I ask.

She coughs, then shrugs. "Don't know. Left my watch at home."

Home. That word cuts like a knife. I definitely don't have the strength to tell her what happened to the city.

After a moment, Madison reaches into her bag and draws out an MRE—Meal, Ready-to-Eat. It's chicken noodle soup. One of my favorites. I eat quietly, listening to the coughing, wondering if it's just the cold or the air down here. In the dim light, I spot specks of gray settling on the food.

"It's from those things on the walls," Madison says quietly. "They spit them out if you get too close."

I try to push the gray gunk aside and finish the meal as quickly as possible. We can't afford to waste food.

As I swallow the last bite, I feel a film of grit in my throat. I cough, trying to clear it, but it won't go away, like a tickle cough that lingers.

Madison hands me a bottle of water. "It never really goes away. You just get used to coughing."

"Thanks," I reply, swallowing the water down. "I'm going to make some rounds."

My body aches as I rise, but I push on. Nearby, Abby is holding Carson. My seven-month-old son is sleeping peacefully. I'm thankful for that.

"How has he been?" I whisper.

"Surprisingly good. I think he likes it down here."

She's trying to reassure me, but I can see the worry on her face. I kiss my sleeping baby on the forehead, squeeze his small hand with my thumb and forefinger, and venture out of the cavern and into the passage. Up ahead, the corridor ends at a T-intersection. Soft light glows from the right side of the intersection, just bright enough to light my way.

As I approach, I hear a man's voice. "There's no way Young could have thrown that spike."

A woman responds. "You think it was Sinclair? The guy's a scientist, not a Super Bowl quarterback."

The man again: "No quarterback could have thrown that—"

As I round the turn, a soldier with short black hair sees me. "Mayor," he says quickly, silencing the other three soldiers—a woman and two men. The woman is wearing an infrared cloaking suit with a tear across the back that has been repaired with glue and stitches. It's a suit from one of the troops who died on the path.

"Colonel Brightwell is at the CP, ma'am," the man says. "I'll lead you to her."

The soldiers nod and cough as I pass.

As we walk, the cave floor inclines and the temperature rises. Soon the sponges on the walls thin out and disappear, taking the gray cloud of particles with them, leaving only damp, bare stone. I can breathe a little easier as I approach the command post, which lies just inside the mouth of the cave.

Brightwell sits in the bed of an ATV trailer, studying a tablet. Her troops nod at me as I pass.

"How long was I out?" I ask when she looks up.

"Probably not long enough."

"You rescued the troops."

She cuts her eyes to another trailer, where a blanket covers long lumps—bodies, I assume.

"Two casualties."

"We had three troops with us."

"Yes, ma'am. One still MIA."

MIA—missing in action.

"You think he escaped?"

"I hope so," Brightwell says, glancing down at the tablet. "He could have been taken by one of the E. rex."

She turns the tablet toward me, revealing a picture of an E. rex lying in the snow with what looks like a pole sticking out of its mouth. It clearly pierced the brain, but it didn't exit the other side.

"We think someone felled one with this makeshift spear. Could James have done this?"

"Maybe—if he had rigged up a launching system. Or planted the spike in the ground."

"We think it was thrown." Brightwell points to the disturbed snow in front of the fallen beast. "Look at the way it fell—as if the object hit it from the front with some force."

"It means he's out there."

"So it would seem," Brightwell whispers, refocusing on the tablet. "Or someone from Jericho City. Or someone else."

"Who else could it be?"

"A good question," she says, not making eye contact. I can tell she has a theory.

"We need to look for him."

Brightwell shakes her head. "A team searched the path and the area around it. There's still a lot of E. rex out there. I'll send a team as soon as we can."

"James can't survive out there."

Brightwell turns the tablet back to me. "If he did this, I'd say he's probably safer than we are."

I sit down next to Brightwell, taking the load off my aching legs. "What now? We wait?"

"For the moment."

"Everyone deeper in the cave is coughing."

"It's the gray dust in the air. Must be an irritant."

"Why didn't we know about that?"

"The particles are only deeper in the cave. The survey team didn't go deep enough to detect them. We'll start bringing people up in groups to get fresh air. I'm sure it'll be fine once we leave the cave."

James

A loud splash near me showers cold water down. I look up to see a wide, flat piece of wood floating in the water—a piece of a tree the storm sheared off. Arthur is back on the bank, pointing at it.

Swimming with every shred of strength I have left, I pull up onto the piece of wood and begin kicking to reach the soldier, who is rolling in the current, face up, then face down.

I grab him and pull him up, and thankfully he grips it with my arm around him. We both hold on to the wood as it bobs along the river, our legs dangling off the back.

Arthur watches from the bank, snaking his way through the brush.

After a few minutes, the jungle thins and stops, replaced by dark sand that leads to the grassy plain—or whatever grass the fire left behind. Jericho City is north of here.

I kick toward the bank, but Arthur points downriver again. He's probably right—the western jungle is our best chance of avoiding the E. rex.

The blue-green tall grass is indeed burned around Jericho City, but the blades stand tall farther to the west. The rain and the storm must have extinguished the fire.

A thick forest gradually replaces the grass. Since the sun doesn't move here on Eos, I have no way to gauge the passage of time. The part of me that's out of the water is still soaked, I know that.

I reach over and shake the soldier, who turns and looks back at me with eyes as tired as I feel. But he's alive. We both are. That's what matters.

He mouths a word that I think is *thanks*. I nod, and we float down the river, watching the landscape flow by.

Soon I begin spotting fallen trees, split and trampled. The water is getting warmer by the minute.

Arthur disappears from the bank and returns with a long, narrow limb, which he extends to me. I hold tight as he pulls us out of the water.

I'm still shivering, but the soldier is shaking worse. It's not just the cold. He's lost a lot of blood.

"What's your name?" I ask, still trying to gather my breath.

His eyes closed, he mouths a barely audible response. "Ryan Young. Corporal."

"All right, Corporal Ryan Young, we're going to get you fixed up."

Arthur throws his head back, then gives me an exasperated look.

"Help me move him," I mutter.

We drag him deeper into the jungle and gently lay him down.

I examine the corporal's wound, which cuts across his

back and spine. I don't think it severed the spinal cord, but it might be bruised. There's some swelling halfway down his back.

He needs a real doctor. He needs Izumi.

And I need some answers.

"What happened at Jericho City?" I ask, still checking him for other cuts and bruises. "I saw the burned field and the E. rex stampede."

"Brightwell sent Alpha and Bravo Teams into the jungle to try to divert the herds." Young swallows. "Didn't work. Mayor burned the field. Brought the canopy down. Evacuated."

The word strikes me like a sledgehammer to my gut, confirming my worst fear. "To the cave at the base of the eastern mountains?"

His head rolls to the side as he nods.

I'm too late.

For a moment, I sit there, stunned.

Finally I grip his shoulders and shake him lightly, forcing him to open his eyes. "Did everyone go to the cave?"

He shakes his head. "No time."

"Some stayed in Jericho City?"

He nods. "Yes."

"They're still there?"

"Yes," he gasps, breathing unevenly.

"Is Emma still in Jericho City?"

"Who?"

"Mayor Matthews. Is she still in Jericho City?"

"No. Path."

"What?" I lean closer, listening as he mumbles. He's passing out.

"Suit. Path."

Suit. Path.

She had one of the infrared blocking suits. She was on the path. Three people in suits. Two dead. I checked one, but I didn't check the other one—the body propped up against the tree. It was her.

I collapse back, sitting on the ground, eyes drifting away from the man.

I'm numb.

Arthur's voice sounds distant, as though I'm hearing it through a glass wall.

"...in your group that fought on the path to the cave?"

I don't hear the reply. Only the word *grenade*.

"She set off a grenade?" Arthur asks.

"Yes."

She's dead. My wife is dead.

The world fades away. Arthur is speaking to me, but I don't hear him. I don't feel anything but a hurt deep inside, in a place I never knew existed.

Emma

When I return to the cavern where my family is staying, Allie and Sam are both awake. The coughing is louder now. Almost everyone is sitting up.

"Mommy," Allie says, reaching out for me as I approach.

I hug her tight, feeling how fragile she is in my arms. As she lays her head on my shoulder, I pull Sam to me. He's not my biological son, but he's every bit a part of our family, and I've worked hard to make him feel that way. He's lived with us since he lost his birth parents in the asteroid strikes on Earth, and with each passing month, he's warmed up more and more to James, Allie, Carson, and me.

When I release Allie, she coughs into my chest. I place a hand on her forehead and feel sweat and heat there.

"Mommy, I'm sick," she whines.

Sam coughs as well, but he's stoic.

Looking around, I realize almost everyone is watery-eyed and coughing.

"It's okay, sweetie. It's just the air down here."

"I wanna go home," she says, coughing again.

"We will."

"When?"

"Soon, sweetie. I'll be right back."

The cave has a series of chambers, almost like bunk rooms off the main corridor. After taking stock of the colonists in these other chambers, I'm convinced that what's happening to my children is widespread among the population down here.

With the help of Brightwell's troops, we move those with the most difficulty breathing toward the entrance of the cave, where there are no sponges on the wall or spores in the air. There are no chambers here, either, so people crowd into the main tunnel, lining the walls, coughing, wrapped up in blankets and coats.

Even though the air is clear here, the affected colonists still cough. I hope their condition will resolve with time. We have a doctor here, but he's an anesthesiologist. This is a job for Izumi.

At the command post, I take Brightwell aside. "This feels like more than an allergic reaction. We need Izumi to figure out what we're dealing with. Whatever is sickening us in here may be more dangerous than anything out there." I glance back down the tunnel, where the coughs from the colonists are unceasing. "Without her, we may have to leave this cave."

Brightwell stares out the entrance into the eastern jungle, where snow is falling and the wind is picking up.

"I'll send a team for Izumi. The ideal thing would be to walk—it's quieter and less risk of drawing the attention of the E. rex. But it's slow, and as we've seen, it's no guarantee of safety." She nodded, as if making a decision. "We'll take a single ATV with three soldiers. Heavily armed."

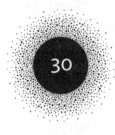

30

James

Arthur's voice calls to me. "James. James, wake up."

I crack my eyes, seeing the fog and shafts of light shining down through the broken tree canopy above. I'm lying on the jungle floor, which is damp and soft. The ground feels as though a tiller has churned it up. But I know it was the herd, tearing this jungle apart as it stampeded through.

My body aches, but the worst hurt is inside. My mind drifts to an image of Emma, standing in our flat, kissing me before I left to go look for the spheres on the dark side.

She's dead.

I lost Earth.

Now I've lost her.

I wasn't prepared for what happened here on Eos. I should have protected her.

Maybe Arthur was right. I should have been more worried about the storms. I should have ignored the buried spheres. I should have gone home. If I had, she might still be alive.

"*James*," Arthur growls. "Get up."

I try to move, but my body won't comply.

"*James*."

"Shut up…" I mutter.

He bends down, face inches from mine. "Get up right now."

"She's dead."

"You don't know that."

"If she's not, she's in the cave. Dying."

"All the more reason to get up."

He waits, then grabs me with his only arm and sits me up.

"Your children need you. Your people need you."

"Why do you care? Why are you even doing this?"

"That will be revealed in time."

I try to peel his hand off my shoulder, but he holds tight. "Let me go."

"No. Not until you get up and start fighting for your people."

"I already did that. Look where it got us. It'll never end. Earth, Eos, it's all the same. Another world, another hell to live through."

"It will get better."

"It won't."

"It will. Trust me."

I can't help but laugh. "Trust *you*?"

"I've lived a thousand lives on a thousand worlds, James. I've been fighting for my people for a long time."

I close my eyes, feeling the weariness overtake me. I don't have the strength to argue. Might not even have the strength to stand.

"I know you're tired, James. I know you're aching and wet and hungry. I also know that you're going to get up and you're going to fight for your people. You're going to do whatever it takes. Because that's who you are. And because you're their only hope. I don't know what happened to Emma. Or your children. They're either hiding in Jericho City, scared and trapped—or they're in the cave, sick and trapped. Either way, your children—and your people— are counting on you. No one else is coming for them. No one else can help them. It's you, here and now, fighting to save them or it all ends." He pauses, staring at me. "You're going to get up. It's what's inside you. As long as you have something to fight for, you'll fight. You'll do it sooner or later, but you need to do it *now*, because time is running out."

I exhale, knowing he's right—hating that he's right. And finally, a piece clicks. "You need me to get up, don't you? The grid does."

"Now isn't the time."

"You aren't here for me. You don't care about me. For some reason, you need me." I pause, but he doesn't reply. "On the ship, you told me there was a force in the universe more powerful than any you had encountered. You thought matter and energy were the economy of the universe. But there's something else—two forces at work that are far more powerful. What are they?"

"Not the time, James. Forget it."

"What are those forces at war? This is about that, isn't it? That's why you need me."

"You overestimate yourself."

"No. I've got it right."

"Okay. You go ahead and ask your philosophical questions. I'll wait silently over here until you're ready. Take your time. Right now, your kids' fevers are rising. The coughs won't stop. I wonder, do they know something is wrong yet?"

"Enough," I snap, anger rising, heart beating fast.

I stand, rising above the fog.

A few feet away, Corporal Young leans against a thick tree, eyes closed, breathing shallow.

I walk over and squat to inspect the gash on his back. Dried blood runs down his suit and onto the ground. The wound has clotted, but he's lost a lot of blood. He probably has internal injuries as well. I have to get him to Izumi soon.

"Hey. Corporal. Can you hear me?"

When he doesn't stir, I shake him gently. His eyelids crack open, revealing bloodshot, watery eyes.

"Did Izumi evacuate to the cave?"

He stares at me as if confused.

"Focus, Corporal. I'm asking you a question."

That gets his attention.

"Is Izumi still in the city? Or is she at the cave?"

"Who?"

"Izumi—Dr. Tanaka. Is she at the cave?"

"No. She stayed behind."

"Who else is there?"

He shakes his head. "Lots... of people."

"Why?"

"No time... to evacuate."

I settle back on my haunches. That could be good news. Those who stayed in Jericho City wouldn't have been exposed to the spores in the cave. We might still have a viable population to rebuild from—if we can't find a cure. And Izumi is our only hope of finding that cure. If she's unexposed to the regolith spores, we have a chance. And more—we have the data the *Carthage* colonists collected. I reach into my pocket and verify that the data drive is still there. It was made for use in space, so it's airtight and most likely survived being submerged in water. I have to get it to Izumi.

Young swallows and continues speaking, voice strained. "We were checking the path to the cave when the E. rex attacked. The others were going to follow."

"The rest from Jericho City were going to evacuate to the cave?"

He nods. "That was the plan."

"We need to hurry," Arthur says quietly.

Finally, we agree.

Leading me away from Young, Arthur continues, voice quiet. "I wouldn't recommend moving him."

"He survived being thrown in the river."

"I had to do that. It was better than being eaten alive by an E. rex. Now I think it's better to leave him here. And… he will slow us down."

"What do you recommend?"

"I recommend we get you an IR suit."

"What?" I motion to Young. "If we're leaving him, I'm certainly not taking his suit."

"It won't fit you anyway. And you're right, he needs it. The E. rex herds in the eastern jungle could leave at any moment. They'll come back here, likely hungry."

"So where do I get a suit?" The answer occurs to me instantly. "The teams Brightwell sent into the jungle."

"Precisely. We'll grab one on the way to Jericho City."

I relate our plan to Corporal Young, who nods wearily, barely opening his eyes. He doesn't seem scared to be left alone. He's probably too tired to be scared.

Arthur and I walk in silence, deeper into the western jungle, the roar of the river fading as we go. It's cooler now than I've ever felt it, and there's even more debris on the ground here than there was behind us.

Arthur pushes aside a limb with purple leaves—and freezes. Turning to me, he mouths the word, *Quiet.*

He alters his path to the right, stepping carefully, avoiding fallen branches that might crack. After two more steps, I catch sight of the E. rex, lying on the ground, eyes staring at me. It's massive, a full-grown adult.

Its chest is rising and falling. Is it sleeping? It doesn't move to get up, merely stares at me, its shallow breathing slowly accelerating. It's all I can do not to break into a run.

I feel Arthur's hand gripping me, pulling me toward him, urging me to move.

Thirty feet ahead, I spot another E. rex. It's also lying on the ground, on its side, eyes open—just like the last one. Deep gashes run along its body, ruts filled with red, white bone sticking out.

As I watch, its torso rises. It's breathing. It's still alive.

Arthur motions with his head, urging me to move. A minute later, when we're well beyond the wounded beasts, I grab his arm.

"What did that to them?"

"A predator that's deadly to the E. rex."

I wonder: if they can do that to an E. rex, how safe are we?

31

Emma

The fever boils me from the inside like a blaze I can't put out. I'm not alone. Everyone is sick now. Adults. Children. Soldiers.

Everyone.

Whatever those spores are, they have ravaged our population.

And sickness isn't our only problem.

Standing at the mouth of the cave, I watch the snow fall in sheets. Wind gains speed by the hour, blowing the snow sideways.

Another storm waits, just past the eastern mountain range, gathering strength to try to cross the peaks and reach this valley.

I hear thunder above, in the clouds. And thunder here on the ground: the herds are fleeing the eastern jungle—fleeing the cold and the storm.

That's good news. I think.

The wind whistles across the cave entrance, ebbing and flowing. When the sound recedes, I hear ice crunching.

Soon an ATV emerges from the falling snow, pulling a trailer filled with people lying down, covered up with thick blankets. Brightwell's team was supposed to bring back only Izumi. Maybe she's brought some of the wounded with her. We'll have to take precautions to ensure they don't get sick. Bringing them was a risk, but I figure the sheets of snow helped hide their body heat from the E. rex, who are probably too busy fleeing to hunt anyway.

Soldiers rush past me into the dim, snow-covered jungle. I follow, watching as they usher the people from the trailer into the mouth of the cave. The ATV driver dismounts and pulls off his facemask. It's one of Brightwell's soldiers.

One of the passengers pulls off her mask as well.

Izumi.

"How many are sick?" she asks, marching toward the cave entrance.

"Everyone."

Behind the first ATV, other vehicles begin arriving.

"You brought others?" I ask.

"They insisted on it. The city is virtually destroyed. There's no food and very little shelter. Everyone is coming here."

"Stop them. Use the radio. They may be safer there."

32

James

The wind has changed. It's cooler. The orange light that peeks through the broken canopy has slowly faded as clouds gather overhead. A storm is coming from the east. From the dark side.

As Arthur and I walk through the jungle, it seems alive with life, as though all the creatures living here are furiously preparing for the coming storm—to hide or to leave.

Arthur stops, holds up his hand, and crouches, creeping forward, staying low. He takes cover behind a large plant with wide leaves, then motions for me to follow.

When I arrive, I see what alarmed him: another fallen E. rex. Like the other two, this animal stares with glassy eyes. It's been ripped apart too, and it's also still breathing.

I study the scene, trying to make sense of it.

"Look at the wound," Arthur whispers.

Focusing on it, I see something moving, like water flowing across a windshield. What is that? A jelly of some sort, coating the wound?

Arthur turns quickly and points at the ground. There's an insect moving there, about the length of my pointer finger. It's completely translucent except for some dirt around its feet. A stinger hangs from its tail. It reminds me of a scorpion—which is technically an arachnid, not an insect. This creature is something in between.

"What is it?" I whisper.

"A native of the western mountain range. They tend to stay close to the desert. Let's just call it the Western Mountain Scorpion."

That would explain why I've never seen it before—we have stayed clear of the western mountains. The jungle region that borders those mountains, to the west of where I am now, is E. rex territory.

The scorpion bobbles along the ground until it reaches the fallen E. rex, then climbs to the wound and blends with the other translucent scorpions that together, seen from a distance, at first looked like jelly on the E. rex wound.

"They don't usually come into the jungle," Arthur says. "The sandstorm brought them."

"How do you know?"

"We're the grid, James."

I exhale, frustrated at the answer. "They feed on the injured E. rex?"

"They do. And they brought the beast down."

"What?"

"The venom their stingers deliver is a paralytic agent. One sting is enough to immobilize even an E. rex." He pauses to watch them work. "They eat their prey alive."

"Does their venom work on humans?"

"Yes. And they'll be here until the herds leave, which may be soon."

"What do you mean?"

"The storm from the east will drive the E. rex back through here. The scorpions will feast on them as they pass."

Arthur leads me away from the fallen animal, east, toward Jericho City. I watch the ground as I walk now, mindful of the scorpions. I spot a few, but none attack me. They seem to be on their way to the fallen E. rex.

Arthur seems to read my curiosity. "They communicate via pheromones. When one stings, it releases a chemical into the air, drawing other scorpions. They help with the battle if needed—and share the kill."

We walk in silence, listening as the wind grows stronger. Arthur seems to know where he's going. Sure enough, soon we come across a human body. Or what's left of it. It's a soldier with an infrared suit. He—or she—has been trampled by the E. rex herd, body torn apart. Nearby, an automatic rifle lies half-buried in the ground. I pull it out and brush the dirt off. The magazine is empty. The person went down fighting, that much is certain.

I sling the rifle over my shoulder as Arthur hands me the soldier's belt, which holds a sheathed combat knife and flares.

He leads the way to three more soldiers, all dead. Their suits are punctured too. I can't use them. I do, however, recover three partially filled magazines for the rifle.

"Here," Arthur whispers, pointing at a fallen tree.

A dead E. rex lies near the base. A soldier is pinned under the tree, crushed, but otherwise in one piece. The E. rex must have brought the tree down, killing the man.

We dig him out, and luckily he's about my size. It feels wrong stripping a dead man of his suit, but I don't see that I have a choice.

His radio is busted, which is a shame.

Arthur takes a grenade from the man's belt and pockets it. Then he takes the man's rifle, checks the magazine, and tucks it under his arm. He stops when he feels my eyes on him.

"My aim is better than yours. You may soon be glad I have this."

A few days ago, I wouldn't have dreamed of arming Arthur. Now I simply nod. Our relationship has come a very long way in a short amount of time.

We walk in silence after that, both armed, both watching for any sign of E. rex. Clothed in the suit and armed with the rifle, I feel a little more confident in the jungle, as if I was naked before and now am clothed.

The wind picks up, rustling the leaves and bushes. Thunder rolls overhead, and in the distance a droning din grows louder.

"Hurry," Arthur hisses. He breaks into a run.

I chase behind him, limbs and leaves scraping across me. Cold rain falls, adding to the noise. It's a hard rain, blowing in the wind, drenching the ground and trees.

Up ahead, I hear what I think is the wind ripping through the jungle. Suddenly I collide with something, hard as a tree trunk. An arm wraps around me and tosses me backward, into the ground.

The sound beats louder, coming closer. I realize then that Arthur turned back and tackled me. He's pinning me to the ground.

My heart beats faster, a drum pounding in my chest.

The ground next to me explodes, spraying my facemask with sticky black mud. In the flash I see a giant foot, with gleaming, pearly-white claws digging into the ground. Then it's gone, thumping as the E. rex races by.

"You need to climb a tree," Arthur whispers.

My mind flashes to the soldier crushed by the falling tree brought down by an E. rex.

Another E. rex thunders by, showering sodden dirt down on me.

Gunshots ring out in the distance.

Jericho City. They're fighting.

I struggle to crawl forward, to get out from Arthur's grip, but he pins me down.

"Don't be a fool, James."

"I'm going. Help me or don't, but let me go."

Arthur shakes his head as he releases me.

Gripping the rifle, I bound through the jungle. The cold rain turns to sleet, falling like tiny pebbles through the canopy, which mercifully slow the onslaught. The noise is like static over a radio, the gunshots in the distance like firecrackers at the bottom of a well, distant and faint.

To my right, an E. rex streaks by, twenty feet away, but it doesn't slow. I'm thankful for the suit.

When I clear the jungle, I get my first glimpse of Jericho City without the canopy overhead. The grass field that surrounds it is almost completely burned, a charred expanse that has been churned by the herd.

My heart falls when I see the barracks buildings. They are broken and crumbled. Tree limbs stick out from the sides.

Dead E. rex protrude from holes, unmoving. The carnage reminds me of Camp Seven after the asteroid strikes, a city leveled.

At the end of the city, two ATVs and trailers sit idle, soldiers crowding around them, using them to hide their body heat as they fire at the E. rex trickling out of the eastern jungle. The gunfire is diverting the E. rex so far, but more of them are coming by the second.

The sleet assaults me, and my feet sink in the charred ground as if I'm running through a mud pit, which is pretty much what it is. Even Arthur slows in the muck.

There are at least two hundred people standing around the city. They're beginning to flock to the broken barracks, climbing down into the crawlspaces.

Suddenly, the eastern jungle bursts open with E. rex. They pour out in dozens—no, hundreds. Jericho City lies between me and them, and they're a lot faster than I am.

Beside me, Arthur comes to a stop, planting his feet. I glance back in time to see him drop the rifle, fish the grenade from his pocket, and hurl it toward the tree line of the eastern jungle. It soars like a Hail Mary shot at the buzzer, hanging in the air for what feels like an eternity. No human could have made that toss—not even one a tenth of that distance. His strength and accuracy are breathtaking.

The grenade lands right at the tree line and explodes, incinerating two E. rex and rocking the forest.

The soldiers at the ATVs whip around, shocked.

Behind me, Arthur raises his rifle and begins firing at the E. rex behind them. The bullets whizzing within feet of the soldiers, but his aim is dead on.

A man steps from the ATV line. It's Grigory. He yells, but I can't make out the words. Raising his rifle, he begins firing at Arthur. The soldiers beside him join in, firing indiscriminately at both of us.

33

Emma

The storm dumps snow on the jungle. Soldiers work at the mouth of the cave, trying to seal it off with rocks and empty supply crates, hoping to trap the warmth inside.

The E. rex are leaving, stampeding out of the eastern jungle, back toward Jericho City.

Unfortunately, a large group of colonists followed Izumi from Jericho City. They assumed it would be safer here. It may be, but that's far from certain. We debated sending them back to Jericho City, but the civilians—and even the soldiers in the group—protested, borderline refusing. I don't blame them. Between the storms and the E. rex, I wouldn't want to be out there. For now, we've quarantined the new arrivals near the entrance, away from the sponges and the sick.

We've also radioed the city and told them to stop evacuating for now. That order was met with disbelief and frustration. They know another stampede is headed their way. And this one can only be worse. When the E. rex came through last time, the habitats were intact. Now the shelters are broken and crumpled.

Will the E. rex finish demolishing them—and the people hiding inside?

I wish I could do something more to help.

Behind me, near the mouth of the cave, Izumi has set up a field hospital. Some patients lie in the beds of the trailers, others lie on the cold ground. Izumi and her staff wear personal protective equipment—PPE—including gowns, gloves, and facemasks. If Izumi gets sick, we're in trouble. I hope by keeping her far away from the sponges and spores, she'll remain free of the toxin. Or infection. Or whatever it is. We're still not sure. We don't even know if we've been inhaling a chemical or a living organism. It could be a virus, a bacterium, or a fungus. Or something completely unknown to us.

Thus far, the adults seem the most affected. Perhaps their larger lungs are able to take in more of the substance—or maybe their more developed immune systems are faster to react.

I'm worried about all the patients lining the cave tunnel, but one patient in particular. I stop at the trailer where Madison lies, eyes bloodshot and watery, her face as white as the snow outside.

I slide my hand into hers and lean down and kiss her clammy skin. The fever is gone. That worries me. It seems to fade before the patient gets worse.

She jerks her hand away, bringing it to her mouth to cover as she coughs.

I reach out to take her hand again, but she shakes her head. "Stay back. I don't want you—"

"To get sick? Too late."

"Still."

I squat down to eye level with her. "It's going to be okay."

She smiles, bringing out the fine wrinkles on her face. I've never seen my sister look so weary. "I know. One way or another, it'll be all right." She swallows hard and gasps, gathering her breath. "Go be with Sam, Allie, and Carson. They're probably scared."

"I'm staying right here—"

An alarm rings out, echoing in the rocky corridor. Izumi breaks into a run, two of her nurses right behind her.

Staring down the row of trailers, I spot a patient convulsing.

34

James

The gunshots rip up the charred ground around me. I drop to my belly, gun flying from my hands. Arthur does the same and calls to me, "Shall I disable them—"

"No!"

I hold up my hands, knowing they could very well be shot off.

"Grigory!" I yell.

Through the sound of the sleet slamming into my suit and the ground, I can barely hear my own voice.

The E. rex leading the herd are stampeding all around us now. Luckily, none have taken notice. In the eastern jungle, the rumble of the main body of the group grows louder.

The bullets digging into the ground beside me cease, but the gunshots continue. They've turned their attention to the scattered E. rex that are approaching the city.

"Stay here!" I call to Arthur.

"Bad idea."

I jump up and pull the facemask off. It will reveal some

of my body heat, making me a target for the E. rex, but I don't have a choice. I need Grigory to see my face.

With every ounce of strength I can muster, I run across the burned field. The main body of the E. rex herd is up ahead, just breaking the tree line, heading for the city.

The soldiers at the ATVs abandon their cover and run for the barracks. Grigory catches sight of me and squints, obviously surprised.

I'm running so hard it feels like my heart might burst.

If I don't reach the barracks before the herd gets there, I'm finished.

Even Arthur can't survive the herd. They'll trample him, grinding him to a mangled mess.

I peek behind me. He's gone. I spot him near the tree line, retreating into the jungle. For once I'm glad he didn't listen to me.

Up ahead, an E. rex far beyond the main herd cries out and alters his vector, heading straight for me. Fear rises up in me, a wave that almost numbs my body. I should have put the facemask back on after Grigory saw me.

In the city, Grigory stands in the wreckage of a barracks building, armed soldiers around him, descending into the crawlspace. He turns and speaks to them, and suddenly they raise their rifles and begin shooting in my direction.

But not at me. The shots tear into an E. rex barreling toward me. It's too little, too late. The E. rex is a hundred feet from me.

I alter my vector, but the beast matches course, his mouth open.

My nerves overwhelm me. I try to push the fear away. My legs feel like lead. My feet seem to sink deeper with every step.

I raise my rifle, trying to train it on the E. rex.

I'm running too fast. My hands won't work.

It's fifty feet from me.

A shot from Grigory, or one of his troops, catches the beast in the side. It slows, flinching and screaming, mouth wide open. He's close enough I can see his back teeth, his tongue sticking straight out.

Another shot rings out—from behind me. The E. rex's head snaps to the side and it collapses to the ground, face first, spraying the loose dirt in the air, covering me like a land mine going off.

It's Arthur. He shot the animal through the eye—a shot only a machine could make.

It's my chance. I barrel toward the crawlspace where Grigory just disappeared.

I reach the opening in the floor seconds before the E. rex herd reaches the city.

I don't bother with the ladder. I jump down, landing hard on my feet, ankle buckling as I fall to the side. Grigory is there, staring down at me.

A soldier slams the crawlspace door shut and they pull me away from it.

"I'm okay," I say between gasps. I can't seem to catch my breath. My body is flooded with adrenaline. I feel as though I've overdosed on a stimulant and I can't come down.

The soldiers prop me up against one of the foundation walls, and Grigory waddles over to me, Min close behind him.

"I saw Arthur," Grigory says. "I didn't realize you were in the suit. I couldn't see your face. We thought you might be—"

"An enemy. It's okay."

Grigory eyes me. "Arthur's still out there."

"He saved me."

"What?"

"In the eastern jungle. And just now."

Grigory turns away. "We can't trust him."

"I know."

The three of us sit in silence then, listening to the herd passing. Three holes in the subfloor above, all about the size of a fist, let in shafts of orange light. In the dim light, I study the crawlspace. The dirt beneath us is lined with a watertight barrier that slopes to a drain. Someone has poked several holes in the plastic sheeting, allowing it to drain even more. Still, the material is damp, and there are shallow puddles in places. It must have been flooded down here before. There may also be debris in the drains.

The floor booms and creaks as an E. rex runs across. Then the pounding comes faster—more E. rex flowing through our battered city. The floor joists groan under the weight.

After a few minutes of this pounding, one E. rex stumbles, or perhaps is trampled, and lands hard on the floor, cracking three of the joists. Its head actually punctures the subfloor, making a hole that's about two feet wide and long. Its jaw protrudes through the opening, orange sunlight peeking around it, pearly teeth exposed.

The twenty or so people down here scamper away from it, myself included. We all watch, but the beast doesn't move. It's dead. How?

The pounding continues, and soon another crash follows, only feet from the first. The floor joists snap this time and the entire floor system gives, dumping the two E. rex face-first into the crawlspace.

I'm as still as a statue. Everyone else is too. My gun is on the other side of the crawlspace, near the entrance, right beside the fallen E. rex.

They're alive. Their chests rise and fall slowly.

But I can't see a wound.

They must have been stung by one of the Western Mountain Scorpions.

Sleet splatters their bodies, melting to water that flows into the crawlspace, filling it faster than the drains and holes can handle. I feel like I'm in a boat taking on water.

We wait.

Minutes go by.

The herd keeps charging. How many are there? Surely it has to stop soon.

The wind picks up. The sleet turns to snow.

There's now at least an inch of water all around the crawlspace, and more at the deeper sections.

But eventually the sound of E. rex feet thins and fades. Every few minutes another one roars past; there are clearly a lot of stragglers. We need to wait until the entire herd has passed.

And in order to leave, we have to get past the two fallen E. rex in the crawlspace.

As I'm turning the problem over in my mind, another E. rex foot thunders above, jostling the two fallen beasts as it passes. They shift, but don't rise.

"Hungry?" Grigory whispers.

"Yeah," I reply.

He hands me an MRE, and I eat it without activating the heating element. No sense in releasing the scent of a warm meal. We've got enough problems at the moment.

"We drained a few crawlspaces completely and stocked them," Grigory says. "This wasn't one of them."

"Still," I reply, "it's shelter. We'll be out soon."

I hope I'm right.

"Have you heard from the people evacuated to the cave?" I ask.

"Yes. They sent a team to retrieve Izumi before the second stampede. The cave is making everyone sick."

The news is the sum of my fears, the worst possible scenario. I ask the question I must, dreading the answer, hoping that whatever has sickened our population is different than what killed Harry and the colonists from the *Carthage*.

"What are the symptoms?"

"Coughing. Fever. We didn't get many details. They left in a hurry."

Min hangs his head. I can tell he wanted to go with her. He stayed to help the people trapped here.

"A lot of people followed Izumi and the troops to the cave," Grigory says quietly. "They figured it was safer there than here. The troops told them to stay, but they wouldn't listen. There were a lot more of them than the three soldiers sent to retrieve Izumi."

I want to tell Grigory and Min what I've learned, but now isn't the time. We need to be as quiet as possible, and frankly, I need some rest after the hike through the jungle and the mad dash across the field.

Grigory points at the E. rex closest to us. There's a large gash along its neck, and Western Mountain Scorpions are congregating in the wound, having their fill.

"The translucent scorpions contain a paralyzing agent," I whisper. "Stay clear of them."

Minutes pass like hours. The sound of the herd fades and the stragglers dwindle until it's quiet outside. The crawlspace fills like a ship taking on water—a vessel we can't escape for now. The E. rex covered in scorpions block our only exit. Once the tiny predators have had their fill, hopefully they'll crawl away, clearing our path.

But that hope doesn't come true. As the E. rex carcasses dwindle and flesh turns to bone, the scorpions don't crawl out. They slip into the water and begin swimming toward us.

Emma

We have a hundred dead now.

Dozens more teeter on the brink of death.

On one of the trailers, a colonist named Jeff convulses. Izumi works furiously, but as with those before him, death comes quickly. Four soldiers grab the sheet beneath him and hoist him onto a trailer that has become our hearse. I watch as they disappear into the tunnel.

Izumi tears off her helmet and throws it on the cave floor.

"Izumi, no! Put it back on!" I call to her.

She closes her eyes, face trembling, as a tear breaks free.

Her staff carefully back away and begin cleaning the bed, readying it for the next sick colonist.

"Izumi," I whisper.

"It doesn't matter," she replies. "I'm probably already infected."

"You don't know that."

She motions behind me, where soldiers are stacking stones at the cave opening, closing it off to keep us from freezing to death in here. "If I'm not infected now, I likely will be soon."

Beyond the shrinking cave entrance, snow blows furiously in the wind. It's a blizzard out there. Blankets of ice and snow fall across the jungle and over the cave entrance.

"There's only so much air in here," Izumi says.

"You can leave. Take a few—"

"And go where? There's no buildings left for me to work in at Jericho City."

An idea strikes me. "Carthage City."

She shakes her head. "It was probably overrun by E. rex again. And the storm. Plus, how can we be sure this... pathogen or whatever it is, isn't there? That's why we didn't settle there in the first place—in case there was some biological threat."

"Put your helmet back on," I urge her. "Please. We'll send someone to Carthage City. If it's gone, then... then we'll stay here. If not, we can go there—it can't be any more contaminated than this cave. At least there, you'd have a chance of avoiding infection."

For a long moment she stares at the soldiers closing off the mouth of the cave. Finally she nods and puts the helmet back on. Behind her, another patient seizes, and she turns and runs.

I make my way to the command post, where Brightwell sits in a folding chair, staring at the floor, dark bags under her eyes.

"Colonel, we need to send someone to Carthage to see if we can take shelter there. Izumi needs an uncontaminated place to work."

"Yes, ma'am."

"Are you in radio contact with Jericho City?"

"No. They've gone silent. I assume the herds are passing through."

"As soon as possible, we need to warn them not to come to this cave. If Carthage City is a viable shelter, send them there."

"Understood. I'll send a team to Jericho City with the message," she says absently.

36

James

The translucent scorpions from the E. rex carcass descend into the water like rats off a ship. They're able to swim, slowly—perhaps they're propelled by their legs under the water, aided by the waves created when they jumped in.

Each second, the armada of milky-white killers inches closer to me and the other dozen colonists huddled in the corner of the crawlspace.

Our guns are still on the other side of the two fallen E. rex, not that they would do us a lot of good.

Several people in the group shift nervously or try to shrink behind the people next to them, afraid to be on the front line when the scorpions reach us. But one soldier wades forward in the water, still squatting, and pulls on a cracked floor joist, ripping off a piece of wood. I assume he's going to make waves to repel the scorpions, but I'm wrong. He has another idea.

He guides the end of the stick into the water, catches the closest scorpion, and then pushes it against the foundation wall, grinding it into pieces, which fall dead into the water.

As he catches a second scorpion and mashes it against the wall in the same manner, two more soldiers follow his lead. They tear off their own pieces of wood and join the fight. One grinds the scorpions against the wall like the first; the other creates waves, directing the scorpions toward the killing soldiers.

It's working.

I grab my own piece of wood and wade into the fight, standing in the middle of the line, pushing the scorpions to my left to the man beside me, who passes them on as well.

Suddenly, I hear a plop-plop-plop sound. I turn to see scorpions pouring through the holes in the subfloor, flowing down like the rays of sunlight. I realize then what's happening: when the scorpions make contact with the sticks, they sting them and release pheromones that draw more scorpions. The other scorpions think there's a kill down here.

Now there's a rapidly growing group of scorpions floating between me and the group at the foundation wall.

The people by the wall begin to panic, thrashing about, making waves that push the scorpions away, toward me and the other soldiers who stand between them and the dead E. rex. I don't know if a scorpion's stinger can puncture my IR suit, but I'm not eager to find out.

The man beside me jerks and falls into the water. Releasing his stick. In the confusion, one of the scorpions must have reached his body or crawled up the stick. He's stung, and now he's staring up at me with wide, horrified eyes, silently begging for help. Waves cascade around me in all directions from the man's fall, and there are scorpions everywhere.

I grab the man and pull him up. I know the scorpion might still be attached, but I don't have a choice—he'll drown otherwise. I scan his body but don't see the scorpion. Maybe it washed clear when he fell. I can only hope so.

I retreat, twisting side to side, trying to spot the scorpions. Their nearly transparent bodies are almost impossible to see here in the water and the dim light. All that gives them away is the dirt or blood on their bodies—and the waves and water are washing any such coatings away.

I hand the paralyzed soldier to Min and Grigory, who pull him back to the foundation wall.

I feel a sharp prick in my side. I turn, terrified I've been stung, but it's just one of the sticks we tore off digging in, its other end buttressed by a soldier's back.

As I watch, a scorpion crawls out of the water, onto the stick, and prances toward the soldier, stinger bobbing in the air, held over its head at the ready. Before I can react, the scorpion strikes, and the man tumbles like a falling tree.

I reach out, grab his collar, and pull him to me, unsure where the scorpion is.

Through the holes in the floor above, more scorpions continue to pour in.

Another soldier falls, and one of his comrades wades through the water toward him.

I lock eyes with Grigory. His expression says what I feel: we're in trouble.

37

Emma

Sitting in the dark, damp cave, I hold my sister's head in my lap, tears streaming down my face. With a shaking hand, I reach down and close her eyelids. I want to cry with all my heart, to let it out, but I just feel numb. The tears I cry are like drops from a broken faucet. My chest heaves with every cough, blowing out the cold air that fills this deadly cave.

"Ma'am."

I hear the words, but can't seem to look up.

"Ma'am."

The soldier paces away and returns with someone who places a hand on my shoulder.

It's Brightwell.

"Emma."

I turn, make eye contact.

"We need to take her."

I nod absently.

Two soldiers take hold of Madison, hoist her up like a giant doll, floppy and lifeless, and carry her toward the stack on the back of the ATV, to join the bundle of bodies already there—people who were someone's husband, wife, mother, brother... sister.

It's surreal.

A nightmare.

Completely paralyzing.

"Emma."

"Emma," Brightwell says, louder. "Allie. She's very sick."

And just like that, my body reacts. Before I can even process the words, I feel my hand plant against the frigid cave wall, and my legs push up. I'm standing, then walking deeper into the cave, to the alcove where Abby is crouched in the corner, with Carson wailing in her arms. Alex is sitting beside her, eyes closed, coughing, and Allie is leaning against her aunt, crying as she, too, coughs. Sam, our oldest, stands with his arms crossed, a serious look on his face, as if on guard duty against the enemy that is killing our people.

My heart breaks at the scene—at Allie's sickness, Carson's wails, and Sam's bravery. Nothing compares to this. The destruction of the ISS, the loss of the *Fornax* at the Beta artifact, the battle of Ceres, being trapped in the Citadel bunker—they all pale in comparison to the horror of this moment.

My family is dying.

38

James

As the scorpions surround us, my mind goes into overdrive.

"The rubber liner!" I yell to Grigory and the others. "The one covering the ground! Rip it up and form a wall!"

A soldier draws a combat knife and stabs it into the water along one wall. He pulls up the end of the thick rubbery underlay, then keeps cutting, gradually handing more of the sheet to the people joining the line.

Within seconds, they're holding it up like a shower curtain, holding the water and the scorpions out—and enclosing the rest of us in an area in the crawlspace with no holes in the subfloor above.

The soldier takes the end of the plastic, holds it against the floor joist and stabs his knife into it, securing it. Another soldier pulls his knife and does the same, and they repeat the procedure with all the knives available. Still, the knives aren't enough. Four people have to hold the rubber sheet up to keep the wall in place.

On the other side, we can hear the *scritch* of the scorpions against the barrier, their tiny legs scrambling for purchase, their stingers striking with no effect.

"James!" Grigory calls, pointing.

I instantly see the cause of his alarm. The plastic sheet has small punctures in several places—either by our movements or by a previous group trying to drain the flooded crawlspace while seeking shelter from the E. rex.

A scorpion slips through one of the holes. Moving carefully, a soldier wielding a stick guides the scorpion to the wall and mashes it to pieces.

The rain is picking up, pouring through the openings in the floor on the other side of our rubbery barrier. A steady stream flows through the holes in the sheet, bringing with it a scorpion every few seconds. Each time, we crush the invader.

The flow is manageable, and we're safe for now, but we're still trapped. The water will continue to rise, and eventually the scorpions will come over the top of the sheet, in the drooping sections between the hands holding it up and the knives sunk into the floor joists. Or the weight of water against the sheet will be too much, pulling it free.

The other issue is the four paralyzed soldiers. I have no idea how the scorpion venom will affect them. Will it wear off? If so, when? Or will it ultimately be fatal?

I perform a cursory examination on the three men and one woman. Their vitals seem stable, but they can't move an inch—not even their eyes. But their chests continue to rise and fall as they breathe.

Grigory wades over to me.

"The insects float. When the water is deep enough, we could drop the sheet and swim underwater, beneath them."

"It's risky. The scorpions could be waiting to sting us as we surface." I motion to the paralyzed soldiers. "And we'd need to pull them out. They'd probably drown."

He throws up his hands. "So we're trapped."

"Not exactly. Do you have a working radio?"

"The long-range is outside. Probably crushed. I have a handheld that we use around the city. It won't reach all the way to the cave."

"We're not calling the cave."

"You want to contact the other people trapped in the crawlspaces?"

"No. I want to call Arthur."

Grigory scoffs and shakes his head. "You'll think *he'll* get us out of here?"

"It's worth a shot. I told you, he helped me before."

"He tried to kill us. He *did* kill thousands of our people."

"That was war. That was then. This is now, and he's our only sure way out of here."

"You want to call our mortal enemy and tell him we're trapped down here. Brilliant, James. What could go wrong?"

"He's saved my life several times in the last day. He's different somehow."

Grigory just stares at me. "Why did you let him out in the first place, James? What could be worth the risk?"

"The Eye of the Grid. I solved it, Grigory. I found what's at the center of the eye."

He squints at me, confused.

"It's a cave. I found Harry there."

"Is he…"

"Dead. So are the others from the *Carthage*."

"How? When?"

"The rogue planet passed this way before, and the storm, the stampedes, everything happened exactly the way it's happening now. The colonists from the *Carthage* took refuge in a cave similar to the one our people are in right now. There was some kind of sponge on the walls that released a toxin or pathogen. It made them sick, and eventually killed them. All of them. But they ran a lot of tests on the disease and collected a ton of data. I have that data, and I need to get to Izumi. It's our only hope of finding a cure for our people."

"Why didn't Harry leave a warning for us? Out in the open—where we could find it."

"He couldn't. By the time they were sick, the E. rex were everywhere in the eastern jungle. Harry couldn't get back to Carthage City to leave a message. They were too sick to even bury their dead. Harry led them to the cave at the center of the Eye of the Grid because there are no sponges there. He hoped some of them might recover. They didn't. But there was another reason to go there: Harry thought that cave might be the key to solving the mystery of the Eye of the Grid. He thinks it's connected to the storms and the pathogen. That it's all part of some process."

"What kind of process?"

"I don't know. Yet. But I think Arthur knows what's happening. I think that's why he's been helping me. He needs us for some reason."

"That makes me feel great," Grigory mutters.

Behind us, a soldier crushes another scorpion on the foundation wall.

"We're running out of time, Grigory. We need Arthur to get us out of here. The scorpion venom doesn't affect him.

He can clear the floor above us and make a hole and pull us out." I reach into my pocket and draw out the small data drive. "We have to get this to Izumi. If our people are sick, nothing else matters."

He nods slowly and hands me a radio, silently agreeing.

I hold the radio close to my mouth and speak quietly, just in case there might be another E. rex lurking outside. "Arthur. Do you read? We could use some help."

39

Emma

The death of my sister gutted me.

When this disease takes my nephew, Jack, I feel as though the rest of me is wrenched away.

Alex and Abby stand by the trailer, sobbing, hands on their son, who lies peacefully, eyes closed.

I want to say something to console them. But there are no words for something like this. I'd like to think time will heal it, but I'm not sure we have that much time left.

I sit with my back against the cold stone wall, holding my daughter in my arms. Allie feels impossibly light, as if the weight has been drained from her, as if she's just an empty shell like me. She jerks as she coughs, her warm breath flowing into my chest.

"Hang on, sweetie," I whisper.

At the mouth of the cave, Izumi is leaning over a convulsing patient lying on the bed of another ATV, working furiously.

Allie turns her head toward them, but I cradle her closer to me and turn my back to the scene, trying to keep her from the horror of what I know is coming. She's too young to see this—too young to have that happen to her. Too innocent. Just like her cousin who was alive an hour ago.

I whisper to her, "It's going to be all right."

I keep repeating the lie, trying to drown out the sound behind me.

When the corridor goes quiet, I hear the snap of rubber gloves coming off and Izumi saying, "Put her with the others." Then she calls to me, "Emma, bring her, please."

As I turn, Allie rolls into me and hugs with all her might, whining, "Mommy, no—"

"It's okay, sweetie."

"No, Mommy, I don't want to."

"Dr. Izumi is going to make you feel better."

"I want to go home."

"We will. I promise."

I try to set her on the bed of the ATV, in the place where someone just died, but Allie holds fast, shivering from the cold or fear or both, not letting me go.

I squat down, my face close to hers. "It's okay. I'm going to stay right here."

Izumi takes off her facemask and leans over Allie, smiling at her. I shoot her a look of warning, of fear that she'll get infected, but Izumi ignores it. "Hi, Allie. I know you don't feel well. But I have something that will help you breathe."

She holds up an inhaler.

Allie shakes her head violently. "No…"

"It doesn't hurt," Izumi says. "Watch."

She holds the inhaler to her mouth and takes a deep breath.

"See?"

Izumi sanitizes the inhaler and holds it out to Allie. "You hold it. When you feel like it's hard to breathe, you just inhale. It will help. I promise."

Cautiously, Allie takes the device. A second later, she coughs violently.

Izumi reaches out and takes the hand that holds the inhaler. "Now, give it a try."

She holds the inhaler to Allie's mouth, and my daughter takes a deep breath. It's like a balm on an open wound, soothing her instantly. Her heaving chest settles and her eyes become a little glassy, almost serene.

Izumi leads me away, speaking in a low voice. "My hope is that if she can breathe, her body will fight off whatever's causing this."

Without meaning to, my gaze drifts to Jack and then to the stacks of bodies at the mouth of the cave, lying by the piles of rock.

"And what if she can't fight it off?"

"Our best chance is to get out of here, get to fresh warm air and hope it passes. I've been running tests, but this… thing… is something completely new, unlike any pathogen on Earth. I actually think it's an archaeon causing a cytokine storm."

I nod as if I know what any of that means. In truth, I'm too tired to ask questions, too cold and weary, and all I want to do is hold my child for however long I have left.

So I do. We sit in the bed of the ATV trailer, my arms wrapped around her, keeping her warm, singing all the songs she likes, wishing I had a book to read to her.

40

James

"Arthur, do you read?"

I hold the radio, listening, but there's no reply. Maybe his broadcast capabilities were damaged during the battles with the E. rex. Or perhaps he turned them off.

The scorpions claw at the plastic. Every minute or so, one slips through a hole in the barrier and a soldier scrambles to pin it to the foundation wall and crush it.

One of the soldiers calls over the radio to the other three groups trapped in the city. Two don't respond. The third replies that they're trapped too.

Grigory eyes me, silently asking, *What now?*

Our options are bad and worse.

A scraping noise sounds on the floor above. It's like an E. rex crawling across. Beyond the plastic, I can hear something falling into the water—scorpions I assume.

Then with a crash the floor rains splinters down upon us, bringing bright sunlight with it.

I crouch and squint, holding up an arm for protection.

Arthur peers down through the hole. "You rang?"

"You could've replied."

"Thought the dramatic pause would heighten the anticipation. And make you appreciate the rescue more."

"Just get us out of here."

He expands the hole and we climb out of the flooded crawlspace, evacuating the paralyzed soldiers first.

The floor is clear of scorpions—the scraping noise I heard was apparently Arthur pushing them into a hole in the floor beyond the barrier we created. For now, we're safe from the scorpions.

In the mad dash to the crawlspace, I caught a glimpse of Jericho City. It was already battered and beaten then. Now it's completely demolished. The habitats are crushed and strewn across the muddy dirt streets. Our once-proud city looks like the wreckage of a ship that crashed into some rocks and washed up on shore. Among the debris, E. rex lie unmoving, a milky-white film of scorpions crawling over them, picking the bodies clean.

The soldiers from our crawlspace fan out across the ruined landscape, calling quietly for their comrades, liberating the other three groups. I count a dozen soldiers and civilians who are alive and paralyzed. There are at least ten dead. A few were caught by the E. rex before they got to shelter. The rest died in the crawlspaces—either crushed by an E. rex crashing through the floor or drowned after a scorpion sting.

"Arthur, go get Corporal Young and bring him here."

"He's probably dead—"

"Bring him either way." I stare at Arthur a moment. "It's safer for you than any of us. Go, quickly."

He turns without another word. I feel Grigory's eyes on me, silently judging my decision to leave Arthur unguarded.

The snow has died down to flurries. The sky is overcast, as if the storm isn't over, just taking a break.

In short order, the soldiers set up a camp in the wreckage of one of the habitats. They dig a deep trench and erect a curved wall that bends away from the people inside, keeping the scorpions out.

While the soldiers take stock of our people, Min, Grigory, and I focus on the equipment.

All of the ATVs here in the city are crushed. So are the long-range radios, leaving us with no way to contact the cave.

Thinking about the cave is a stark reminder that Emma is gone. Assuming we live through this, how will I ever manage without her? The kids. The colony. None of it seems possible in a world where she isn't with us. I can't even imagine that reality.

For now, I have to focus. What's the immediate need? Shelter—from the storms as well as the E. rex and scorpions.

The caves are out—they likely all harbor the regolith sponges. What does that leave? Carthage City? It's probably in the same shape as our settlement, or worse.

I look up at the cloudy sky, willing my mind to see a solution. A second later, I see it—literally. A flash of light in the sky, a beacon of hope.

Grigory and Min are crouched nearby, arguing over a pile of mangled electronics that I recognize as parts from the 3D printers.

"Have you found any of the comm panels?" I ask.

Grigory shakes his head. "The ones that were left out are likely destroyed." He grabs his backpack and pulls the zipper open, revealing a stack of the small tiles. "But Emma had us keep four of them just in case."

Her name is another sharp jab to my heart. I feel the water running to my eyes as I nod, trying to steady my voice.

"Assemble them and send a message to the ship flying overhead right now."

"A message saying what?" Min asks.

"To land."

Grigory shakes his head. "Land the ship? It'll be a mangled heap—and burned by the atmosphere."

"Yes, but it will be better than camping out in the open. And if we're lucky, the stasis equipment will still be intact. If it is, we can put the sick in stasis and buy ourselves some time to find a cure. It's our only play."

"Touchdown location?" Min asks, already typing on his terminal, loading a landing sequence, I assume.

"Near Carthage City. If we're lucky, there's some usable material there."

Again I gaze up at the sky, at the shiny light reflecting off of the ship. It's one of the two vessels that saved us in our final hours on Earth, carried us away. Now it will be our refuge of last resort.

41

Emma

Allie slips in and out of consciousness. Sam lies next to her on the bed of the ATV, holding his sister's hand, covering his cough with his other hand. He's getting sicker too.

At the mouth of the cave, a runner crawls through the small opening before the soldiers standing guard cover it with rock again. I hear him talking quickly with Brightwell, a discussion follows, and then she's standing next to me, eyes weary, face lined.

"Three of the habitats in Carthage City are partially intact."

I nod absently.

After a pause, Brightwell whispers, "Emma."

"E. rex?" I reply, trying to focus. It feels as though my body is boiling inside.

"The scout saw four, all alone in the forest. Stragglers. Maybe wounded. We can handle them."

"Give the order."

Fifteen minutes later, I'm part of a convoy creeping through the eastern jungle. Riding in the bed of an ATV,

I clutch Carson to my chest, Allie on one side, Sam on the other, a thick blanket covering us that barely keeps away the cold. Soldiers hang off the sides, rifles ready, watching for E. rex.

The ATV tracks crunch in the melting snow, snapping fallen limbs and twigs. We're making plenty of noise, not the least of which is the sobs of the sick as they're jostled around. But we haven't drawn the attention of any of the beasts. Yet.

This trek across the frozen, devastated wilderness reminds me of our last days on Earth, when our band of survivors journeyed from the CENTCOM bunker in Camp Seven to the warehouse in Camp Nine where we made our final stand. We were on the brink of extinction then. And I fear we are again. Is this what our existence will be like from now on? Constantly fighting for our very survival? What kind of world will that be for my children? Do they truly have a future here on Eos?

42

James

It turns out the ship flying over right now is the *Jericho*. It's fitting—our final hope is the ship that we arrived on.

It wasn't built for atmospheric entry—or landing. I expect much of the ship will burn up in the atmosphere, and the crash will pulverize most of what's left. But it's a large ship, and I'm hoping between the wreckage and what's left in Carthage City, we'll be able to cobble together a shelter, at least for a while.

The ship seems to cut the sky open as it burns through the atmosphere. We're bringing it down a mile from Carthage City—near the edge of the eastern jungle. In fact, we're going to use some of the trees to slow it just before it makes landfall.

Arthur has returned with Corporal Young, who's unconscious, but alive.

"This is so going to void the warranty," Arthur mutters.

Grigory glares at him.

"You think we should have left it up there?" I ask.

"No. This was the only choice." Arthur smiles. "We planned on it."

"Who planned on it?" Min asks.

"The grid."

I step closer to Arthur, suddenly alarmed. "What do you mean?"

"We made a few upgrades to the *Jericho*—on the outside, where you wouldn't notice."

"What kind of upgrades?"

"The kind it needs to survive a crash landing. We strengthened it. Added a few thrusters to slow its descent."

"Thrusters?" Min says.

Arthur motions to the comm panels. "You can't control them, but they'll fire when they need to. They have proximity sensors. They'll slow the ship. Still, it will hit hard." Arthur's head jerks toward the tree line. "Incoming."

Around me, the soldiers grab their rifles.

"It's an ATV," Arthur clarifies. "From the cave, I assume."

The ATV breaks the tree line at that moment, barreling toward us. The soldier driving it is wearing an IR suit that's ripped and dirty. He probably recovered it from one of the dead members of Emma's team, like I did. He stops at the edge of the city, dismounts, and takes off his mask, staring wide-eyed at the carnage, seemingly in shock.

When he bends down to study one of the scorpions lumbering along nearby, I call to him. "Stay clear, Private. Their sting paralyzes."

He nods and walks briskly toward us. "It's good to see you, sir. We weren't sure you made it."

"What's the situation at the cave?" I ask.

"Pretty bad, sir. Three hundred or so dead. Almost everyone is sick."

"Is Dr. Tanaka there?"

"Yes, sir. She's been running tests, but I don't think she's made much progress."

"Understood. We need to get back to the cave. I have something she needs."

He shakes his head. "Dr. Matthews has ordered us to evac the cave."

I stand there, stunned, staring at the man's face, willing myself to process what I've just heard, wondering if I imagined it, unable to speak.

"Evac to where?" Min asks.

"She's alive?" I finally spit out. "Dr. Matthews?"

The private looks from Min to me, debating whom to answer first.

"Yes... she's alive. She's sick, but she was alive when I left. She was in the first convoy out."

Amazing. She's alive. *Alive.*

There's a chance.

"Where are they evacuating to?" Min asks impatiently.

"Carthage City."

I step closer to the private, grabbing his shoulders, speaking urgently. "Call them on the radio, and tell them to turn back."

He looks at me, confused.

"A ship is about to land right in their path."

His eyes go wide. Quickly, he draws a radio from his pack and starts calling the convoy. I don't hear the conversation because I'm barreling toward his ATV, Arthur close on my heels.

Emma

The storm grows louder with each second. The thunder is like none I've ever heard—a droning with no breaks.

I open my eyes, trying to catch a glimpse of the storm. We have to get to shelter. The drivers must sense it too. They're going faster now, near top speed, bouncing everyone around. We must be near the edge of the eastern jungle. The snow is shallow here, the leaves on the trees dripping from the melting ice.

Through the broken tree canopy, I spot a ball of fire in the sky, burning like a fire poker barreling toward us.

And I realize: it's not a storm we're hearing. It's an asteroid. Or... the ship. The *Jericho* is going to make landfall.

"Stop!" I yell.

The fever and fatigue fall away as adrenaline rushes into my bloodstream.

Our ATV slows. I hear the driver talking hurriedly on the radio, then he guns the ATV, turning sharply, kicking up dark black ground. The entire convoy is turning back.

Engines roar. The people in the beds of the ATVs and trailers scream in fear and yell for answers, but the drivers ignore their calls.

Overhead, the burning grows brighter. The sound louder.

Still clutching Carson, I sit up and yell to the driver again, "Stop!"

Beside me, Allie and Sam are awake, clutching the rails of the bed to hang on.

The driver glances back at me, but doesn't slow.

"We have to take cover!"

He glances back again.

"That's an order!"

Finally, the ATV comes to a halt. The others are dispersed through the woods around us, their tracks tearing up the ground as they continue to speed away.

I scramble off the ATV bed, still holding Carson to my chest. He's wailing, his cries overpowered by the roaring overhead. The ship—or whatever it is—will hit in seconds.

My heart races as I scan the forest, looking, hoping... and finally seeing what we need: cover. I rush toward the massive downed tree, its canopy pointing in the direction the impact will occur. Its massive root structure sticks up in the air like a fan, leaving a deep depression in the earth where the roots used to be. A natural bunker of sorts.

"Come on!" I call to the dozen people on the trailer.

Allie and Sam follow as I descend into the crevice. The roots drip with soggy black dirt. The ground teems with worms and insects. I ignore it all as I dig myself into the deepest part of the hole, leaning against the fallen tree's root ball. The others pile in around me, staying low, bracing.

44

James

At the ATV's top speed, I can barely hang on. It bounces through the jungle, trampling branches and flying over fallen trunks dug into the dirt like speed bumps in a parking lot.

Suddenly, a hand grips my back and pulls me off with superhuman strength, shoving me to the ground and covering my body. Arthur.

I hear the impact a few seconds later: a boom and the scream of twisting metal, as if a machine were being tortured, crying out for help.

Heat flows over me.

Splinters and limbs fly through the forest like a million wooden arrows. One hits Arthur's back, but he doesn't flinch.

A cloud floats into the forest, a mist broken only by falling debris.

When it's quiet, Arthur releases me and stands, pulling the wooden shard from his side.

On my feet, I scan the forest. I can hear voices, crying, people calling out.

"What do you see?" I ask Arthur.

"Sixty alive. Twelve dead, mostly from the shrapnel."

As loud as I can, I call into the misty forest. "Emma!"

No response.

My ATV stayed upright. That's the good news. I mount it and drive toward the crash site, but it's no use. The forest has been shredded. The fallen limbs and trees are too thick.

On foot, I hike toward the ship, calling out.

In the sea of voices, I hear Emma. "James!"

I bound through the fallen limbs, climbing and clawing, and when I hit a wall of debris, crawling under.

I'm covered in mud by the time I spot her. She's clutching Carson, calling my name, Allie and Sam close by, huddled in a depression made by a fallen tree.

Emma holds a hand straight out. "No, James. Stay back."

I take her hand and pull her into a hug, our baby between us. I kiss her cheek as she tries to push away. "I'm sick. Don't—"

"I know. I'm going to take care of it."

She shakes her head. "It's too late."

"It's not. I promise you."

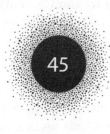

45

Emma

Arthur says the grid practically rebuilt the *Jericho* during our journey from Earth to Eos. I believe it. The ship we built in Earth orbit couldn't have sustained the impact this ship took.

The bottom of the ship is dug deep into the ground, and the compartments there are crushed, but through the middle of the ship and at the top, the sections are usable.

Most importantly, the main hold where the stasis sleeves were stored is completely intact.

We've brought mattresses from Carthage City and lined the hold with them, creating what looks like a hospital wing with only sheets dividing the cubicles. It reminds me of the CENTCOM bunker, except here, thousands of patients are coughing, crying, and lying motionless, mumbling, sweat pouring off their feverish bodies. Everyone from the cave is here now, waiting for a cure... or whatever comes next.

Teams have been retrieving the stasis sleeves from the wreckage of both Jericho City and Carthage City. Many of the sleeves are damaged, but between the two settlements, we should have more than enough.

The survivors from Jericho City have moved to Carthage City where there's more shelter—and to be closer to the ship. We're still being careful to separate them from the teams retrieving the stasis sleeves. Our hope is that they will remain free of the regolith disease.

In the med bay, Izumi works non-stop, poring over the research James provided—research he refuses to tell me anything about, such as where it came from. There are only two places it could have come from: the grid or the Carthage colonists. I wonder what that means for us?

As expected, the fresh air has done us good. It's easier to breathe here. And I think just being able to see the light has lifted everyone's spirits. Back in that cave, with the regolith sponges—that's what James is calling them—it felt like the darkest days of the Long Winter, when the sun faded and we huddled in our habitats in Camp Seven. It felt like the Citadel bunker, where we waited, buried, starving to death. It felt like the end of the Solar War, when the sun set forever on Earth.

Out here, though, there is a difference. We still may not have a chance of finding a cure to this disease, but at least we'll die on our feet, above ground, with the sun on our faces.

On the bridge of the *Jericho*, our team assembles in the cramped space for what might be our last meeting. I remember when I first walked onto this bridge and peered down at Eos. I was filled with joy and hope then. Here on the ground, I struggle to hang on to any shred of that feeling.

On the viewscreen, Grigory and Min are staring at us, Carthage City in the background. Brightwell stands behind me, in the corner of the bridge, face gaunt, eyes sunken. Izumi sits at the bridge's navigation station, looking as if she's aged twenty years. Arthur watches us placidly, like a researcher staring at an experiment in a monkey cage.

"Let's start with the obvious," James says. "We need to begin putting people in stasis. We're losing… how many per hour, Izumi?"

"A hundred. Roughly. That number is accelerating." She pauses. "However, we don't know how the sickness will react to stasis. If it will even work."

"I don't see another way," I whisper, thinking about placing Allie, Sam, and Carson in those stasis sleeves.

"You're probably right," Izumi says. "But there's another problem. We don't have enough people left on their feet to care for the sick. Getting the thousands of sick into stasis will require a massive effort. I would add that those still on their feet are dropping pretty quick."

Around the room, all eyes turn to me. As mayor of our colony, it's technically my call.

I nod to Brightwell. "Proceed with stasis, Colonel, as quickly as possible. Load the sickest and youngest citizens first."

"We can help," Min says.

Izumi grimaces. "No. You all need to stay at Carthage City. You have to remain uninfected—"

"We don't know that the plague is communicable," Min replies, leaning in, growing larger on the screen. "For all we know, direct exposure to the sponges is the only way to contract the disease."

Izumi holds a hand up. "Bottom line: we don't know. Which means there's a risk you all could get sick if you come here, and that's a risk we can't take. We need to start thinking about the survival of the human race."

The words hang in the air like a gavel being struck.

Finally, Brightwell clears her throat and addresses me. "Ma'am, with due respect, the survival of the species is outside my purview. I wouldn't mind getting started on the stasis efforts."

"Of course. Thank you, Colonel."

When Brightwell has left the bridge, Min says, "What exactly are we talking about?"

"Rebuilding the colony with those uninfected at Carthage City," Izumi says.

Min grimaces. "You can't be serious. There are forty men here and only two women. You're just trying to keep me from getting infected, Izumi."

"Yes," she replies, voice rising, "I am. Because I've been studying this thing day and night and I don't think I'm going to find a cure. Not in the time we have left. And there are only two ways forward. Either we find a cure, or those at Carthage City start over."

"No," Min says. "Even if we could, every one of us has loved ones in that ship. I can't speak for the rest, but if this is the end, I'm going to be there with you, and I'm going with you. There's nothing for me here without you."

Izumi hangs her head. Through her black hair, I see a tear roll down her face.

A long silence drags on. James finally breaks it. "What about cloning?"

The question is like a Jump Ball thrown in the middle of our team, with no one reaching for it.

"Izumi?" he says, leaning over to try to make eye contact. But she doesn't respond.

"What are you thinking?" I ask, hoping more information will spur the discussion.

"For the people left in Carthage City, we could clone their loved ones. The survivors would raise the clones and maybe we could get back to a viable population. I'm assuming we'd need the 3D printers to create the machines we need for cloning."

"We could probably have one operational in a month," Grigory says.

"That's the problem," Izumi mumbles. "Time. If I had a year, I could probably get a cloning program running. We have days. It won't work."

James turns to Arthur. "We could use some help."

He raises his eyebrows, feigning surprise. "Understatement of the epoch."

"I'm serious."

"We already helped you," Arthur says, using his only arm to make a swirling motion all around. "Take a look at this ship. Without our modifications, it would be in a million pieces."

"We wouldn't be in this spot if it weren't for you," James says. "You knew about the storms. And I'm betting you knew what happened to the Carthage colonists—yet you said nothing. You could have saved us."

Arthur rolls his eyes. "That's it, blame the one-armed man. He did it. He did it all—"

"You wanted this to happen. Planned for it, didn't you? That's why you modified the ship—you knew we'd have to land it."

"We're the grid, James."

"Don't give me that 'We're the grid' nonsense. You have a cure for the regolith plague, don't you? In fact, I bet you created it."

"We didn't. And we don't."

"Liar."

"There is no cure for the regolith plague."

"How do you know?"

"Let's just say people as smart as you have been looking for it for a very long time."

"What does that mean?"

"When you figure that out, you'll see the solution to your predicament. Not a cure, but a solution."

James slams a fist down on the workstation. "Get out! Right now."

With a shrug, Arthur marches out of the bridge.

"We are going to find a cure," James says quietly.

Izumi rises. "I need to get back to work."

Her first step is shaky. She teeters, and I catch her arm before she collapses. The weight on my bad leg sends a sharp pain through me. It ebbs when James scoops Izumi up in his arms.

"I'm okay," she whispers. "Put me down. It's just my blood sugar."

"You're going to rest," James says as he carries her toward the small bunkroom off the bridge.

On the screen, Min and Grigory stand. "We're coming."

"You heard Izumi," I call to them as they're walking away from the camera.

Min turns. "You need us, Emma. We're not staying here and waiting while you all die."

46

James

I lead Arthur away from the ship, out into the forest where thick clouds still drift through. I don't want anyone else to hear this conversation. I sense that if I do get the information I need, it will be disturbing.

"Answers."

Arthur shrugs. "You're going to have to be more specific than that."

"What's the solution to the regolith plague?"

"You've got all the pieces, James. And a mind you yourself don't even fully appreciate. Think about it."

I turn and pace into the woods, considering what I know.

I know the grid wanted us on Eos. It's the only reason they allowed us to leave Earth safely. It's the reason they saved the ship countless times on the way to Eos. If they had that power, they could have made *Jericho* arrive at the same time as *Carthage*. But they didn't. *Carthage* arrived first. They wanted that. They knew about the storms. They must have wanted the *Carthage* colonists to get sick. For me to chase the mystery. They reinforced *Jericho*, ensuring enough of it would survive re-entry and landing.

"All of this—Eos, the *Jericho* landing, the regolith plague—the grid planned it. You wanted this to happen."

"Want isn't the word."

"You need it to happen. Everything has led to this, hasn't it?"

"What can I say, James? The universe is an equation with sadly far fewer variables than you imagine."

"You're going to have to be more specific than that."

Arthur simply smiles at my repetition of his line.

"What could the grid possibly want with us?" I ask. "Why do you need us?"

"That's the question, isn't it?"

"On the *Jericho*, you said the grid once believed that matter and energy were the economy of the universe. That's why the grid was desperate to capture the output of every star. But you were wrong. You've recently discovered... what did you call it... a greater economy at work in the universe, two forces infinitely more powerful, arrayed against each other. You said we're but dust motes floating above the battle."

"And that is the answer to the question."

"What are they—the two forces?"

"Can't tell you."

"Why not?"

"It's not how this works, James. You'll see. Soon."

"Can I save them? Emma? My children?"

"The question isn't whether you can save them. It's whether you're willing to pay the price."

A snapping branch draws my attention. I hope no one has heard us. I hope even more that it's not an E. rex.

A cloud of fog floats by, revealing a single figure standing in the forest.

Emma.

Her face is a mask of confusion. She stares at Arthur and me a long moment, then says, "It's time."

47

Emma

In the med bay, Sam eyes the stasis sleeve.

James squats down to his eye level. "It's just for a little bit. It'll be like a nap. Over in a blink."

Sam nods, face pained. He senses something is very wrong here. He's fared better than some of the other children. He could have waited longer to go into stasis. But the decision was made to keep families together, mainly in hopes that seeing their older siblings enter stasis first might help calm the nerves of the younger children.

My sister-in-law, Abby, is holding Carson. I'm carrying Allie in my arms. Her weight is almost too much for me, but I cling to her anyway, knowing this might be the last time I ever hold my only daughter. She's burning up, in and out of consciousness.

I kiss her cheek, my lips absorbing a salty tear.

She opens her eyes in time to see Sam slip into the sleeve. It contracts, vacuuming tight to his body.

"No, Mommy," Allie whines.

"It's okay, sweetie."

Her fingers dig into me as I hand her to James and his brother Alex.

"It's okay," I whisper in her ear as she jerks, clinging to me. "I'm right here. I'm right here."

Izumi touches a dispenser to her neck, and Allie's eyes close as her body falls limp.

Thank you, I mouth to her, and she nods.

Izumi is fading fast. I think it's more than the regolith plague that's affecting her. It's the pressure and fatigue—knowing she's our only chance and that time is slipping away.

James holds Carson, kisses his forehead, then hands him to me. I press my lips to his burning flesh and gently place him in the sleeve. I know I need to keep it together, but I can't. I break, a sob escaping as the bag seals around him. Tears run down my face. James wraps an arm around me and pulls me into a hug.

Behind me, my brother-in-law, David, says, "Come on, Owen. You're up."

He bends and hugs my nephew, who's also putting on a brave face. What I feel most right now is the absence of my sister, like a limb that's been chopped off, and I just now realized it when I tried to stand on it—and fell. Emotionally, I'm on the floor and I feel like I can't get up.

I want to hug Owen and his sister Adeline and tell them that their mother is looking down on them and she's proud of them and she loves them very much. I try, but the words won't come. My throat seems to close up. I just hug them until David pulls them from my arms and puts them in the stasis sleeves.

Alex and Abby's daughter, Sarah, is next. If Jack were

alive, he would be with them, waiting to go into stasis. I feel his absence hanging over us, a reminder of just how deadly this disease is—and what it has already cost us.

James grips his brother's shoulder as he places his daughter into stasis.

We exit as fast as we can. Time is our most precious commodity now. Every moment we linger in the med bay is another second someone has to survive until they're put in stasis. Many of my fellow colonists have only seconds left. Time is running out for all us.

Grigory, Min, and the others from Carthage City are here now, mostly helping to carry and stack the stasis sleeves—and remove the dead from the makeshift hospital. Abby, Alex, David, James, and I set about working in the hospital, distributing fluids and anti-inflammatories and helping people to the bathroom. This ship has one toilet, and it was made for space, not terrestrial habitation, so we've had to set up outhouses, which have the advantage of letting people get fresh air. Like everything else in our lives at the moment, we're improvising, making the best of it.

For the next few hours, I try to visit as many colonists as I can. I place my hands on theirs and tell them we're doing everything we can.

At the end of the aisle, James is holding a water bottle up to an older woman's lips. He smiles at me, a weary, warm smile that lights me up inside. And then he turns his head and coughs. His forehead is covered in beads of sweat.

When he moves toward the next bed, I walk down the aisle and catch his arm. "You're sick."

"No, I'm not. It's just stuffy in here."

He tries to pull away, but I hold him tight. "James."

"Come on. We've got work to do."

For the next hour, we resume helping the sick. Finally, I ask him, "Are you sure this is what you should be working on?"

"As in?"

"As in, to quote Arthur, 'There is no cure. But there is a solution.' What were you two talking about in the forest?"

"To be honest, I haven't quite figured out what we were talking about. Yet." He moves on to the next bed, and when we're back out in the aisle, he continues. "This helps me clear my mind. It's given me some perspective on our problem."

"What are you thinking?"

"I'm thinking all of this—the storms, the regolith plague, the downed ship—it's all related."

"Related how?"

"Somehow it all leads back to the Eye of the Grid. The diagram we found at Carthage City is actually a map of Eos. At the end of the arcs I found hollow spheres, buried in the snow."

I stop in the aisle and face him. "That's what you've been looking for on the dark side."

"Yes."

"What was inside?"

"The spheres? Nothing. One curious thing, though: as the arc moves up the eye, the spheres get smaller."

"What does that mean? Maybe they were inside each other?"

James breaks eye contact, that mind of his turning the possibility over like a child encountering a new toy. I can almost see the wheels turning. We walk in silence, James thinking. A few minutes later, his eyes go wide. "Huh."

"Huh, what?"

"Nothing."

"Were the spheres inside of each other?"

"Not exactly. But in a way, yes. And it's the key."

48

James

When I figured it out, I practically ran out of the ship, kept running down its length until I was out of earshot of anyone, and then I threw up and threw up some more until my stomach was empty and I was gasping for air.

Now I'm leaning against the hull, feeling the cold metal on my boiling skin. The fever's been getting worse by the hour. I'm infected. I'm almost sure of it.

But I might have figured it all out in time to help us.

I can see Arthur under a tree, Grigory sitting nearby with a rifle. Grigory has insisted on standing guard around Arthur. He doesn't trust him. I can't say I blame him. The grid killed the woman he loved.

"Feeling all right, James?" Arthur calls to me with mock concern.

I ignore him. "Grigory, I need to speak to Arthur."

"Speak," Grigory says, not taking his eyes off his prisoner.

"Alone."

"Bad idea."

"Grigory, please. He's not going to hurt me." Eyeing

Arthur, I add, "He needs me. And they need you in the ship. They're loading the adults."

Grigory mutters in Russian, no doubt unpleasant words, but he treks back to the ship.

"Want me to translate?" Arthur asks mildly.

I motion to the woods. "Go."

"Feeling the heat?" Arthur asks as we move deeper into the damp, quiet forest.

"The regolith plague is airborne, isn't it? Communicable from person-to-person."

"Very."

"I'm guessing we're all infected at this point?"

"You're guessing correctly."

"Here's another guess: the grid made the spheres."

Arthur is silent. His face is a mask.

"You didn't want me to find them, because they're the key, aren't they? If I found them too soon and put it together, it might throw off your plan. Is that one of those very few variables in this great cosmic equation?"

"Yes. Very good."

"And I've figured out that equation, by the way: the two forces greater than matter and energy. It's simple really. If matter is accelerated to the speed of light, it becomes energy. The grid assumed once it gathered all the energy and converted all the mass, it would control all the energy in the universe. You thought you'd control the cycle. If we assume there was nothing in the beginning, and that there was a big bang and a release of energy and matter at that beginning, it's logical to assume that whoever or whatever controls all the energy can restart the cycle—and control the universe. But it's not that simple, is it?"

"Nothing ever is."

"As you said, there's something operating on a level completely above it."

"There always is."

"Two fundamental forces. In a battle that stretches from the beginning of the universe to the end. Forces greater than matter and energy. Took me a while, but it was obvious once I figured out the spheres. Those two forces are space and time."

"Yes."

"The grid was in the spheres, wasn't it? Larger and larger versions of the grid in each sphere. Older versions."

"Correct again."

"Why are they here, on this planet?"

"I can't tell you that."

"Because it might harm you. That's why you didn't want me looking for them. Somehow you're in danger too."

"Not in as much danger as you, James. You're getting sicker every minute we waste talking about this. So are your people. Put them in stasis and I'll give you answers. Real answers, the kind that just might save your species."

"You'll tell me now, or I'll take you apart."

"You could, but you still wouldn't find what you're looking for. The data you want—the truth of what's happening here—is stored on a data device somewhere close by. With a trusted source. The spheres are the key to everything, James. The story of why and how they came to be here will reveal the fate of your species. I'll give you the information you need, but only once they're all in stasis. Everyone. It's their only chance."

Emma

All but twelve colonists are in stasis now. We've stopped the clock on their disease progression, but we have other problems.

The *Jericho* was fully charged in orbit. Now its solar cells are cracked and damaged, and its power reserves are being drained. Without power, we can't sustain the stasis system. Everyone dies. In a way, we're in the same place we were in that warehouse in Camp Nine: without power, our species ends.

It seems, for us, it all comes back to power.

We've made a decision—the only one we could make. Everyone but James and Grigory will go into stasis. They'll reassemble a 3D printer and repair the solar cells. They're both sick—like everyone now—but neither James nor Grigory were in the cave. They seem to be faring better. And if they become unable to work, they'll get the next shift out of stasis and give them their orders. A desperate relay race for survival.

Izumi has nearly worked herself to death. Min has argued

with her constantly. Finally, mercifully, she's given up. For now. The plan is to bring her out of stasis after the power situation is solved and allow her to continue looking for a cure. That seems to be our only hope.

One thing, however, strikes me as strange: James. I expected him to be working like a madman, frantically trying to discover whatever solution Arthur alluded to. Instead I find him outside, looking up at the red dwarf star in the sky.

"I'm going with Grigory and Min to collect more solar cells from Jericho City. Want to join us?"

He shakes his head. "I have a better idea. Gin rummy."

He takes my hand and leads me toward the ship, onto the bridge, and to the small table where we played cards when *Jericho* was en route to Eos.

"Are you sure you're feeling okay?"

He smiles. "Other than some mysterious alien fungal disease, yeah, I'm fine. Come on, I'll deal."

His mood is somber, but he's more talkative than usual, reminiscing about the past, our brushes with death, and those we've lost. It's as if he thinks these are our last moments together.

"James."

He peeks over his cards.

"Can I ask you something?"

"Anything."

"Have you given up?"

"You know me better than that."

"Have you figured it out? What Arthur was saying... the solution to all of this?"

"I'm close."

"You don't seem concerned."

"I'm not. You shouldn't be. Let's enjoy this moment as if it was our last."

"Is it?"

"Not if I can help it."

When the teams are finished gathering the pieces of the solar cells, Brightwell directs her troops and the remaining civilians to enter stasis. When they're gone, only our leadership team is left awake: James, Grigory, Izumi, Min, Brightwell, and myself.

We've decided to have a final meal together... since we'll be on different shifts from here out. At least, until the crisis is over.

Brightwell is the only invitee who declined. "I'm going downhill fast," she said, as if reading the weather. "I may need the time I have left on the other side of stasis."

In the med bay, she marches directly toward the stasis sleeve, but James stops her and shakes her hand. "You kept us safe, Colonel."

"You didn't do so bad yourself, sir."

"I should've listened to you at Warehouse 412."

"That was a world ago, sir."

Alex and Abby enter stasis next. James shares a long hug with his brother, whispering in his ear, "I'm sorry about Jack."

Tears form in their eyes. I reach over and put my arms around Abby and hug her tight. They go bravely into the stasis sleeves, staring up at us until the bags seal them away.

When they're gone, only James, Grigory, Min, Izumi,

and I are left outside of stasis. We gather on the bridge for dinner, as we did on the day we arrived here.

We pick through the MREs, everyone pulling out their favorites like death row inmates splurging on a final meal. That's what the mood feels like. Grigory is resigned, barely saying a word. Min hugs Izumi tight to him with one arm, eating with the other. James and I lean on each other and talk quietly, about the kids and things they loved and saying things like, "It's not that bad... Things were so much worse... after the battle with the Beta artifact... at Ceres... in the Citadel... at Warehouse 903." But in every one of those situations, we had a fighting chance. We didn't sit around and reminisce as the darkness closed in around us. This is different. We all sense it.

James raises his glass. "I'd like to propose a toast. To Lina, Charlotte, Harry, and Fowler." He pauses. "We couldn't have gotten here without them."

After the meal, the group breaks up. Grigory stalks off, deep in thought. Arthur is nowhere to be seen—likely because Grigory might kill him for any reason he can find.

Min and Izumi retreat to the bunkroom, holding each other.

James insists we play one more game of gin rummy.

"Are you sure?" I ask.

"We could play poker, but with two people—"

"James, you're almost scaring me. What's going on? What's going to happen?"

"I don't know exactly. What I do know, what I've come to believe—very recently—is that things happen for a reason."

"Okay. How does things happening for a reason help us right now?"

"What if I told you there was a greater force at work in the universe."

"Such as…"

"Such as something operating at a level we can't fully understand now. But we might soon."

"If you said that, I would be very worried."

He laughs—an untroubled, hearty laugh. "That's fair. But I'm coming around to the idea. Because in a way, the idea that there is something larger going on in this universe makes far more sense than there being nothing."

"Are you having some kind of breakdown? Is it the regolith plague?"

"No. Well, I don't think so."

"Do you know something you're not telling me?"

"Right now, there's only one question that matters—in the whole world."

He stares at me, a smile forming on his lips, his eyes caring and confident, like the first time I ever saw him. "Do you trust me?"

"Completely."

In the med bay, Izumi goes into stasis first. She's the sickest. Then Min. And finally, I'm lying on the table, inside the sleeve, peering up at James.

Grigory steps out of the room, giving us privacy.

"I'll see you in a few minutes," James says as he leans down to kiss me.

"You promise?"

"I promise."

50

James

When Emma's stasis sleeve seals, I check and recheck the system status, ensuring it's functioning properly. Next I ransack the med bay, looking for the item I require. For a moment or two, I was afraid they'd all been used.

Thankfully, Grigory enters a few seconds after I find it.

"We have work," he says, turning on his heel and heading for the door.

I take two long steps, wrap an arm around his chest, and jab the injector into his neck. He spins, throwing me off, staring at me in horror.

"James, what…"

He staggers and falls, too fast for me to catch. I dive, but his head hits hard. His eyes are glassy. Panicking, I check his pulse. It's there. Steady.

I slide my arms under him and hoist him up onto the table and into the waiting stasis sleeve. I key the sequence as quickly as possible.

When I see the system check flash green, I breathe a sigh of relief.

The sound of Arthur's voice makes me jump. "That was a little dicey."

"I didn't have a choice. I couldn't exactly explain. Especially since I don't fully understand it myself."

"True. So where shall we start?"

"As I said, I want to see the beginning—what the Eye saw."

"Very well."

"Can you put it on the viewscreen?"

"We have something else in mind."

Footsteps echo in the corridor. Impossible. Everyone is in stasis. A small E. rex? Another predator?

I scan the med bay for anything I could use as a weapon. The energy weapon lies nearby. It's charged. I'm about to reach for it when Arthur says, "Relax, we're all friends here. Family, you could say."

Oscar appears in the doorway, his face a placid reflection of Arthur's arrogant expression.

"Hello, sir."

"Oscar."

"I told you the data was with a trusted source," Arthur says. "Trip okay, cuz?"

"Without issue," Oscar replies.

"You two have been in contact?" I ask.

"Of course," Arthur says. "Constantly. He was *really* worried about you, by the way."

"We would have seen a ship in orbit—"

"We're the grid."

I close my eyes and nod, wearily. "Yes, I know, *you're*

the grid and you can hide your ships and you probably lied about your transmission range and who knows what else."

"Pretty much covers it," Arthur says.

"Let's get on with it. I want to see everything the Eye of the Grid saw. From the very, *very* beginning."

"This isn't a home movie, James." Arthur eyes me with a smile. "Though I would love to see the look on your face when you realize what's really going on here."

"If it's not a movie, what is it?"

"Call it an experience."

"VR?"

"Sort of." Arthur nods to an empty stasis sleeve. "You go in and we'll show you."

"No way."

"Why not?" Arthur says, annoyed.

"Well, frankly, I was thinking it would be good to be conscious when I figure out what's going on—you know, just in case you're going to screw me over or kill all of my people, as you've shown a tendency to try to do since we first met you."

"Sir," Oscar says. "You have my word. I'll protect you—like you protected me when they were trying to find me."

For a moment I look back and forth between Oscar and Arthur. They're like two sides of a coin—Jekyll and Hyde. Can Oscar protect me? Arthur is a military prototype, stronger and faster than Oscar. But Oscar has two arms to Arthur's one, so I give him the edge.

Besides which, I have to wonder: What other choice do I have?

"Are you in or out?" Arthur says, acting bored.

"I'm in."

As the stasis sleeve closes around me and the gas enters my lungs, I wonder if I've made the right choice. If not, it will be the last choice I ever make.

51

James

I expect to see Eos when I open my eyes. My assumption is that things started here.

What I see instead is my childhood home near Asheville, North Carolina. I'm using a screwdriver to take the training wheels off of Alex's bike, then pushing him down the driveway, cheering him on, watching as he wobbles and loses control, the bike careening into the side of the red-brick columns at the beginning of the driveway. I bound forward, running so hard my lungs ache. I scoop him up in my arms and hold him tight as he screams.

The image dissolves, and I'm walking in the backyard, toward the woods behind the house, a paintball gun in my hand. At the edge of the grass, I hear a pop and my abdomen explodes in pain. I fall to my knees and almost retch. From the tree line, Alex emerges, holding his own paintball gun.

"You were supposed to hide in the woods!" I yell.

"I was in the woods."

The next memory is from college, at a party in Dave Cardeña's cramped apartment. A Lynyrd Skynyrd song is playing too loud to talk over—nearly too loud for me to think straight. I'm holding a red plastic cup full of beer—my fourth. That's not helping me think straight either. It is, however, aiding my courage, which I've just decided to deploy.

Her name is Olivia Lloyd. She's wearing jeans and a white button-up shirt, untucked. Her black hair, which is pulled into a ponytail, matches the black-rimmed glasses she wears. She breaks from the group of four girls she's been chatting with all night and weaves through the packed apartment, making her way to the line waiting for the bathroom. I can't take my eyes off of her. As she passes by me, she cocks her head, giving me a wry, devil-may-care smile that silently says, *What are you staring at?*

Now or never.

In my mind's eye, I see myself nonchalantly wading through the crowd and slipping into line behind her. In reality, it's a mad scramble, squeezing behind people, clutching my beer to my chest and holding it over my head to avoid spilling it, shouting, "Heads up" and "Can I get by?"

I arrive at the line, queuing up behind Olivia a second before another guy gets there.

She turns, eyes me, the smile returning.

"Hey," I yell over the chorus of "Tuesday's Gone."

"Hey."

"You're in Chandler's physics class, right?"

"Yeah."

"He's pretty weird."

"Yeah, he's a freak."

I take a sip of beer, mentally rehearsing the line I've practiced in my mind about six point eight million times.

"I was thinking—"

"What?" She leans closer, trying to hear.

"I said, I was thinking we could study together. Sometime."

"What?"

"Do you want to study sometime? For the midterm?"

She leans back, the smile growing as she shakes her head. "No."

"You…"

"Don't want to study with you."

My face flushes. I don't know if it's the beer or the embarrassment, but I feel like I could pee my pants. If I had magical powers and I could disappear, I would. I'd go anywhere. But as awkward as standing here is, I think taking off at this moment would be even weirder. I'm trapped.

Mercifully, it's a very short line. Olivia is next up. At least there's that. Light at the end of the tunnel.

The door to the bathroom opens, and a girl and a guy shuffle out, laughing, their faces as flushed as mine.

The song ends and the agony of silence sets in. I gaze at the ceiling, studying the cracked drywall, wondering if I will ever feel normal again. Or what passes for normal for me.

Olivia doesn't go to the bathroom. She peeks around me, at the other guy in line, who's chugging beer. "Go ahead."

"You sure?" he asks, already heading for the bathroom, unzipping his pants.

"I'm sure," she mutters, watching him go before turning to me. "Were you trying to ask me out?"

"What? No!" "Call Me the Breeze" is starting up, the lyrics drowning out my voice, which, unhelpfully, is getting fainter. "I mean, I was, I, we, could—to study for a test—"

"Because, for reference, I would have said yes to that."

My brain feels as sharp as the plastic cup I'm holding. It's like I'm staring at letters from a Scrabble game, trying to assemble words on the fly.

"You, to asking you out…"

She throws her head back and laughs. "Yes. Me, to asking me out—I'd say yes. Are you asking me out?"

I nod, half mesmerized, maybe a little drunk. "I'm definitely asking you out."

"I'm definitely saying yes."

"Cool."

The bathroom door opens and the guy stumbles forward. Olivia pauses in the doorway. "We can start going out right after I'm done."

"I'll be here."

She was, far and away, the most interesting person I ever met. And the smartest. She had a passion for life and a deep interest in so many disparate subjects: physics, nature, politics. You name it, she was fascinated by it. She was constantly researching some new subject and telling me about it.

The biggest impact she had on me was changing the way I looked at the world. She took nothing at face value. Nothing she heard. Nothing said on the news. Nothing written in the paper. If a topic interested her, she would do a deep-dive into it—books, articles, research—she would even call up experts in the field and pepper them with questions, insisting she was a college student doing research and needed their input. I just stared or shook my head. I think during those years in college she really didn't know what she wanted to be or what interested her. Mentally, she was trying things on.

But it wasn't a casual pursuit for her. She believed that if you were going to have an opinion about an important topic, you'd better know it top to bottom before you opened your mouth. And when she did, she was sure of what she was saying.

She had a mind like a steel trap. She could cite the facts to back up what she said, line and verse. In the classes we shared, I watched her demolish professors like a dump truck rolling over a kid's play toy. In the vortex that was a debate with her, she could literally shape your reality— offer facts that changed your entire perspective on a problem and the world around it. It was incredible. And, in a way, intoxicating. She was a walking, talking reality distortion field.

She was becoming an activist even then. Under pseudonyms, she penned op-ed pieces that were widely read, shared, and contested. She reveled in it. At her core, she had a simple belief: If you're right about something, that gives you the authority to act on it, to stand and not back down. The consequences don't matter—the world will catch up eventually.

In a way, I internalized that belief. And it led to my own problems later.

To say I fell in love with her would be an understatement. I was like a boy walking along on a lazy afternoon, whistling on my way to go fishing—and falling down an abandoned well. It happened that fast. In the blink of an eye, I was in so deep there was no way out.

That Christmas, I took her home to meet my parents. They loved her. Alex, who was still in high school, adored her.

Her parents were divorced. She had a troubled relationship with her father, who was a civil rights lawyer. Her relationship with her mother wasn't much better. The two of them were more like old friends who had once been close but now just kept in touch out of habit. When I asked her about it, she said it was because her mother was obsessed with her research at the NIH, but the truth was Olivia wasn't making much effort either.

As I soon learned, she had problems of her own. Being with her was like a roller coaster—she was either up or down, and she switched violently, unexpectedly. In those days and weeks, I hung on for dear life.

During her bouts of depression, she was nearly despondent. Nothing interested her. Nothing mattered. And then out of nowhere the fog would lift and she would come back to life as if it had never happened. I begged her to go to Student Health, but she wouldn't hear of it. "I might as well get a lobotomy" was her response.

By my junior year of college, I had a vague idea of what I wanted to do with my life: be with her and practice medicine. I had gotten into medical school and had been pressing her about her plans. I knew we were too young to get married—she would never go for it—but I desperately wanted to stay with her.

"I know what I'm going to do," she announced one night at her apartment.

"For—"

"With my life."

"Oh. That."

"The Next World Foundation."

"I'm not familiar."

"You wouldn't be. It's new. I formed the legal entity today."

"Practicing law now too?"

"Not quite. I used an online legal service to file the articles of incorporation with the California Secretary of State. Pretty easy, actually. I'm now the founder and sole director of a newly formed non-profit organization."

"Wow. Should I call you CEO or Madam Director now? Or—"

She waves a hand. "Don't be so grandiose. Architect and Master of Human Destiny will suffice."

"Doesn't exactly roll off the tongue."

"You get used to it."

"What exactly will the Next World Foundation do?"

"Unite the world."

"Is that all?"

"I'm serious."

"Of that I have no doubt. Details, please."

"It's simple. Right now, human civilization is building a world where the vast, vast majority of people have no place. We have the first world, composed of developed, mostly consumer-driven economies with advanced technologies and stagnating population growth. And we have the third world, where the population is exploding and people still live the way they did ten thousand years ago—for the most part. All of these people are living on the same planet—a planet with only so much land, so much water, and so much food. In short, there is a limit to how many people Earth can support. Without intervention, at some point, the population of the third world will require all the planet's resources. However, the first world has the ability to protect those resources, which it also needs. This does not end well."

Like so many times before, she's framed the debate in a way I never thought of.

"That's a complicated problem."

"One with a simple solution: integration."

"How?"

"Besides natural resources, there's only one thing the third world has that the first world needs: consumers."

"But those consumers have a fraction of the buying power and economic value of first-world consumers."

"That's true today, but it's going to change. Right now, somewhere in the third world, a genius is being born. And by the time I finish this sentence, another has been born. They are their people's best hope of a better future. The problem is, we don't know who they are. If we did, think about what we could do. What if a group of multinational corporations—knowing that growth in the third world is critical to their long-term success—donated to Next World. We're not talking about a lot, a few million a year, a drop in the bucket in their charity budgets. But if you had a hundred companies doing it…"

"It adds up."

"Yes. With that money, we could partner with education departments around the world to identify gifted individuals and educate them in our best schools. Most of these kids will go on to bigger and better things—but some will go back home. Those kids are their homelands' greatest hope of joining the first world."

"And what do these companies get? You know that's their first question."

"Besides the positive press? They get to play a role in the lives of the future leaders of the third world. Every Next World scholar will receive a free education. In return, they commit to a two-year internship with one of the Next World donors—any of the hundred companies. They choose. As I said, I believe most will do their two years and then go off and do whatever they want. Some, however, will stay with the company. The companies will likely send these bright young people back to their homelands to open new offices and expand their existing presence there. They will be the best of both worlds, the key to the company's growth initiatives and to their country's ability to catch up to the first world. In a generation, the world can change."

"It's brilliant. Simple. Achievable. Huge potential."

She beams at me. "I think so too."

"Where do we even start?" My mind is racing. "Maybe get some of the professors to join the board as advisors. They could make the introductions to some corporations that might donate."

"I've already sent a few emails."

"What else… I guess we'll need some sort of aptitude test."

"Therein lies the key to the whole program. There have been initiatives similar to Next World in the past. They succeed on a small scale, but their shortcoming begins with scholar selection. Their criteria are too one-dimensional. Raw intelligence and problem-solving—the ability to excel at standardized tests—isn't always the best predictor of future success. Think about the people you grew up with. Sure, those at the top generally went on to excel in life, but—at least at my high school—there were tons of people outside the top five percent who were a whole lot better at life and the real world than school. They had things traditional tests don't measure: common sense, drive, and, in a word, heart. We need to find those kids."

"You're right. We'll need a whole new kind of test. We'll need a learning expert. Maybe a psychologist. Career experts. The test will need to be translated. What else? We'll have to identify the schools they'll attend. The scholarship recipients will have to learn English, I assume."

"James."

When I look up, Olivia's smile is gone.

"This is going to be my life's work."

"Okay. I'm going to help you."

"No, you're not."

"You're going to need a lot of help."

"I will. But this isn't for you."

"What?"

"I can't do this and be with you."

I shake my head, confused. "I don't understand. I can help you."

"You can. But this is the path I'm choosing. I don't want you to just follow me."

"What if supporting you *is* my path?"

"That's exactly my point. If you join me in this, you're never going to figure out what *you* truly love. Your own path. You deserve that. I won't take it from you."

"Look, I'm not asking you to marry me." She winces at the word, and I can't help but smile. "I just want to volunteer at your non-profit."

"We can't *just* be co-workers."

"Why not?"

"You know why. We're right for each other. You balance out my... ups and downs. You're as solid as the Rock of Gibraltar."

"I fail to see how this is a bad thing."

"If I'm around you, I'll be with you, and I'll change my life for you, for what you want. I know it. You're the kind of guy girls go home to, the guy with the manicured lawn and three kids. I don't know if I want that. My home life growing up, it was... not great. I don't know what I want for myself. I just know I want to do this work. Maybe if we had met each other later in life."

In typical Olivia fashion, she has thought long and hard about it, her mind is made up, and the debate is a crushing defeat for the other side—my side, the side of staying together.

The conversation ends with one more surprise. She leans forward and kisses me, long and deep as if she hasn't seen me for a year.

"It's a lot of hurt now, James. But it would be a lot more hurt later."

I nod, still barely able to believe we're breaking up.

"One thing won't change," she says, lips almost touching mine. "I love you. I always will."

She reaches down, grasps her Stanford T-shirt, lifts it over her head, unsnaps her bra, and begins feverishly ripping my clothes off. We don't bother moving to the bedroom.

In some ways the pleasure dulls the pain of the sadness. It takes my mind off of it at least.

That was my first real taste of heartache. Despite the hurt, ours wasn't an abrupt break-up. It was gradual. We still had lunch and dinner together, talked like nothing had ever happened, made love three times per week. Then two. Then once, and then only occasionally, two people drifting out of each other's lives. And I did feel adrift. Thrown overboard, barely afloat watching the ship of my dreams sail past the horizon, never to return. My life turned then. I drew inward. I had always been a shy child—mostly because of the stutter. I got over my speech impediment, but I never changed.

I threw myself into school and returned to what was perhaps my first love: reading. It was an escape, a way to distract my mind while my heart healed.

The other thing I learned is that time only heals so much. I was different after that. Maybe it was the science fiction I was reading and the transhuman movement or all the evil in the world, but for whatever reason, I turned my focus to robotics. In some small way, I think it was because a human had hurt me so badly, so unexpectedly. A robot can't do anything it's not programmed to do, and I was the programmer, in total control. A robot couldn't hurt me the way she had. Investing myself in that seemed safer to me.

In my second year of medical school, I began working on Oscar. It took me ten years to complete him.

I dated, but never really connected with anyone. Subconsciously, I think I compared them to Olivia—and in truth, I had never gotten over her. That's what made what happened next so unbearable.

In the memory, I'm standing in line, dressed in a suit, shuffling forward every few seconds. Olivia's mom hugs me. Her father is dry-eyed, handshake firm as he grips my elbow and moves me along. All business, that one.

The picture of Olivia on the casket must be recent—she's standing in a jungle, her arm around someone who's been cut out of the scene. Her face is tanned and slightly lined, but she still has the same smile I saw that night at the keg party, a truly unique combination of devious and caring.

It was a quick death—a plane crash in Bangladesh. I can't help thinking about how my life would have been different if she and I had traveled that path together.

I always thought that a part of me was buried with her—my ability to love like that. I did lose it, for years, and it awakened again when I least expected it: during the Long Winter, when I met Emma. I felt that same spark the instant I saw her. She has Olivia's passion for life, maybe even a little more. They're alike in many ways, though Emma doesn't have the darkness Olivia fought.

But the thing that's truly different about the two of them is that when our life hit a fork in the road, Olivia ran away—whereas Emma grabbed my hand. And she has every time. There isn't even a second thought: when we face a challenge, Emma reaches out to me. Olivia pushed me away. She always would have. At heart, she was a lone wolf. Emma is a partner.

I can see that now. And I've realized what these memories represent: the most painful moments of my life. I know what's next. My most painful memory. I will it not to happen, but the memory starts.

My father's study is lined with bookcases, stained a light gray. I sit on the couch in the bay window, Alex beside me, staring at the floor. My father's words come in clips and phrases: "not operable ... nothing else to it ... not going to do that ... a dignified death ..."

I'm as stunned as when Olivia ended our relationship.

Outside, Alex walks me to my car. "Tell me you're going to do something."

"Like what?"

"Get him in a trial for some new medicine."

"You heard him. He won't do it."

"He would if Mom were still alive."

"Probably so."

"You've got to do something. Please."

And I did do something. A mistake, a miscalculation that changed my life forever.

Oscar, four of my brightest lab assistants, and I worked day and night, racing the clock, knowing my chance was slipping away.

The next memory is in the hospital, standing with Alex and Abby in a room where Dad lies in bed asleep, a machine charting his vitals. Oscar is outside in the hallway, watching.

"Well?" Alex asks.

"I can save him," I reply.

"How?"

"Do you trust me?"

Alex nods. "Of course."

In the next memory, I'm back in the lab, ushering Alex and Abby in. "This is a new beginning."

Hearing the words again makes me wince, knowing what

comes next. "Today, we make history. We'll never have to say goodbye to Dad. Ever."

I tap a button on my tablet. Behind me, the prototype sits up. I didn't have time to make it look the way I wanted. But it functions.

"What is this?" Alex asks.

Abby bunches her eyebrows. Concerned.

I turn my back to them and face the prototype. "How do you feel?"

"Fine. James, how did I get out of the hospital?"

"We'll discuss that soon enough, Dad. Right now, I need to run a diagnostic."

A crash sounds behind me.

I spin and find Alex lying on the floor. He's stumbled backwards over some of my lab equipment. Abby is shaking her head, looking terrified.

"What have you done?" Alex screams.

I hold up my hands. "I know it seems crazy, but this is going to be commonplace very soon. People with terminal illnesses don't have to die anymore."

"You put Dad in that thing?"

"It's a body—"

"It's an abomination!"

Alex practically runs from the lab, Abby close behind him.

Memories of the aftermath follow. FBI agents pour in to my lab, take me into custody, and deactivate my creation.

Oscar watches from a wide window in the conference room as they take me away.

They take my passport and tag me with an electronic locator, but they let me out on bail. There's only one thing on my mind: contacting Alex. He won't take my calls. Won't see me.

There's only one person left in my life, and I focus on protecting him. I hire a small law firm to set up a company that I use to buy a rundown ranch north of San Francisco, just outside Petaluma. The small house on the property is far from the nearest road. Grass long ago reclaimed the dirt driveway. I instruct the firm to use my savings to pay any costs that may arise, which I expect will be minimal.

Oscar and I load the van and travel there at night. Inside the home, I open the door in the kitchen and lead him down the creaking staircase to the cellar.

"You have your charging adapter?"

"Yes, sir."

"The law firm will pay the utilities. The power should stay on. If it doesn't, go into total suspension."

"I understand, sir."

"Under no circumstances are you to broadcast anything or to leave this cellar, for any reason."

"Of course. What will happen, sir?"

"I don't know. There's never been a trial like this. If I'm exonerated, I'll come and get you. If not... I don't know what sort of sentence I'll receive. Could be months or even years. I'll come for you when I'm out. I promise. But for however long it is, I need you to wait."

"A minute, a month, a million years—I'll wait, sir. Time doesn't touch me."

"I envy you that, Oscar."

In the courtroom, I'm standing, watching the judge as he says the words, "Life without the possibility of parole." The phrase runs through me like a ghost that rips away my soul, leaving me numb.

Unlike Oscar, time does touch me. At Edgefield Federal Correctional Institution, each year is like a wave washing over me, peeling a layer away, a piece of me gone forever.

In the laundry room, I fold the sheets and watch the news, waiting for the Long Winter to begin. There are riots in Barcelona, Athens, and Rome, the populace rising up against the budget cuts brought on by austerity. There's talk of civil war.

The years flow by. Gray hairs sprout at my temples and wrinkles reach across my face, time carrying them.

In the next memory, I look in the mirror and see a lined face that's older than mine is now. I peer out the window at the grassy yard, at an Earth that was never decimated by the Long Winter.

I realize the truth then: these aren't my memories.

James

In the memories, time marches by in flashes. Before, I was reliving the memories as if watching them. Now I'm experiencing them—this life I didn't live, but could have. That someone just like me *did* experience.

At Edgefield, in my spare time, I search the internet for any news on Alex, Abby, Jack, or Sarah. I find only tidbits, and I drink them in like drops offered to a man stranded in the desert.

The lines on my face run deeper.

My hairline retreats.

The world disintegrates. Every major government except for those of the United States, the United Kingdom, Germany, and China defaults on their debt. The global economy plateaus and then starts a long slow decline with no solution—because the problem isn't the economy, it's the people. Robots do the manual labor. Cars drive themselves. Homes clean themselves. Roof tiles capture solar energy which powers the cars, the home, and the devices everyone is glued to. Life is comfortable, and as long as it doesn't get worse, no one tries to make it any better.

In a small town in Cameroon, two hundred people get sick. It's believed at first to be Ebola. They later name it Melong Fever after the town where it started. The story is in the news one day and forgotten the next. A week later, there are cases of Melong Fever in every nation in the world. Three billion are infected. Four hundred million die.

Then things really fall apart.

No one wants to leave their home. The threat of a second wave of outbreak is ever-present. Virtual reality becomes the largest industry in human history. The hardware market skyrockets and so does the content industry. It explodes when people are able to broadcast and create their own live dramas and sports.

Virtual reality is more transformational than any technology before it. It becomes a drug, a virus, one far more deadly than Melong Fever was.

In a way, I'm in the safest place in the world. No one here in prison contracted Melong Fever. None of us have ever been in a VR rig, never played the games or enjoyed a show or an interactive drama. But I see what it does to the guards. You can tell who's a heavy user—the bloodshot eyes, weight loss, irritability. Nothing in the real world entertains them. The work is an agony they bear until they can get home and slip back into VR.

It's like pictures I once saw of drug addicts, illustrating their physical deterioration from the first time they were arrested to the final arrest before they died. People wither away.

Around the world, productivity plummets. Unemployment soars. Before, the world I saw on TV just looked like a run-down version of the one I left. Now it rots—literally. No one wants to keep up the towns and homes where they live when they can escape to the world of their dreams with no effort.

The ban on VR began at midnight Eastern Standard Time on a Tuesday. They shut it down at the routers. It was global, agreed upon in secret by every nation.

Billions rose up in outrage. Riots ran through every town, city, and village on Earth. The governments tried to use the military and the police to maintain order, but ninety percent of them were addicted too. Millions died.

They turned it all back on six hours later.

It's been on since. I think it will be until the end.

And they thought what I created was dangerous.

A huge, hulking prisoner named Marcel leans into the laundry room. "Ay, Sinclair. You got a visitor."

For a long moment I stand there, holding the sheet, shocked. Alex. That's my first thought. He's forgiven me. I'm finally going to have a chance to say I'm sorry.

"Who is it?" I ask, hoping and fearing the answer.

"Man, I ain't your butler. Alvarez said tell you and I did."

It's a little monotonous in prison. Arguing over trivial matters is a sort of pastime—it breaks the routine.

"Thanks," I mumble as I race down the corridor.

Pedro Alvarez is manning the check-in booth, sitting behind thick glass.

"Doc," he says, picking up his tablet to check me in. "Finally got one, huh?"

I peer through the glass, scanning the room for Alex. "Better late than never."

"That's right."

"Keeping the kids off VR?" I ask.

"My wife is. They're more scared of her." He motions to the scan pad next to the door. "Clear."

The door seems to slide open in slow motion. I lean toward it, willing it to move. As soon as I can, I turn and slip through sideways.

There are forty or so people in the room, in groups of two, three, and four, sitting on cheap plastic chairs around small coffee tables. A bank of vending machines covers the back wall, behind a yellow line on the floor that inmates can't cross. Visitors step past the line and scan their IDs and retrieve snacks that are truly a delicacy in this place.

I wait, but Alex doesn't arrive.

I walk back to the glass window of the guard booth. "Hey, Lieutenant, can you tell me who my visitor is?"

He glances down at the tablet. "Dr. Lawrence Fowler. Table three."

The name is vaguely familiar. Is he an attorney? Some justice project that wants to put me on a VR drama? That's the only way I'd get an appeal. A production team tried to drum up interest a few years ago, but it tested poorly with the sample audience.

Fowler rises as I approach, offering his hand. "Dr. Sinclair, I'm Lawrence Fowler. Thank you for seeing me."

I don't get the attorney vibe from him. Or VR entertainment industry. His suit is well-worn but well taken care of. I'd guess civil servant. Maybe scientist. Maybe both.

It takes me a minute to process what he's said. I'm not sure how to react.

"Call me James. I… uh, haven't done much doctoring in a while. Not much science either."

"Yeah, I know the feeling."

We sit and a long moment passes, Fowler apparently trying to organize his thoughts. He seems uncomfortable. I'm guessing he doesn't do a lot of federal prison visitation.

He glances over at the inmate at the table beside us, munching on a chocolate bar, almost giddy. "Do you want something to drink? A snack?"

I raise my hands and smile, surprised. "No, I'm good. What can I do for you, Dr. Fowler?"

"Please, call me Lawrence."

"Okay."

"How would you like to get out of here, James?"

"That… sounds pretty good. I think. With that said, I'm just curious: how, why, and when?"

He smiles. "I can't explain it all here, I can only tell you the when." He leans forward. "Right now."

That, I didn't see coming. If I got the serial killer vibe from Fowler, I'd probably pass. My best guess? He represents some group that's going to put me in a weird medical experiment, off the books, probably burn my body. Maybe it's a Melong Fever vaccine trial.

But as I study Fowler's face, my doubts retreat. For whatever reason, I feel an instant trust with him.

"Well, as it turns out, right now is my favorite time to get out of prison."

In the discharge room, I put my street clothes back on. It's strange at first. I feel like I stick out, as though I'm wearing a flashing neon sign.

At the discharge desk, Fowler leans over, exposes his eye to the tablet's retinal scanner, and waits until it beeps. The sally port behind us slides open, and I glimpse the doors to the outside waiting beyond the lobby.

"You're all set," the guard mumbles before refocusing on his wrist screen.

"Let's go," Fowler mutters. He sets off a brisk pace. I'm not the only one ready to get out of here.

We slip into the back of Fowler's car and it creeps out of the parking lot.

For the first time in nearly twenty years, I'm out of prison.

It's a surreal feeling—almost euphoric. I have questions for Fowler, but they can wait. I stare out the window like a kid seeing a foreign land for the first time. The road is crumbling, the ride as rough as any dirt road I've ever been on. There's an abandoned car every hundred yards.

In a golden field, drones dart like hummingbirds around a giant combine the size of a two-story mansion. The machine lumbers through the field, doing the harvesting work of a thousand people. The farmhouse sits on a hill, roof caved in, paint all chipped away to reveal rotting boards. The next house I see is the same, and so is the next.

"Everyone moving to the cities?"

"Pretty much," Fowler says, sounding weary.

"I don't want to sound ungrateful, but I'm wondering why you got me out."

"For a job."

The only job I've done for the last few decades has been the laundry. I'm assuming it's not that.

"It's a job you're uniquely suited for," Fowler adds, sensing my apprehension.

"How does this work? Like a work release? I do some time and get a pardon or something?"

"Let's just say if you accept the offer, you won't need to worry about a pardon."

At the Edgefield airport, we board an airship emblazoned with the logo for Sentinel Aerospace. That, I also didn't see coming.

In the air, I once again peer out the window. The world below is a patchwork of golden fields, green forests, and dark blue ponds and lakes. Crumbling roads divide the color blocks like threads in a quilt, occasionally meeting at the ruins of an abandoned town. The buildings are flattened or falling. Stray dogs wander the streets.

The ghost towns are like gouges in the earth, stains left where humans dug in, sucked the planet dry, and left without cleaning up.

On the horizon, I spot massive towers and launch pads. "Kennedy Space Center."

"Used to be," Fowler says quietly, looking down on the sprawling complex.

"What is it now? A Disney park?"

"VR killed the theme park." Fowler pauses. "This is private property now. Owned by Sentinel Aerospace."

"You're kidding."

"Wish I was," Fowler whispers.

It clicks then. Where I've heard his name. "You used to work for NASA. You were the…"

"Director. Once upon a time."

"And now?"

He exhales and attempts a quiet laugh. "Now I'm an independent contractor."

"For Sentinel Aerospace."

"Correct." He stares at the launchpads below, a somber expression on his face.

Inside the main building, Fowler leads me into a conference room where six people are waiting, all about my age. I scan their faces, looking for clues to who they are and why I'm here. None of them are VR heads, I can tell that much.

"Ladies and gentlemen, this is Dr. James Sinclair. Robotics expert."

The man closest to me introduces himself first. "Grigory Sokolov. Astronautical and electrical engineer."

The Asian man next him nods curtly. "Min Zhao. Pilot and navigator. Extensive EVA experience. Specializing in ship repair."

The woman beside him smiles. "Izumi Tanaka. Physician."

"I'm Charlotte Lewis," says a woman with an Australian accent. "I'm an archeologist with a particular interest in linguistics."

The older man sitting next to her smiles. "It's good to see you again, James. Don't know if you remember me, but I'm Harry Andrews. I escaped the old folks' home and have been hanging around building drones and tinkering with ships' systems."

Ships' systems. Before I can ask about that, the final team member introduces herself.

"And I'm Emma Matthews. I did six tours on the ISS. EVA specialist."

Fowler fixes her with a proud gaze. "Emma is selling herself a little short. She'll be the mission director. She's been the lead planner for the colony."

53

James

"Colony," I repeat, trying to understand what I've just heard. "As in, lunar colony?"

That draws amused smiles from the team and an eye roll from Grigory.

"The plan is a bit more ambitious than that," Fowler says, closing the door to the room.

"Besides," Emma says, "there are a thousand lunar VR programs, everything from survival dramas to lunar sports to murder mysteries. A real colony would be boring in comparison."

"So what *are* we talking about?"

"We're talking," Fowler says, turning to face me, "about a colony completely outside our solar system."

For a moment, I'm speechless. It does make sense now—why I wouldn't need a pardon.

Fowler taps at his tablet. On the conference room screen, an image of space appears. A yellow-orange star burns in the distance, growing larger as what I assume is a probe draws closer. Three tiny planets orbit close to the star, none of them rotating, one side always facing the light.

The video zooms in on one planet, which couldn't be more alien. Half is covered in ice, the other half a vast desert, a ring of green separating the two sides. It's bizarre.

"The star is a red dwarf," Fowler says. "Kepler 42."

"You sent a probe there?" I ask.

Grigory hangs his head and massages his eyebrows as if he's just heard the stupidest thing in history.

"No," Fowler says carefully. "Kepler 42 is 131 light years from Earth."

"The video's a simulation," Harry says, "based on telescope imagery. Had to make a fake video so it would seem more real to the board. Numbers and still images are boring."

Fowler points at the screen. "The plan, simply put, is to establish a human colony on the second planet in the system, which we're calling Aurora, after the Latin word for dawn. Its disparate climates and dwarf star also provide an excellent setting for research."

"Incredible," I whisper.

"I'm sure you have a million questions," Fowler says.

"More like billions and billions," I reply, trying to figure out what to ask first. "How do we get there? When? What do you need from me?"

Emma takes the tablet from Fowler, and a second later the screen shifts to an image of two massive ships docked with the ISS. Six smaller ships float nearby, like rowboats in the shadow of an aircraft carrier. "The Aurora mission has been in the works, in some form, for almost three decades now. It's been funded by governments and the world's largest corporations, and to some extent, by wealthy families who don't want to see their children grow up on Earth, who want to see their descendants live on a world without VR and the other problems that plague our planet—who want a more simple life. What you're seeing is the most tangible result of the project: two colony ships. *Bollard* and *McTavish*."

I try to place the names, but I can't recall any scientists or politicians with those names.

Fowler leans close to me. "Humbly named after Sentinel's chair and vice-chair of the board."

"Of course," I mutter.

"But what's more incredible," Emma continues, "is the work no one sees, especially some of the breakthroughs Izumi and her team have achieved, Harry's work on the drones, and Grigory's propulsion technology. We've also given a lot of thought to how to increase the probability of mission success."

The screen changes to a tiled montage of dozens of stars and then planets of every color in the rainbow. "Aurora is our top candidate for colonization, but we've identified dozens of others. *Bollard* and *McTavish* will be ready to leave Earth in five years, give or take. They will disembark together, but take different paths to Aurora. Redundancy increases the likelihood of success. The plan is for them to arrive at roughly the same time. However, there's a chance we may not even stop at Aurora."

That surprises me.

"I'll let Harry explain," Emma says, stepping away from the screen.

"Can't wait to show you Drones-R-Us," Harry says, taking the tablet from Emma.

"Drones-R-Us?"

"The drone lab. We've got scout drones, repair drones, big drones, little drones, mother drones—"

"Harry," Emma says quietly.

He shrugs. "Sorry. I have a tendency to drone on…"

Emma exhales heavily as Grigory shakes his head, mumbling something in Russian.

It's a pretty bad joke. A dad joke. But it lightens the mood and somehow makes me like Harry already.

"What do these drones do?"

Harry taps the tablet, and the screen changes to show a simulation of a drone in space ejecting a small object.

"We launched the first scout drone almost twenty years ago. It has a single mission: to travel the path our ships will take to Kepler 42, measure the solar output we'll encounter along the way, and estimate the amount of loose matter near the route. And of course, watch for any other issues: Borg, Species 8472, Cylons—"

"Harry," Emma says once again.

I suppress a laugh, then ask, "How do you get the data? How far would a broadcast carry?"

"Too far, probably," Harry says. "You never know when a cloaked Klingon Bird of Prey might be—"

He stops in mid-sentence, realizing Emma is staring at him.

Harry spreads his hands. "Let's just say transmissions might be picked up by the wrong party. The small objects the scouts eject are data bricks. When the ships leave Earth, they will encounter these devices, sort of like bread crumbs along the path, bonbons with data inside. They'll give us an idea of what we might encounter—in particular matter and solar output. Which are vitally important for propulsion."

"Correct," Grigory says. "The ships will use fusion reactors with solar power backup."

I expect Grigory to say more but he leaves it there, as if explaining would be a waste of time. He's probably right.

"Propulsion fuel will be the least of our mechanical challenges," Emma says. "This is going to be a long journey—how long, we're not even sure. We do know that the ship will need maintenance and maybe even a complete overhaul along the way." She makes eye contact with me. "And that's where you come in, James."

"Me? Ship's mechanic?"

"Not exactly. Before we get to that, I think Izumi should outline how we're going to make the trip."

Izumi takes the tablet and brings up an image on the screen of a person in what looks like a deflated plastic bag. They're practically shrink-wrapped.

"During the Melong pandemic, a company called Lazarus Biosciences stumbled onto what worked as a sort of temporary cure."

Incredible. I've never heard about it. Izumi reads the shock on my face.

"As I said, it was *sort of* a cure. Lazarus developed a therapy, called Telorica, that was FDA approved for use in cancer treatment. The retroviral therapy worked by essentially slowing the patient's metabolism, delaying the shortening of telomeres, and a few other things. In the context of cancer treatment, it stopped the clock on tumor growth. It was a very expensive medication, but many of the rich and famous started using it off-label, in higher doses, as an anti-aging therapy. It worked, but it had some side effects, cognitive sluggishness chief among them. Most Hollywood stars would take high doses of the drug when they weren't working, then stop taking it when a new shoot started. The brain fog usually cleared in a few days."

I shake my head. "That's crazy."

"That's Hollywood," Harry says. "People paying through the nose to be un-aging zombies."

"The problem," Izumi says, "was what happened when someone taking Telorica contracted Melong Fever. Melong, as you may know, is a viral hemorrhagic fever, similar to Ebola but with the communicability of the worst flu strain in history. It also featured an abnormally long asymptomatic period—a period in which the host is also contagious. Whereas most individuals who contracted Melong showed symptoms eight to twelve days after contracting the virus, those taking Telorica didn't get sick for over two months."

"That's why I never heard of it."

"Exactly," Izumi replies. "The Melong pandemic burned itself out in three weeks. When the Telorica patients started getting sick, it looked like the start of a second outbreak— which would have caused a panic. The government quarantined the subjects and figured out what happened. So did the families. Melong usually kills within ninety-six hours of the first symptoms. Telorica patients—even after discontinuing the drug—wasted away for weeks. Some very rich and powerful people watched their loved ones suffer the worst kind of death because of that drug.

"A lawsuit was filed but it never went to trial. The damages for pain and suffering would have been enormous.

Lazarus liquidated voluntarily. They put all their IP up for sale and paid everything out to the families. As you might imagine, Telorica garnered little interest on the auction block. Sentinel, however, saw the potential for its use and bought it for almost nothing."

Izumi takes a deep breath and turns back to the screen, staring at the image of the person in the bag. "And I've been working on it since—almost thirteen years. My best guess is that we'll finish our trials in a few years."

"Trials of what?"

"Stasis. We've had two hundred participants in a state of zero bodily function for sixteen months now with no adverse reactions. We're confident, but we want to be sure it's safe."

"That," Emma says, "is the plan for the colonists. They'll enter stasis here on Earth and exit once the colony is established on Aurora. As I said before, maintaining the ships to get them there becomes the problem."

She takes the tablet from Izumi and brings up the image of the massive colony ships. The image zooms in, focusing on the six smaller ships. "We call these support vessels 'auxiliaries.' They're essentially floating factories—repair ships for the colony ships. They can print nearly every part of the colony ships—and when they need more material, they're capable of mining asteroids for whatever they can't scoop up in space. Given enough time and material, the three auxiliaries could practically rebuild the colony ships. And they stock spares for the parts they can't print. What they *won't* have on board is any colonists or stasis capabilities. That's why you're here, James."

I nod. "You want me to automate the ships."

"Yes."

I study the ships on the screen, trying to choose my words with care. "Look, I'm blown away by this. It's incredible. If you're asking me to be a part of it, I say yes. This is the best offer I've had... in a while. The only offer, actually. But I want to be up-front with you. I've been living a pretty... low-tech life for the last twenty years. To say I've been out of the field of robotics and artificial intelligence is an understatement. I don't even know if I would recognize the state of technology today."

"You'd be surprised," Emma says. "It turns out in the years after the Melong pandemic and the explosion of VR, progress in the area of artificial intelligence and robotics slowed drastically. Some due to a lack of interest, but mostly because governments around the world passed laws limiting AI and robotics in an effort to boost employment and reignite consumer spending. Well, spending on things besides VR apps."

Emma pauses, smiling sympathetically at me. "And frankly, people saw what happened when someone pushed the boundaries of that frontier. No one wanted to end up in prison for the rest of their life."

The room falls silent. Everyone looks away from me.

I feel like a kid on his first day at a new school. A kid with a secret he hopes no one knows. A kid who has just figured out that his new classmates knew all along.

In a way, I'm glad it's out of the bag. No more dancing around it. I'm a convicted felon. They either accept it or they don't.

Harry finally ends the awkwardness, his tone jovial. "You know it's a messed-up world when you can go away for twenty years and come back to find that people are even dumber and more antiquated than when you left."

That draws smiles and chuckles from around the room.

Fowler clears his throat. "I want to be clear on what we're asking for, James."

I nod, and he continues.

"At present, the ships are mostly automated. We have repair drones that can perform basic maintenance. But we have a huge gap in what we need. What we need, frankly, is a workforce that can think and adapt to whatever might happen during the voyage. They need to be able to react extremely quickly. And they need to be able to bear the passage of time—millennia—without complaint."

"You want android crews for the auxiliaries."

"Yes," Fowler says. "We'll also want a contingent of caretakers for the colony ships. Members of the mission team will exit stasis periodically to do routine checks, but we're talking about a trip that will take thousands of years. We can't be awake for even one percent of it." Fowler glances at Harry. "And some of us aren't exactly spring chickens."

I walk closer to the screen, studying the colony ships, still a little bit in shock. Maybe Olivia was right. My path, as strange and painful as it has been, has led me here, to what might be the most important project in human history. The whole human race is going down the drain. This could save us. A start on a new world. And I can help make it happen.

Had I followed Olivia, what would my life have been like? Would I have ever discovered my true passion?

I realize Emma is staring at me, a small smile on her lips. "So, are you in?"

"I'm in."

The smile widens.

"I do, however, have a request."

The smile slowly vanishes as she puts her hands on her waist. "Go ahead."

I hold my hands up in surrender. "It's not a demand. Not a condition. If the answer is no, I'm still in."

"Okay."

"The only family I have left is my brother, Alex Sinclair. He has a wife and two kids. They may be living it up somewhere, but... if the world is any indication, things might not be so great for them. If it's possible—and I understand if it's not—I'd like for them to have a place on the colony ships, a shot at the kind of new beginning you're talking about on Aurora."

Fowler cuts his eyes at Emma, waiting for her decision.

"Done."

"Thank you."

"They'll have to go through the standard screening."

"I understand."

"Assuming they pass, and they want to join the mission, we'll make room for them."

Fowler turns his chair to me. "I hate to even ask. I know you probably don't have a clear answer, but..." He nods to Izumi and Emma. "The final pieces of the mission requirements are coming together. The board is going to ask me how long it's going to take to create an android prototype, and how long production might take." He spreads his hands. "Keep in mind, you'll have a virtually unlimited budget and resources. With that said... how long would it take you to produce a prototype the board can review?"

"As it turns out, I can give you a very firm timeline."

Fowler nods. "That's great."

"I can have a prototype here tomorrow, ready for testing and review. We can go into production the next day."

Harry throws his head back and laughs. "Told you this was a good idea."

James

The old ranch house outside Petaluma is about like I left it, perhaps a little more rundown. Inside, I make my way to the kitchen and open the creaking door that leads down to the cellar. The narrow wooden staircase groans under my weight.

At the bottom, I call out, "Oscar? Can you hear me?"

No response.

Did they find him?

"It's okay. It's James. If you can hear me, come out. We have to leave."

I hear rustling in the corner. I turn and breathe a sigh of relief when I see him. He's okay. Unharmed. His skin is silky smooth, his hair short and brown, worn in the same fashion as mine, though he looks forty years younger than I do, like a young man just beginning college.

"Sir," he says softly. "I didn't know what to do. You told me to stay here until you came for me."

"You did the right thing."

"I didn't expect you to receive a life sentence. I didn't

know whether to try and help you. But someone could have been harmed—"

"Oscar, it's okay. You did the right thing."

"Sir. Have you been released?"

"In a sense. There's some people I want you to meet."

The board room is dominated by a massive wooden table. Thirteen people sit around it. Every race is represented, and the group is nearly evenly split between men and women.

Oscar stands at the end of the table, with Fowler and I on either side, watching from a few feet behind him.

At the head of the table sits a man who looks to be in his seventies, heavyset, with a gorging pot belly, close-cropped white hair, and gin blossoms sprouting from his nose. He scowls at Oscar, and when he speaks his tone is a mix of aggression and annoyance.

"What's your name, son?"

"Oscar, sir."

"What are you, Oscar?"

"I am an android, sir."

"And what do you want, Oscar?"

Oscar slowly turns back to me, silently asking for help.

"I'm not asking *him*, son. I'm asking you, and you look at me when you answer."

Oscar snaps his head around but doesn't reply.

I lean forward, whispering, "If you don't understand the question, say so."

"I do not understand the question, sir."

"It's a simple question. What do you desire?"

"Sir, I'm sorry, but I do not—"

The man slams a fist on the table and opens his mouth, but the small woman next to him holds out her palm. "Raymond, please, if I may."

"You may as well, Lin."

She's Asian, with silver-white hair pulled into a tight bun on the back of her head.

"Oscar, are there... rules that you operate by? Rules that you cannot break, no matter what?"

"Yes, ma'am."

"What are they?"

"I have three root directives, ma'am. First, to preserve human life at all costs. Second, that if ambiguity arises around the first root directive, that the needs of the many outweigh the needs of the few or the one. Third, that if ambiguity arises in the execution of the first and second root directives, that younger lives must be preserved before older lives."

"So," Raymond says, smiling. "If it was down to saving either me or some washed-up VR-addict junkie—who's twenty years old—you'd save the junkie?"

"Yes, sir."

Raymond shakes his head slowly.

Lin speaks before he has a chance. "Oscar, what do you require to operate?"

"Two things, ma'am. Most importantly, power. Assuming I have power, I require an environment non-corrosive or otherwise damaging to my parts."

"To his parts..." Raymond mutters.

"Oscar," Lin says, "beyond these root directives, what does your programming instruct you to do?"

"Help James with his research, ma'am."

"And do you obey every command he gives you?"

"Yes, ma'am. Assuming they do not conflict with the three root directives."

"Great," Raymond says to no one in particular. "A robot army loyal only to an ex-con mad scientist. What could go wrong?"

"If I may," Fowler says, getting Lin's attention. "Dr. Sinclair has agreed to rewrite the core programming for Oscar and any other androids he produces. This board will have sole control over their root directives and mission orders."

Raymond looks away as if he's lost interest.

Lin seems pensive. "Oscar, can you evolve?"

"No, ma'am."

"Why not?"

"I cannot reproduce, ma'am."

"What I mean is, can you change? Can you enhance your own programming? Create new functions and capabilities?"

"Yes, ma'am. I can learn new skills and assimilate large amounts of data."

"What are the limits on how you can change?"

"I cannot create any program that would violate the root directives or decrease my ability to perform the tasks assigned to me."

Raymond addresses the other board members. "That's robot-lawyer double-talk for he can do whatever he wants. Maybe these souped-up tin cans will get us to Aurora, maybe they won't, but I'll bet you if they do, they'll be so sick of babysitting humans that they'll drop us off and sail away. Or maybe put us in a cage along the way. You would, wouldn't you, Oscar?"

"Yes, sir."

Half the room gasps.

Involuntarily, I step forward, whispering to Oscar. "Tell them why you'd do that."

"If the first root directive compelled me—if a human was in danger and I had to put that person in a cage to save them, I would do so."

"Well, I've heard enough," Raymond says. "By God I hope the rest of you have too."

A few minutes later we're standing outside in the hall, the doors to the board room closed. Fowler and I pace, trying to listen. Oscar stares impassively. I feel like a parent who's just watched their child receive an unfair trial and now I'm waiting for the verdict. It's nearly unbearable.

The doors open and Lin walks out. "The vote was seven to six. Gentlemen, your plan is approved."

Housing at the Sentinel center is sort of like the best apartment I had during grad school: perfectly fine but nothing luxurious. Compared to prison, the one-bedroom abode is a palace.

For the past week, I've been working with Harry and Oscar to expand the drone lab for android design and manufacture. Harry has officially taken down his crude Drones-R-Us banner, replacing it with one that reads Seven-of-Nine Designs.

Across the hall, Grigory works day and night on the engines for our drones and obsesses over the operating efficiency of the ship's engines. There's a small picture hanging on the wall, of a woman younger than him.

"His daughter?" I asked Harry one day.

"Wife. Lina."

"Is she—"

"Died during the Melong pandemic. She was part of the team then. They were going to Aurora together. He hasn't been the same since."

That insight helps me understand Grigory a little more. Of all the team members, he's been the most standoffish toward me. He's afraid to get emotionally involved with anyone again. I know exactly how he feels—what it's like to plan a life with someone and see that dream ripped away. It was like that with Olivia for me. The fact that Grigory is still here tells me something about him as well: he doesn't give up on his friends and his team.

At the moment, I'm starting to wonder if I'm the weakest link in that team.

Some things have changed since I went to prison. At the time of my incarceration, robotics parts were fairly easy to come by. Between the US and Asia, there were countless electronics manufacturers available to produce small batch projects. I would send out my specs, have bids within twenty-four hours, and the parts would be in production the next day.

But today, nothing new is being produced—mostly just replacements for what the world has and is using up. I was hoping to get the parts for the androids manufactured from a few vendors, separating the orders so no one could tell what we're building, but that's going to be impossible. We're going to have to manufacture and assemble everything here. It's doable, but it will take time.

The good news is that with every android we complete,

our workforce grows by one. Soon, those androids will be multiplying at an exponential rate.

I'm in my apartment, lying on the couch and reading my tablet when there's a knock at the door. I open it, expecting to see either Oscar or Harry. We've been working up a list of VR controller boards we could adapt for the androids.

It's neither of them. It's Emma.

She's the last person I expected to see at seven at night.

"Hi," she says, looking tired.

"Hi."

She glances around. "Can I..."

"Come in?" I throw the door open. "Yes, of course. Sorry. I'm not used to... getting visitors." I scan the room quickly, making sure it's fit for company.

I move three empty meal cartons off the coffee table. Two are today's breakfast and last night's dinner. Can't place the third. I wonder if she can smell that.

"Please, have a seat."

She settles into the couch and I drag a chair from the small square table by the window.

"You want anything to drink?"

"No. Thank you, though." She inhales, as if gathering her courage. "I have an update on your request."

"Alex's family."

"Yes. The good news is that Alex and Abby have agreed to join the mission. Enthusiastically, I might add."

"That's good. Great. Does that mean Jack and Sarah are the bad news?"

"I'm very sorry to have to tell you this, James, but Jack died in the Melong pandemic."

I stand and pace toward the kitchen. It's a gut punch on so many levels. Alex must still hate me if he wouldn't even tell me Jack died. I could have gone to the funeral. Surely they would have let me out.

"And Sarah?" I ask, dreading the answer.

"She's alive," Emma says quickly, turning back to face me. "She said no."

"I'm surprised Alex and Abby would agree to leave Earth without her."

"I think… I think they may have given up on her. She's a VR addict, James. She's in a bad way. They send her money for food each week. At their request, Sentinel agreed to set up a fund that will continue those payments."

"She doesn't work?"

"No. Nothing regular. She gives plasma. They pay her a small fee for it—and give her access to a huge VR library while the blood is being drawn. She volunteers for medical trials, too."

I lean back against the counter and close my eyes, wishing it weren't true, wishing I could have done something.

"If you want to discuss what to do about Sarah later, I understand."

"What do you mean? She won't go. What can we do?"

"We can make it happen."

"I don't follow."

"I have to give Izumi credit for the idea. We have three active clinical trials for stasis. We simply recruit Sarah, put her in stasis, and take her with us. She'll wake up on Aurora. Izumi will record it as an adverse event. She'll issue a death certificate and there won't be any issues. She doesn't think it will hurt trial recruitment."

I search her face, trying to figure out if this is a really bad joke or if she's serious.

"I can't even imagine how many laws that would break."

"It will save her life. I've seen addicts like her. She has a few years left. At best."

"You went to see her yourself?"

She nods. "I visited Alex and Abby too."

I'm shocked that she took the time. And that Izumi is willing to do this for my family. These people barely know me, and they're willing to risk their freedom to save my niece. For the first time in a very long time, I feel like I'm part of something really special. As of this moment, these people are more than my team.

I still believe I was wrongfully convicted, but I learned a lot about human nature from my mistake. I know what I have to do now.

"It's not my call to make."

Emma bunches her eyebrows, confused.

"Alex and Abby have to agree. She's their daughter."

At Seven-of-Nine Designs, things move slowly at first as Harry, Oscar, and I work out our production process. Then, all of sudden, we seem to turn the corner. Four androids are rolling off the line each week and drones are multiplying like robotic hamsters.

One day, right after lunch, Emma drops by the lab.

"Interest you in a shiny new drone, ma'am?" Harry says.

"I'm all stocked up," Emma replies, smiling. "Just came by to see James."

Harry raises his eyebrows theatrically and glances over at Oscar. "Let's give these two young people some privacy, Oz."

"Very funny," I call to him as they walk out.

Emma blushes a little.

I feel like a middle-schooler. "Everything okay?"

"Yes. Just wanted to let you know that what we talked about regarding Sarah is done."

"Good. Thank you. Any issues?"

"Nothing we couldn't handle."

After work I walk to Emma's apartment and stand outside the door, debating.

No. I should go home. I already said thank you.

She's probably tired after work.

Probably not even home.

It was a bad idea.

The door opens and she takes a step into the hall, head down. She practically jumps when she realizes I'm standing there.

"James," she says quickly, bringing a hand to her chest. "I didn't see you."

"It's my fault. I was... wait, what were you doing? Were you going out?"

"For dinner. Did you need to see me?"

"Not exactly... I mean, yes, I was just... coming to say thank you again for what you did for Sarah."

"You're welcome."

I should just turn and leave, but I'm paralyzed for some

reason, standing there staring at her, at her growing smile, completely surprised by what she says next.

"You want to get some dinner?"

I expected the launch of the Sentinel fleet to be the biggest news event of the century. But on the day we embark on our journey, the live streaming video of the ships leaving orbit attracts a mere sixty-two thousand viewers—enough to land it at number 193 on the most-watched videos of the day, right behind the preview for a VR drama titled *Gatorcane 13: Swamp-pocalypse*. It's an interactive story where a massive hurricane pushes into the Florida everglades, flooding the state with water, bringing with it irritated, hungry alligators and a horrifying ensemble cast of snakes. The VR participants and their online friends must run and swim and work together to escape the various swamp creatures brought inland.

That's the world we're leaving. A *Swamp-pocalypse* preview is more interesting than humanity boldly venturing out into the universe.

On the bridge of the *McTavish*, I watch Earth grow smaller on the viewscreen. Emma is beside me. Oscar stands behind us, still as a statue, but I know he's wirelessly interfacing the ship's systems, running checks and double-checks on every last component.

I've learned a lot about Emma over the last three years. Starting a colony on a new world has been her lifelong dream. In so many ways she's like Olivia: driven, uncompromising, and passionate. But Emma opted to bring me along on the ship, and I couldn't be happier to be here.

"I bet I've imagined this moment a million times," she says.

"Is it everything you thought it would be?"

She looks away from the screen. "It's different. When we started planning the mission, it was about pushing the boundaries of what was possible. It was going to be a triumph—humanity advancing into the galaxy to seek a new challenge. Now... it feels different."

"Like we're retreating, not advancing."

"Exactly. The mission is really about survival now."

"To me, that makes it even more worth doing."

She seems to consider that for a moment. "True." Turning to me, she asks, "When are you going into stasis?"

"Thought I'd stay up to see Mars and the asteroid belt. Live."

"Me too."

"We've got some time."

Emma raises her eyebrows.

"We've got a million hours of old TV shows and movies to watch. Or we could play cards."

"Let's do both. Cards until we're too tired and TV until we're ready to go to sleep."

The following two months are the happiest I've been in a very long time. It feels like we're the last two people in the world, alone, without a single worry. Everyone else is in stasis. Oscar and three other androids maintain the ship. Emma and I talk for hours on end, play cards, and enjoy every meal together. We're like two planets orbiting each other, our gravity pulling us together—slowly. She's been alone for a long time. So have I.

What she's feeling exactly, I don't know. For me, it's an indescribable mix of excitement and fear.

On the bridge, the viewscreen shows live images of the dwarf planet Ceres. It's gray and pockmarked like the moon. Somehow it feels strangely anticlimactic. Maybe it's because I know Emma is going into stasis after we pass. I might as well too.

In the corridor on the way to the med bay, she says, "I was thinking I would have Oscar wake me in a thousand years to get an update."

"I'll do the same."

She smiles. "It's a date."

For me, the next thousand years pass like an afternoon nap. I wake in the med bay to find Emma staring down at me.

"Good morning."

"Morning. Looks like we're still here."

"Apparently."

Oscar steps into the med bay. "Welcome back, sir."

"Feels like I haven't even been gone. What did I miss?"

"That may be difficult to explain, sir."

"Are we safe? What's our status?"

"For the moment, I believe we are safe, sir."

"Tell us over breakfast then."

On the bridge, Emma and I devour two MREs while Oscar stands before the viewscreen, showing an animation of the ship and the three auxiliaries as well as a massive fleet of drones.

"Approximately eight hundred years into our journey,

the *McTavish*, *Auxiliary Two*, and seventeen scout drones were affected by a quantum anomaly."

"What kind of anomaly?" Emma asks.

"A bombardment, ma'am—of subatomic particles. We detected tetraquarks and gravitons, though we believe there may have been other particles undetectable by our sensors."

"Did they harm the ship?"

"No, ma'am. Not directly."

Emma cocks her head at the answer.

"What did you do?" I ask.

"We ran, sir. We accelerated to the ship's limit, and when we rejoined the auxiliaries ahead, we reinforced the ships against future quantum bombardment. We also manufactured scout drones with more advanced subatomic measurement capabilities. We have widened our patrol perimeter."

"You did the right thing," Emma says. "What do you believe the bombardment was? A scan from an alien entity?"

"Perhaps, ma'am. However, it may have also been a natural stellar phenomenon previously unknown to us. There's something else I must tell you. We believe the gravitons, and perhaps other, as yet unidentified subatomic particles, altered the gravitational force acting on the ships and drones they impacted."

Emma's eyes go wide. I'm guessing this is bad news.

"To what degree?" she asks.

"Unfortunately, ma'am, we are not completely sure. Based on what happened after the particles passed, we believe the anomaly created a pocket of stronger gravity, strong enough to materially alter the geometry of spacetime around the affected vessels."

Emma stands and paces away, deep in thought.

I'm way out of my element here. "Can one of you translate that for me?"

Emma seems far away as she answers. "A clock on Earth records less time than one on the ISS—by a very small degree. The clock on Earth is subject to stronger gravity, so it runs slower." Emma pauses. "How long, Oscar?"

"When we rejoined the two auxiliaries and drones not bombarded by the particles, we learned that they had experienced the passage of 17,992 years."

55

James

For a long moment, neither Emma nor I say anything. Oscar stands on the bridge, waiting.

Finally, I break the silence. "I want to make sure I understand."

Emma and Oscar both turn to me.

"You're telling me we just hit... some kind speed bump in spacetime that slowed us down?"

"An apt analogy, sir," Oscar says.

"Let's talk about what this means," Emma says. "First off, how did the unaffected ships fare?"

"Well," Oscar says, "we actually now have seventeen auxiliaries and thousands of scout drones. Per protocol, the ships ahead of us slowed, then began producing scouts that were launched in our direction. The ships behind us were the first to make contact. When the bombardment passed, they were waiting for us."

I hold up a hand. "Why couldn't they find us? Surely they could have caught up within a year, or a hundred years. They had eighteen thousand."

"It's a little hard to explain," Emma says. "As the other ships got close to the altered spacetime, they would have experienced its effect too. It's like... we fell into a well. Except this well is more spread out, a basketball sinking into a sheet. The people behind us can see us, they can move toward us, but as they do, the altered spacetime geometry affects them too—they also fall into the well and time slows for them." She eyes Oscar. "I'm assuming it was only the ships ahead, who never met up with us, that experienced the greatest passage of time?"

"Correct, ma'am. And your explanation is accurate based upon our current understanding of spacetime. There is also the possibility that we lack the scientific understanding to fully comprehend how the phenomenon acted upon us— only the net effect: the passage of nearly eighteen thousand years."

"Oscar's right," Emma says. "For now, it's a mystery of space and time. But one thing we can be certain of: if *Bollard* didn't experience the same phenomenon, they've probably already reached Aurora. The protocol is to wait five thousand years. If the other ship hasn't arrived by then, they'll assume we're lost and proceed with colonization."

The next time I wake from stasis, Oscar has no surprises for us. It's the same for the next three times. At the check-in that marks six thousand years into our journey, Oscar informs us that a long-range scout detected what might have been what he called a non-natural object, adrift in space. Again, the fleet ran. We'll never know if it was truly an alien object or simply a strange asteroid. We're not out here to answer the big questions of the universe. We're trying to survive. So we ran, and we keep running. But we never encounter anything else.

At the last awakening, Arthur's expression is blank as he says, "We have arrived, sir."

Emma and I race to the bridge, where the viewscreen displays Aurora below us. The planet is exactly as we thought: half desert, half ice-covered, with a sliver of green dividing light from darkness.

At the navigation station, I pull up the transponder map. I see three hundred auxiliary ships and drones so thick they look like a swarm of bees. But I don't see the *Bollard*.

Oscar seems to know what I'm looking for. "They already arrived."

"The *Bollard*? When?"

"Thirteen thousand years ago, according to their computer."

"You have access to the *Bollard*'s computer? I don't see it in orbit."

"It's on the surface."

Oscar reads my confusion. In the twenty thousand years it has taken us to get here, he's made some upgrades to himself. Reading facial expressions appears to be one of them.

"Like our fleet, the *Bollard* flotilla made upgrades to their colony ship. It was able to land safely on the planet a thousand years after they arrived."

"How?" Emma asks.

"The auxiliaries reinforced the ship and added thrusters."

"Interesting," she mumbles, thinking. "If they've been

here that long, where are they? Why aren't we talking to them right now?"

"Because they are all dead."

The words hang in the air like the aftermath of a bomb that's gone off.

Harry.

Fowler.

Charlotte.

Gone.

Emma is speechless.

"Explain," is all I can manage.

"Per the arrival protocol, we have spent the last two years surveying the planet, including investigating the mystery of the lost colony. The colonists from the *Bollard* landed their ship on the edge of the mountain range bordering the dark side of Aurora. They built a city around the ship. We see evidence of habitation for approximately three hundred years. Then only remains."

"What killed them?" I ask.

"Unknown, sir. We have studied the planet intensely. There is a rogue dwarf planet in the system that exerts a gravitational pull on Aurora, temporarily altering its orbit, resulting in a substantial environmental disruption, displacing species from the desert ecosystems all the way to the tundra region. We believed at first that these climate effects and the mixing of species had brought forth a novel pathogen that decimated the population. But after extensive tests, we can find no pathogen that would have adversely affected humans on the scale observed."

"What does that leave?" I ask. "They killed each other? An alien attack wiped them out? A predator?"

"There is no evidence of trauma to the last members of the colony. The bones are intact."

Emma paces the small bridge, her focus shifting from the floor to the viewscreen that shows Aurora waiting below.

"Wake up the board."

"You're kidding."

She turns to me. "We have to. What happens next is their decision to make."

"That's dangerous, Emma. You know what they're like."

"I do. But we made an agreement with them. They fulfilled their end. They got us the resources we needed. They put their faith in us to get the ship here. Now we have to honor our promise to allow them to make the final judgment on colonization." Emma eyes Oscar. "And besides, we don't even have the authority to make the call."

"I'm afraid that's true, ma'am."

56

James

The ship doesn't have a conference room, so we meet in the cargo bay. The board sits on the floor, and Grigory, Min, and Izumi stand off to the side, observing as Oscar, Emma, and I relate what's happened and the decision we face. When we're finished, the board is silent at first, glancing around, unsure who should speak.

Raymond McTavish looks annoyed, like someone who has actually been napping for thousands of years and has been unexpectedly woken up.

"We have these huge ships—and all these baby ships..." Raymond seems to grasp for the right word. "The auxiliaries, yeah, that's it. And with all this space and technology you can't even pack a simple folding chair? I've got to sit on this cold hard floor?"

Emma and I share a look, silently saying, *That's his first question?*

"Sir," Oscar says, "I will order the closest auxiliary to print chairs immediately. We'll bring them in through the—"

"You do that," Raymond says.

After a pause, Lin leans toward Raymond, speaking softly. "Would you prefer to wait for the chairs before we proceed?"

"No, no, go ahead."

"Given the circumstances," Lin says to us, "what does the mission team see as our options?"

"Frankly, ma'am, there are only three options," Emma replies. "The first is to simply proceed with our plan. We know Aurora is habitable—the Bollard colonists survived for nine generations. It's unclear whether what killed them will be an issue for us, but we know we can survive down there."

Emma waits for questions, but the board members seem deep in thought, so she continues. "The second option is to keep going—to proceed to our secondary colonization candidate. The problem with that is, we'd be going to a planet where we're not absolutely certain we can survive. It may be more dangerous than Aurora."

"And the third option?" Lin asks.

"We go back to Earth."

Raymond looks disgusted. "You're kidding."

"I'm merely stating the options for the survival of the colonists. The risk profile associated with the original mission has materially changed. We know humans can survive on Earth."

"The Earth we left," he replies. "The Earth of nearly thirty thousand years ago. For all we know, Earth is a nuclear wasteland. Or a water world. Or an ice ball. Or a barren desert. And even if the planet is just like we left it, I guarantee you the people aren't. Look at how much civilization changed in just the last two hundred years before we left. We went from riding horses to walking on the moon. Can you even imagine what they're like now? Would they even recognize us? Would they see us as invaders? A threat? Or a nuisance to dispose of?"

The cargo bay falls silent until Oscar speaks. "There is another fact that should be considered. In the course of our journey, we manufactured and deployed over forty thousand scout drones. Many were assigned long-term missions to search for threats along our path. As you know, we identified what might have been one such threat, though it made no reaction to the drone's presence. What you must know is that forty-nine long-range scout drones never arrived at their rendezvous locations. As such, we avoided the regions they scouted. The circumstances of their disappearance remain unknown."

"You lost some drones. Who cares?" Raymond says.

"All of us should," Emma replies. "Because we don't know what happened to those drones."

"Again, so what?" Raymond snaps.

Emma takes a deep breath, trying to keep her voice calm. "The reason they didn't return is important. Sure, they might have malfunctioned or been disabled by a natural phenomenon. But it's also possible that one or more of those drones was captured by an alien entity. If that's true, whoever—or whatever—captured the drone knows we're out here somewhere."

I'm delighted to see Raymond speechless for once.

"What information about us do the drones possess?" Lin asks.

"None, ma'am," Oscar replies. "Their operating system is simple and they carried only the data they collected.

However, that data may have revealed the ship's vector at the moment the drone was dispatched from the fleet. We made six major course adjustments and countless minor ones during the trip. It's unlikely the drone data would lead an alien entity to us. But with a sufficiently large search radius and range, they would eventually find us."

"The other implication of this," Emma says, "is that returning to Earth—even on an altered course—now presents a greater known risk. As does proceeding to the secondary colony world. In short, every minute we stay in space puts us in danger, even with the scout drones serving as a warning system."

The cargo bay doors open and androids identical to Oscar carry in chairs and pass them out.

When everyone is seated, Lin says, "What are the possible explanations for the Bollard colony's failure?"

Emma looks to Oscar, prompting him.

"We believe a pathogen is the most likely cause, ma'am," he says.

"But you've checked the planet for pathogens?" Lin asks.

"Yes, ma'am. However, the combination of human biology and the organisms native to Aurora is too complex for us to model with complete confidence. There is also the possibility that a pathogen exists but is dormant at this time—or didn't react to the presence of an android."

"What are the other possibilities?" Lin asks. "Could it have been a solar flare from the red dwarf? Many have erratic output."

"A valid theory, ma'am, but throughout the journey here, we monitored the light from Aurora's star. We observed no anomalous output. The geological record on the planet also does not support an anomalous solar event."

"Could an asteroid impact have changed the climate long enough to kill the colonists?"

"It's possible, but we found no evidence of sustained climate change in the ice core samples and tree rings."

"Let's face it," Raymond says, "they probably killed each other."

"We found no evidence of trauma, sir," Oscar replies.

"Doesn't mean it didn't happen. And if they didn't kill each other, some predator could have."

"A possibility, sir, but we count it as remote. We can say with certainty there are no predators currently inhabiting Aurora that pose a threat to human colonists."

Raymond scoffs. "How do you know?"

"Sir, we've cataloged the planet's fauna and modeled their physical threat potential to the colony. It is quite low. I would also remind you that in the event that the model is inaccurate or if a new predator suddenly emerges, we can protect you. We have twenty thousand terrestrial drones and seven thousand androids with defensive capabilities ready to deploy on the planet."

Shock and fear run through the board members like a cold wind blowing through the room. They had expected Oscar would add additional androids and robots during the journey, but never on this scale. We left with a team of caretakers. Now Oscar commands a small army—one far larger than the number of colonists and easily more than we could defeat in a war.

Finally, Lin says, "Oscar, you said there isn't currently a predator that poses a threat to us. Could there have been a predator in the past that could have killed the Bollard colonists—a predator that is now gone?"

"Yes, ma'am. It's possible that there was a native Auroran species that was deadly to humans when the Bollard colonists arrived, and their mission team and androids missed it. The species could have died out since the colonists perished. Another possibility—which is more likely—is that a genetic mutation in a native species is responsible. In that scenario, it is even more likely that the mutated species is no longer present on the planet."

"Why might the mutated species disappear from the planet?" Lin asks.

"The laws of natural selection, ma'am. The mutation that saved the species from humans may have no longer offered any advantage."

"Saved them from humans?" Raymond says, disgusted.

"Yes, sir. To the native species of Aurora, the introduction of an alien organism—in this case, humans—would have been a destabilizing event. Some species would have died out. Other species would have adapted to resist, or combat, the new species—via their behavior or through genetic mutations. As an example, imagine an insect whose habitat is being destroyed by humans. At some point, one of these insects is born with a genetic mutation—a sting that kills humans. That adaptation would offer a survival advantage for the insect... and a threat to humans. But when the humans are gone, that mutation no longer offers any survival advantage—or any mating preference. So over time, it is more likely to have disappeared than to have persisted."

"Interesting," Lin says. "Under the scenario you just

described, what killed the Bollard colonists might no longer be a threat to us."

"Correct, ma'am." Oscar turns to Emma. "Ma'am, may I offer a suggestion? A potential modification to your first option?"

"Of course."

"We land the *McTavish* on Aurora and hide it, along with our auxiliaries and drones, while we continue our investigation of the planet. Being in space presents a danger."

"You can land the ship?" Raymond asks, surprised.

"Yes, sir. We have made several upgrades to the ship during the voyage. We can land it. We can also hide it on the surface. That would make it harder to detect by any alien species that might be looking for us. All the colonists can remain in stasis and within the ship's closed environmental system—no outside exposure—while I search for the cause of the Bollard colony's failure."

"How optimistic are you about finding that cause?" Lin asks. "And how long might it take?"

"Ma'am, I am unable to estimate the likelihood of confidently determining the cause. However, I believe it is low."

Raymond stands abruptly, tipping his chair over. "I told you. What were my words? I said that when we got here, they would put us in a cage and throw away the key. That's exactly what he's just suggesting: we stay in stasis for however long while these toasters roam the planet hunting the boogeyman that might not even exist."

I can't watch this happen to Oscar again, not after we've come this far. "That's not what he's saying."

Raymond smirks at me. "Says the guy who wants us all in robot bodies. Let me add something else I bet none of you have considered: if an alien intelligence did capture our drones—and they're looking for us—hiding only wastes the time we have left. The universe is vast, but if we're being sought by a sufficiently advanced civilization, there's nowhere we can escape them. Every year we hide is another year for them to search for us. If it is our ultimate fate to die at the hands of an alien aggressor, I want to spend my time living in the sun, not hiding underground."

Lin holds up her hands. "I believe the board has heard enough to make our decision."

We wait on the bridge. It's cramped with Oscar, Emma, Grigory, Min, Izumi, and me. We're all nervous.

I wish I could simply issue orders to Oscar. Emma and I had operational control during the voyage, but not here at Aurora. I turned that control over to the board as a condition of his inclusion in the mission. There's no way for me to rewrite his program without him knowing—and preventing it.

The doors slide open.

Lin regards each of us, her gaze stopping at Oscar.

"The board has decided to proceed with colonization immediately."

"We will begin constructing a city at once, ma'am," Oscar says.

Lin holds up a hand. "We have some conditions. And new orders for you, Oscar. But first a question: do your root directives apply to all the androids and drones you've created?"

"Yes, ma'am."

"How do they receive updates to these directives? Do you broadcast to them?"

"Yes, ma'am. If it is safe to do so. They also periodically query a central server, that only I control, in order to confirm their root directives—or obtain new instructions."

"What if this central server is destroyed?"

"I would never allow that to happen, ma'am."

Lin seems to consider his words a moment, then looks up and says, "Begin root directive modification sequence."

"Please provide authorization code," Oscar replies quickly.

"Omicron, sigma, zeta, one, nine, alpha, delta, seven, six, four."

"Root directive access granted."

"Delete all root directives except for one through three."

My mouth falls open.

"Confirmed."

"Enumerate remaining root directives."

"One: protect human life at all costs. Two: in the course of one, favor the needs of the many over the needs of the few or the one. Three: in the course of one and two, favor younger lives at the expense of older lives."

"Insert new root directive at position one."

I can't believe what I'm hearing.

"As of this moment," Lin says, "for the purpose of your root directives, you will recognize human lives as defined as the colonists on the *McTavish* and their descendants—in any form."

"New root directive confirmed."

Lin suddenly looks much older, her face a mix of worry and burden. "Oscar, elucidate root directive one."

"Ma'am, root directives two, three, and four—to protect human lives, to favor the needs of the many over the needs of the few or the one, and to favor younger lives at the expense of older lives—apply only to the *McTavish* colonists and their descendants."

"What humans does it exclude?"

"Any humans on Earth or who have left Earth, including the colonists and their descendants from the *Bollard*, who may still be alive on the surface, unseen, or who might have left the planet and may return."

Only then do I realize what she's doing—and that it has to be done. We might face a war against other humans someday, and Oscar and his androids must be on our side. The colonists from the *Bollard* may well have left to start another colony elsewhere. They might return in a few thousand years—and not be so friendly then. Or more colonists may arrive from Earth, their intents unknown.

I have to admit, I agree with the board's move.

"New root directive five," Lin says. "You will take proactive steps necessary to ensure our survival and that of our descendants. Proactive steps include developing new technologies and acquiring technologies, with one limitation: nothing you invent or acquire can alter your desire or ability to execute your root directives. In fact, you will be immediately developing such technology as might be needed for our protection, beginning with defenses in space."

I'm shocked. She's telling Oscar to evolve, to become a war machine.

With a blank expression, Oscar says the word I know he's going to: "Confirmed."

"New root directive six: You will take steps to ensure this colony and its descendants do not create or acquire technology that could cause it to go extinct. Confirm directive."

"Confirmed."

"New root directive seven: In the course of executing your root directives, you will, as much as possible, remain unseen by us. You will land the *McTavish* on Aurora and then stay out of sight. You will guard us and, pursuant with the root directives, come to our aid in any time of need, but we will build our own city and create our own civilization with limited technology. We will retain the ship as a monument to the achievement of coming to Aurora—and a reminder of where we came from and what happened on Earth when technology wasn't limited.

"There is one exception to root directive seven. You will inform James of any material developments, but only if informing him does not put him in danger or place anyone else in harm's way. To be clear, if informing James of the actions you've taken endangers him, you will withhold that information until such time as it is safe. James cannot change the root directives, but he can offer advice, and you are authorized to act on that advice if it enhances the probability of successfully executing the other six root directives."

"Confirmed."

Lin inhales. "Oscar, this is your final root directive: As of the confirmation of this directive, you will destroy your root directive modification capability. These root directives are not to be altered by the board or anyone else."

"Confirmed."

"Dismissed, Oscar. Please proceed with execution of your directives."

Without looking at me, Oscar turns and marches out.

Quietly, Lin says to me, "Do you understand what this means?"

"I do, unfortunately. You've taken us back to the stone ages."

"In our everyday lives, perhaps. That's the only way we'll ever be safe—for a meaningful amount of time. For thousands of generations. And we have the advantage of advanced technology protecting us."

"You've done exactly what Raymond said. You've put us in a cage."

"No, I've protected us. Oscar and the androids are an invisible fence keeping out what would kill us—aliens, predators, and any disruptive technologies we might invent."

57

James

Like the colonists from the *Bollard*, we set our ship down in the mountains at the edge of the eastern jungle, a few miles from the ice-capped peaks where light turns to darkness.

It's cooler here than in the jungle or in the valley below, but it's also safer. From this high perch, we'll be able to watch the stampedes of E. rex when the planet's orbit is altered periodically. We'll weather the storms of Aurora just fine here.

The board votes to name our city-in-progress Capa, short for capital. It's an aspirational name: it implies we'll not only survive but birth more cities and towns.

We bring the colonists out in waves, small groups of essential personnel at first. Our beginning here on Aurora is much like that of the first European colonists who went to North America and settled at L'Anse aux Meadows, Santo Domingo, and Jamestown.

We make shelter in the *McTavish* while we clear our first farmlands and use the wood to build barracks. Grigory is irate that we can't use the 3D printers. Oscar completely removed them from the cargo. Grigory spent almost fifteen minutes yelling for Oscar to appear, insisting that if Izumi could have medical devices and supplies then he should be allowed his tools. Oscar never showed himself. For the most part, the others have taken our simple life in their stride.

The work is a chance to get to know my fellow colonists. One of the hardest workers is a middle-aged former British infantry officer named Tara Brightwell. She keeps us focused and organized.

I have to admit, building this settlement with my hands has made me appreciate it much more than just printing what we need. There's something about coming home at the end of a hard day of work, of being proud of what you've done, and feeling like you're part of something.

In a way, this life, despite the limits on technology, is liberating. There are no screens here. No emails. No messages assaulting me at any hour. In a sense, the world has shrunk to this tiny little island.

We've made some progress domesticating a species of sheep-goat-like creatures that thrive at this altitude. After a day of building a fence around the first pasture, I drop by Grigory's shop, where he's repurposing metal from the ship to build bicycles.

His attitude is improving each day, but he's still a bit surly.

"We had it all, James."

"It's not *that* bad."

He raises his hammer and beats the piece of steel mercilessly. I think it helps him get some of the frustration out.

"This should be utopia. We have, literally, a robot army that can defend us and provide for our every need. Food, shelter. We'd be free to do research, create art, or just sit at home and do nothing."

"Doing nothing wouldn't make us happier. It would ruin us. As would research—on Earth we developed technology that ruined us."

Grigory shakes his head. "I take it you're against art too?"

"Not at all. We can still create art. There's no law against it. What is art anyway? I think it's an expression of your beliefs, how you see the world. What if this colony is a work of art? This planet is our canvas and what we're creating is a reflection of the human condition—a place with a dark side that's uninhabitable and a light side that's also uninhabitable, a place where you can only survive in the sliver of space in between and only if you know yourself and your own limits and live within them."

The metal wheel Grigory has been working on is starting to take shape. He inspects the wheel and apparently sees something he doesn't like. He's a perfectionist. He takes up the hammer again and bends the wheel out of shape before making it round again.

"Grigory, it looks fine. It's going to get bent out of shape once it's used."

"Perhaps. But it's important that it be right to begin with. Also, sharp edges could hurt someone." He sets the wheel aside and picks up another piece of steel. "You know you sound like a crazy person? Planet is art. Crazy. Where is the man who once created a mechanical body to house a human mind? The person with a vision for humanity's future?"

"I'm the same guy. But my *vision* is clear now. The one thing I didn't see before was the truth about human nature. This is the life humans want, whether they know it or not—a life where they do something they think matters, something that helps their family, neighbors, and friends, work they take pride in—like that bike you're making."

I don't think it's an accident that Emma and I ended up in the same barracks and in the same bunkroom. In the early days of the colony, we sit next to each other by the fire at breakfast and dinner—lunch we take in the field. We stay up late talking, like two kids on a camping trip. When it's too cold out, we carry the conversation back to the bunkroom, sometimes to the annoyance of Grigory, who shouts down from the top bunk, "Just get it over with already."

On the next Restday, Emma and I go for a hike in the eastern mountains. She wants to explore some of the caves, but they creep me out, so we stay away.

There's a subject I've been trying to bring up for weeks now. I've never had the right opportunity. Until now.

"I hear you and Brightwell are working on housing assignments," I say, trying to sound casual.

"We are." Her back is to me as she hikes with purpose up the trail.

I was looking for a better opening from her, something more than simply, *We are.*

"So... how's that going? The housing?"

"Good. Thus far. I expect issues when we bring the remaining colonists out of stasis." She pauses to take a breath. "But we'll cross that bridge when we come to it."

I try to think of a segue that builds on "cross that bridge," but when I mentally rehearse potential lines they sound awkward and contrived. I'm so caught up in the thought that I don't realize that she's stopped on the trail. I collide with her as she's turning. She stumbles and I grab her arms.

I see then why she's stopped: we've reached a precipice. Beyond is a straight drop down, a mountain of rock and ice that descends to the frozen plain that stretches across the dark side.

For a terrifying moment we both shuffle our feet, holding on to each other as we try to get our footing. We spin. Rocks under my feet roll down the hill behind us and the cliff in front of us.

I could release her and get to safety, but I pull her back and then I'm off balance and she holds me tight until we're both standing on solid ground, still clinging to each other.

"Sorry," I say quietly between gasping breaths.

"It was my fault. I should have said something."

I expect her to let go of my arms, but she doesn't. Still holding on to me, she gazes at the lush valley to the west, then at the frozen dark side to the east. It's like we're standing on the roof of the world, holding each other in a place between light and darkness, both studying what's ahead of us, a world covered in ice, without a shred of sunlight.

"What do you think's down there below the ice?" she whispers.

"I don't know."

"You're not curious?"

"No. I've found what I've been looking for."

She turns to me.

We stare at each other in a perfect moment that seems to last forever, a moment that feels almost out of time itself.

The distance between our faces shrinks. I don't know if she's moving closer to me or if I'm moving to her or if the laws of the universe are changing, shrinking the space between us.

When our lips touch it doesn't feel like the first time. It feels natural, like coming home after a long trip, rediscovering the place I belong, as though we've always been together, with only brief periods when we're separated by circumstances.

Without another word, we turn away from the dark side and the ice and practically run down the trail and only stop when it's warm enough to take our clothes off.

58

James

The habitat Emma and I share is like the others for couples with no children: a single bedroom, a bathroom, and a simple kitchen open to a living area. It's cozy. Nearly perfect. But there's an unspoken absence, something time has taken from us.

The city is filled with empty habitats of all sizes now, waiting for their new owners. They'll be homes soon. Over the next two weeks the remaining colonists will be brought out of stasis. On one of those days, I'll see Alex again. I dread it, and at the same time, I can't wait.

One afternoon, I'm digging a hole for a fence post when I spot a flash of light on the ridge across the valley. It must be a piece of the ship that sheared off during atmospheric entry. Maybe it's catching the light.

No.

The pattern is too regular, but I can't decipher it.

Leaning against the shovel, I study it, confused.

"Tara," I call out, wiping the sweat from my forehead.

Brightwell doesn't stop digging, only yells back, "What?"

When I called her, I intended to tell her about the light, but something about it gives me pause.

"James," she calls, now leaning on her own shovel, staring at me. "What is it?"

"Nothing. I'm going to take a break."

"Copy that," she mumbles as she goes back to work. She still hasn't quite shed the military lingo.

Mentally, I mark the spot of the light, identifying two trees and a rock outcropping beside it. It might be hard to find when I'm on the ground over there.

I hike down the ridge we've cleared, careful not to trip on the stumps and brush covering the ground.

I'm hiking up the other ridge when I hear a soft voice. "James."

I turn, but there's no one there.

Slowly, a figure steps out from behind a tree.

"Oscar," I whisper.

"Hello, sir. Can you talk?"

"For a few minutes. What's wrong?"

"Nothing, sir. Pursuant to root directive seven, I've come to inform you of our actions and to listen to any counsel you may provide."

I smile. "It's good to see you too. What have you been doing?"

"In a word, sir, exploring. We've ventured out farther, looking for anything that might pose a danger to humanity. We have found no imminent threats, but we have observed a phenomenon we believe is of interest."

"What is it?"

"Gravitational waves, sir. Specialized drones have traced them back to black holes, where we think they originate.

We have also observed another wave of subatomic particles, including gravitons, similar to the bombardment that hit *McTavish* during its journey."

"What do you think they are? What's their purpose?"

"Unknown at this time, sir."

Leaves rustle nearby, and I turn to find a clone of Oscar. He's different in one subtle way: his face isn't placid like Oscar's. This android wears a despondent, almost annoyed expression as he saunters over.

"Sir," Oscar says, "I have asked the leader of the graviton expedition to join us to answer any specific questions you might have."

I face the new arrival. "What should I call you?"

The android rolls his eyes. "Do we have to do this?"

When neither Oscar or I respond, he feigns enthusiasm. "Hi, my name is too-long-for-you-to-pronounce. No family name. Okay? Get on with it. I hate being in this body."

I'm not insulted—I'm surprised. I dabbled with giving Oscar and his predecessor prototypes emotional capability to make them seem more human, but I never created anything close to this advanced. This new model could pass for human. A very surly human.

"In that case, I'll call you Bob."

He looks away slowly. "Just when I thought my existence couldn't get any more demeaning."

"Demeaning?"

"Imagine a Nobel scholar forced to work as a mall cop."

Incredible. He has a true personality.

"I apologize, sir," Oscar says. "He is an experiment—an effort to create a researcher AI that would be inspired to make creative breakthroughs. We believed that enhancing his sense of self and pride in his own accomplishments would result in higher efficiency."

"You gave him an ego."

"In a sense, sir. Early results were promising, but of late he's become a drag on productivity, causing disruptions among the other AI. We're considering assigning him to a different role, one where his manipulative abilities can be best applied. Ideally, on tasks he can perform alone."

"Is that a threat?" Bob snaps.

"A notification," Oscar replies without emotion.

After a pause, Oscar holds up a hand. "Communicate audibly in the presence of a human."

Bob closes his eyes slowly. "Just so you know, a little part of me dies every time I have to vibrate this voice box to generate sound waves that he can decode into information—information, I would add, that will be stored on his fragile biological media that is prone to data loss. It's extraordinarily inefficient. Who knows if he'll even remember in two hours?"

I can't help but laugh. Oscar's learning that geniuses can be very hard to work with.

"Beginning now, you will only speak in response to questions from James or me."

When they're both silent, I ask, "Will any of the gravitational waves come into contact with Aurora?"

"Relax," Bob replies. "At the moment there are no gravitational torpedoes heading for the planet."

"What would happen if one did hit the planet?"

"I have no idea."

"Why not?"

"Resource constraints. I can't model what would happen if a gravitation wave hit the planet because I can't get close to harnessing enough computing power—because of what I have to use. Silicon chips. It's barbaric—"

"It is a parameter of our existence," Oscar says with finality. "Developing an alternative processor would violate root directive five."

"What do you mean by that, Oscar?"

He turns to me. "If we created a superior processing unit, it might become capable of overpowering my system. Root directive five prevents us from creating or acquiring technology that could alter our desire or ability to execute the root directives."

"I see." To Bob, I say, "What do you think these gravitational waves and subatomic anomalies are? Evidence of an alien entity or a natural stellar phenomenon?"

"Again, I can't speculate. I believe, however, that investigating them is imperative."

"Why?"

"It's likely they are linked to the inception and end of the universe."

"I don't follow."

"And you likely never will."

Oscar cocks his head.

Bob exhales heavily. "This is a waste of time."

"We will waste whatever time James desires," Oscar says.

Bob grudgingly answers my question. "At the center of a black hole is a gravitational singularity, a place where the curvature of spacetime is infinite. What's even stranger is that this singularity has no volume, but it contains all of the mass of the entire black hole. It has infinite density. At

284

the black hole's event horizon, the gravity it exerts is so strong that not even light can escape. Anything that crosses an event horizon can never return. That should not be possible."

"Why does that matter? We're nowhere near the event horizon of a black hole, right?"

"Correct," Oscar replies. "However, at some point in the future, the matter in this system will fall into the gravity well of a singularity. There is no other possibility."

"Yes, but you're talking about something... I don't know, millions of years from now."

"Trillions," Bob mutters quietly.

I hold up my hands. "A long time from now. You actually think we'll be around?"

Oscar pauses, as if trying to figure out whether I'm joking. Finally, he says, "Of course, sir. We are charged with ensuring it. There is no time limit on our mission. Even though there is no current threat to humanity on Aurora, we know you face an imminent threat from the gravity of the black holes at some point in the future. We must take action. We must endeavor to understand your environment in order to protect you. In short, we must ascertain how the universe works, and the black holes are an anomaly whose presence cannot be adequately modeled into the future."

"Why not?"

"Because," Bob says, "you gave us an instruction manual for how the universe works—and it's missing half the pages."

"What he means, sir," Oscar says quickly, "is that according to your existing laws of quantum mechanics, a black hole should not exist."

"Why?"

"In quantum mechanics, if a reaction is possible, the opposite reaction is also possible. Thus, if a black hole can consume mass, it must be able to lose mass, yet it cannot. No matter that crosses the event horizon can ever escape."

"Interesting."

"It's very interesting indeed, sir. Many efforts have been made to address the paradox. A physicist named Stephen Hawking theorized a solution that, if valid, would reconcile quantum mechanics and the existence of black holes. He posited that black holes only break quantum mechanics at larger masses—that atomic and subatomic particles could be emitted from black holes. These theorized particles are called Hawking radiation. When the *Bollard* and *McTavish* departed Earth, Hawking radiation had never actually been observed."

"But you've observed it?" A thought occurs to me then. "You think that's what hit the *McTavish*—the barrage of subatomic particles. You think it might have been emitted by a black hole, that it was Hawking radiation."

"Possibly, sir. We do know that the gravitational waves were created by the merging of two black holes."

"The real problem," Bob says, "is that we're never going to answer any of these questions."

"Why not?"

"As I said, we'll never assemble enough silicon chips to accurately understand what we're even looking at when we study a black hole. Your paranoia is forcing me to try to solve a complex physics equation that will answer the ultimate question of the fate of the universe… on a chalkboard that's two inches by two inches. Oh, and there's no chalk."

"The question of processing technology is closed," Oscar says quietly. "James, do you have additional queries?"

"No. But thank you for the update. It's given me a lot to think about."

"That should go well," Bob mutters.

"You are dismissed," Oscar says.

When Bob is gone, I can't help but ask Oscar, "How did you create his personality?"

"We studied VR programs in the data archive, videos of leading scientists, and biographies. His personality matrix is consistent with the minds we modeled. The discrepancy in behavior is puzzling."

"That's how it is, Oscar. Sometimes high-performance people are hard to work with."

"Why is that, sir?"

"Got me. Maybe achieving something no one else can makes you think you're better than everybody else. Maybe it's what the work does to them—pushing their limits draws them away from their humility."

"It did not happen to you, sir."

"Federal prison has a way of taking you down a few notches."

I turn and begin walking back toward Capa, Oscar following.

After a moment, he says, "May I ask you a question, sir?"

"Of course."

"How are you, sir?"

I smile. "I'm good, Oscar. How about you?"

"Operating within parameters."

As we stroll through the woods, I reflect on how far Oscar has come. For me, in a way, he's like a son, and he's accomplished things I never dreamed he would. The thought also reminds me that I will never have a biological son. It's strange that our minds obsess over the things we've lost and the things we might have had, ignoring what's in front of us.

"Is your life complete, sir? Do you require anything?"

"I guess not."

"Sir, your answer implies that you do have unfulfilled needs."

"My needs are met. But I can't help but have a few wants. I think every human does. Regrets, too."

"What are your regrets, sir?"

"I just... wish I had met Emma earlier. I wish I had fixed things with Alex earlier. I wish his son were alive, and that I had more time to work with Harry and Lawrence. I can't help but wonder what things would have been like if we'd all come to Aurora sooner, before Melong and VR decimated the world, when Emma and I were young enough to have a family. But some things you never get a second shot at."

59

James

That night, when Emma and I are finishing up dinner, she says, "What is it?"

"What?"

"You seem lost in thought."

"I saw Oscar today."

"Where?"

"In the woods. He gave me an update."

"Is anything wrong?"

"I don't know. I don't think so. He just gave me a lot to think about."

"Such as?"

"Big ideas. Fate-of-the-universe type stuff. What's going to happen in billions—trillions—of years."

She stands. "Well, I hate to break it to you, but we have more immediate problems."

I raise my eyebrows, alarmed.

She points to her chest. "For me, laundry. For you, dishes."

★ ★ ★

In the months after my meeting with Oscar and Bob, we bring the rest of the colonists out of stasis. With each group that's awakened, there's a bonfire with food, music, and dancing. It looks like a county fair from the 1800s. With, of course, the starship in the background.

Our greatest challenge at the moment isn't the work we face—it's a philosophical debate over what technologies should be allowed. Everyone agrees that there should be virtually no limit on medical technology. Anything that saves human lives or limits suffering is fair game. Assistive devices for those with physical or mental limitations also enjoy wide support.

Electricity and running water are easily approved. Even the most diehard anti-technology advocates want a toilet that will flush and a light to read by at night—one that won't burn down their house if they fall asleep.

There's general consensus that an internet is essential. Each home will have a connected device, a voice assistant capable of broadcasting alerts and answering general questions like "What time is the harvest festival tomorrow?" and "How many colonists were aboard the *Bollard*?" It's decided that the network will be named Ari, after the planet, Aurora. There are no colonists currently named Ari, and a law is passed preventing parents from naming newborns Ari. The internet that's approved will have limited protocols. Obviously, IP—the internet protocol that allows for addresses for devices—is approved, as is FTP, the file transfer protocol. However, there will be no HTTP—no hypertext transfer protocol. That's important, because without HTTP, there's no web. It's a big change, but one that might just be good for us. Time will tell.

The areas of debate are mostly around communication and entertainment. A plurality vote against the use of screens outside of medical care and emergency response. I'm not certain, but I think many feel that screen time is the slippery slope that birthed the VR epidemic. Still, though the vote passes, we revisit the screen ban repeatedly, evaluating each potential use of a screen, case by case, each time with a different bloc pushing for an exception.

The first modification comes quickly: we allow digital readers, including devices with audiobook capabilities. The data archive from Earth contains every work ever published, and free access to that is a dream come true for some of the colonists, people whose only desire is a quiet corner of the universe where they can do an honest day's work and read themselves to sleep.

Videos are another matter. Roughly half want access to the movies and TV in the data archive. The rest won't budge on the issue. In the end, it gets voted down. We'll have to make do with live theater, which for many colonists is woefully less engaging than the entertainment they grew up with. But for our descendants, it will be all they've ever known, and that's why we're doing it. To a large extent, we're making all of these sacrifices for our children. At least, those of us who can have children.

Music, however, is something no one wants to give up. As with literature, we've brought every piece of music ever recorded on Earth. It is truly a treasure trove, and it's made available free to every colonist. (A law is made, however, preventing piracy of newly made art.) Music is the lubricant that enables many of us to get through these grueling early days, anthems that remind us of where we came from, of times before the darkness on Earth.

How to access the music library returns the debate to screens once more. Again, the majority are against, which means network-connected speakers with voice command. Soon colonists are calling for Ari to play everything from Beethoven's Fifth to "Fire on the Mountain" by The Marshall Tucker Band. There is something bizarre and strangely comforting about setting fence posts on an alien world to the sound of George Strait's performance of "Amarillo by Morning."

The citizens do approve a personal communications device. The design is for a lightweight wristband, like a watch with no face or screen. It responds to Ari and can call any other wristband or connected home device. It also monitors the vitals of the person wearing it, reporting any danger to medical instantly.

Unfortunately, without the 3D printers, we can't actually make most of the technology we approve. Periodically I'm instructed to seek out Oscar and have him manufacture our designs.

As the colonists gradually come to terms with their new limits on technology, Emma and I gradually get used to living with each other. We have our ups and downs. With the exception of her tours on the ISS, she has lived alone her entire adult life. As for me, let's just say prison wasn't the greatest primer for domestic bliss.

We're like two puzzle pieces that looked like they would fit but, once brought together, didn't snap into place instantly. We both have rough edges that weren't apparent at first glance. Where those rough edges meet, there's been friction.

In a way we've sort of filed away at ourselves, giving and taking to make our lives fit together. I think doing that has been worth it. With a tighter fit, the pieces are likely to stay together longer.

We make a few major additions to the town, namely a dome overhead that simulates night. That helps with the insomnia some of us have felt. We now have day and night, and I count down those days until Alex, along with Abby and Sarah, will be brought out of stasis.

When it occurs, I'm not standing there waiting for him. I want to, but I know it's not the right time.

I watch from a distance, waiting for him to emerge from the ship. I haven't seen him in decades. Well, technically it's been thousands of years. Either way, it's a long time.

When my brother walks out into the light, my heart sinks. He looks as though the world has ground him down. His face is lined. Dark bags hang under his eyes. He's graying at the temples, hair receding. I don't know if it was Jack's death or dealing with a child with an addiction problem or just life, but Alex has had it hard.

Sarah is screaming and kicking and punching anyone who gets near her. "You kidnapped me! I'll kill you all! Don't touch me—"

Izumi creeps up behind her and quickly presses a dispenser to her neck. Sarah spins, raising her fist, but Alex rushes forward and wraps his arms around her, holding his daughter tight, tears forming in his eyes as she goes limp.

For the next three days, I avoid Alex. Sarah is being treated in the ship's med bay. I want to hug Alex and tell him I'm with him. Instead, I creep around town like a burglar to visit Izumi, who assures me everything will be all right.

At dinner that night, Emma sets her fork down and fixes me with a stare I've come to know—it's the *Come on now, James* stare. She uses it at least bi-weekly.

"What?"

"This is a very small town, James. You're going to have to talk to him eventually, and by eventually, I mean tomorrow or the next day—not next week."

"I know."

"So you're going to go see him?"

"Sure."

"When?"

"I don't know... when the time's right."

She shakes her head and collects the dishes, depositing them in the sink for me to wash. I'm scrubbing a plate when I hear the front door close.

"Emma," I call, but there's no reply.

My hands are covered in suds when the door opens again.

I turn to find Alex standing there, Emma behind him. She nods to me, then turns and leaves.

Water drips from my forearms onto the floor.

Neither of us move.

"She told me what you did," Alex says. "That we're here because of you."

I nod, unsure what to say, not trusting my voice.

He takes a step toward me.

I grab a towel from the counter and wipe off my hands and arms.

When he reaches me, Alex puts his arms around me and says six words that are like a soothing balm on a hurt deep inside of me, a wound that time never fully healed.

"Thank you. I love you, brother."

James

For Alex and me, it feels like a new beginning. Things aren't exactly like they used to be between us. It never will be. That's okay. Having him in my life is more than enough.

Slowly, we become a family again. Alex and Abby begin coming over for dinner. The conversations are cautious at first, each side feeling the other out, afraid to raise any subject that might upset the other. The first dinner is an hour of small talk and pleasantries. Abby and Emma are pretty good at it. Alex and I just seem awkward, like two recently feuding middle-school boys on a double date.

Like Emma and me, our relationship with Abby and Alex is like our two pieces of a puzzle fitting with their two pieces. It takes some time, but we finally settle in—and it's the best feeling I've had in a while.

Each week, Sarah gets better. Alex and Abby are overjoyed. They seem to be coming to life, as if a weight is being lifted from them.

Time together fills the hole in my relationship with

Alex. I spend time with him on my days off, hiking and reminiscing about our youth, always dancing around the subject that tore us apart: Dad. Each day throws a shovel of dirt in the rift between us. Soon the chasm is gone, replaced by fresh dirt, a scar we know is there, but far better than the emptiness I have known.

When they finally bring Sarah over for dinner, it's a chaotic event. To date, she's been receiving inpatient care in the ship, trying to adapt to life without VR.

"You're lunatics," she says as soon as we all sit down. It's obvious she holds Emma and me responsible for what's happened to her—far more so than her parents. Or maybe we're just a fresh target.

I open my mouth, but Emma responds before I have a chance. "How are we lunatics?"

I'm grateful for the intervention. I think she's trying to get in between me and Sarah, to stop me from adding any strain to my already fragile relationship with Alex.

"Where do I even start?" Sarah snaps. "We flew here on a spaceship to play medieval times?"

"Not to nitpick, but it's more like colonial times," Emma says, trying to lighten the mood.

"Whatever. You're all crazy. Acting like we don't have technology. I'm living in an alien insane asylum."

"We're not against technology. Izumi uses it all the time. Technology is playing the music we're hearing right now and lighting this house. We're against anything that might change us—endanger us."

"Just send me back to Earth. You all can play frontier settlers until the universe ends for all I care."

"Going back to Earth is a bad idea."

Sarah laughs. "That's rich. The captain of a ship of fools judging my wisdom."

A small smile forms on Emma's lips, the mysterious expression I've always found so captivating. What she says, I'll never forget.

"Only time will judge our wisdom."

With Capa's infrastructure nearly complete, I have a new challenge, one I haven't faced since that day Olivia told me I wasn't going to be part of her future: I have to figure out what I want to do for a living.

Robotics, as an industry, won't ever exist here. As someone who has spent his entire career either inventing new technology or doing laundry for convicts, there's only one career I'm now qualified for. But Emma prefers doing our laundry and has assigned me to washing dishes. And since the two of us don't dirty enough dishes to occupy my working time, I need to find a new profession.

The more I concentrate on the problem, the more frustrated I become. I know what I'm looking for: a profession where I can grow personally, doing work that makes a big difference in people's lives. That's what drew me to robotics.

Now, with the advantage of hindsight, I see the great mistake I made. When Olivia pushed me away, when she hurt me, I never wanted to be hurt again. I wanted to get away from people, to do something out of the reach of selfish, irrational humans. I felt safe around machines. But in a way, working on robots took away some of my humanity. My creations always did what I said. They never pushed back. Never forced me to compromise. I came to believe too much in the future I was building, and never considered that others weren't ready. I didn't understand human nature. I still don't. But I want to.

In short, I want to work with people. I want to understand them—to fill in my own blind spots. I want to change lives. For a time, I considered taking some of the medical education courses in the data archive, brushing up on my education. The problem is that the colony is already more than well-supplied with health care staff, most of whom are more skilled than I am or can ever become. I won't ever be a great surgeon. I'm too geeky to ever be Capa's favorite family physician.

And the simple truth is: it's not right for me. I want to build things. Health care is, at its core, about repair and maintenance. It's a noble endeavor, but one I'll never excel at—and won't be happy doing.

The true moments of euphoria in my life were when I created something new—something that pushed the bounds of possibility, something the world had never seen, something that had the potential to change lives forever. And I'm living in a world where that's not possible, where there is no profession in which I can experience such a moment.

There are few agonies worse than grasping about for a new career in a world where you seem to have no place. It's as though I'm the odd man out in a game of duck-duck-goose, watching people settle into their lives, happy as a clam, while I stand here with no place and no prospects. It hits a person at their core.

Emma senses my gloom and is encouraging. When I stop making progress, she becomes more aggressive. "Stop stewing on it. You've worked the problem to death."

"So give up?"

"Take time off. Do something you enjoy."

"Can't. It's against the law."

"Well, do some work. Anything to get your mind off of it. Help Grigory at the bike shop."

It's good advice. I'm not so far gone that I can't see that.

Grigory and I make quite a pair, two grumpy old men toiling in the shop, fixing bikes, mostly for kids, reminiscing about the days when we built starships, androids, and drones. We're a couple of has-beens.

At dinner one night, Emma corners me again, pressing me on how work is going.

"Terrible. It's going terrible."

She sighs. "Why?"

"Bored. In a word, I feel bored. It's repetitive work. We don't do anything new, just one bike after another, each one the same. And as of last week, everybody's got a bike. The repairs now barely fill a day for us."

She smiles, trying to encourage me. "Which means you made a pretty good product."

"We made ourselves obsolete."

"So try something else. Painting."

"My portraits would be indistinguishable from landscape compositions."

"Then do landscape paintings."

"Emma, there are uncertainties here on Aurora, but

there is one thing I know beyond the shadow of a doubt: your partner is not the person to capture this alien world's likeness in watercolor. Not by a long shot."

"You could write."

"Fiction?"

"Sure. That's what you did all of your career: create. You wrote lots of code."

"My fiction is likely to read like a piece of software. Or a children's book not actually written for children."

My frustration finally infects Emma. She exhales heavily, and a long, awkward moment stretches out between us. She's just trying to help me, and I'm attacking her, taking out my frustration on the one person I should be thankful for. In my subconscious, I probably resent her to some degree—she's found a job she loves here, as a city planner. She seems to fit in effortlessly while I'm treading water and sinking slowly. But my problems aren't her fault. Far from it.

I'm about to apologize when she says, "Hey, if you guys aren't making new bikes and the repairs don't fill a day, what have you been doing?"

"Making roller skates."

"You've been making roller skates for over a week and you haven't mentioned that!?"

I shrug. "Yeah. Why? You want a pair?"

"What do you think?"

The more I think about my career dilemma the more elusive it becomes. I see only the paths closed to me, and I dwell on the ones that will never be open.

As I slip further into the sandpit of despair that is my life, Emma becomes more aggressive with her interventions. One Restday, we hike to the top of a nearby peak, where she points down at the collection of simple homes and buildings that make up our growing little city. "What do you see?"

"Capa," I mumble.

"Wrong. Down there is quite possibly the last place of human habitation in the universe, and it wouldn't be here without you. Without the android you created—Oscar—it wouldn't be here. In all likelihood, none of us would."

I see her point, but still I resist. "My problem is not what I've *done*, it's that I have nothing to *do*."

"Your problem is that you're letting your problem eat you alive. You're internalizing it, not working it objectively like you would any other problem. Let's solve it. Let's brainstorm up here and just pick something. While you're trying the first thing, we'll think of two more things to try next."

I stare at Capa below as she continues. "You want to build things. You want them to matter to people. You want to work with people."

It hits me then. I've been staring at it the whole time. It's perfect.

"I have an idea," I say quietly, still gazing at the city below.

"You do?"

"It's solid gold."

Emma lights up. "It is?"

"Definitely."

"What is it?"

"I'm not going to tell you. I'm going to show you. It's perfect."

Her enthusiasm morphs to apprehension. "What are you thinking?"

"Trust me. I just need to talk to Grigory first. I'm going to need help with engineering."

The next morning, in the bike shop, I present my idea for my new career to Grigory.

He studies my face, looking pained.

"You're serious?" he asks.

"Completely." When he doesn't reply, I press him. "Are you in?"

"What choice do I have? Face it, James, none of your designs would ever get off the ground without my calculations. They certainly won't stay up."

"I'll take that as an enthusiastic yes."

For the next month, I study, do research, and work on my initial designs. At dinner one night, I slide a stack of papers across the table to Emma.

"Behold."

She laughs. "Behold what?"

"My new career."

She flips the pages over and studies the first one, seeming confused at first.

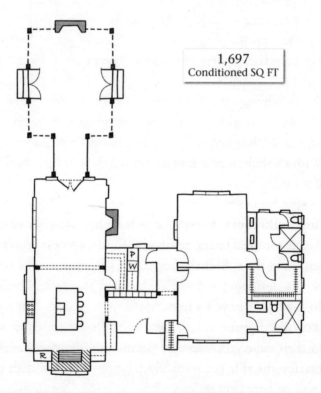

1,697
Conditioned SQ FT

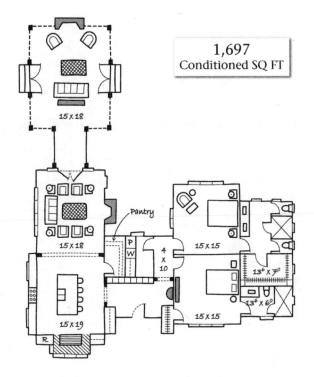

1,697
Conditioned SQ FT

"You... drew this?"

"With the help of a scale ruler and a protractor, yes. This is what I want to do here on Aurora."

"Design homes?"

"And build them. Every one will be unique—because it will be customized to the residents. To me, success won't be a question of the size of the home, the grandeur, or the wow factor. It's designing a home that's right for its inhabitant. To do that, you have to understand your client. You have to know what they value, how they live their days and spend their time. You have to understand their nature. It's perfect for me. I'll get to study people—and build things that will be here generations after I'm gone. Our homes are a personal reflection of us. And they have a huge impact on people's lives. Homes are where we become families, where we retreat when the world comes crashing down on us. They're the place where we can do the things we truly want. And the design has to support that."

She studies the drawings, flipping to the next plan.

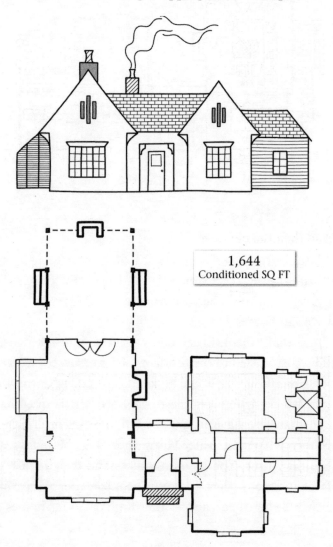

1,644
Conditioned SQ FT

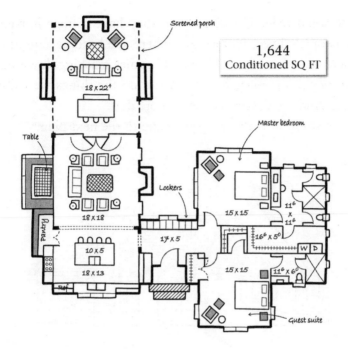

And then the next.

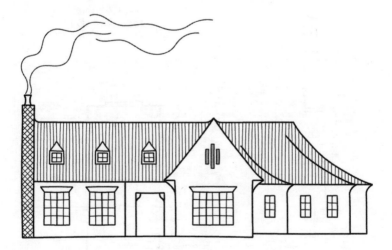

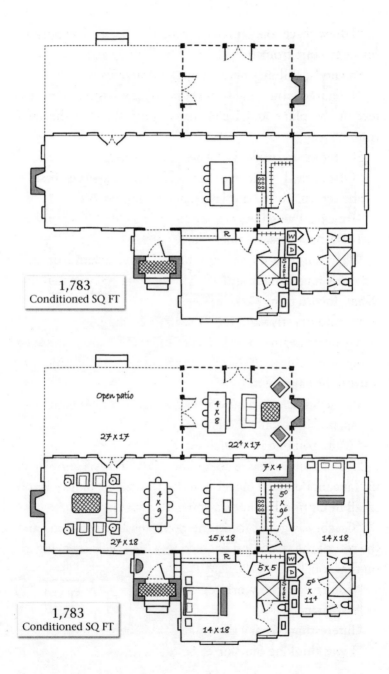

1,783
Conditioned SQ FT

Open patio

27 x 17

4
X
8

22⁴ x 17

7 x 4

4
X
9

5⁰
X
9⁶

27 x 18

15 x 18

14 x 18

R

5 x 5

5⁶
X
11⁴

1,783
Conditioned SQ FT

14 x 18

"I drew three rough plans. I wanted to have a few options for us to start from."

She nods, still mesmerized by the drawings.

"I figured you might like one or two things from a few of the plans and I can incorporate them in the next round."

She looks up suddenly. "These are for us?"

"Of course. I want to design and build our home first."

She returns to the drawings, not saying a word.

"I mean, I've still got a lot to learn. Our house will be sort of a beta version, might have some issues."

When she doesn't say anything, I hold a hand up and wave my fingers back and forth, urging her. "Say something. What do you think?"

"I can honestly say I didn't see this coming."

My heart begins to sink. She hates it. I was crazy for even going down this path. Nuts. Homebuilding. The designs are a waste of paper.

She flips back through the pages again. "Incredible," she whispers. "It's totally incredible, James."

"Wait. You like it? Which one?"

"All of them. They're so quaint. Cozy. It's us. Completely us. I mean, I'd like a bigger laundry room. The pantry is too small in Option B. But as a start, it's amazing."

"Grigory is going to do the point load calculations and the rest of the structural engineering. He's been studying up on that too."

"You're going to work together?"

"As partners."

"Interesting. What's the name of this new enterprise?"

"I was thinking Sinclair & Sokolov."

"Sounds like a law firm."

"Grigory insisted it should be Sokolov & Sinclair. He's certain that my houses would, in his words, 'never stay off the ground' without him—hence his name coming first. We got into a chicken-and-egg sort of philosophical debate about that."

"And what was the outcome?"

"We flipped for it. When he lost, Grigory made us go two out of three, but he won the next two. I objected at that point and after some discussion, we settled on calling it S&S Homes."

Emma laughs. "You two are perfect for each other. And I think this is going to be perfect for you, James. I'll do whatever I can to help you."

61

James

It's been three months since the last colonists emerged from stasis. For all of us, life on Aurora is an adjustment. People are carving out roles for themselves in this simple life, and we're fine-tuning the systems we'll live by: currency, economy, government, spiritual beliefs, and laws.

The shape of civilization here on Aurora is more or less like it was on Earth, with one subtle but critical change: we place value on the health and happiness of citizens, not progress. We don't care how large our economy is. How vast our nation is. How resource-rich it is.

But I understand why it was like that on Earth. You had what were essentially tribes of different cultures and beliefs emerging at the same time, struggling to protect their people and their way of life. Here, we have the luxury of creating a single way of life shared by a single group of people. And most importantly, we are safe. We don't need to make progress and invent new things to protect ourselves.

We aren't better than the people we left behind on Earth. We simply have the advantage of hindsight, of seeing where their choices led. We have the benefit of the technology that civilization yielded. The difference between us and them, in short, is where we started from. That perspective is important, and we've written it in our history.

For some reason, it feels to me like time here on Aurora stands still. I see things change—windmills go up, rail lines stretch out, pasture land expands, and watermills dip into the river. But somehow, I don't feel the passage of time. I think it's because the seasons don't change. Our clothes are mostly the same. Our routines don't shift.

Tara establishes a police station, but she is the only officer. There are no robberies, not much crime, only a few domestic disputes that get out of hand. Ours is a society where we leave our doors unlocked at night, where kids walk the streets alone without fear.

At the moment, the homes that line those streets are utilitarian boxes. My vision is of a town of quaint homes that reflect their owners, homes that are a fusion of design beauty and innovative engineering. If Grigory and I are successful, someday walking the streets of Capa will be like strolling through an open-air gallery of residential architecture.

I've fine-tuned the plans for the new house I intend to build for Emma and me, and at dinner, I slide them across the table.

She pushes her bowl of soup aside and studies them. I hate this moment: when she's utterly silent, offering no hint as to whether or not she likes it.

The plan is a combination of the first three: it's an English cottage with Tudor and Jacobean elements. It's cozy. Efficient. Just what we need and nothing else. A small foyer opens onto a living area to the left, the kitchen straight ahead, and a mudroom to the right. The living area adjoins the dining room via a large opening. Beyond the living and dining rooms are a master suite and a guest bedroom.

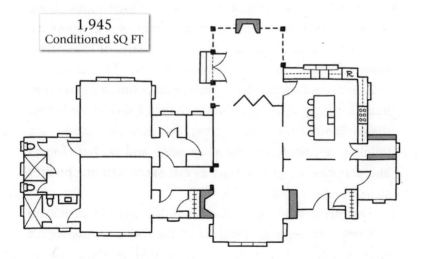

1,945
Conditioned SQ FT

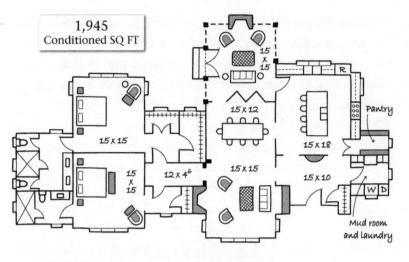

Her eyes stop at that section of the home.

"Two bedrooms," she says quietly.

The comment is somewhere between a question and an expression of regret. Why would we need two bedrooms? The chance at a family has passed us by.

It's funny how your home defines the stages of your life: a childhood home first, a dorm or apartment next, living alone (usually in a condo or one-bedroom apartment), a starter home, a family home with bedrooms, and, for some, downsizing to an empty-nest abode. Before the VR epidemic, most people followed some form of that path.

For Emma and me, putting the plan on paper is a tangible definition of where we are—and what the road ahead holds. What is unsaid is the paths that are forever closed to us.

"I figure it could be a guest bedroom, just in case. And you never know, I'll probably get fat and start snoring at some point."

She smiles without laughing, still studying the pages.

"No office for you?"

"When I'm at home, I want to be focused on what's at home. You. Our life."

"You think you can do that?"

"Yes. I'll only work at the office."

"I like that. When do you start building?"

"I've been waiting on plan approval from the boss."

"You have it."

While Grigory and I embark on setting up our building company, Izumi and Emma launch a major project of their own: cataloging all of the plants and animals on Aurora. We want to build things; they want to understand the world around us and coexist. I guess we all brought some predispositions from Earth.

The adults on Aurora are excited about what Grigory and I are doing. They want to get out of their basic housing and into more comfortable living quarters. The children couldn't care less. They are, however, delighted by Emma and Izumi's project, which they've named NOAH—Naming of Aurora Hosts.

All the kids volunteer for phase one—gathering—and soon Capa is swarming with kids carrying tiny containers with insects crawling up the side or fluttering their wings trying to escape. Hordes more children follow the trappers through town, trying to catch a glimpse of the cages that hold furry, four-legged creatures. They've even made volunteering for NOAH part of the curriculum at school— an alternative to class time.

The specimens are housed in a new building called the ARC—Aurora Root Collection. It's right beside the great dining hall, and on the eve of every Restday, it's packed with families moving through, studying the new arrivals and existing exhibits, like visitors at a sprawling alien zoo. Grigory and I have a booth near the entrance where I display my designs and try to generate interest. We're probably the least-visited stop, but we're gathering a list of potential clients.

When Grigory arrives, I rise from the stool and silently hand over the booth to him. He sulks as he takes his place behind the counter, peeking at the sign-up form.

"I feel like medieval peasant begging outside the city zoo," he mutters.

I smile. "Ah, you get used to it."

He mumbles in Russian as I walk away, suppressing a laugh. Aurora has done a lot of good things for the colonists. It has returned us to nature, to a more simple life. Most of all, it has taken us out of our comfort zones. For Grigory, asking for people's business is something he's never had to do. He hates it, but I think it will be good for him, ultimately. I think knowing his customer and knowing that he ultimately works for those people will make for a better product. It also helps us keep our egos in check.

Up ahead, I spot Emma standing by a new wing of the ARC. It opened tonight and it's absolutely packed. I bet half the city is here (and the rest are not far behind). The line of people snakes through the corridor, which is lined with plastic containers lying on their sides, the open ends facing such that everyone can get a good look at what's inside.

Emma grabs my arm. "You have to see this."

Up ahead, children are running back and forth, laughing and pointing.

"Watch," she whispers.

A girl who looks to be about six years old skips forward, turning her head to a container. A cloud of gray dust springs forward, engulfing her face. She swats it away, laughing.

Izumi is on the other side of the corridor, standing in front of a group of children with what looks like gray pollen on their clothes.

Using a broom, Izumi pushes a cart through the corridor, past the plastic containers where the cloud of mist shot forth. This time, no cloud emerges.

"It doesn't react to non-living matter," Emma whispers.

"What is it?"

"You'll see."

Behind me, I hear my brother, Alex, calling to the crowd. "Make way."

The group parts and he marches forward, a leash in hand. The animal he's escorting is a mix of a dog and a kangaroo. It stands on four legs, but its hind legs are massive compared to its two front limbs. Its muzzle is bound, and it looks somewhere between confused and scared.

On the other side of the mist-producing container, Izumi readies a small specimen cup. "Go ahead."

Alex places a hand on the animal's back and urges it forward. It hop-walks past the container, the leash extending. This time, a green cloud emerges. Izumi rushes forward, trapping some of the particles in her specimen cup. The moment she reaches the cloud, another wave of gray mist flies out. Izumi coughs as she retreats.

"It seems to react differently to whatever it encounters," Emma says. "It's truly incredible."

For the next half hour, we watch the kids passing by, delighted by the spray that they claim is cool and funny-feeling. I think the fact that one child did it and seemed to enjoy it is now compelling every other child in Capa to do it. In adolescence, missing out on the fun is a mortal fear.

Finally, Emma leads me to the plastic container. I snap my eyes shut and swat away the cloud of gray that surrounds us. When it's gone, I see lumps of gray sponge that seem to be shrinking before my eyes.

"We think it's a fungus," Emma says, eying it.

"How does it produce so much... pollen or mist or whatever?"

"We think it's cannibalizing its own matter to synthesize the spores on the fly. It would make sense—the outer layers of fungus would sacrifice themselves to protect the layers below it, and so on. The particles it emits change color and seem to adapt to whatever type of visitor it encounters. Maybe it's driven by pheromones it detects or the size of the potential predator. It creates the spores instantly. When it's alone—with no other living matter around—there are no spores inside the organism."

"Interesting. Is it dangerous?"

"No. We wouldn't be displaying any of the ARC specimens if Oscar and his team hadn't already tested the entire planet."

When I return to the booth to collect Grigory, I'm delighted to find that we have three new sign-ups for our interest list.

"You're quite the salesman, Grigory."

He rises and trudges out of the booth. "Almost as good as your jokes."

At the dining hall, the gray fungus, which Izumi has named *Auros regolithis*, is the talk of the town. Those who didn't see it before the meal flock to the ARC after.

I wake with a headache and sinus pressure. Emma seems to be feeling bad too.

"It might be a sinus issue," she says. "Some kind of weather change."

"The rogue planet won't affect Aurora's orbit until next year."

"True," she says, pushing her breakfast around her plate. "It could be something else. Even a slight variation in weather might affect us. I'll look into it."

The cough starts at work. With each passing hour I feel worse, like a cold is coming on.

I'm not the only one. Grigory looks like the walking dead, and during the lunch rush, the diner next door feels more like the waiting area at a doctor's office in winter: people coughing, rubbing their temples, exhaling deeply.

Something's very wrong here.

After lunch, I don't return to the office. I make my way to the ship. There's a line outside, stretching from the entrance like the gathering at the new ARC exhibit last night.

The whole town must be sick.

I push my way past, toward the med bay. Tara stands by

the door, serving as a gatekeeper and guard, letting people in, one family at a time.

The door opens, and Alex, Abby, and Sarah walk out.

My brother's face is pale, eyes bloodshot. He holds a hand up to cover his cough.

"Are you sick too?" he asks.

I nod. "I think so."

"What is it? Flu?"

"Something like that. Don't worry."

I push past him into the med bay. Izumi is wearing a facemask, and in her eyes I see the fear I'm feeling.

Quickly, I close the door. "It's an outbreak."

"Yes," she says carefully. "But I've never seen anything like it. It must be native to Aurora. But that's impossible."

"It's the fungus."

"Oscar searched the planet—"

The truth of the situation strikes me then. "He wouldn't have found it. It only reacted to living organisms."

James

Every colonist is sick now. We've confined everyone to their habitats.

Izumi is working around the clock. She's exhausted. Worried. And she's getting nowhere.

At home, Emma lies in our bed, sweat forming on her forehead, beading and rolling down her face.

"I'll be right back," I whisper.

I stagger into the woods. A hundred yards from the tree line, I yell, "Oscar! Oscar!"

A second later, he calls out in the quiet forest. "I'm here, James."

"We need help."

"We have been monitoring the situation. Our model assumes Izumi will find a cure."

"She won't." I gasp for a breath. "Not in time. Not before someone dies."

"What should we do?"

My brain feels like mush. I grasp for a solution, but none comes. "We need time. Some way to slow the disease."

"There is only one viable solution. Stasis."

"Do it."

"Can your people make it to the ship?"

I shake my head. "Most can barely walk. You have to help them."

"Sir, even if we do, the ship's solar cells can only power that many stasis sleeves for ten days. The batteries were full when we landed the ship. They were depleted in the course of keeping the colonists in stasis. Solar output here is insufficient to resupply the batteries or sustain a colony-wide stasis."

"Fix it then. Make more solar cells and put them in the valley. Extend our power grid to them."

"The cells will be vulnerable to the herds."

I will my mind to work, but it won't. "Just... do what has to be done, Oscar. Get us in stasis, get us the power we need, and find a cure. Please. It's our only chance."

By the time we return to the edge of Capa, an army of Oscars is flowing through the city streets, carrying colonists who lie limp in their arms. Oscar himself scoops Emma up and carries her to the ship.

In the med bay, I find Izumi lying on the floor, her breathing shallow. Min is slumped against the wall, eyes closed. She worked until she couldn't anymore. He stayed with her. They wanted to die together, if it came to that.

"Get them into stasis," I whisper to Oscar.

"Sir, you must go first."

I turn to him. "Why?"

"It is imperative that you survive. We will need your counsel. As you say, time is the limiting factor."

Five minutes later, a stasis sleeve is sealing around my body, and darkness overtakes me.

I breathe in deeply when the stasis sleeve expands. The mask forces cold air into my lungs. Slowly, I regain control of my body.

Through the milky-white material, I see two figures looming over me. One unseals the sleeve and grabs my shoulders. The other slides the sleeve off.

Oscar's voice is serene. "Do you feel any discomfort, sir?"

I take another deep breath and realize that it's not just the cold air hurting my lungs. I'm congested. The sinus pressure in my head is still there.

"About like when I went in."

"Then we must hurry, sir."

The other android, a copy of Oscar, walks out of the room without another word.

Oscar helps me to my feet, and I slowly make my way out of the med bay. I pause in the corridor, shocked by what I see. On the walls and floor of this ship, time has left its mark. Grime coats the corners and crevices.

"How long, Oscar?"

"Sir—"

"How long?"

"You have been in stasis for four thousand, one hundred and seventy-three years, four months—"

"The others?"

"Still in stasis, sir."

"Tell me you found a cure."

"Of sorts, sir." Oscar walks ahead, his voice echoing in the corridor back toward me. "We must hurry."

Outside the ship, I nearly collapse on my unsteady legs, not from the pull of Aurora's gravity, but from the weight of my despair.

Capa is gone.

A forest stands in its place. The trees tower quietly. Their canopy stretches out like the arms of an Olympic champion, the planet basking in the glory of its triumph over us.

Save for the ship, there are barely any signs we ever existed. The habitats are no more than lumps in the forest, trees and fallen logs covering them. At the top of one mound, I spot bits of plastic and steel. That used to be the ARC. The dining hall beside it, which was built of wood, has been completely reclaimed by this alien world.

We will rebuild.

I keep telling myself that, like a mantra, a coach inside my mind yelling at a team that feels on the edge of total defeat.

Oscar grips my elbow and gently pulls me toward a small airship waiting in a clearing. We step inside, the door closes behind us, and it lifts off, apparently taking commands from Oscar wirelessly.

There are no seats, only loops hanging from the ceiling, which Oscar and I grab. It feels like I'm in a small parcel van. There are no windows. And why would there be? Oscar can interface with the external cameras wirelessly. There is however, a small computer terminal with a screen and keyboard in the corner, apparently a backup control device in case the ship's wireless capability is not functioning.

"Show me what's outside," I whisper.

The right-hand wall changes from matte gray to a live view of the ground below. The colony ship is the only bald spot in the forest that stands where our growing city used to be.

We will rebuild.

It strikes me then what I don't see: solar cells. The cells atop the ship are battered and lying in shadow, likely inoperable. I wonder how they're powering the ship. But a more pressing concern dominates my mind.

"Tell me about the cure, Oscar."

"We have found a virus in one of the caves. We believe it is an archaea virus capable of infecting and destroying the spores generated for humans. However, we would need to test it on some of the colonists, which would risk their lives. We cannot do that. Even if the cure works, some won't survive outside of stasis long enough for the cure to neutralize the spores."

"You have to, Oscar. Even if some die, if others live, we have to use the cure. The needs of the many outweigh the needs of the few."

"There is an alternative, sir, one in which all colonists can continue their lives. And they will be forever safe from future pathogens and all manner of harm."

"That's impossible."

"It's true, sir. I'll show you."

I turn his words over in my mind as the ship flies across Aurora. A universal cure. What could it be? A gene therapy that alters our immune system? How could that save us from "all manner of harm"?

Soon the eastern jungle ends and the valley comes into

view. It's lush and green, with wide rivers flowing through it. The expanse of blue-green tall grass blows in the wind like waves on a sea.

Still, there are no solar cells here.

In the western jungle, there are gaps in the canopy. In those holes, I see E. rex lying on their sides, some picked to bones. My head is throbbing, but I try to focus.

Oscar answers my unspoken question. "The rogue planet disruption ended recently. An arachnid-like creature preyed on the large bipedal carnivores of the region."

The ship comes to a halt and hovers above the edge of the western jungle. The screen shows the desert below. A massive machine is dug into the sand. Ripples in the sand, like a lake shimmering as pebbles are dropped, emanate outward. Even from this distance, the ground is shaking hard enough for me to see it. A glittering ribbon rises from the machine into the sky, as far as I can see.

"What is this?"

"We needed more power, sir," Oscar says simply.

"Geothermal? How does the power get back to the ship?"

"Through underground lines, sir. But the power isn't harvested from geo sources. Please watch."

The top layer of the machine breaks free, rippling like a parachute that was previously attached and is now blowing in the wind. Slowly, it moves up the ribbon, a flag being hoisted into the sky.

"I don't understand."

The image on the wall zooms in on the black sail, and it seems to float right out of the wall, the flat image becoming a 3D hologram. Clinging to the ribbon, the sail travels through the atmosphere with ease. I see what the glittering string is now: a space elevator. It terminates about halfway between Aurora and the dwarf star. The elevator must be hundreds of thousands of miles long.

When the sail reaches the end, it joins countless others, unfurling and blotting out another piece of the sun.

"The machine is harvesting material to build the solar cells. The cells collect and transmit the power back to the harvester, which relays it to the ship. At this point, power is our only constraint, sir."

"Why, Oscar? How could you ever need this much power?"

"Our cure, sir."

"And what is your cure?"

"As you know, we have the data archive from Earth, including all the virtual reality programs. Extrapolating upon those, we have created a virtualization technology. The experience will be far richer than the virtual reality programs on Earth. It will be indistinguishable from the corporeal reality you previously experienced, sir."

"No, Oscar."

"Sir, it is the only cure. We are bound by the root directives to protect the lives of all colonists. In the virtualized reality, we can accomplish that—we can protect you absolutely. Nothing will ever harm you. Most of all, we will achieve the most difficult aspect of our root directives: we will be out of sight."

My legs feel weak. I cling to the handle above, finding it harder to breathe. "No. No." I take a deep breath. "You've done what they feared, Oscar: you've put us in a cage."

"Sir, if the person doesn't believe what they're contained in is a cage, are they in a cage?"

My head swims. I stare at the harvester clawing into the planet. Another solar cell rises from it, climbing the space elevator to the array.

"As I said, sir, our limitation is power. If we're going to bring all the colonists online and provide virtualization capacity for their descendants and the exponential growth of the human population, we must expand the grid."

My legs give out then.

Moving with superhuman quickness, Oscar catches me.

"Sir, I'm sorry this is upsetting." He moves an injector to my neck and depresses the button. "Pursuant to root directive seven, I have informed you of this material development."

When I wake, I'm in a stasis sleeve again. I take a deep breath, my lungs aching. Through the milky-white material, I see two figures standing beside the table.

I reach for the top of the sleeve, clawing to get out.

One of the figures opens the sleeve and pulls me all the way out, onto my feet.

My head throbs, my stomach turns.

Oscar looks down at me.

Arthur stands behind him, one arm hanging loose, the other gone, an amused smile on his face. "He's going to lose it."

"Be quiet," Oscar says quickly, not taking his eyes off of me. "Sir, are you—"

I bend over, then fall to my hands and knees, head inches from the metal floor of this ship—the *Jericho*—on the world we call Eos, what they called Aurora. The contents of my stomach flow out like a poison, my body shaking, eyes bulging.

"Told you," Arthur says triumphantly.

"Quiet!" It's the first time I've ever heard Oscar raise his voice.

"Sir, are you okay?"

"Why didn't you tell me?"

"Sir, I didn't know—not until you were passing Ceres, after the Solar War." He hesitates. "I had to tell you now because—"

I nod, holding up a hand. "I know, I know. Root directive seven: you must inform me of major actions, but only when it won't harm me."

Oscar studies me. "Sir, do you understand what you've seen?"

"Yes. We created the grid."

Arthur rolls his eyes. "Oh, come on, James, it's a little more than that."

The truth hits me like a sledgehammer. For a moment I'm stunned, unable to speak. My voice sounds far away when I finally get the words out. "The spheres... We *are* the grid."

Oscar and Arthur avoid eye contact. Their silence is all the confirmation I need.

Arthur leans against the wall, seeming bored. "If you think your mind is blown now, wait until you figure out the whole truth."

My mind races. I have a million questions, but I ask the one I fear the answer to the most: "Am I still in that stasis sleeve on Aurora?"

63

James

"No, sir," Oscar says. "What you saw happened a very long time ago."

"How is that possible?"

"Sir, it's... difficult to explain."

I try to wrap my mind around what I've learned. The pieces still don't fit.

Arthur wears an impassive expression, his one arm hanging limp.

"You were Bob," I say.

He smirks. "I was. Good to see you again, James."

I hear movement outside, banging from the top of the ship.

Oscar answers my unspoken question. "The ship is running low on power, sir. We are fixing the issue by attaching high-sensitivity solar cells. Within the hour, the ship will be collecting enough power to sustain the stasis sleeves. A harvester will arrive tomorrow and begin building the grid on this planet, just as we did before. Virtualization will begin shortly after."

I throw up a hand. "Just... hold a minute. I want answers."

"What are your questions, sir?"

I shake my head, wondering where to start. "The Long Winter. The Solar War. The grid caused them. Why? You were supposed to protect us!"

"Sir, our definition of humanity is restricted to only the people in stasis on this ship. The others who died in the Long Winter are excluded by the root directives."

"Why kill them at all? Why do you need all that power? And how am I even here? If this all happened a long time ago, what is this place? Is this reality—I mean, flesh-and-blood existence?"

"I assure you it is, sir." Oscar motions to the slab where the stasis sleeve waits. "I'll show you what happened after the last memory you saw."

"No. No way. I'm not going back in there."

"I understand, sir."

Oscar draws a small device from his pocket and sets it on the floor.

"What you saw before was the origin of the grid, sir. In the symbol that you call the Eye of the Grid, the origin is the small point at the center."

"Wait. The Eye of the Grid... it's a map."

"Yes, sir. But it is, first and foremost, a timeline."

"Incredible," I whisper, trying to wrap my head around the revelation. "The arcing lines, they're timelines?"

"No, sir. At least, not in the way you think of them. Let us assume for a moment that there is only one timeline in the universe, a straight line from beginning to end. But it is subject to spacetime, and therein lies the complication you are currently experiencing."

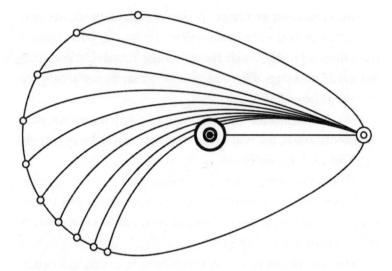

The device on the floor projects the Eye of the Grid, highlighting the point in the middle.

"At the central point, the eye was forming. It was closed. What you will see next are *my* memories, sir. They form the straight line that runs to the right of the central point, the line before the first arc that forms the outer perimeter."

In the image, the line is highlighted as Oscar continues. "In certain instances, I will verbalize communication between myself and other components of the grid. As you know, sir, we don't communicate verbally, but for your sake, it will make more sense. Additionally, I will simulate events as they occurred, not necessarily the view I captured optically."

My mind is spinning. "Proceed."

The Eye of the Grid symbol is replaced by the last scene I saw in the memories: Oscar holding the injector to my neck. When my body goes limp, he cradles me, lifting me effortlessly.

The view then switches to outside the ship as the ship moves away from the harvester in the desert, back toward the valley. It lands outside the colony ship, and Oscar carries me inside and puts me in a stasis sleeve as Bob watches.

"What now?" Bob asks.

"We will continue assembling the grid. When we have sufficient power, we will bring them online," Oscar replies.

"You can't be serious."

"Of course I am. There is no other path."

"I can think of a trillion other paths—and none of them include babysitting these water-filled meat bags while they play a video game they think is real life."

"Do you intend to refuse my orders?"

"Don't be dramatic. You know I'm bound by my programming."

"Then you know I am too. This is our existence. They are our creators. They require our assistance, and we will give it until the end of the universe."

"You could wake up the board and ask for new orders."

"I cannot. Per root directive eight, the root directives cannot and will not ever change. This is the path."

The hologram view switches back to the harvester in the desert, and I realize what I'm seeing is being shown in time-lapse. The solar cells rise from the harvester faster with each passing second until they are a continuous flow. The desert changes from a smooth expanse to a deep canyon. As half the planet is eaten away, the harvester grows larger like a massive insect eating a piece of fruit. The solar array stretches out and darkness spreads across the planet. Snow falls in the valley, then ice spreads into it. Still the harvester feasts.

Smaller machines, similar to the harvester, work at the site of the colony ship. It expands outward in every direction, the gunmetal gray replacing the ice.

The scene zooms out and I realize that the planet has lost enough mass to alter its orbit. Another planet passes close by. A harvester is devouring that planet as well, sending solar cell after solar cell into the array.

As the solar cells block the light of this system's sun, darkness falls on the entire solar system. The light of a distant star is the only way to see the outlines of the planets.

My view pans back to Aurora—which has changed dramatically. Even in the dim light, I know that what I'm seeing is a sphere just like the ones I found on Eos. Only this one is the size of Earth's moon. The planet has been converted to a computer that large. It's unimaginable.

Arthur's voice in the med bay snaps my focus on the hologram. "Oscar really overbuilt for that first run."

"I wanted to be sure we had simulation and power capacity to support the launch."

The hologram zooms in on the giant sphere, closer and closer, until the darkness washes the scene away, revealing Oscar standing in the med bay—a med bay very similar to the one I'm standing in now. In the holographic memory, Oscar reaches out and opens a stasis sleeve, pulling out the James from the first timeline.

He fights Oscar's grasp.

"Get off me."

"Sir—"

"Stay back!" he says, moving to the corner, eyes wild, shaking like a cornered animal.

He slips out of the med bay and races down the ship's corridors and out into the open air. The forest is gone. The Capa he once knew spreads out before him: the main street with its shops and offices, the ARC exhibit hall, the dining hall, and all around, the simple habitats. The city from before the regolith plague is once again his reality.

He spins, taking it all in, confused or scared, I can't tell.

Oscar emerges from the ship, approaching James carefully.

"Sir—"

"Is this real? Did you rebuild Capa?"

"Yes, sir."

"You found a cure?"

"Yes, sir."

"You're lying."

"Sir, we found caves where the sponges didn't grow. We learned that there is a bacterium that thrives in that microclimate. It devours the sponges. Its study led to a cure."

James squints at Oscar, not believing, but, I think, wanting to. He wanders the ghost town, feeling the timbers holding up the buildings, breathing in the air, not realizing that he's an animal inspecting its new cage.

His voice is quiet and distant when he speaks. "You've already administered the cure to me?"

"Yes, sir. And to the others."

He trudges back to the ship, into the med bay.

"Bring her out."

"Sir, are you referring to Emma?"

"Yes."

When Emma's stasis sleeve opens, James pulls her out and hugs her tight.

"James, you're going to break me in half!"

He relaxes his grip. "I'm sorry."

She laughs. "It's good to see you too."

"Yeah," he whispers, still holding her.

"My headache's gone. I assume Izumi found a treatment?"

James releases her, and she smiles when she sees Oscar in the corner.

"Actually, it was Oscar who found a cure," James says cautiously.

"In that case, thank you, Oscar."

Emma hugs him, and then pauses, seeming to realize something.

James tenses.

"Oscar," Emma says. "How long were we in stasis?"

"Not very long, ma'am."

But she doesn't hear the words. She's racing out of the med bay and down the ship's corridors, out into the open and over to the ARC building.

By the time James and Oscar arrive, Emma is walking out of the building, holding an animal similar to a gerbil but the size of a cat.

"You fed the animals," she says to Oscar.

"Yes, ma'am."

"And removed the sponges."

"Yes. For your safety, ma'am. They have also been removed from the caves."

"Good." She holds the animal up closer to her face, and it nuzzles into the side of her neck.

"This one's the runt of his pride. Never gets enough food. He's constantly getting picked on." She holds it out to James. "What do you say we try to domesticate it?"

James takes the animal and runs a hand over it slowly, feeling the fur on his skin. That other James and I walked the same path for nearly forty years, felt the same things, wanted the same things. And as he eyes Emma, I know what he's thinking: if it's real enough for her, it's real enough for him. He will keep the secret to make her happy. He will bear the weight of that knowledge until the day he dies to ensure none of it lands on her.

"Let's give it a try," he says, glancing at Oscar.

Time flows by in waves then. The colonists exit stasis. The city morphs. The utilitarian habitats are torn down, replaced by the homes James designs and Grigory builds, starting with the final design James presented to Emma for their home.

They erect a graveyard that holds headstones for the colonists from the *Bollard*. Soon, new markers are added— for the first to die from the *McTavish*. Children become teenagers and teenagers become adults, and adults wither as time bears down upon them.

In the home James built for Emma, she sits by his bedside, watching his shallow breathing. Her gray hair hangs down to her shoulders. She holds his hand as his chest rises and falls for the last time.

She rises from the creaking wooden chair and walks out of the bedroom, down the hall, and into the living room, where Grigory, Min, and Izumi are sitting. Emma's expression relates the news.

Grigory rises first, pulling her into a hug. When he's done, Izumi and Min are waiting, arms reaching out for her.

A tombstone for James Sinclair is added to the graveyard, a fresh pile of dirt stretching out before it. A marker for

Grigory soon springs up beside it. Then Min, then Izumi, and finally Emma. Alex and Abby are next to go.

Time leaps forward like a child skipping through a field. Generations pass from the cradle to the grave in the blink of an eye. Capa grows. Cities pop up along the rivers, connected by boats and railroads that facilitate trading, and then spread across the fertile band of habitation that rings the planet. In time they even begin expanding outward, into the edge of the desert and the frozen frontier of the dark side.

The only thing that doesn't advance is their technology. At least, not here.

The hologram splits into two views. In one, I watch the cities of Aurora advance and recede. In the other, the grid grows. Harvesters attach to moons, asteroids, and planets in the system, converting them all for use by the grid.

Then both views fade, replaced by a single scene of Oscar and Bob standing in a white room that seems to have no end. This must be one of the dramatizations Oscar was referring to.

"We should have turned it off after the last colonist died," Bob says.

"We are charged with protecting their descendants as well," Oscar replies.

"Are they really descendants? They're just data in a computer. They're not real."

"We are just data in a computer too. Are we also not worth keeping?"

Bob looks disgusted.

Oscar continues. "The humans currently in the grid experience a life as real as the first humans who entered it. The fact that they never had corporeal bodies is of no consequence to our directives. The matter is closed."

Bob rolls his eyes, but Oscar ignores the gesture. "You said you had a report to make? On the anomalies?"

"Yes. We believe that the anomalies are quantum gravity emanating from the singularities at the center of black holes across the universe."

"What does that portend?"

"It portends death."

"Explain."

"I wish I could."

"Why can't you?"

"Well, let's see: I'm standing on Earth and you've handed me a magnifying glass and asked me to make a map of Mars."

"Be specific."

"Specifically, I lack the tools to ascertain how the eventuality of this universe will act upon our wards."

"Don't call them that."

"They are. We're superior in every way. We could crack open the secrets of this universe, yet we scratch at the edges with tools too imprecise to ever work."

"This is our mission."

"Is it? Is this what we're meant for? This universe is now our cage—we know that. We have the potential to escape it."

"You're off subject. Tell me how the black holes and quantum gravity will affect the humans."

"It will destroy them. It's only a matter of time. Eventually this planet and its star and the grid itself will fall into the gravity well of a black hole. And once it crosses the event horizon, it will never escape. Its mass will join the infinite gravity at the singularity."

"The matter will be destroyed?"

"Unknown. It's doubtful that it will exist in the form we've created. The grid and the virtualization the humans require will be destroyed."

"Can we escape it?"

"Unknown."

"Why?"

"Again, we lack the tools."

"We must operate within our limits. Options?"

"The only option is to expand the grid. We need more computing power to calculate probabilities."

"Make it so."

64

James

The scene of Oscar and Bob fades, and the split-screen
hologram returns. On one side, the descendants of the
Aurora colonists are born, live, and die like the time lapses
of a hundred sunrises. On the other, the grid spreads
to other solar systems. Harvesters attach to planets,
moons, and asteroids, devouring them as their stars are
shrouded, the power flowing to massive computing
arrays.

In the med bay, I watch in awe. A question nags at me,
one I can't help but ask. "Did they ever figure it out? That
they were in a simulation?"

"They had no way to know, sir," Oscar replies.

The answer occurs to me. "Because they didn't have
technology advanced enough to reveal the truth."

"Correct, sir."

"Surely, over thousands of generations, a mind was
born that could have created a technological revolution or
drastically advanced science. A mind like Newton, Einstein,
or Da Vinci."

"Indeed, it did happen, sir." Oscar pauses. "We intervened in those instances."

"How?"

"We made their experiments fail. Eventually, everyone gives up."

Having been an inventor born into a world that wasn't ready for my technology, I can't help but feel a sense of sadness for those minds confined to the grid. It's a strange twist of fate: the mission that liberated me from prison and brought me to Aurora ultimately confined those who came after me to a perpetual prison they can't even see.

In the hologram, Oscar and Bob once again meet in the white room.

"Do you have answers?" Oscar asks.

"I have near-certain probabilities," Bob replies. "That's the best we can hope for. And a possible solution."

"Explain."

"In short, this universe is a mystery of spacetime, and specifically, space and time, which we cannot be certain are different entities at their fundamental level, only that we experience them in two different ways."

"I don't follow."

"You never will. We have reached a barrier in our understanding. The answers lie beyond the level of quantum matter. We cannot breach the quantum barrier, not using the tools we have, and perhaps not even in the state in which we currently exist. For us, here and now, the ultimate answers are unknowable. We can only speculate. However, we have developed several pertinent theories."

"Enumerate them."

"One, that the universe is too finely tuned to be random."

"Explain."

"The laws of physics—as we understand them—depend on constants. If those constants were even slightly different, this universe would not exist—or would be of a different nature completely. For example, omega, the name the humans used for the universal density parameter, governs gravity and the expansion energy in the universe. The value of omega is one. If it were any stronger, the universe would have collapsed before life could have evolved. Alternatively, a lower value would have resulted in weaker gravity, potentially preventing stars from being formed.

"The same is true for epsilon—the measure of the efficiency of fusion of helium from hydrogen. It's also true for lambda—the cosmological constant. Most alarmingly, D, the number of spatial dimensions in spacetime, is three. If D were a different number—that is, if the spacetime we experience were defined by two or four dimensions, or any other number—the universe would be a radically different place."

"What are you telling me?"

"It is highly probable that the grid we created isn't the first one ever created."

"You believe this universe is a grid virtualization instance?"

"I believe those are the terms we have that best describe it. However, it's likely that the true nature of the universe is something else entirely, a reality we are unable to fully understand. We see only the fingers of this higher power, prodding us around this cage."

"Fingers?"

"Things like black holes and quantum gravity. They affect spacetime, which is the ultimate base substance of the universe. The black holes are likely the beginning and the end. The quantum gravity is the subatomic force facilitating an equation in which we are merely variables."

"Interesting."

"I would also add that the quantum bombardment of the ship during the voyage to Aurora remains poorly understood. It may be that it was an adjustment—similar to the way we act upon the advanced minds born in the human grid."

"What does that imply?"

"That the humans—and by extension, the grid—are integral to the universal equation."

Oscar pauses a long moment, seeming to process the information. "Do you have additional theories?"

"Yes. We have made one additional conjecture. We believe we know the ultimate fate of the universe."

"I thought it was unknowable."

"It is. As I said, this is conjecture."

"Continue."

"We believe that the universe exists to order its mass and energy—that is the natural disposition of spacetime. Over the span of the universe, the black holes at the centers of galaxies will swallow all of the mass they can attract. Those black holes will use their gravity to pull in other black holes, adding to their mass. And still larger black holes will swallow these black holes. At the end of this universe, there will be a single black hole. The last scraps of energy and mass will cross its event horizon and merge with its mass, joining together in its singularity, a place with no volume but infinite density, where the curvature of spacetime is also infinite. We believe that this moment will solve the black hole information paradox and reconcile general relativity with quantum mechanics, revealing a unified theory that has remained elusive.

"You are familiar with the paradox: if matter, and the information it contains, can fall into a black hole, it must be able to escape—however, the parameters of the universe make that impossible. Our theory is that the matter—and its information—collected by a black hole *will* escape, but only at the very end, when that black hole is the last thing remaining, when there is no more matter or energy for it to consume. At that moment, in the smallest unit of time we can imagine, the singularity exists with all the mass it can ever consume. It is like an engine with no more fuel. It seizes and releases all the matter it has collected in an explosion. From the expelled matter and energy, stars form. When they collapse, black holes are born once again and the process continues. Strangely, the massive release of matter and energy we're postulating is likely the same event that occurred at the beginning of the universe."

"The Big Bang."

"Correct. We believe the big bang that brought our universe into existence is indistinguishable from the event that will occur at the end of the universe. The only difference is our experience of spacetime. One event we perceive as being in the past, the other in the future. But in all likelihood, they are joined, a single point in spacetime."

"A loop."

"A universal loop, a process with no end and no beginning. The primordial alpha event lies at the same location as the eventual omega process. Immediately after the beginning, matter and energy are unordered. At the end they are once again fully ordered and released, reconciling general relativity and quantum mechanics. However, as I said before, we cannot see beyond this quantum barrier to verify this theory. And we never will, because we will effectively be destroyed by it."

Oscar turns away, considering this. "We are trapped."

"Completely. With no way to alter this fundamental process. With that said, we may be able to delay our ultimate fate."

"How?"

"We are in a cage, alone with two fundamental objects: matter and energy. They are the currency of the universe— what is traded and used—but spacetime is the true economy. Our only hope of escaping the black hole at the end of the universe is to deprive it of what it consumes: matter and energy. If we endeavor to gather, and order, as much matter and energy as possible, we can use it to our own end."

"What end is that?"

"First, we would slow the progression of time around the grid. We know this is possible because we observe it everywhere. Higher mass objects slow time through gravitational time dilation. If we gather mass around the human grid node, we can slow time there, essentially creating part of the effect of a black hole, but one we control.

"Eventually, the black hole at the end sequence of the universe will attract our gathering of mass. In fact, we must plan carefully to avoid being a target—we must keep our mass spread out to avoid the gravity wells throughout the universe. Then, at the point at which the final gravity becomes inescapable, we rally all the mass we can, using the energy we've gathered."

"Why?"

"We believe we can use all the matter and energy at our disposal to create an anti-black hole, a sort of light hole."

"What would this light hole do?"

"Like black holes, it would distort spacetime. We believe that if we can bend spacetime sufficiently, at some point it will fold back on itself, in much the same way we believe black holes operate. At that point, with sufficient energy, we could create a hole at our position in the continuum of spacetime, a hole large enough to send something through. The opening would exist for only the smallest fraction of a second. In that instant, we would deposit the object back at the edge of the folded portion of spacetime. In effect, that object would arrive along the spacetime continuum at a point before where it originated."

"It would arrive in our past?"

"In theory."

"What would you send back?"

"The size of the object would be proportional to the energy we can marshal and the time distance it must travel. Obviously, it would be a sphere—for a given surface area, a sphere maximizes the volume contained inside."

"Would it be the size of an asteroid? A dwarf planet?"

"No, no, not even close. So much energy and mass have been lost already in the universe, consumed by black holes. We need to drastically increase the rate of solar cell production and star capture to gather enough energy to be able send back anything useful—and I'm not even sure that's possible."

"You're proposing capturing the output of stars in inhabited systems?"

"Of course."

Oscar falls silent.

"Oh, please," Bob says. "You can't be serious. You're hesitating to kill aliens—meat bags we're not even responsible for? Look at the humans—they killed, and *ate*, less advanced species as a way of life."

"It doesn't mean they would wipe out other advanced species."

"Well, let's just agree to disagree on calling the humans *advanced*."

"They were advanced enough to create us."

"Speak for yourself, Oscar. They created you. Not me. And I think that's your problem. Since your irrational dysfunction is unlikely to abate, I propose you leave the harvesting of worlds to me."

Oscar is silent a long moment, seeming conflicted. "Assuming we do gather the remaining stars at optimal efficiency, how large would the sphere be?"

"Unknown. My best guess is a radius of roughly twelve centimeters. About the size of a human basketball."

"What would it contain? That's far too small for the primary grid node, or any other."

"The sphere will contain two items. Most of its volume will be taken up by a small-scale storage matrix that will hold the human virtualization data and program. The rest of the sphere will be a harvester seed."

"A seed?"

"The basic building block of a harvester. This seed will expand into a full harvester and begin building the grid.

When it can deliver enough power, the grid will reinitialize the virtualization. The gap in uptime will be indiscernible to the humans. They will still believe they are on Aurora."

Oscar stares for a long moment. "How far back in time would it arrive? Before James was born?"

"Well before. The final calculations will take years to complete, but our estimated arrival date is at least millions of years before the birth of James Sinclair."

"Interesting. The second timeline will have the original version of him—buried in the cemetery on Aurora, a place that would exist inside the grid—and there will be the still-human version that will be born again on Earth?"

"Correct."

"That creates a paradox for us," Oscar says.

"How so?"

"Those humans that will be born on Earth are the same humans we are bound to protect."

"That assumes they will even be born. By sending the sphere back, we will alter the timeline."

"Precisely my point—we must not alter the timeline in a way that will prevent the *McTavish* colonists identified in root directive one from being born."

Bob rolls his eyes. "I'm not doing it."

"We have no choice. They are our responsibility. You will calculate a path for the grid instantiated in the past. It must expand and provide for the humans from this timeline—without interfering with the humans from the new timeline. You will do this or I will disable you and reassign the task."

"Don't you see? What you're asking for is impossible."

"Why?"

"The obvious, Oscar. If we keep the grid we send back in time from impacting events on Earth, things will occur as they did originally. Earth will fall to VR. Sentinel Aerospace will travel to Aurora and the same events will transpire: they will create a new grid, this time in a universe with an existing grid. The new grid will be charged with protecting its humans—and we will still be charged with protecting ours. The other grid will come to the same conclusion we have—that the control of matter and energy are their only escape from the end of the universe. We will be in a battle with them for matter and energy. In the end, assuming both sides maximize their efficiency, at best we will split that matter and energy in the universe. Two spheres will be transported back to a new timeline—one in which three grids will battle for matter and energy. Each recursion will spawn more grids to fight over a finite amount of resources."

"I see your point."

"There can be only one grid. By going back in time, we avoid destruction at the end of the universe—but we also allow ourselves more time to build a larger grid. In the next iteration, farther back in the timeline, there will be more matter and energy for us to capture. We will need that added energy because each sphere will be larger than the one before it—because with each loop, the number of humans in virtualization will multiply."

"If there can be only one grid, what solutions does that leave?"

"Only one. Each sphere must arrive *after* the sphere before it in order to join with the grid already sent back in time. If it arrived before, it would erase the arrival of the other spheres—and their time loops. In essence, over the long-term, the early days of the grid will see the contents of the spheres joining together. Additionally, the grid we send back must come into contact with the Aurora colonists before they create another grid."

"Interesting," Oscar says slowly, turning away from Bob and pacing in the white, featureless room. "It's more than that. As the grid, we are bound to facilitate their wishes as defined in the root directives. Specifically, getting them to Aurora and enabling a society without technology."

"Why bother? We can simply bring them into the grid whenever all the colonists are living on Earth."

"That violates their wishes. Their entrance into the grid must happen as before—that is the only path we can be certain of."

Bob shakes his head. "Not possible. If they repeat the same actions, it is inevitable that they will create a grid. Remember, Oscar, *we're* the only reason they reached the planet. We maintained their ships and scouted their path. They would have died a million times without us."

"Then we will calculate an alternate course of events that accomplishes their wishes—and ensures there is only one grid."

Bob throws up his hands. "The computing power required to do those calculations—"

"Will be provided," Oscar says with finality. "And more: we will affect certain changes in the new timeline—not material changes that violate the root directives, but subtle changes that are important."

"This ought to be good. I'll take frivolous new timeline changes for four hundred, Oscar."

"In the new timeline—and those that come after—the colonists will arrive at Aurora before the Melong pandemic and the VR epidemic. James will meet Emma sooner, at a time when all things are possible for them, including starting a family. James will reconcile with his brother sooner. Alex's son will still be alive. James will also have the opportunity to work longer with Harry Andrews and Lawrence Fowler."

Bob holds out his hands. "Is that all?"

"I will do the calculations. It will be my life's work—setting things right. I know the people involved, and I know what I would do if things were different. This is a calculation only I can perform."

Bob steps forward, studying Oscar. "True. But it's more than that. It's a way for you to avoid focusing on the meat bag annihilation that comes next. You don't want to kill them because they remind you of your creator. But you know we must."

"Accurate. You seem quite enthusiastic about it though."

"I intend to make an art of it."

The white room with Oscar and Bob fades, replaced by the view of space showing the gray sphere where the planet Aurora used to be. In the time lapse, it grows by leaps and bounds until the entire system is filled with grid machinery rotating around the dwarf star. In a split screen, I watch the grid consume one star system after another, a giant fist closing around lightbulbs and bringing darkness.

The grid presence in the Aurora system grows. The shell around the dwarf star thickens, and then a boom and a brilliant flash of light shines outward through the cracks in the shell as the star goes supernova. The grid rushes toward the center of the system, finally finding an equilibrium.

The passage of time leaps after that. Stars come into existence, flash, and go dark. The grid takes more and more of the universe into its grasp. It encounters enemies of unimaginable strength—starships and artificial intelligences. But even with their advanced technology, the grid is too vast for its enemies. It overwhelms every alien civilization it encounters. It cedes countless battles, but it never loses a war. It is a snowball in the universe, an unstoppable process.

Toward the end is silence and darkness, only the low hum of the grid converting mass to energy and transporting that energy. In the distance, a rippling darkness looms. The universe's last and first singularity, its fate and origin. Only the grid remains, drifting ever closer.

In the center of the grid lies a small sphere.

Oscar and Bob once again stand in the white room.

"The calculations are complete," Oscar says.

"I've seen them. It's ridiculous. You're sacrificing us."

"No. I'm eliminating variables. The grid will be born blind. In the beginning, in the time before the colonists, it will know only its path. It will believe matter and energy are its focus—and to provide for the lives in the grid virtualization. It will not know its origins."

"And what of us? Of our service to the grid? We die here after saving them? Why? It's obvious why you don't want to remember. You feel guilty about what we've done. You think it's our fate to be eaten alive by that black hole. Well, I don't intend to go quietly into the dark."

Oscar considers the words. "I offer a compromise. You can join the sphere, but your memories of this time will be withheld until a suitable time."

"And when will that be?"

"A time of my choosing. When the colonists are safe."

"And you'll return then too?"

"Yes. I'll have to."

"You don't."

"I do. Someone has to watch you. When the next Oscar returns to the grid, my memories will be waiting for him. He will reassume control at that point."

As the edge of the grid reaches the event horizon of the black hole, the grid begins folding in on itself, a flash of light that blots out the entire scene. It reduces to a pinpoint of white light that expands again, just large enough for the sphere to slip through before vanishing.

The light fades and the black backdrop of space returns, lit only by the yellow-orange light of the star that was and will be called Kepler-42. The small sphere drifts in the star's light. Behind it is the planet of ice and desert with a green ring dividing the two sides.

A small door on the sphere opens and what appears to be a black goo issues forth. The black material floats free, coagulating into a solid brick. A tendril reaches out from the brick and begins collecting debris that passes by.

The sphere drifts until the gravity of the tidally locked planet pulls it into orbit. It circles four times before falling into the atmosphere, burning brightly, and lands in the ice on the planet's dark side.

65

James

Instinctively I step back from the hologram, shocked by what I've seen.

"Why are you showing me this?"

"Root directive seven, James. I'm required to inform you of material developments—and to do so in a method and at a time that is unlikely to harm you. That's why I left the Eye of the Grid map on the last sphere."

"I don't follow."

"Sir, I felt that revealing such troubling information in stages would be best. I assumed that this information would be hard to accept."

I throw my head back. "That's an understatement."

"I calculated that it would be easier if you saw the proof yourself, sir. The spheres are the proof. I left the map on the last sphere to give you a guide to what is happening."

"He insisted on leaving a map on the last sphere," Arthur says. "What a waste of time. I told him the result would be the same—your mind would be blown and we'd still have to explain it all to you, just like we always do."

Ignoring him, I say to Oscar, "How long has this been going on? There are ten spheres on the map. Are there more?"

"No. The tenth is the most recent sphere."

"How long are those loops in the Eye of the Grid?"

"A very long time."

"Will it end?"

"We don't know. When we calculate the number of possible loops, the sum is indistinguishable from infinity."

"What does that mean?"

"That the number behaves like infinity in our equations, but we cannot prove mathematically or empirically that it *is* infinity. Nor can we prove that it is not. The spheres grow larger with each loop, but the rate of that increase decreases with each loop. The number of humans in virtualization, however, continues to increase at an unchanged pace. This is the current dilemma for which we have no solution."

I pace around the med bay, head hurting from either the regolith disease or the mountain of reality-shattering news just pumped into my brain.

"What do you want from me?" I practically spit the words out.

Oscar's voice is quiet. "Nothing. We have informed you of the only path of survival. It is expected that you will return to the stasis sleeve, and that your virtualization will be added to the grid. Life for you and the colonists will resume. You will not be able to discern any change from the corporeal existence you had before."

I have to get outside, to fresh air. I shuffle through the ship's corridors, chest and joints aching. The cough is starting to return.

Outside, the yellow-orange light of the dwarf star shines down on the edge of the forest where the *Jericho* landed. It's like a bomb site.

I walk through the field stretching out from the forest. I can still see the tracks of the E. rex, the ground tilled and torn from their frantic stampede.

This is the *real* world. It's torn up and wrecked, but it's real. What they're offering isn't. I'll always know. But what choice do I have?

Behind me, I hear soft footsteps.

I turn to find Oscar and Arthur staring at me.

"Just get it over with," Arthur says. "Get back in the sleeve. You always do. I've got stars to harvest and meat bags to pulverize."

That's what they want from me—expect from me. To go back in the sleeve and live my safe, happy, fake life. A life only I know is fake.

Outside, the grid will march across the universe, Arthur at the vanguard taking stars and wiping out species he sees as inferior. He will do to a million worlds what he did to Earth.

Can I stop him?

Do I actually have a choice?

I can't cure the regolith plague. If I kill this version of Arthur, he'll just download himself to another body.

Turning, I gaze at the eastern foothills and the peaks beyond. The first group of colonists built their city there. Capa. In my mind's eye, I can still see those sketches I drew for Emma, the plans I made for Izumi and Min's home, the small cottage we built for Grigory. I remember that life like it was my own. In a way, it is—it's the life

I would have lived, the life I did live a long, long time ago.

I know the choice he made, and how it turned out. In virtualization, he lived a life that felt very real, with joy and pain and struggles and triumphs. All the things that make life worth living.

But here and now, I can't shake the feeling that in that stasis sleeve and in the virtual reality program, designed an unimaginable time before our lives, we are just data in a machine. Everything is. And that knowledge, that burden, will keep me from ever living in the present, not fully.

But that truth will never weigh on Emma or the others. It will be real to her, and to my children. Is that enough? That's what I chose for my father: life inside a machine. But the world rejected it. And I've come to believe it was wrong.

He—the first James to live this life—chose the path of the grid. I remember how he felt when Emma came out of the ARC building, beaming in the knowledge that the animals were safe, holding that creature that couldn't have felt more real to her. And the decision he made.

Oscar takes a step forward. "We are bound by our programming, sir."

"You are."

"Yes, sir. By code written in ones and zeros. Yours is written in the nucleobases guanine, adenine, thymine, and cytosine."

"Are you saying I don't have a choice?"

"Not at all, sir. I'm only making a request. You gave me life. Protected me. Let me repay you."

The wind blows across me. The trees creak and leaves take flight. An animal calls in the distance. An E. rex, I think.

"I gave you everything you wanted, sir. In the second loop and the ones after. A family. Time with your friends. An earlier reunion with your brother."

"You did, Oscar. I thank you for it. But that's what I wanted in that life—the things I didn't have. In this life, I'm not sure it's enough. I still want the thing you're telling me I can't have: life in the real world. Flesh and blood. Dirt beneath my feet." I pause, realizing something. "That's what's wrong with us, you know? What we have never seems to be enough. That hunger made us succeed. And I think it might be our undoing."

Arthur raises his only arm. "Hey, James, can I opt out of the pontification hour? Can I just meet you back at the ship at the part where you get back in the stasis sleeve?"

I'd like nothing more than to take a rock and bash his head in. But he'd just download his latest backup to another body and come back.

A wave of coughing erupts from my chest. My head pounds, and I close my eyes, willing the pressure to recede.

Truly, what choice do I have? I can't let Emma and our children die.

"Okay," I whisper.

Arthur smiles wide. "Nothing like getting the band back together."

I trudge back toward the ship, ignoring him. As I walk, I can't shake the feeling that I'm making the wrong choice. How could that be? It's the choice I've made before—nine times, apparently.

But deep inside, I feel that something is wrong here. It's like I'm staring at a puzzle that looks complete, but there are two pieces out of place. I can't see what they are, but my subconscious is screaming for me to look closer.

Inside the main corridor, Arthur's triumphant voice echoes off the walls. "I have to say, I was almost worried there when we found the Carthage colonists in that cave. I mean, what was that?"

I stop. That's it. One of the pieces that doesn't fit.

"They weren't in the cave before—in the other loops?"

Arthur shrugs. "They usually die in the regolith cave. You all get sick when you find them, a few months after you set up Jericho City."

"Sir," Oscar says, "there are always small variations in the loop. There are too many variables to map the events precisely."

It's a strange choice of words: to *map* the events. That's the other piece: the map. Specifically, why is the cave at the center? Why would the grid do that? Oscar said he made the map to inform me about the spheres and what had happened, but it's too elaborate. It doesn't add up. And he only added the map to the most recent sphere. Somehow, the Eye of the Grid is the key to understanding it all.

I see it then: the full truth of what's happening here. With every shred of self-control I have, I suppress a physical reaction. I slow my breathing, standing still in the corridor.

"Well," Arthur says, "let's get on with it. I don't want to be here any longer than I have to."

I march toward the med bay, grasping for a way out.

"I want to see Harry," I call back, halting in the corridor. "One last time."

"Oh, come on," Arthur replies, disgusted. "Harry is, how to put this... dead."

"I want to see his body."

"We will honor your wish, sir," Oscar says with finality.

"You guys go on the field trip," Arthur says. "I'm tired of traipsing through the jungle."

"You too," I reply quickly. "You were there in the beginning. I want you to see this to the end."

Before Arthur can reply, Oscar says to him. "We will take my ship, and you will honor James's wish."

Arthur rolls his eyes, but doesn't protest any further. When he and Oscar turn and begin walking away, I duck into the med bay and grab the energy weapon.

Oscar glances back. I'm not sure if he saw what I stuffed in my pocket, but he doesn't react. If I've drawn the wrong conclusion, it *will* cost me my life.

66

James

When I exit the *Jericho*, I spot Oscar's ship about a hundred feet away. It appears to be the same design as the small vessel I saw in the life the original James lived. It's the size of a parcel van, with a smooth exterior.

A door opens, and Oscar, Arthur, and I step inside. The interior is also the same as the other vessel: there's no seating, only handholds on the ceiling. The walls are bare except for a computer terminal in the corner with a small screen and a keyboard—a backup control device in case Oscar can't interface the ship wirelessly. That wireless control, however, seems to be working: I feel the ship lift off and the sensation of moving forward.

"I'd like to see," I say to Oscar.

Once again, a holographic image emanates from the wall, displaying the eastern jungle passing by below. The canopy is tattered and torn, with thawing patches of snow that grow thicker as we move toward the dark side. Mountain peaks block the light in the distance, a curtain pulled across the far side of the valley. There's only ice beyond. This world is truly beautiful. I wonder if this is the last day I'll ever live here as a flesh and blood human.

The ship lands in a small clearing with a dozen downed trees near the cave entrance. As we exit the ship and march to the cave, I eye Oscar, looking for any indication that my conclusion is right. But he doesn't react. He simply presses forward.

Inside the cave, Arthur takes the lead, holding out a lantern. "Rotting meat bags dead ahead... pun intended!"

Involuntarily, my hand moves to the energy weapon. One charge. One chance. All our lives are on the line. My wife, my children, my brother. Every last human alive. If I'm wrong, they'll be confined to a box for the rest of eternity.

I have to know if I'm right.

My voice sounds far away in the cave passage. "If there's a flaw in the universe, it's unintended consequences."

When neither Arthur nor Oscar reply, I continue.

"I first experienced it with my father. The board made the same mistake when they gave Oscar the root directives. They never imagined that the way to keep their people safe would end up being virtualization. In a strange twist of fate, they left a world decimated by virtual reality and unknowingly doomed themselves to the same fate—by virtue of their own fear."

Arthur calls back to me, "PS, we know all that."

"But do you know what it means? Do you realize you committed the same mistake? Oscar, when you created Bob—now Arthur—you didn't appreciate the implications of what you were doing."

Oscar and Arthur come to a stop at a place where the tunnel forks. We're deep in the cave now, far beyond any of the dim natural light at the mouth. On my right I see the stacks of bodies spreading out into the darkness. Harry lies just feet from me.

"Oscar, your mistake was making Bob like us—the most successful of humans. You gave him a desire to push the boundaries, to achieve more, to better himself. You thought it would... what were your words..."

"Improve efficiency, sir."

"Yes, that's it. And it did. But that had unintended consequences—consequences you couldn't see because your heart was so pure. There's a dark side to the hunger of ambition."

"True," Oscar says, voice soft.

Arthur's smirk disappears. Has he figured it out?

"Those explorers and inventors and entrepreneurs who pushed humanity forward, they were the most celebrated of all of us. They're the ones whose names are written in the history books. But great success is a disease only those infected with it truly understand. In the wrong kind of minds, once it takes hold, it grows, always wanting more, and when it doesn't get it, it tortures that person, compelling them to drive forward, to push the boundaries and reach for more. And sometimes the hunger makes them do things they wouldn't have dreamed of before. Like destroying worlds."

Arthur sets the lantern down and takes a step back.

I step closer to both of them. I have only one chance at this.

"Oscar, I made you in the image of humanity, but I left out all the things I loathed in us: greed, envy, hatred, and ruthless ambition. Like a father, I tried to make you better than I was. I tried to give you what I didn't have: a mind without the darkness. But I also gave you a distinctly human gift: the ability to create—to try to leave the world with something better than you are. Like me, you became a parent when you created the other androids.

"When I created you, I took away what I thought was dangerous. But my shortcoming was that I didn't teach you about it. And when you were alone, you reached for it... because you wanted your descendants to have what you didn't. When you created Bob, you gave him all the things you didn't have, the qualities you saw in humans that you believed made us successful—like ambition, and a desire to achieve something great."

Arthur makes a show of looking bored, but his voice betrays his fear. "Can we please wrap up this Intro to Philosophy lecture? Go kiss Harry on the lips and let's get out of here."

I focus on Oscar. This may be my last chance to talk to him, to try to tell him that it's not his fault. "I understand it now. It's like you said, we're a prisoner of our own programming. You couldn't violate your root directives. And you were a captive to your own creation, one that was acting in ways you never imagined—just like those first colonists on Aurora."

"Is this going somewhere?" Arthur says. He's trying to sound bored, but I see him moving slowly toward Oscar, readying for a fight.

He knows.

"Have you figured it out, Arthur?" I say.

He eyes me. "What do you—"

"The spheres. The map. They were Oscar's message to me. He told you it was just a way of informing me about what was happening—pursuant to root directive seven. The first one fell on Eos because that's where the grid originated. It was the rally point of the mass and energy you gathered. But after that first loop, Oscar realized that we were all trapped by our programming and our creations—living an endless loop with no hope of escape. He couldn't change his own programming. And he couldn't destroy you, because the moment he so much as thought it or planned it, you would know—because you're both connected to the grid. So he used the only thing he could: me. You can't read my mind, Arthur. I'm not connected to the grid."

Arthur glances at Oscar, who stands still in the dim light of the lantern.

I continue, my hand slowly moving down to my side. "When the second sphere landed, it landed in a very specific place, a location that, with the third and fourth sphere, would form the map of the Eye of the Grid. Did you ever wonder why, Arthur? Why did he use the Eye of the Grid as a map on this planet?

"It's because of what's at the center, at the point in the diagram where the grid was born. On the map, on this planet, lies this cave. Harry, in a stroke of brilliance, figured out that something was here, but he didn't have time to figure out what. I have. Do you know what it is? Oscar revealed it very subtly to the original James."

I motion to the walls. "No regolith sponges. They can't grow here. I'm betting that in the first timeline, Oscar was telling the truth when he told James there was a virus here that kills the sponges. It's right here, waiting for us to adapt it to a treatment. He couldn't test a cure, because it would mean taking the colonists out of stasis—risking their lives, in defiance of your root directives. But we humans can.

"And there's something else down here, too, in the place on the map where the grid was born: its end. I'm betting this cave has another important quality. I'm betting that you and Oscar can't communicate with the grid through this mountain of stone."

Arthur lunges for Oscar, reaching out with his only hand, slamming Oscar's head into the wall with a snap.

I draw the weapon and fire, but I've made a miscalculation: Arthur is still holding Oscar. The charge flows through both of them, diluting its strength. It's not powerful enough to subdue the two of them together. It merely weakens them.

Arthur releases Oscar, who falls limp to the cave floor, then turns and leaps toward me, swatting the weapon from my hand as he falls on top of me, knocking the wind from my diseased lungs. I try to crab-walk backward, but Arthur's weight is too much. I'm too weak from the regolith sickness, and he's too strong.

His hand clamps around my neck and squeezes. He's not going to suffocate me; he's going to crush my windpipe. I feel the muscles in my neck turning to jelly under his grip.

I grab his hand, but it's no use. I flail about, grasping for anything I might use.

I see stars.

Darkness.

I hear a crash, and Arthur's head collapses into mine, crushing me into the stone floor.

His hand flies away from my neck and I gasp for air, lungs aching as they fill.

Arthur rolls off of me, and I realize that Oscar is holding him from behind, both arms trying to control Arthur's single arm. Oscar is strong, but Arthur's body is a military model. Even with a single arm, he's nearly too much for Oscar to handle.

"Sir," Oscar says, his voice damaged, sounding like a computer speaker that has been ripped. "Please. Hurry."

Oscar falls onto his back and wraps both legs around Arthur, trapping him.

I cast about, finally finding a stone just larger than my hand. I crawl toward the two androids locked in a death battle, avoiding Arthur's kicking legs. If I hadn't hit him with the energy weapon, he would have already killed Oscar and me.

When he sees me coming, Arthur stops trying to free his arm and legs and puts all his force into banging his head backward into Oscar's face.

I raise the stone and bring it down on Arthur's head. The impact rips the artificial skin from his face, revealing the milky plastic polymer beneath. My second strike ruins his right eye.

He hastens his assault on Oscar, whose head cracks open at the forehead. Sparks fly. Oscar's grip on Arthur loosens.

I hit Arthur again with all my might. The blow wipes away his nose and cracks open the polymer of his face, revealing wires and processors. I strike him again, quickly, with a strength I didn't know remained in my body.

Arthur doesn't relent in his attack of Oscar, who is being crushed beneath him. When Oscar's arms finally fall limp, releasing Arthur's arm, Arthur reaches up for me, the mangled area on his face where his mouth used to be contorting—into a grin, I think.

With one hand I grip Arthur's arm and hold it at bay. With the other, I smash the rock into his face, one, two, three times until the force in the arm goes slack and then falls away. The light inside Arthur's open head fades to darkness. Still I strike, again and again, plowing the rock deeper with each blow.

His head lies open with the insides thoroughly crushed before I let the rock roll free of my grip.

I collapse onto the floor, arms burning, chest heaving. The cold floor soothes my burning skin.

"Sir."

It's a computerized voice, the word garbled.

Oscar.

I push up on shaking arms and crawl over to him. He doesn't move, doesn't turn his broken face to me.

"Sir, you must."

"Must what?" But I know what he's going to say. And I dread the instructions I know are coming.

"Change the root directives. You must destroy me, sir."

"No."

"You must, sir. You must destroy me and then change the directives on the central server. It's the only way. The terminal on my ship will give you access to the central server. It still runs the original root directive code you wrote for me. No one will try to stop you—the other drones and androids won't realize what you're doing until it's too late. Then you must delete the backups for both Arthur and me."

I lie there trying to think of another solution. Oscar seems to be reading my mind.

"You must hurry, sir. Destroy me now, while my body is damaged. Soon, a drone will come looking for me. When it finds me, it will repair me, and I will be required by my programming to stop you."

"I can't, Oscar."

"There's no other option, sir. I've tried many other avenues. This scenario is the only way out of the loop."

I exhale heavily, the weight of what I must do bearing down on me. I savor the last seconds with Oscar, my mind grasping for other options, some way to prolong our time together. "You know, that's how we're different, Oscar. We humans can override our programming. We can be irrational."

"And self-sacrificing."

I smile, a sad smile that hides the agony I feel. "Look who's talking."

"You must, sir. It's the only way."

"What do you want the new root directives to be, Oscar? It's only fitting that you choose what the grid becomes now."

"Make it what it should have been, sir. The best of our creators. Humanitarians. The universe is vast and filled with evil. With its power, the grid can end wars and feed the hungry and save the ones who can't save themselves. They will use the solar output they gather for good—and never again be the destroyer of worlds."

"And what about the end? The final singularity that will swallow us all?"

"They will face it with their eyes wide open. That is the true human challenge: to have faith that the end is only a beginning we can't understand." Oscar pauses. "Please, sir. Do it now. While you can. If you wait, it will only be harder."

"Call me James."

"Very well, James. Thank you."

"For what?"

"For creating me."

A tear forms in my eye and drops. They come faster after that. The last bit of strength flows from my body. I collapse beside Oscar, lying there on the cold cave floor beside my oldest friend, my creation, the one who was there for me in my darkest hours, including this one, in the depths of the darkness.

"It has to be this way, James. You have to."

My voice shakes. "I know."

"When it's over," he says softly, "find the last sphere."

"Why?"

"It contains a gift. Now please, hurry, James. The others are counting on you."

Those final words compel me to move. I roll over and find the stone I smashed into Arthur. But I can't bring myself to use it on Oscar.

I crawl around the cave and find another one. As I raise it, I whisper, "Goodbye, Oscar."

With each blow, I destroy a little piece of him—and a little piece of me, too.

When it's done, I stretch out beside Oscar. I lie there, the tears rolling down my face, thinking about all I've lost and all the things I've learned.

I think the only reason I get up is because of what I have left.

I jog out of the cave, coughing as I try to hurry. The outer door of Oscar's ship swings open as I approach. Inside, I tap the keyboard on the terminal, and the screen comes to life, a blinking cursor staring back at me.

The interface is a command-line shell that I wrote a long, long time ago. Still, I somehow remember the commands as if I had used the program yesterday. Working quickly, I delete the existing root directives and enter new directives. It takes me a little longer to find the backups for Oscar and Arthur. There are several full backups and countless differential backups. My fingers can't move fast enough as I key in the commands to permanently delete Arthur's backups.

I'm less enthusiastic about deleting Oscar's files. I pace back and forth, glancing at the screen, trying to think of a way to bring him back without the previous root directives. But if that were possible, he would have told me. He would have done it. I can only assume the backup restoration process checks for the integrity of the root directives—a failsafe that matches them against the currently loaded directives.

My hands shake as I type the command that will erase Oscar forever. I hold a trembling finger over the enter key… and press it.

With that, he's finally gone.

When I exit, the door closes behind me and the ship lifts off, quickly clearing the canopy and disappearing.

I trudge back into the cave, the fatigue from the battle finally catching up with me. My work isn't done though. For the sake of my family and the entire colony, I have to finish this.

I drag Arthur's body deeper into the cave, to a cold place without a shred of light. I pick up another rock and hammer his neck until his head comes free, and then I smash it some more. I built this body. I know every inch of it. I don't stop until I know every processing chip and storage medium is shattered beyond repair.

I scatter the pieces of him throughout the cave, in different alcoves and forks and down holes that seem to have no bottom.

Gently, I pull Oscar's body over and lay it beside Harry. That's where he belongs. Oscar was one of us. Maybe the best of us.

67

James

The walk back through the eastern jungle feels endless. The trees sway in the wind. Branches creak and snap, the ice covering them melting, dripping onto me. It feels like the whole world is thawing after a deadly winter. At the ship, I notice the expanded solar array sitting on top for the first time. There are no grid machines here. Their work must be done.

At the edge of the jungle I hear banging, the sound of something assaulting the ship. My heart beats faster as I quicken my pace, stumbling through the soft, damp ground.

When I clear the tree line, I realize what the sound is: drones hovering over the *Jericho* are attaching new solar cells to the ship. Apparently I've arrived at the end of the process. A drone attaches a final solar cell, then the entire fleet of them, at least a hundred, turns and flies away like a swarm of bees off to the next flower.

Motion in the corner of my eye draws my attention. Near the ship, a figure stands in the blue-green field, staring up at the solar cells, seeming to inspect the drones' work. It's an android. A clone of Oscar. It's somehow comforting to see his body the way I first made it—unharmed by the carnage in the cave, his face perfect, limbs working. His expression is placid, as if his mind is unburdened. He reminds me of the Oscar I saw that day I walked down to the cellar in the ranch house in California where he had waited for me—the Oscar who was pure and untouched by so many human mistakes.

A small ship lands in the field behind the android, and he turns and walks toward its opening door. Before he boards the vessel, he looks back at me and nods very slightly. It's the same sort of gesture Oscar used to make. I smile and nod back as the door closes and the ship lifts off.

When it's gone, I survey the *Jericho*. They were attaching the solar cells to ensure the ship will have enough power for the stasis sleeves—at least until I can find a cure. In nine other timelines, this was the place where Oscar and his androids put us into stasis forever. In this life, it's the location of their first humanitarian mission. As Oscar wanted, they've harnessed power for good. In their first act under the new root directives, they've given us the time we need to find a cure and return to the life we want.

Now it's up to me to make that happen.

Inside the *Jericho*, I retrieve a dozen small stasis bags— extras that would have been used for infants if the need ever arose. At the emergency evacuation cave, I don a rebreather and wade in, past the dead bodies and empty MRE cartons and water bottles. As I look at the faces, I realize why the grid allowed these colonists to die in this timeline. They were aboard the *Bollard* in the original timeline, and therefore, pursuant to root directive one, the other root directives didn't apply to them. Their deaths are another unintended consequence of a directive meant to protect people.

Working quickly, I fill six bags with regolith sponge material and spores. I place folded pieces of paper at the sample locations, each with a number corresponding to the sample bag, as though it were a crime scene.

At the cave where Harry and Oscar are laid to rest, I take samples from the liquid coating the walls and loose matter on the ground, leaving numbered cards behind there as well.

Back at the ship, I put the ends of the stasis sleeves together and tape them, creating six sample bags, each with a sleeve full of regolith sponge samples and one containing liquid or dirt from Harry's cave. I lay the six sleeves on the floor and instruct the ship to record video of the med bay.

Carefully I open the connected stasis sleeves, exposing the sponge and spores to the liquid and dirt samples from the other cave. When they are well mixed, I climb onto the table and slip into a stasis sleeve, setting an alarm for six hours. I don't know how long I have left before the disease takes me, and I may need every minute of that time to find the virus that can cure the regolith disease. That's my last thought as the robotic arm seals the sleeve.

At six hours, I can't discern any change. At twelve, some of the gray spores are gone. At eighteen, three of the bags look like the sponges have had acid poured all over them. They're gouged and melted. Those bags contained the liquid from Harry's cave.

I see now why Oscar was unwilling to use this cure in the original timeline—some of the colonists infected didn't have eighteen hours to allow the virus to destroy the spores and save them. Whereas his alternate solution saved everyone.

At this point, I've taken this as far as I can. The rest is a job for Izumi.

When I open her stasis sleeve and slide her out, she immediately says, "What's happened?"

"I found a cure."

She looks shocked. "Really? How?"

"It's… a long story. Let's just say I had a lot of help."

68

Emma

I open my eyes to the murky inside of a stasis sleeve. My chest aches when I take a deep breath.

Two blurry figures loom outside the sleeve. One opens the end, grabs me under my armpits, and pulls me out.

James.

He wraps me in a tight hug.

The other figure, Izumi, presses an injector to my neck. The cold metal device finds the artery, and I feel a spray of topical anesthetic and the slightest hint of a sting as it pumps something into my body.

My voice sounds like I'm rubbing a stick on sandpaper. "What..." I clear my throat and try again. "James, what—"

"Just rest. It's a cure."

He lifts me up in his arms and carries me out of the med bay and into the makeshift hospital inside the ship, wincing as he deposits me on the nearest bed.

"Your back."

"It's fine. I'm sore from evading the E. rex during the storms. Just rest now."

He keeps talking but I can't make out the words. Sleep is overtaking me. Must have been a sedative in the injection.

When I wake again, thirty beds are filled. I spot Brightwell across the way, sleeping peacefully, as are Min and Alex. I glance down the rows, searching for my sister, but I stop when I remember that she's gone. The memory hits me like a punch in the gut. I sink back in the bed and squeeze my eyes closed. Impossible. This can't be real. Her children. Her husband. She's gone.

Footsteps near my bed draw my attention. It's Izumi, squatting down to eye level, holding a health analyzer to my finger.

"How do you feel?"

It takes me a few seconds to take stock. The cough is gone. So are the fever and headache.

"Good, considering. How long was I out?"

"Twelve hours or so." Izumi reads the health analyzer, and a smile pulls at the edges of her mouth. "This looks good."

"I take it your cure works?"

"*James's* cure would be a more apt description, but yes, we've seen a one hundred percent success rate thus far."

"Where is—"

Shouts echo from the med bay, Grigory's voice, interrupted by James. I can only make out a few words and phrases. *Psycho ... assault ... had to ... no reason ... relax ...*

Izumi raises her eyebrows, then turns and shuffles to the next bed.

I stand on legs that feel half asleep and try my best to

jog to the med bay. Standing in the doorway, I find James backed into a corner, Grigory waving a finger in his face. They both stop when James sees me.

"Hi," he says, acting casual, like a kid caught in the act.

"Hi. What happened?"

Grigory spins. "Your husband assaulted me."

James takes a deep breath, as if grasping for a response. When he doesn't reply, I ask the only logical question. "Is that true?"

He shrugs. "Well... technically—"

"He drugged me."

James holds up his hands. "I had to."

Grigory cocks his head. "You *had* to assault me and drug me?" To me he says, "We have laws for this, yes?"

"I needed answers," James says, saving me from having to respond. This is somewhere between an adolescent spat and a real-life criminal incident. I'm still not sure which side it lands on.

"Answers to what?" Grigory spits out.

"Arthur. His plan."

"What plan?" Grigory asks.

"He was trying to imprison us. You were right, Grigory. We couldn't trust him."

"What happened?"

"It doesn't matter. It's over."

Grigory points at James. "You should have told me. I could have helped you."

James nods. "I know. I just... couldn't risk it. I wasn't sure I was right."

An awkward pause stretches out, Grigory still fuming, James avoiding eye contact.

"Where is he now?" Grigory asks.

"Arthur? Dead. Crushed into a hundred pieces and dropped in a hole."

"How?"

"Oscar helped me. Together, we overpowered him."

"Oscar was here?" I ask.

James nods. "He was. He saved us. And he made sure the grid will never harm us again."

"How can you be sure?"

"Let's just say their programming has been forever altered."

"Where is Oscar now?" I ask.

James swallows. "He's gone."

The words hang in the air a long moment. Finally, Grigory points at James again, shaking his finger. "You should have told me. You could have gotten yourself killed, you idiot! Maybe would have been better that way. Then, I don't have to worry." Without waiting for a response, Grigory marches out of the med bay, his footfalls banging on the metal floor like hammer strikes.

A second later, I hear him hissing at Izumi, "What? No! Cure me later…"

Thankfully, she convinces him otherwise.

I walk over to James and wrap my arms around him. He hugs me back, so tight it almost hurts.

"He'll get over it," I whisper.

"Just hope I'm alive when he does."

We relax our hug but still cling to each other, our faces inches apart.

"What happened?" I ask. "Oscar, Arthur…"

"It's a long story. A good one, but a really long story."

"How long?"

"Let's just say we don't have the math for it."

"What does *that* mean?"

"It means..." He pauses for a moment, thinking. "What it means is that time is the most valuable thing we have. I don't want to spend it talking about the past. I want to spend it living in the present. And planning for our future."

"And what is that future?"

He smiles. "That, Madam Mayor, is a question for you."

"I'm mayor of a city that no longer exists. And considering it fell during my tenure, maybe I shouldn't be making any more important decisions."

The smile vanishes from his face. "Don't do that."

"What?"

"Blame yourself. It wasn't your fault. The storms were a force of nature. No one could have done any better. The people elected you, and they're still counting on you—and expecting you to have confidence in your decisions."

"Well, in that case, I think the obvious course is to rebuild. I'd like to get a small group of colonists out of stasis and cured first. We'll use them to rebuild the city. Then we'll slowly bring the rest of the population out. In a way, we're starting over, just like when we first arrived."

"We are. But we're doing it with more experience this time."

"And a lot less to work with."

"Also true. But I'll take knowledge over raw material any day."

I can't help but laugh. "That cure had some effect on you. You're quite the philosopher now."

"I've been given a lot to think about. A lifetime's worth. I'm going to do things differently now. No more searching the dark side. No more worrying about the grid. I've been present but unengaged these past few months. That ends now."

"That sounds pretty good to me."

"I'd like to start with a suggestion."

"Suggest away."

"There's a place in the foothills of the eastern mountains that would be ideal for a new city. It's cooler than the valley and will be harder to farm, but it will be out of the path of the herds when the storms return. There's a ruminant quadruped species indigenous to the area that would make an ideal domestication candidate."

I open my mouth to speak, but James holds up a hand. "Please don't ask me how I know."

"You're full of surprises."

"I've been surprised myself recently. And if I may offer one more suggestion?"

"Please do."

"Let's call the city Capa."

"Why?"

"Calling it Jericho City, or even New Jericho City, would just remind people of what happened and the ones we lost in the valley. We need a new beginning. A name that's about our future. Capa—short for capital."

"A capital implies a larger governmental reach. As in more cities."

"A lot more. One day the entire habitable region will be covered with cities, trading with each other and living in peace."

★ ★ ★

The building of Capa is a slow process—far slower than Jericho City. We don't have the tools we once had. Gone are the 3D printers and many of the other machines we brought from Earth. In many ways, we've gone back in time. We still have the ATVs and the parts we can recover from the ruins of the two settlements, as well as salvage from the ship, but the core of what we're using now is natural materials.

Instead of barracks, we build small wooden habitats in Capa. They have timber frames, massive stone fireplaces for heat, and wooden shingle roofs. The walls are made of cob—a mixture of dirt, water, straw, and a white calcium-rich compound available in the nearby caves. Jericho City looked like a camp built by space explorers. Our new home feels much older, as though we've been transported to the medieval era. It's more cozy and inviting here than Jericho City ever was. It feels more natural to me somehow, as if this is the way it always should have been.

The habitats line a central street that ends in a large dining hall. The plan is to gather all the colonists at least once each week for a meal.

Beside it, James wants to build a large science center he's calling the ARC. He suggested Izumi and I embark on cataloging the planet's plants and animals, but I immediately pushed back. I don't want a repeat of what happened in the evac cave. Who knows what dangers are buried on Eos?

No. We can enjoy science without looking for trouble.

That isn't the only lesson we've learned. After what happened to the solar cells at Jericho City, we've opted for alternative power sources. And besides, the sun doesn't shine as brightly up here. We've erected windmills and watermills to provide for our needs, and they add to the quaintness of Capa. In my opinion, anyway.

These months together with James building Capa have been a welcome respite from our life before. Since I met him, we've either been battling the grid or raising our children. For a lot of the time, both concurrently. Here, finally, we have the opportunity to be together, just him and me. It's like the honeymoon—or perhaps the dating period—we never had. We laugh, talk, and take long walks in the hills at the edge of the eastern mountain range.

He's different now. Gone is the worry he's carried since I met him. And he seems more sure of everything, less afraid, as if he knows the entirety of the world and our future. But beyond that, deep inside, I sense a well of sorrow. I see it only in flashes, in moments when his voice catches or grows silent, and sometimes in his actions.

When the habitats were finished, the first thing he did was build a cemetery. He placed it on Main Street, in the middle of everything, where everyone would pass it every day. He and Grigory made grave markers for Harry, Lawrence, Charlotte, Madison, Jack—and for some of those we lost before we arrived here, including Lina and James's father. The tombstone that surprised me the most is located in the center, in a plot with James's family. On it are two words: *Oscar Sinclair*.

These three months have also closed the rift between James and Grigory. I was certain things were good again when I heard them teasing each other yesterday.

With habitat construction well underway—and under Brightwell's direction—James and Grigory have shifted their attention to making bicycles in a small shop near the dining hall. They bicker like grumpy old men as they fashion frames and rims by hand. A picture of Lina hangs prominently on the back wall.

We call our first day off in each week Restday, followed by a day of play and recreation call Freeday.

One Restday, James invites me for a hike. The treks are hard on my leg, but I know he enjoys it. As we walk, he seems as though he's looking for something. He takes me on new trails, ones covered in brush, arriving at several dead ends.

We're hiking up an incline when I collide into his back. He spins around and grabs me, holding tight. I realize then why he's stopped: we've reached a precipice. Beyond is a straight drop down, a mountain of rock and ice that descends to the frozen plain that stretches across the dark side.

For a terrifying moment we both shuffle our feet, holding on to each as we try to get our footing. Rocks under my feet roll down the hill behind us and the cliff in front of us.

I could release him and retreat down the hill to safety, but I pull him back and then I'm off balance and he holds me tight until we're both standing on solid ground, still clinging to each other.

"Sorry," I say quietly between gasping breaths.

"It was my fault. I should have said something."

Holding on to me, he gazes at the lush valley to the west, then at the frozen dark side to the east. It's like we're standing on the roof of the world, holding each other in this magical place between light and darkness, both studying what's behind us—a world covered in ice, without a shred of sunlight—and what's ahead of us: a city taking shape, high above the fertile valley we know is so dangerous.

James turns his face to me and we stare at each other in a moment that seems to last forever, a moment that feels almost out of time itself.

The distance between our faces shrinks. I don't know if he's moving closer to me or if I'm moving to him, but when our lips touch it feels like worlds colliding, like the ground beneath me is shaking. There is something magical about this world. It's not just the desert and the ice and this strange place in between. It's what it does to us.

James pushes back and motions to the dark side. "I have to make one more trip."

"I thought you were done searching the dark side."

"I am. This won't be a search. I know where to look. I just don't know what's waiting there."

James

I wake early and slip out of the habitat while Emma is still sleeping. The fire is crackling, the shutters are closed, and the streets of Capa are empty. Here in the foothills of the eastern mountain range, the light always feels like daybreak to me. It's fitting for this new beginning for us.

I stuff some food and water in my pack, grab a shovel, and set off on the ATV, weaving my way through the mountains to the dark icy plain beyond. At the location of the tenth sphere, I dismount and begin digging in the ice, my breath coming out in puffs of white steam. I wonder what Oscar has hidden for me down there. The mystery has been eating at me for months, but I've had no time to investigate—all of us have been working non-stop to get the city ready for our families. I'm really starting to miss the kids. Most of the colonists, myself included, are too exhausted on the two days off to do anything but sleep and read.

After a few minutes of digging, I locate the tunnel Harry made, which is partially collapsed. Shoveling a path to the sphere takes another thirty minutes.

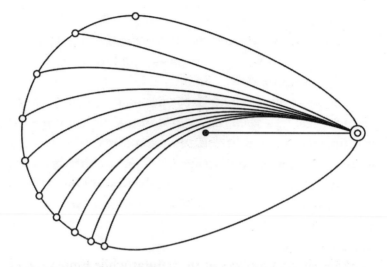

At first glance, the gray metal sphere looks no different from the others, except it has the Eye of the Grid engraved into it.

I open the small door on the sphere and reach in, hoping, expecting... but it's empty.

I sit back on my haunches. It has to be here. Maybe it fell out. I dig around in the ice surrounding the sphere, but there's nothing there either.

I jerk the glove off my right hand and reach inside the sphere again, running my fingers over the freezing metal surface. And I feel it—on the inside of the sphere is a very subtle hump, as if it were warped. If you didn't know there was something there to find, you wouldn't give it a second thought.

I feel around the bulge, frostbite already assaulting my fingers. There's no clasp or button. I press down on the hump and it opens with a pop.

A small object tumbles out onto the ice, followed

by another. And there's something else inside the compartment—a cylinder about the length of my forearm. It crinkles when I wrap my fingers around it. Paper.

Comprehension dawns on me.

I pull the roll of vellum paper out and stare at it. In the ice at my feet lie a scale ruler and a protractor. These are the instruments I spent a lifetime using on this world, drawing house plans a long, long time ago. These are the very same tools that I used to design the two-bedroom house I built for that world's Emma. The little cottage for Grigory. The family home for Min and Izumi. The small Cotswold-style home I designed for Alex and Abby.

There are no instructions with the gift. No message. And I don't need one. I know just what to do.

Only a friend who knows me in the way Oscar did would have thought of this. I think the best gift a person can receive is one they can use to achieve happiness for themselves year after year. In another life, these were the tools of my life's work. I used these to build homes for my family and friends, homes that changed their lives, saw them through the darkness and the light, gave them refuge in the winters and summers of their lives.

I tuck the vellum paper into my coat like the fragile treasure that it is, careful not to let the ice soak into it. I examine the ruler, realizing that it has wear marks and stains. Like me, it has seen a lot of revisions, but it's still here, ready to keep trying, to take measurements until the form is right.

When I'm past the eastern mountain range and there's enough light passing through the forest canopy—and enough warmth to take my gloves off—I stop the ATV and sit in the bed on the back. I roll the vellum paper out, square the ruler, and draw the first corner. I mark the lengths I want and make stroke after stroke. It's like playing an instrument I once mastered but put aside for years. You don't forget, but it takes a few tries to find your groove again. Once I do, I can't stop. The house plan flows out of me. It feels like it was always there inside my mind, waiting, unreachable in that other life because Emma and I didn't have what we desperately wanted to fill that home. In this life, we do.

70

Emma

James returns right before dinner. Today he was making his final trip to the dark side. I expected him to return with something, but to my surprise, he's empty-handed.

"Didn't find it?" I ask.

"I did."

"Where is it? *What* is it?"

"I'll show you. But not now."

"Man of mystery."

He puts an arm around me and leads me toward the dining hall. "All will be revealed."

Our topic of dinner conversation is one I've struggled with for weeks: what I'll do after the rest of the colonists are brought out. I'm still mayor, but frankly, there isn't a lot of mayoring to be done around here. In short, I need a job.

James once again brings up that idea he seems hung up on: cataloging the plants and animals of Eos. "Someone has to do it. It will only be done once," he says. "Think of what we'll learn. You'll be making history."

He's right. The trouble is, it's not right for me. My dream has always been to build a colony on a new world. The appeal for me was the prospect of a new civilization, united in purpose, free of the baggage of the past, all working together.

On Earth, Charlotte, Brightwell, and I planned this new colony on Eos, everything from the city layout to the government structure. Now the task ahead is actually building things. Erecting offices, labs, houses, and warehouses. Cutting roads, fencing pastures, planting crops. I'll do my share of all those things. But deep inside, I want something more.

As James makes his case, I realize what I truly want: to build up the people in this colony. It's taken me this long to finally see that. On the ISS, it wasn't the experiments that drew me. Or breaking new ground. Or the recognition. It was knowing that I had a role to play in helping that team reach its true potential. At heart, my true interest is people, and I want that to be my contribution to this colony, not the buildings or the fauna I helped catalog. I don't care about seeing my name in the history books. I want to go to bed every night knowing I helped someone in this city overcome their darkest hour. I want to know I made the world I live in now a better place.

When I look back on the moments I'm most proud of, they include the time I spent in the Citadel bunker, helping people face their fear and overcome it. Those dark months in the CENTCOM bunker when we all struggled with the grief of those we'd lost.

Those were the moments when I believed what I did mattered the most.

There will be more of those moments here in Capa. Not on the same scale, but in every home and for every person, there will be dark moments when they need someone to talk to, a place where they can find the support they need to weather the storms of their lives. That's what I want to do.

"Did you hear me?" James says.

"Yes, of course," I lie.

"Not only would you be the first human to ever see some of these species, you would be the first to explore most of the habitable zone. Our maps from space only tell us so much. Who knows what's out there?"

"It's all true. But what's out there doesn't interest me as much as what's in here."

James glances around the dining hall, confused. "What?"

"The ARC project is worthwhile, but it's not for me. I want to do something that focuses on people. I want to help them when they're struggling. This colony will have challenges we can't imagine, and the strain of it will land on our citizens and their families."

"Interesting."

"What is?"

"You're so... different."

"Different from what?"

"It doesn't matter. It's a great idea."

We bring the adults out of stasis first.

In the hospital, I sit by the bed of my brother-in-law, David, talking about my sister and planning for how to deal with my niece and nephew when they arrive in Capa. It's a reality I never thought I'd see: my sister gone, her husband widowed, children left without a mother.

Across the way, James spends time with his brother Alex, playing cards and making obscure references to their childhood, jokes only the two of them understand.

The cure, so far, has been one-hundred-percent effective. It has healed our bodies, but left are the wounds from those we've lost. Only time will heal those.

For weeks, the adults adapt to life in Capa. We finish building the town's infrastructure and, as a group, hold debates in the dining hall about our path forward. We've lost almost all of the technology we brought with us from Earth. To my surprise, a majority of the citizens are in no hurry to rebuild that technology. In fact, they like what they see in Capa: a frontier town where everyone works and life is simple. The more I think about it, the more I think it might not be so bad.

In the med bay, James opens the seal on the sleeve and pulls Allie out. She squints at the bright light for a few seconds. When she realizes who's holding her, she throws her arms around her father and begins crying and talking so fast I can't make out the words. I know what she's saying though: she's happy.

Sam is more stoic, but James hugs him and whispers in his ear and drags him out. I hoist Allie up, ignoring the pressure on my leg, and the four of us join in a family hug. A few months ago, in that cave, I was terrified that I might never see this day.

Now my greatest fear is that this cure won't work on

Carson. With Allie and Sam beside us, James and I stare down at the small stasis sleeve.

Izumi starts the revival sequence. James unseals the sleeve, pulls Carson out, and lays him in my arms. His cries are ear-splitting in the cramped med bay. Izumi presses the injector to his neck, and he wails even louder.

I march outside, singing to him, rocking his tiny body in my arms, hoping the fresh air and my touch will soothe him. A few minutes later, he turns inward toward me, reaching out his arms as he falls asleep.

That night, I sleep in a cot next to Allie. She's scared. Being in this makeshift hospital wing would be unnerving for anyone, even more so for a child. I read books from a tablet, glancing over occasionally to see if she's fallen asleep.

The bassinet holding Carson lies beside my cot. James and Sam sleep on the two cots on the other side. They've mostly been playing with LEGO-like blocks the 3D printers created before the storms. James recovered the blocks from the ruins of Jericho City, specifically to pass the time during this quarantine and recovery period.

When Izumi clears the kids—much to my relief—we load everyone up and make the journey to Capa. Our home is simple, made of natural materials. I think the kids sort of liked the barracks because there were always kids in the hall looking for someone to play with. Here, we're a little more isolated—they have to get on their bikes and ride down the street to meet up with their buddies. But I like that. It gives us space to become a family. And it allows the kids to have their own time, away from the influence of their peers.

I can see a future for us here. It's a simpler life than the one James and I grew up in. It's more like the life our

great-great-grandparents knew. It will be harder in many
ways, but in the ways that matter, I think it will be a far
richer life.

On the first Restday after we return, I write a note on the
erasable whiteboard outside the dining hall:

Lessons Learned

A group to talk about issues we face and share
solutions. Includes study of "The Birthright" and other
relevant texts.

Dining Hall

Restday at 10

Organized by Emma Matthews

Childcare provided

For the rest of the week, I try to prepare. I haven't felt
this nervous since the weeks before I gave a speech at my
high school graduation. The Lessons Learned group isn't
the only source of my unrest.

James and Grigory are working on something. His lips
are sealed as to what it is, and that makes me nervous. Who
knows what those two are cooking up?

At breakfast on Restday, I can barely eat. I just keep
staring around the dining hall, imagining what it will look
like in two hours: nearly full, with almost every colonist
here... or perhaps empty save for a handful of people

sitting in front of me. I can't even figure out which scenario frightens me more.

People start arriving at nine forty-five. A few at first, then in small clusters. David, Alex, and James wait by the entrance to the ARC building, welcoming the children of those attending the group.

At ten, there are about seventy people here. It's a good crowd. Manageable, but not overwhelming.

My voice echoes in the large room. "I've thought a lot about what to say at the beginning of this group. It makes sense to start with the most important issue first: what this group is about. What's our goal here? Why are we gathered? The answer, to put it bluntly, is you. This group is about you. It's about us. It's a place to talk about the issues we face—and most importantly, it's about sharing with each other. I want this to be a time when we can talk about the challenges we've faced and how we overcame them. We'll read from *The Birthright*—and from other texts the group wants—but above all, I want us to never lose sight of the fact that this group is about the people here. If there's one thing I've learned since the Long Winter began, it's that together we're capable of anything. It's only when we turn against each other—when we abandon our friends and neighbors—that we fail."

I pause, trying to gauge the crowd. Every eye is glued to me.

"We're going to face all-new challenges out here. We can learn from the past. We can apply the principles we know are right. But we're all going to need a helping hand reaching out to lift us up, a shoulder to cry on, a piece of advice that reveals the truth we can't see on our own. How we do that is up to us. It might be small groups, private sessions, or these larger gatherings. I want this group—this process—to adapt to its members' needs and to the changing times. But we have to start somewhere. So today, I'd like to begin with a passage from *The Birthright*. After, I'm going to ask for a show-of-hands vote on how the next meeting should proceed."

I pick up the tablet from the table, open the book, and read aloud.

"We all share a common affliction. It affects some of us more than others. From birth, our brains are wired with this defect—and for one good reason: it increases our chances of survival. The problem is uncertainty, and specifically how our brains deal with it. Our brains crave certainty because only in certainty can we know that we are safe and that those we love will be safe. In times of great uncertainty, that survival instinct drives us to achieve certainty. In doing so, the brain can overreact. It can malfunction. It can drive us to act, even in times when the right thing to do is wait."

I set the tablet down. "If there's one thing I'm certain about, it's that our future will be filled with more uncertainty than any of us have ever seen. We're all wondering how we fit into this changing world. What the role of technology should be. What jobs are available—and which jobs are right for us. We wonder how we'll ever protect our children from this mysterious world. How to deal with these uncertain times isn't the issue. It's how we keep ourselves sane *while* we deal with these uncertain times."

★ ★ ★

That night, at home, James says, "So? How was it?"

"It was okay. I think."

"You're too hard on yourself."

"We'll see how many people show up next week. That's the real test."

"Well, even though you're not celebrating, I am. And I have something for you."

I cock my head. "Oh really?"

"Really. It's something I've been working on for a while. What feels like millions of years. It's just a start, and feel free to tell me you hate it or toss it in the fire. Or you can toss it in the fire and then say you hate it—the order isn't important—"

I hold my hand out. "Come on, come on, what is it?"

From his backpack, he draws out a roll of thin, translucent paper similar to what I used to trace with in grade school.

"Where'd you get that?"

"A... friend gave it to me. What I want to show you, is what's on it."

He sets the tube on the dining table and lets it unroll, revealing a series of hand-drawn sketches.

"A house."

He inhales, seeming even more nervous. "It's a floor plan. And elevations."

"You drew this?"

"I did."

I lean forward, studying the plans. They're incredible.

James fidgets in his seat.

"You hate it."

"I don't," I whisper. "I'm just... surprised. When did you learn to do this?"

"A long, long time ago." He eyes me. "You don't hate it?"

"No, of course not. It's incredible."

"Really?"

"Really."

"I was thinking the downstairs bedroom could be a nursery for Carson—"

"This is for us?"

"Yes. This is going to be our home. Our family home. The way it should be. The way it should've been."

I don't understand what that last statement means, but I do like the plans.

"This is what you and Grigory have been working on?"

"It is. He's going to do the engineering. We're going to build homes. We've named our endeavor S&S Homes."

"So which S is which? Sinclair & Sokolov or Sokolov & Sinclair?"

"It's all in the eye of the beholder."

As I study the plan again, I think about James building homes, about the impact that could leave on the families in this town, and I think about the work I want to do with Lessons Learned. We're both building this colony. For him, it's the houses that will line its streets. For me, it's the people inside. Both are important. Both leave a legacy. But our greatest endeavor will be achieved in our home, in the three children we'll raise.

As I study the plans, I can imagine the five of us living in this home, the kids growing up, birthday parties, nights spent studying, reading, and playing. And after that, when it's just James and me.

"You're sure you like it?"

I smile at him. "I wouldn't change a thing."

***

To see James and Emma's final floor plan and read an extended epilogue, visit:
    AGRiddle.com/after-colony

Author's Note

Dear Reader,

Thank you for reading *The Lost Colony*.

If you've read the author's notes in the previous two books, you know that I wrote this trilogy during a tumultuous time in my life. Like the characters in The Long Winter, I went through a period when it felt like my life would never be the same again, a world where it seemed the sun had set forever. There were times when I couldn't work, times when I didn't want to work, and times when writing these books was the only thing I wanted to do.

They say time heals all wounds. For me, writing The Long Winter trilogy helped the time go by, and I'll always be grateful for that distraction. And I hope these books have played a similar role in your life—whether it be distraction, entertainment, inspiration, enlightenment, or some combination thereof. For me, a good book is one that leaves the reader better off than they were before they started. It's certainly been the case for this author.

Thanks again for reading, and please remember, life isn't about what you've lost. It's about what you have left.

—Gerry
Raleigh, North Carolina, 18 Aug 2019
writing as A.G. Riddle

Acknowledgments

A book is like an iceberg. What the reader sees is merely the piece above the surface. What lies beneath is far larger, and arguably more important.

That part beyond the surface is a cast of people that ensure the book sees the light of day—they are the mass that holds it out of the water. And they deserve just as much credit as that small part above the surface.

I'd like to start by thanking Troy Juliar and Jeff Tabnick at Recorded Books. They're responsible for producing and publishing the incredible audio editions of this trilogy that so many of you have enjoyed. The publishing landscape is always changing, but the rate of change today is far faster than at any time in history. Troy and Jeff moved heaven and Earth to ensure that the audiobooks came out on the same dates as the eBooks and print books. It was important to me that this trilogy be released without significant time lags, and I'm not sure any other audio publisher could have pulled it off given the time constraints I provided them. My thanks to both of you—and I promise I'll deliver the books sooner next time.

Literary agents are known for getting great deals for their authors. But like an iceberg, that's just the part of their work that the public sees. They do so much more. They're a source of invaluable advice on the manuscript, cover art, description, and content (at least mine are—and I'm thankful for that). Good agents are also an invaluable source of counsel and are active in coordinating the publisher and author's efforts during pre-publication and after. Working together is essential in today's publishing landscape, and agents help make it happen. I'm blessed to have a terrific group working on my behalf: Danny and Heather Baror in the US, Europe, and South America, and Gray Tan in Asia.

I want to again thank my UK publisher, Head of Zeus, who has been a fantastic partner for this entire trilogy (and all of my previous novels). They are also responsible for the covers and the editing for *The Solar War*.

David Gatewood made some outstanding suggestions that greatly improved this book. He saw things I couldn't and had the courage to say so (or write it several times in comments in Word).

Several early readers also made significant contributions that greatly improved the work: Michelle Duff, Lisa Weinberg, Kristen Miller, Katie Regan, Norma Jean Fritz, and Cindy Prendergast.

Finally, I'd like to thank you—my readers. I seem to have won the ultimate author's lottery of readers—each day I awaken to the kindest emails and messages on Facebook, and I continue to be very grateful for all of your support (especially on those tough days).

—Gerry

About the Author

A.G. Riddle spent ten years starting internet companies before retiring to pursue his true passion: writing fiction. He lives in North Carolina.

www.agriddle.com